Vampire Game

JUDAL

Vampire Game Vol. 8
Created by Judal

Translation - Patrick Coffman
English Adaptation - Jason Deitrich
Associate Editor - Tim Beedle
Copy Editor - Peter Ahlstrom
Retouch and Lettering - Dave Sharpe
Production Artists - James Dashiell and James Lee
Cover Design - Anna Kernbaum

Editor - Nicole Monastirsky
Digital Imaging Manager - Chris Buford
Pre-Press Manager - Antonio DePietro
Production Managers - Jennifer Miller and Mutsumi Miyazaki
Art Director - Matt Alford
Managing Editor - Jill Freshney
VP of Production - Ron Klamert
President and C.O.O. - John Parker
Publisher and C.E.O. - Stuart Levy

A  Manga

TOKYOPOP Inc.
5900 Wilshire Blvd. Suite 2000
Los Angeles, CA 90036

E-mail: info@TOKYOPOP.com
Come visit us online at www.TOKYOPOP.com

ISBN: 1-59182-560-1

First TOKYOPOP printing: September 2004
10 9 8 7 6 5 4 3 2 1
Printed in the USA

VAMPIRE GAME

Volume 8

by

JUDAL

HAMBURG // LONDON // LOS ANGELES // TOKYO

VAMPIRE GAME

The Story Thus Far...

This is the tale of the Vampire King Duzell and his quest for revenge against the good King Phelios, a valiant warrior who slew the vampire a century ago. Now Duzell has returned, reincarnated as a feline foe to deliver woe to...well, that's the problem. Who is the reincarnation of King Phelios?

Sir Keld has informed Ishtar that her Aunt Sonia, the benevolent lady of Zi Alda, is dying. But when Ishtar, Duzell and Darres rush to be by her side, they find Lady Sonia in good health, her "fatal" illness little more than a head cold. Convinced this is more than a simple misunderstanding, Ishtar figures that Sir Keld is plotting again. After all, if she were to wed Sonia's son Yuujel, Keld would become part of the royal family.

However, Ishtar has no interest in marrying Yuujel. In fact, she flat-out despises him. Besides, there's the matter of finding Yuujel first, as the prince of Zi Alda has been notoriously MIA for the past few months, a fact that's perfectly fine with Ishtar. She has enough on her plate, what with Duzell's newfound ability to appear as his old self, her pending revenge against Keld, and the unwelcome attention of Lady Leene and her raven-haired sorceress, Diaage. Leene, you see, is in love with Yuujel (despite being married to his best friend) and she's positive that Yuujel has set his sights on Ishtar. Which in turn means that she must set her sights on her as well, and squeeze the trigger.

And what better way to do it than a morning ride? Especially when you've replaced the princess' horse with the untamed, unbroken and completely unpredictable Backbreaker. But the last laugh may be on Leene. After all, her beloved Yuujel has been spending quality time with Ishtar for well over a year now...as her magic instructor, Yujinn.

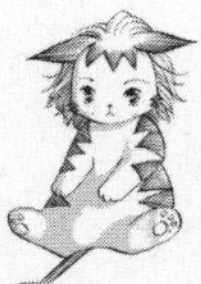

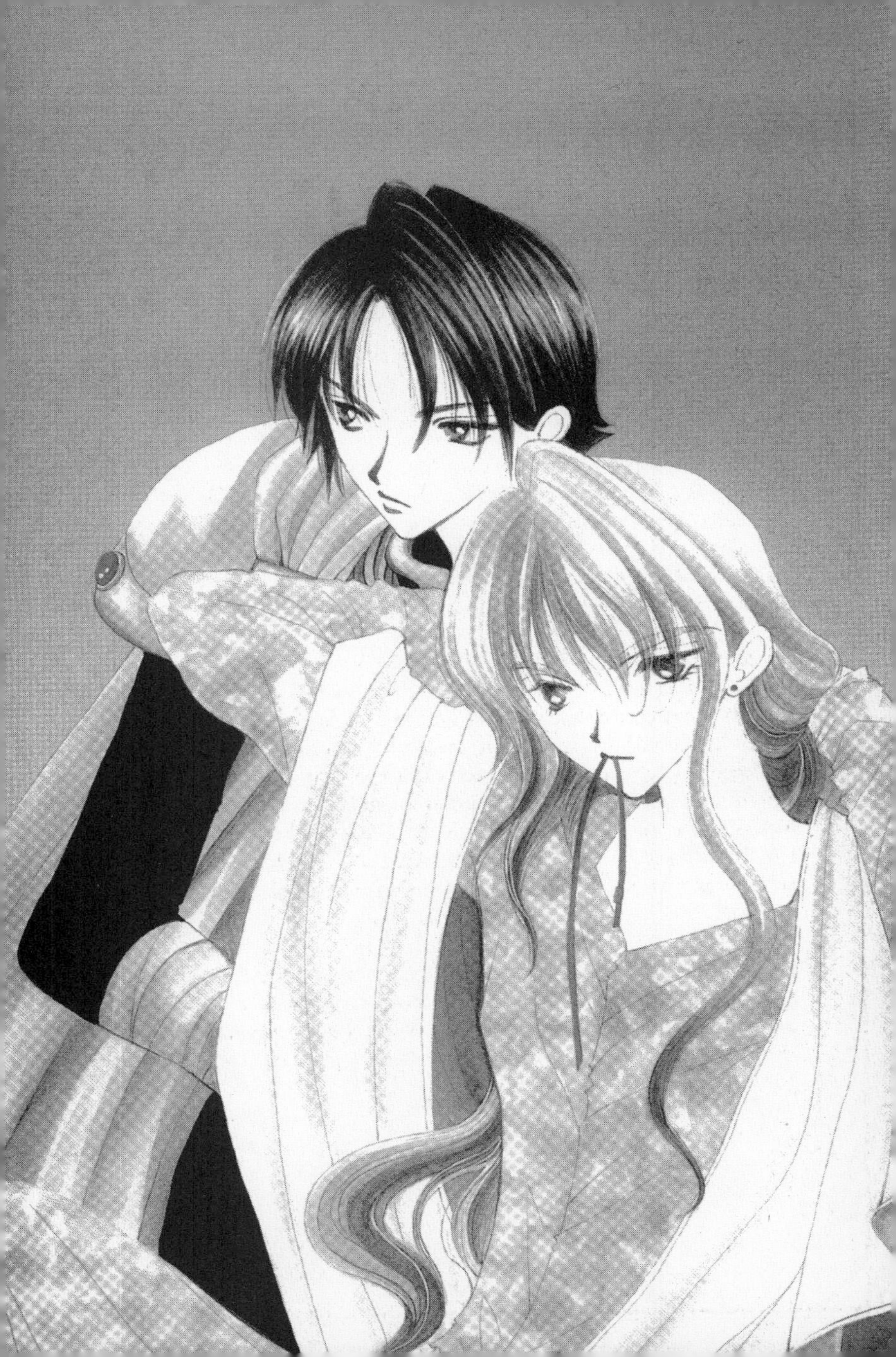

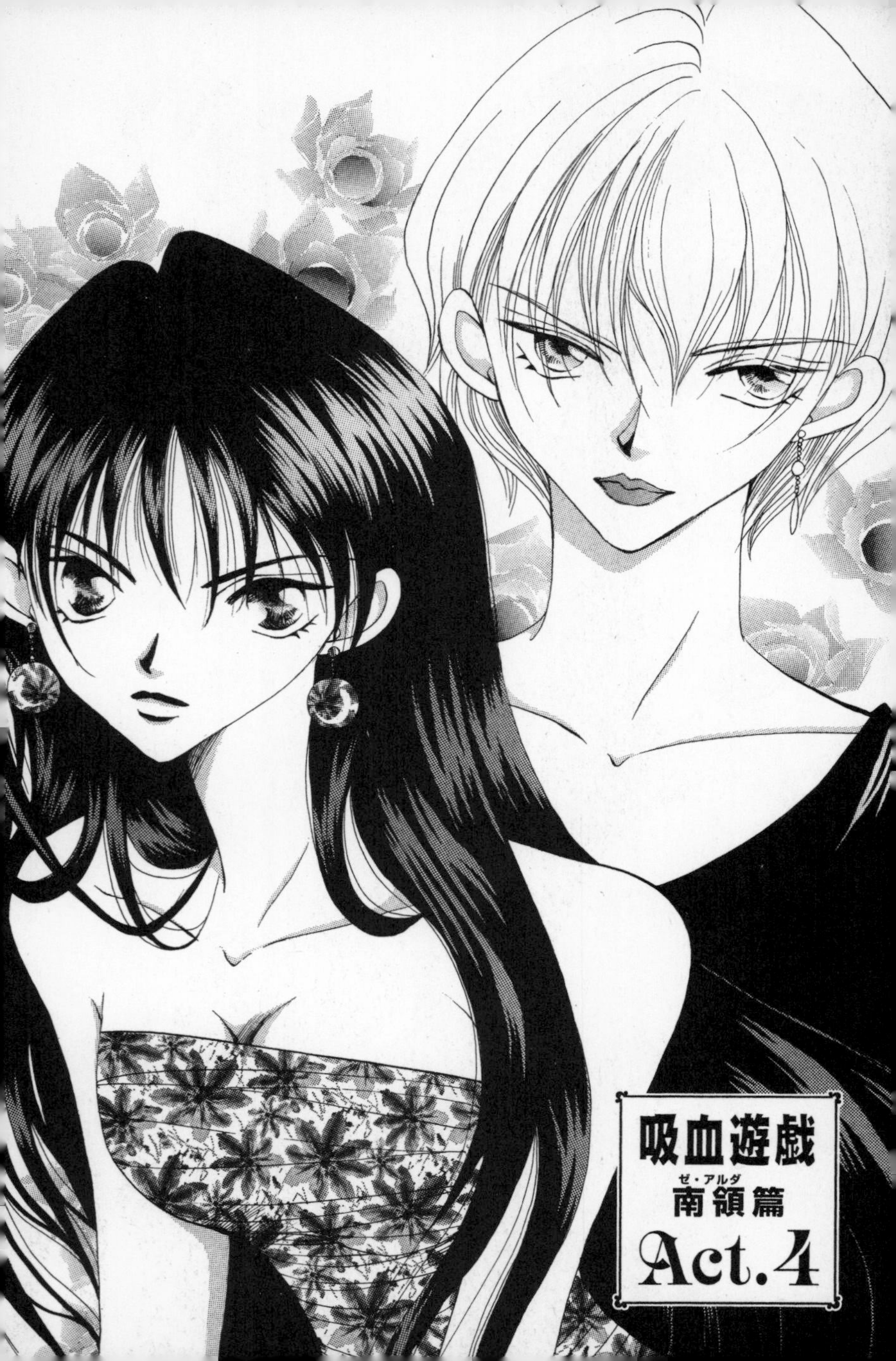
吸血遊戯
南領篇
ゼ・アルダ
Act.4

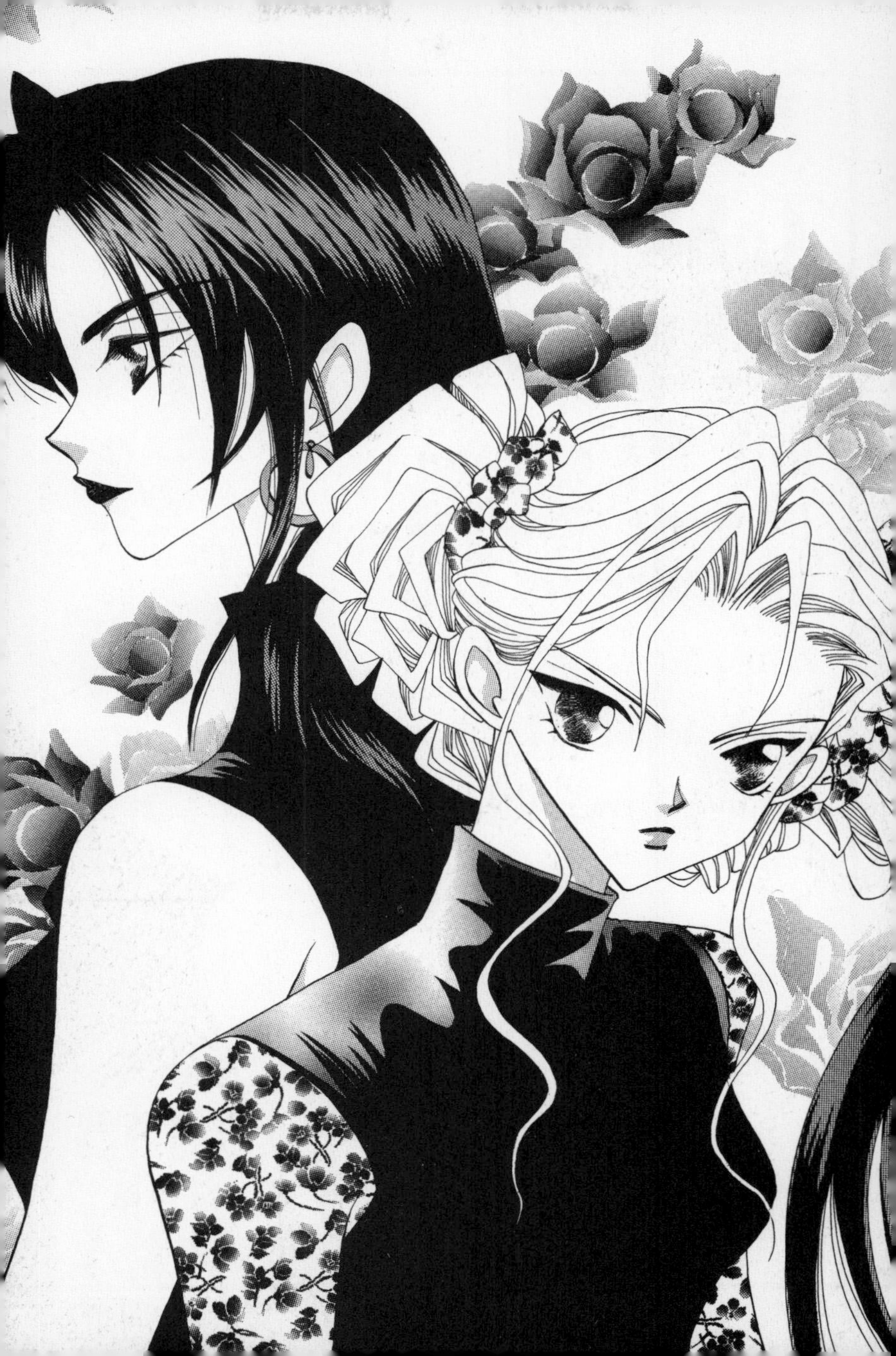

Table of Contents

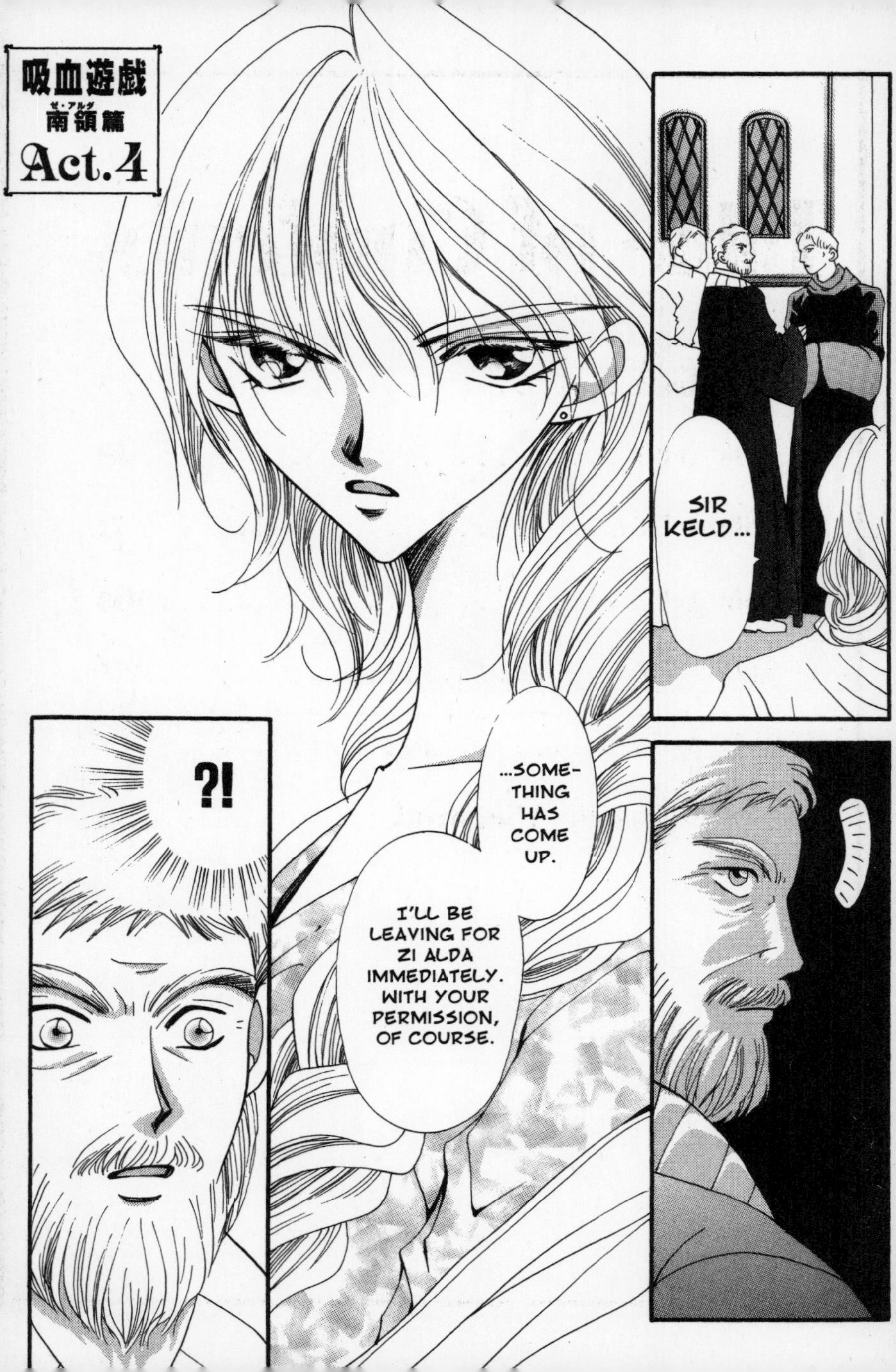
吸血遊戯
ゼ・アルダ
南領篇
Act.4
SIR KELD...
...SOME-THING HAS COME UP.
I'LL BE LEAVING FOR ZI ALDA IMMEDIATELY. WITH YOUR PERMISSION, OF COURSE.
?!

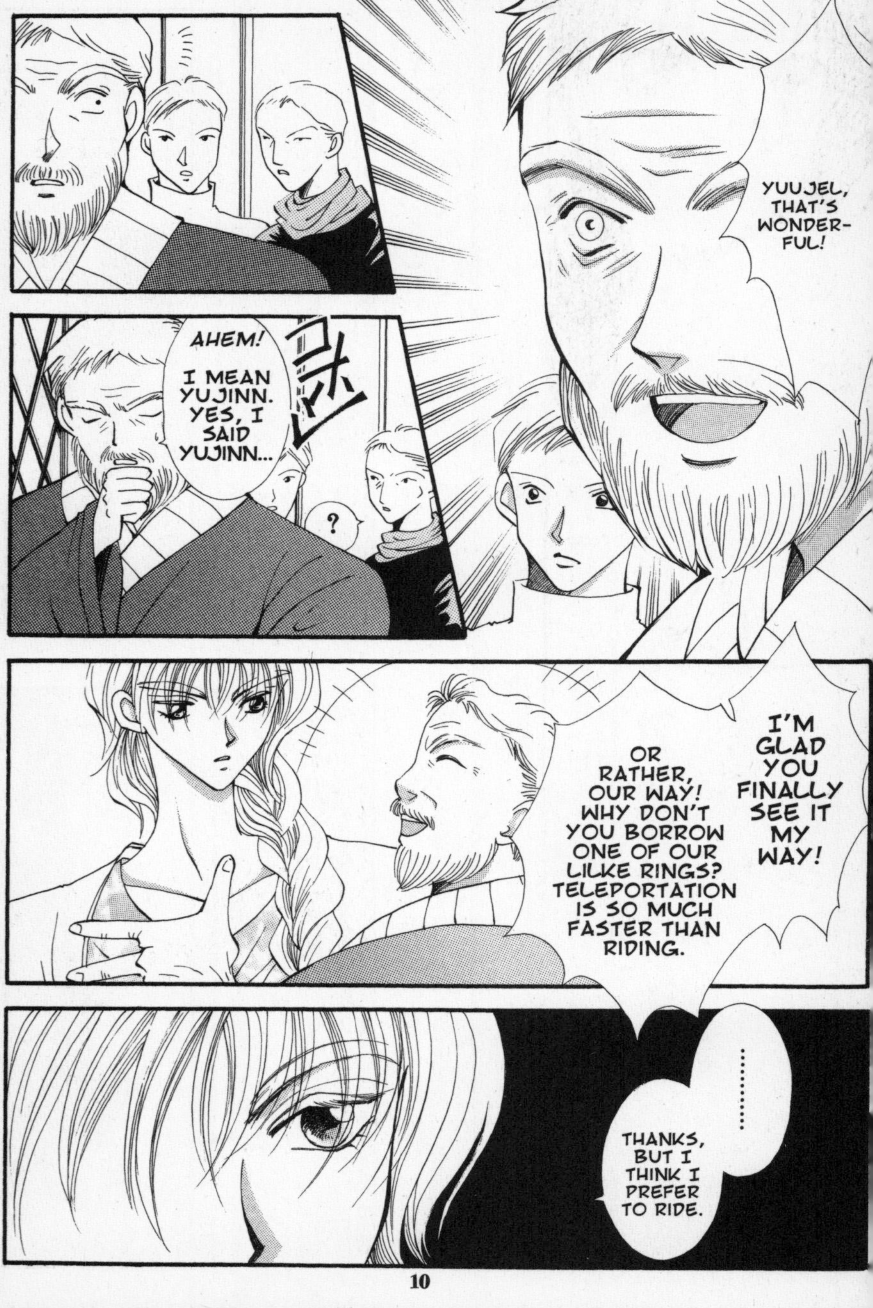
YUUJEL, THAT'S WONDERFUL!
AHEM!
I MEAN YUJINN. YES, I SAID YUJINN...
?
I'M GLAD YOU FINALLY SEE IT MY WAY!
OR RATHER, OUR WAY! WHY DON'T YOU BORROW ONE OF OUR LILKE RINGS? TELEPORTATION IS SO MUCH FASTER THAN RIDING.
......
THANKS, BUT I THINK I PREFER TO RIDE.

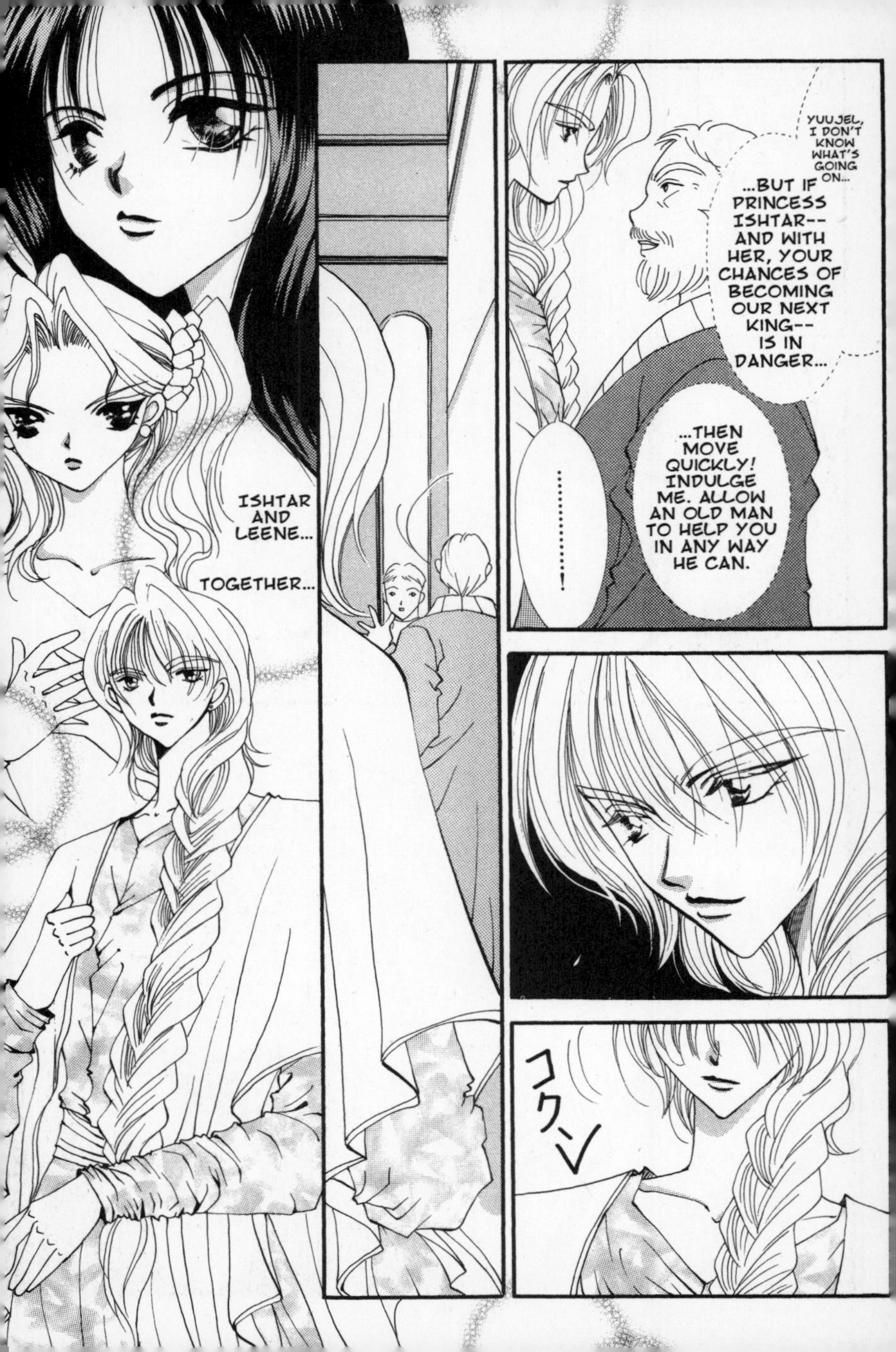
YUUJEL, I DON'T KNOW WHAT'S GOING ON...
...BUT IF PRINCESS ISHTAR-- AND WITH HER, YOUR CHANCES OF BECOMING OUR NEXT KING-- IS IN DANGER...
......!
...THEN MOVE QUICKLY! INDULGE ME. ALLOW AN OLD MAN TO HELP YOU IN ANY WAY HE CAN.
コクン
ISHTAR AND LEENE...
TOGETHER...

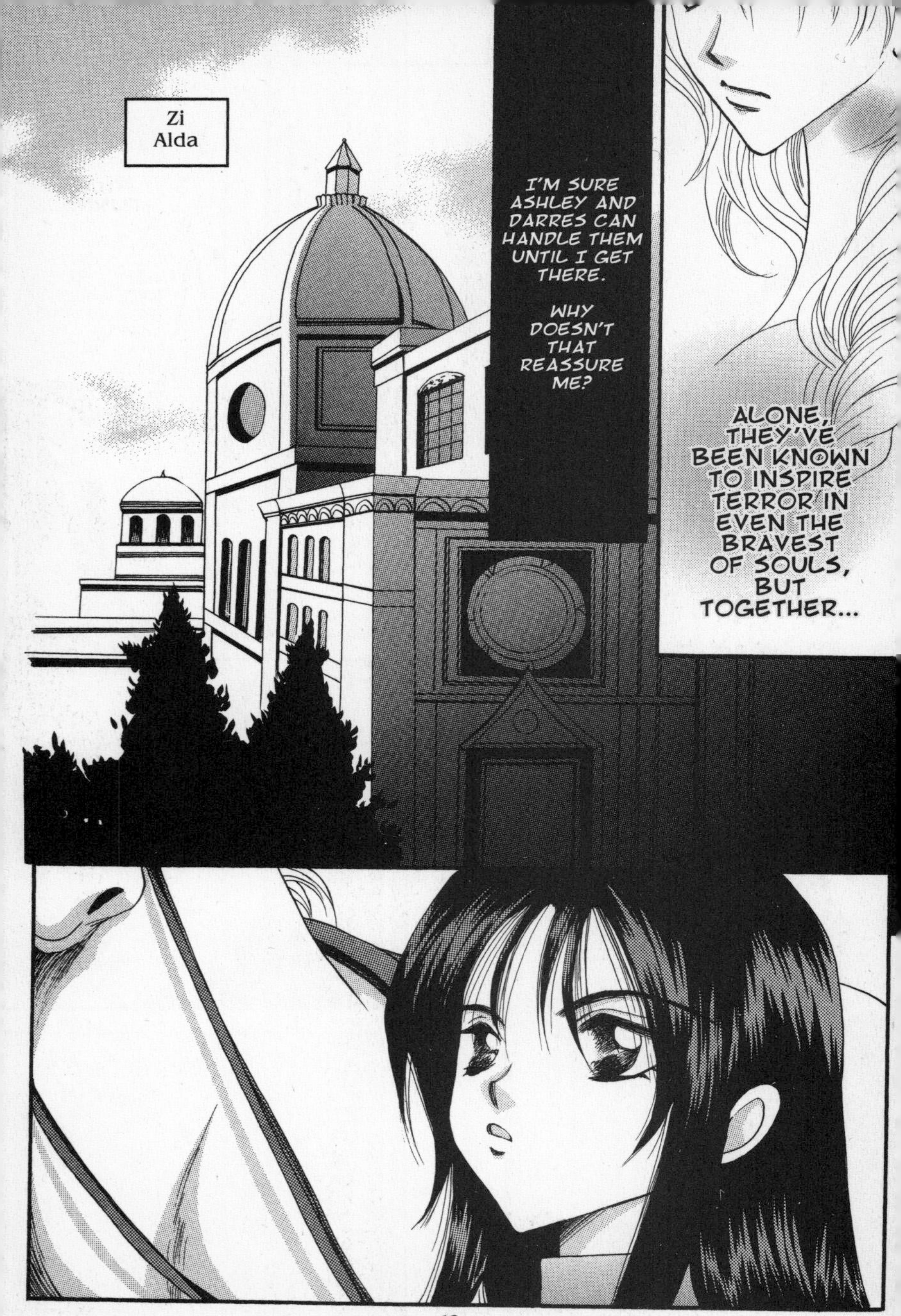
ALONE, THEY'VE BEEN KNOWN TO INSPIRE TERROR IN EVEN THE BRAVEST OF SOULS, BUT TOGETHER...
I'M SURE ASHLEY AND DARRES CAN HANDLE THEM UNTIL I GET THERE.
WHY DOESN'T THAT REASSURE ME?
Zi Alda

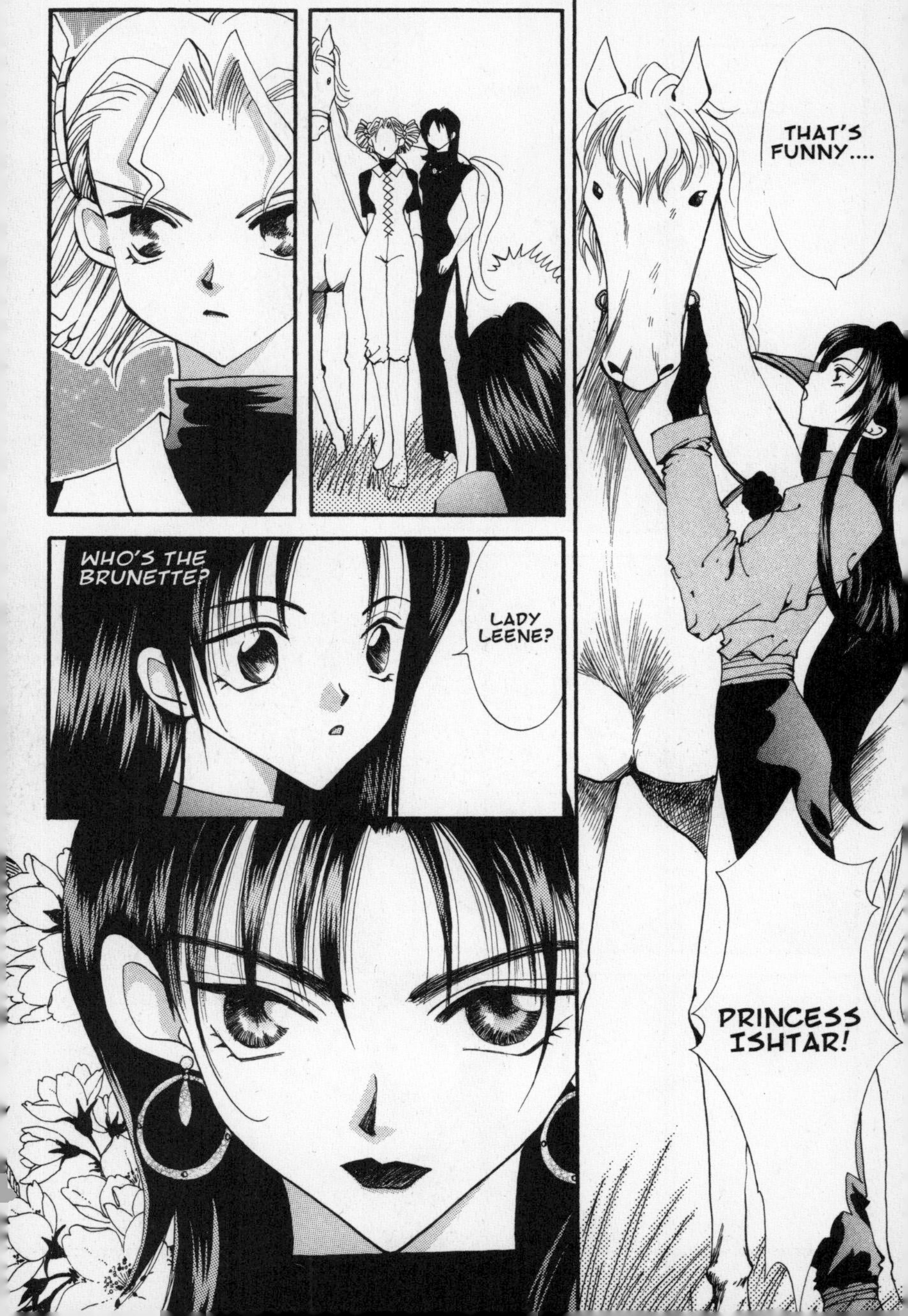
THAT'S FUNNY....
PRINCESS ISHTAR!
LADY LEENE?
WHO'S THE BRUNETTE?

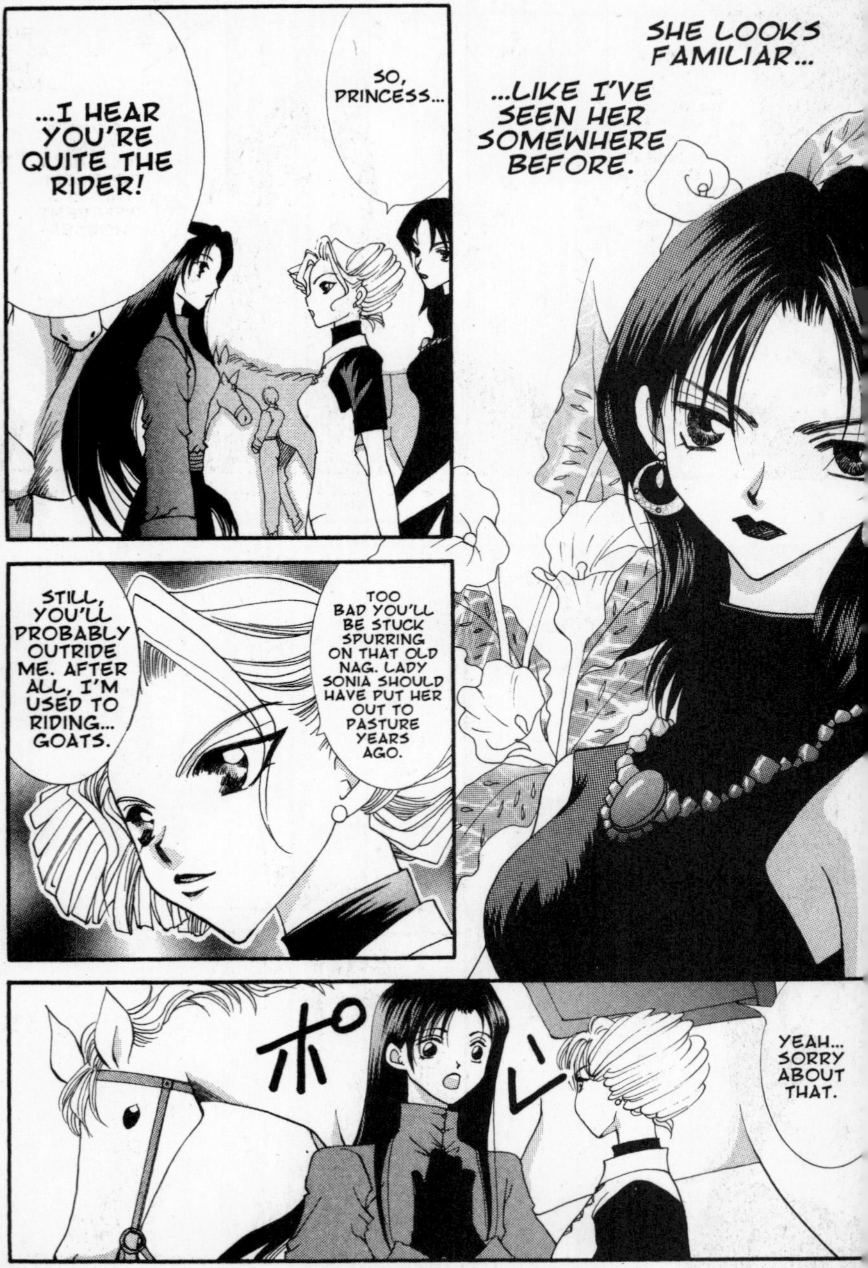
SHE LOOKS FAMILIAR...
...LIKE I'VE SEEN HER SOMEWHERE BEFORE.
SO, PRINCESS...
...I HEAR YOU'RE QUITE THE RIDER!
TOO BAD YOU'LL BE STUCK SPURRING ON THAT OLD NAG. LADY SONIA SHOULD HAVE PUT HER OUT TO PASTURE YEARS AGO.
STILL, YOU'LL PROBABLY OUTRIDE ME. AFTER ALL, I'M USED TO RIDING... GOATS.
YEAH... SORRY ABOUT THAT.
ポン

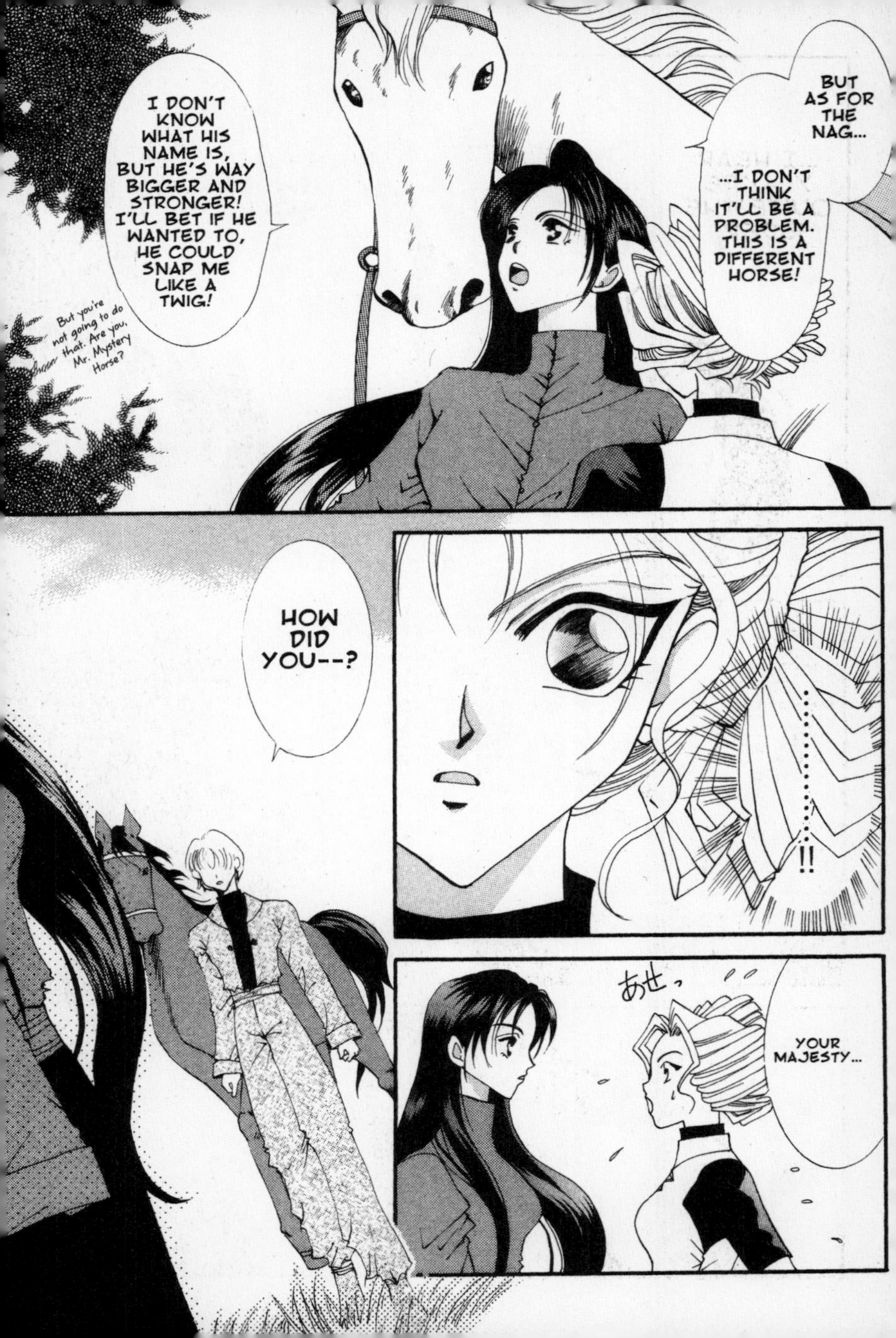
BUT AS FOR THE NAG...
...I DON'T THINK IT'LL BE A PROBLEM. THIS IS A DIFFERENT HORSE!
I DON'T KNOW WHAT HIS NAME IS, BUT HE'S WAY BIGGER AND STRONGER! I'LL BET IF HE WANTED TO, HE COULD SNAP ME LIKE A TWIG!
But you're not going to do that. Are you, Mr. Mystery Horse?
.........!!
あせっ
YOUR MAJESTY...
HOW DID YOU--?

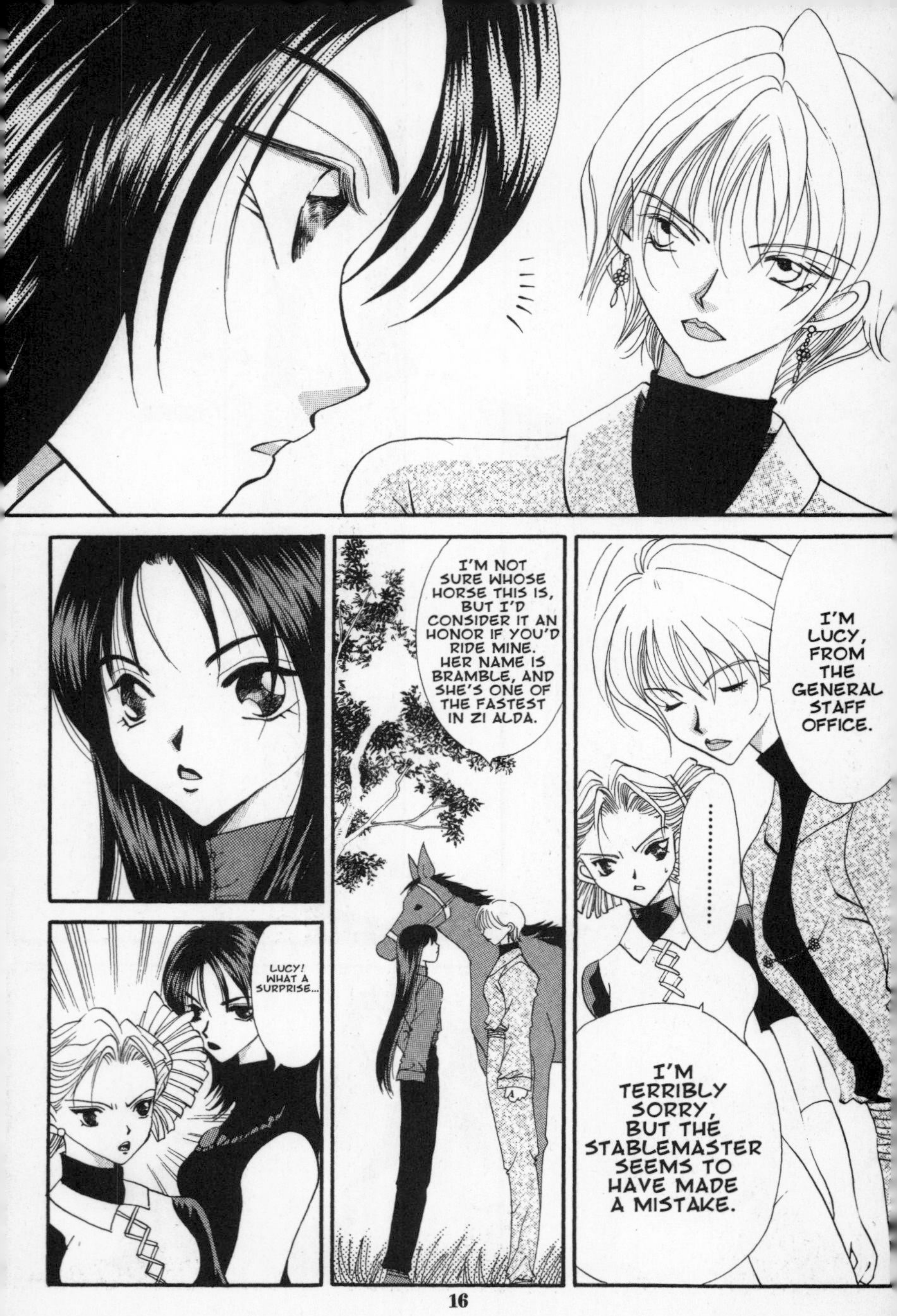
I'M LUCY, FROM THE GENERAL STAFF OFFICE.
......
I'M TERRIBLY SORRY, BUT THE STABLEMASTER SEEMS TO HAVE MADE A MISTAKE.
I'M NOT SURE WHOSE HORSE THIS IS, BUT I'D CONSIDER IT AN HONOR IF YOU'D RIDE MINE. HER NAME IS BRAMBLE, AND SHE'S ONE OF THE FASTEST IN ZI ALDA.
LUCY! WHAT A SURPRISE...

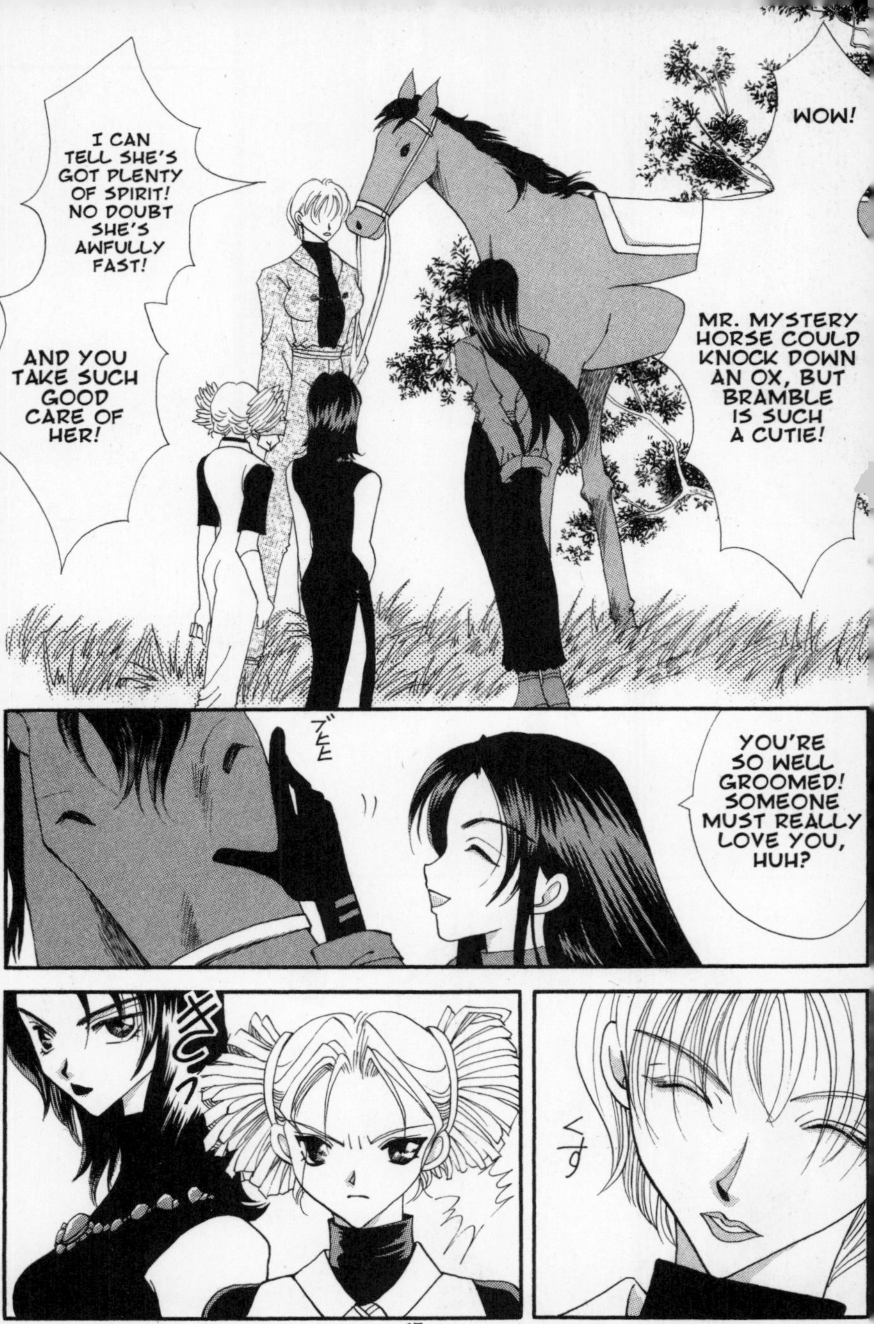
WOW!
MR. MYSTERY HORSE COULD KNOCK DOWN AN OX, BUT BRAMBLE IS SUCH A CUTIE!
I CAN TELL SHE'S GOT PLENTY OF SPIRIT! NO DOUBT SHE'S AWFULLY FAST!
AND YOU TAKE SUCH GOOD CARE OF HER!
YOU'RE SO WELL GROOMED! SOMEONE MUST REALLY LOVE YOU, HUH?
ブヒヒ
くす

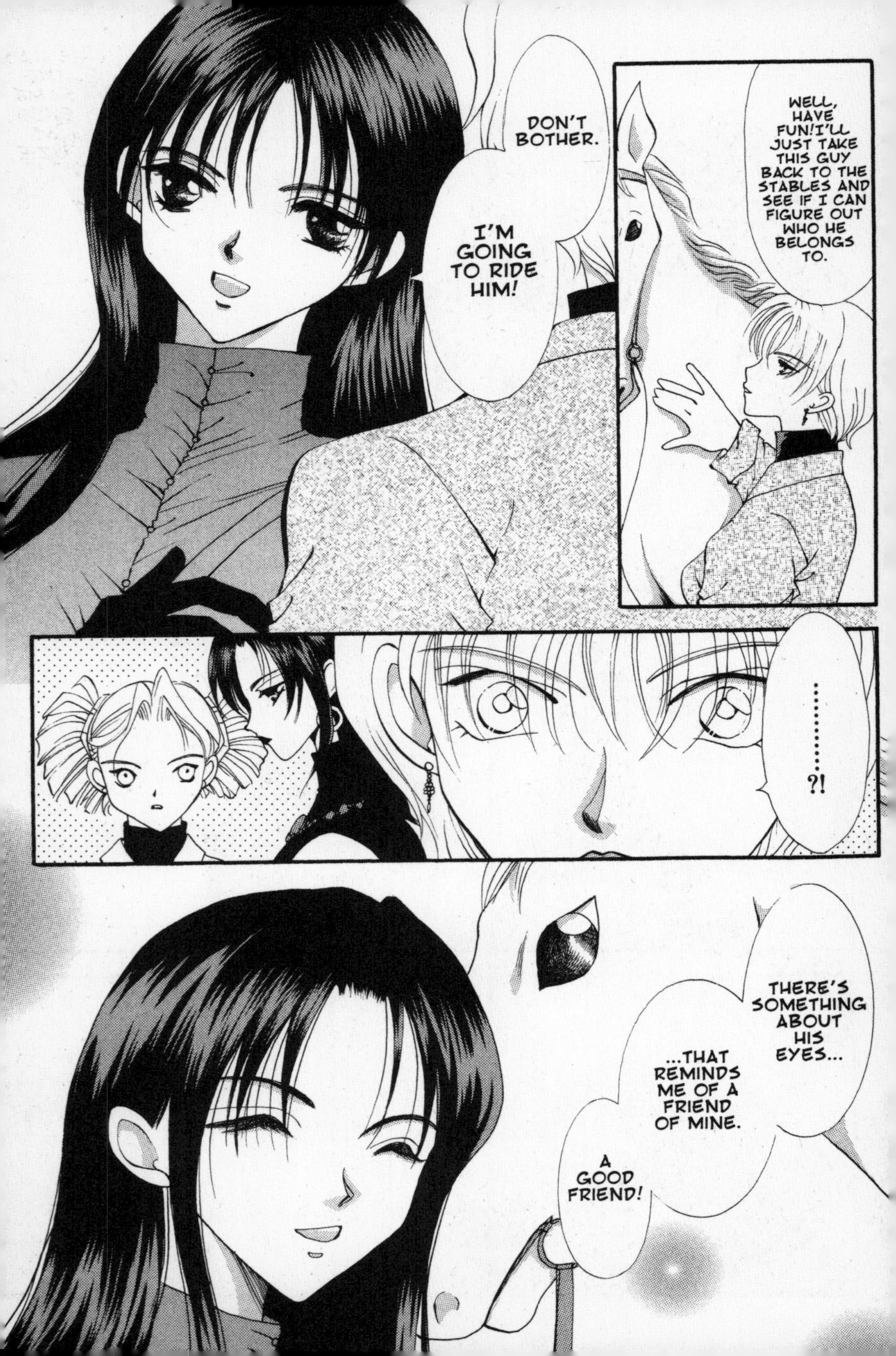
WELL, HAVE FUN! I'LL JUST TAKE THIS GUY BACK TO THE STABLES AND SEE IF I CAN FIGURE OUT WHO HE BELONGS TO.
DON'T BOTHER.
I'M GOING TO RIDE HIM!
........?!
THERE'S SOMETHING ABOUT HIS EYES...
...THAT REMINDS ME OF A FRIEND OF MINE.
A GOOD FRIEND!

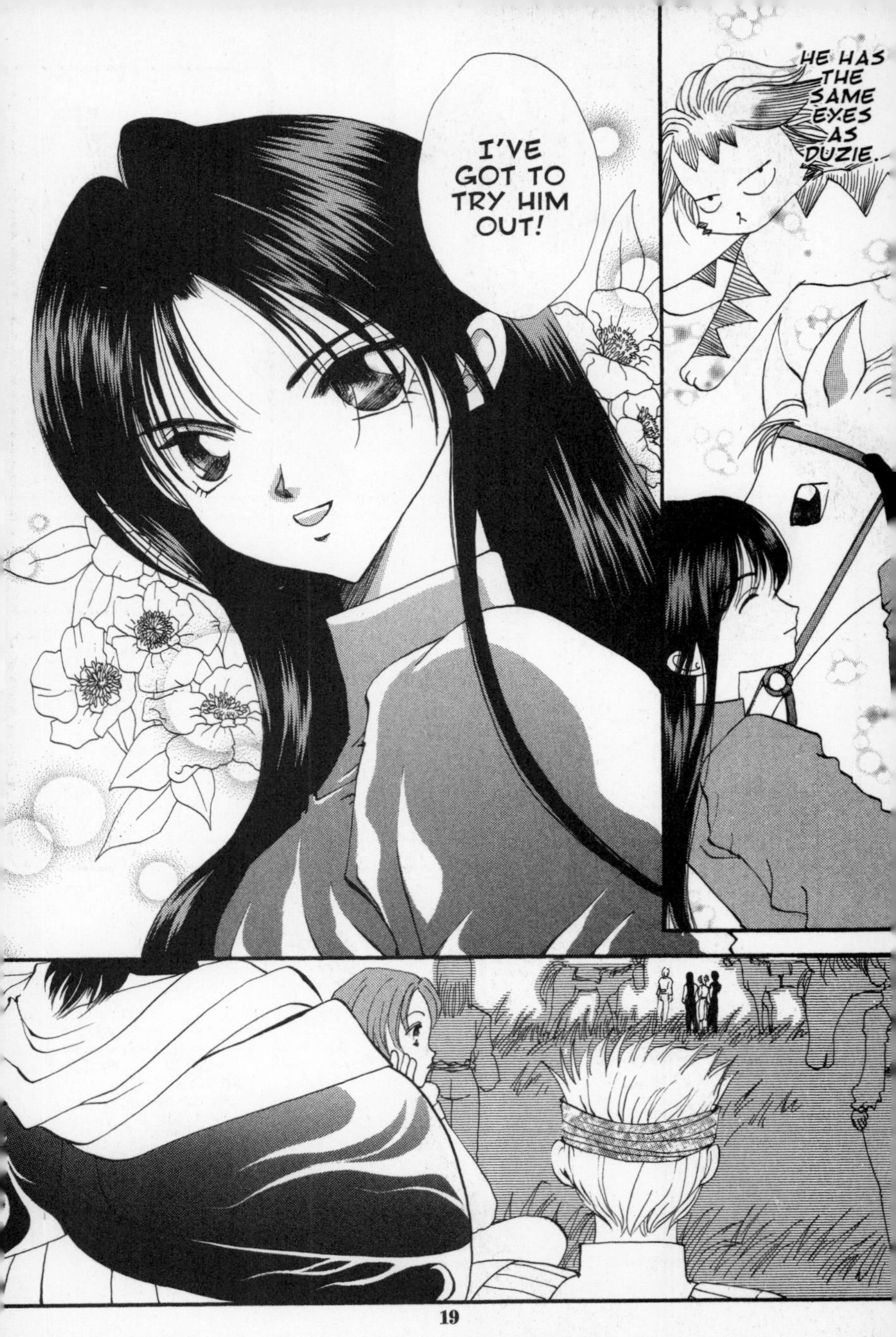
HE HAS THE SAME EYES AS DUZIE.
I'VE GOT TO TRY HIM OUT!

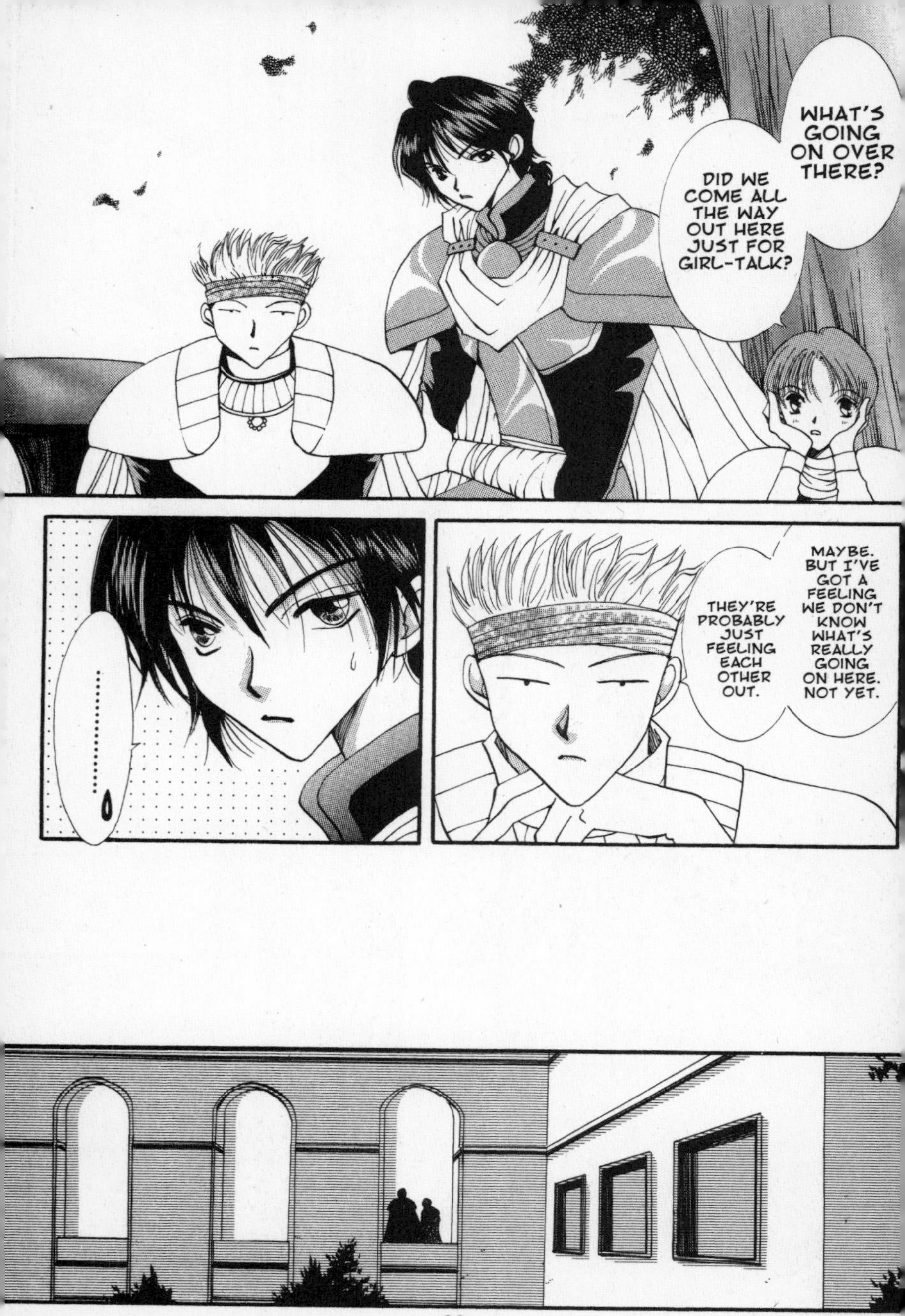
WHAT'S GOING ON OVER THERE?
DID WE COME ALL THE WAY OUT HERE JUST FOR GIRL-TALK?
THEY'RE PROBABLY JUST FEELING EACH OTHER OUT.
MAYBE. BUT I'VE GOT A FEELING WE DON'T KNOW WHAT'S REALLY GOING ON HERE. NOT YET.
......

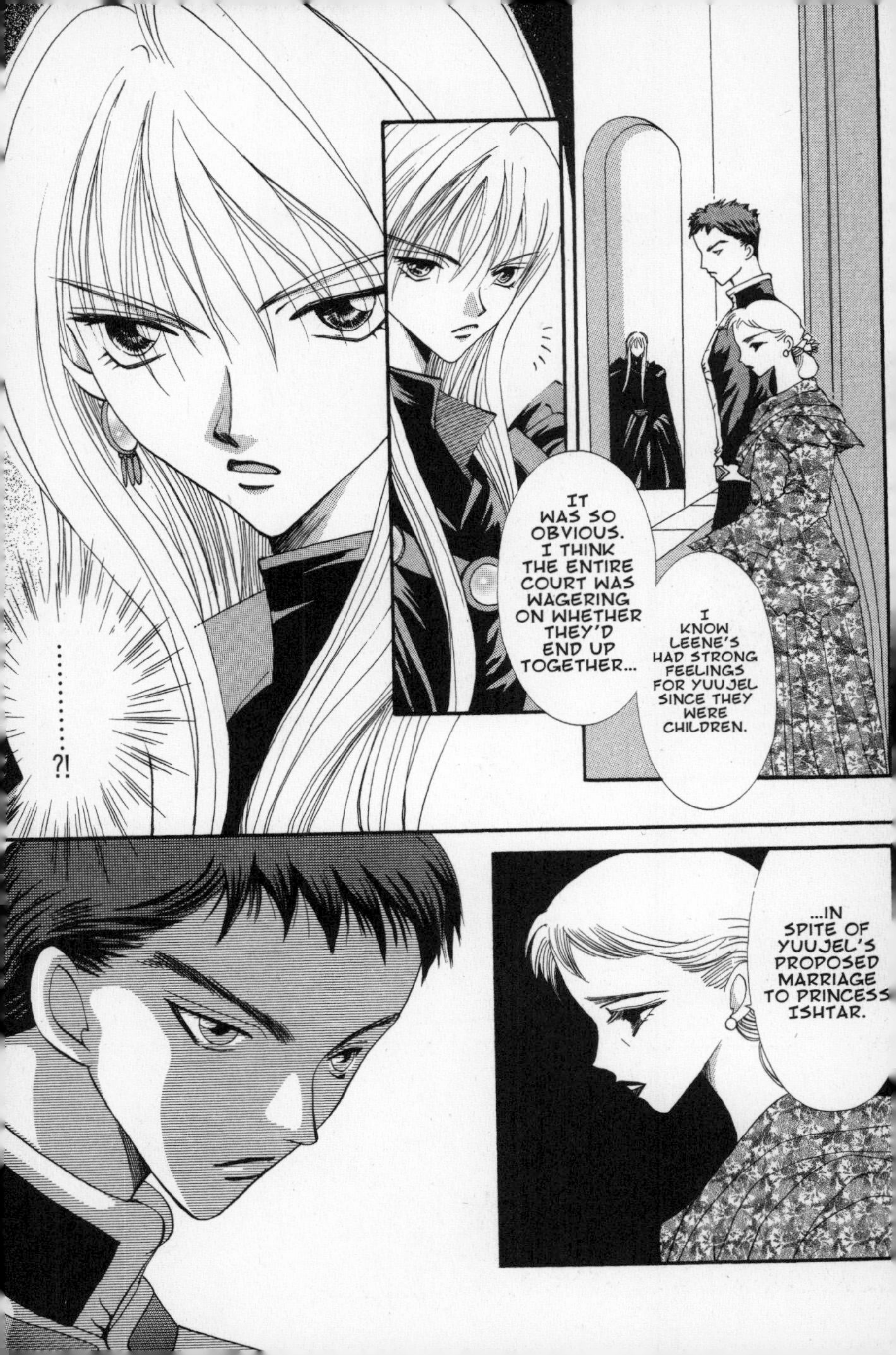
IT WAS SO OBVIOUS. I THINK THE ENTIRE COURT WAS WAGERING ON WHETHER THEY'D END UP TOGETHER...
I KNOW LEENE'S HAD STRONG FEELINGS FOR YUUJEL SINCE THEY WERE CHILDREN.
......?!
...IN SPITE OF YUUJEL'S PROPOSED MARRIAGE TO PRINCESS ISHTAR.

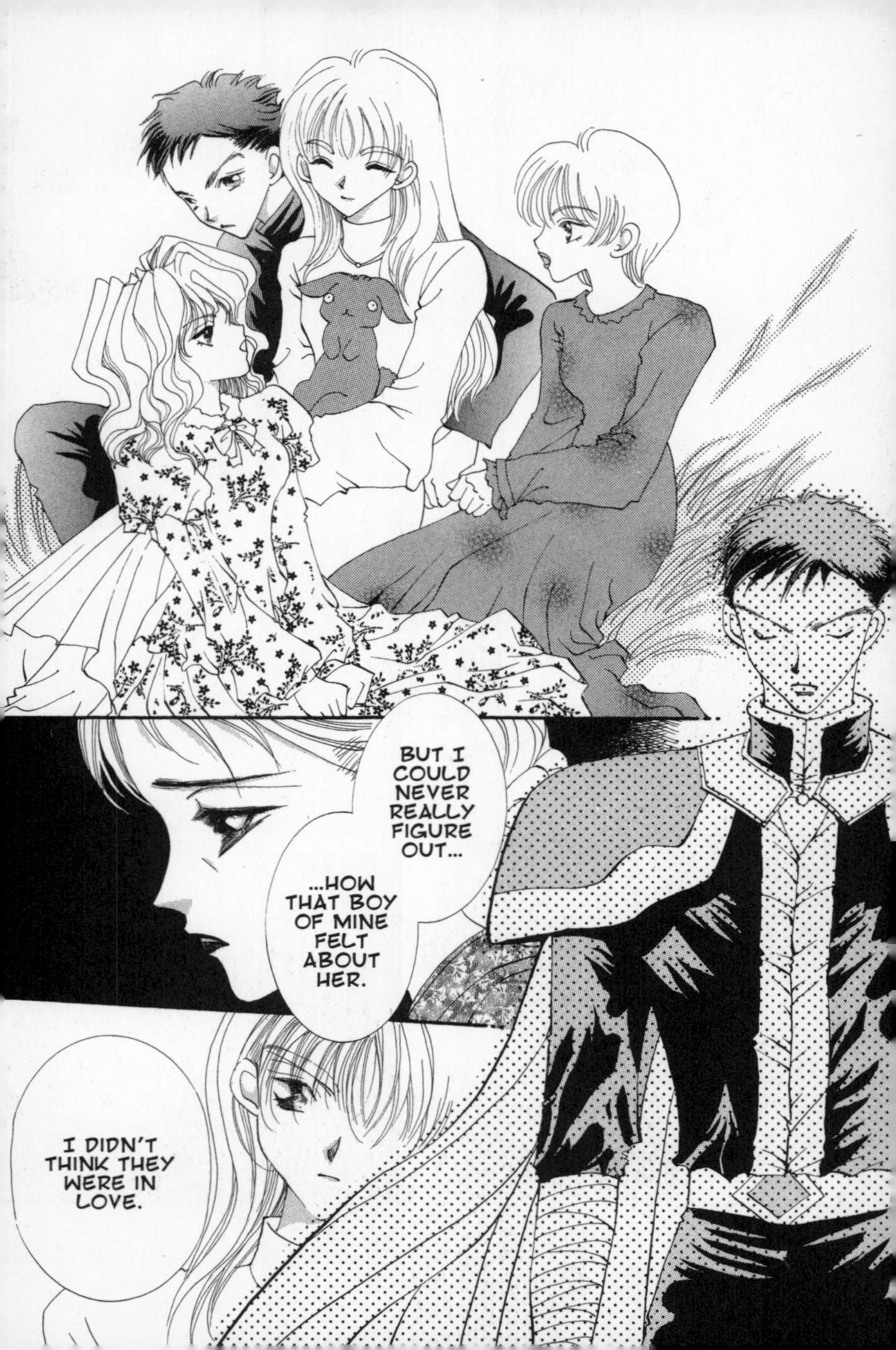

BUT I COULD NEVER REALLY FIGURE OUT...
...HOW THAT BOY OF MINE FELT ABOUT HER.
I DIDN'T THINK THEY WERE IN LOVE.

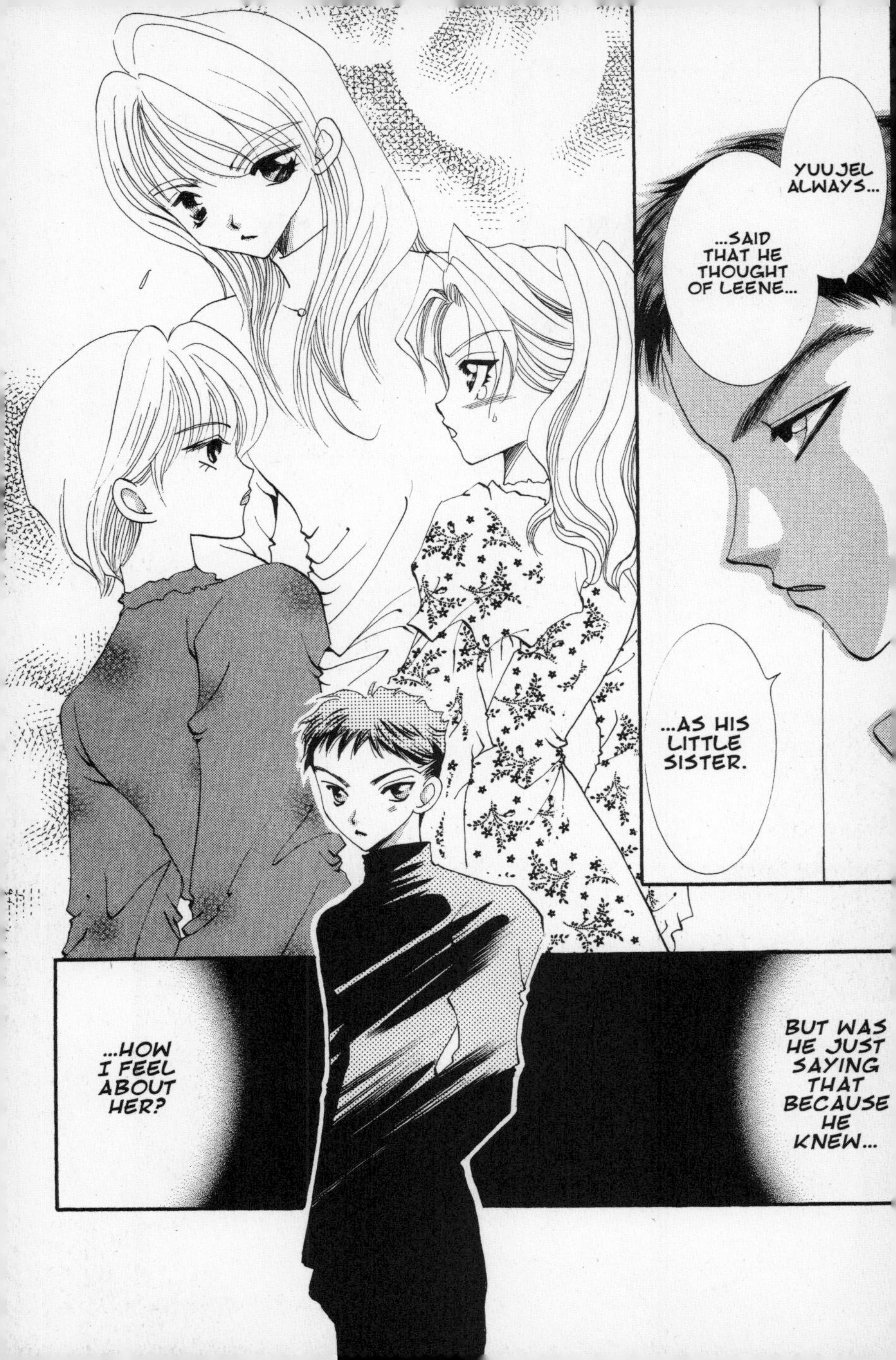
YUUJEL ALWAYS...
...SAID THAT HE THOUGHT OF LEENE...
...AS HIS LITTLE SISTER.
BUT WAS HE JUST SAYING THAT BECAUSE HE KNEW...
...HOW I FEEL ABOUT HER?

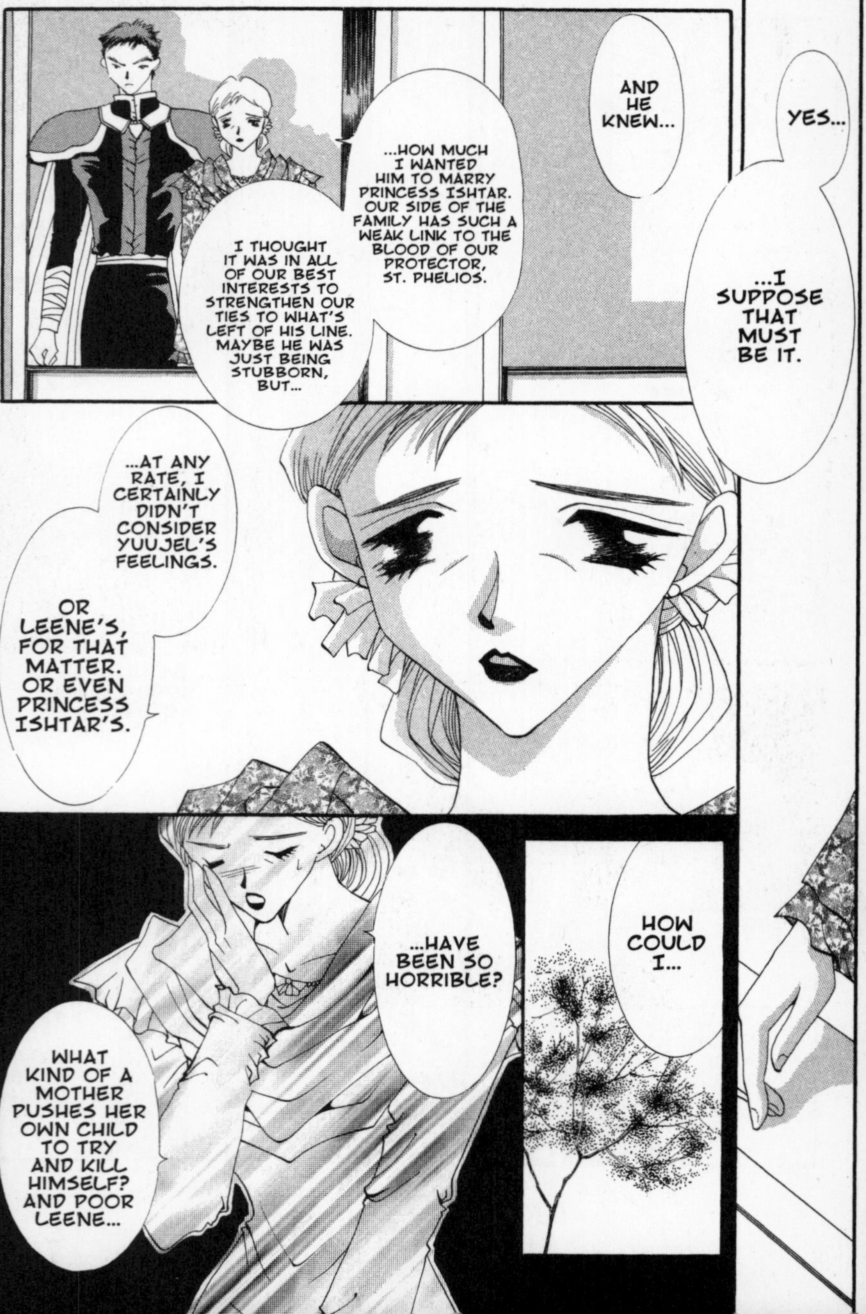
YES...
...I SUPPOSE THAT MUST BE IT.
AND HE KNEW...
...HOW MUCH I WANTED HIM TO MARRY PRINCESS ISHTAR. OUR SIDE OF THE FAMILY HAS SUCH A WEAK LINK TO THE BLOOD OF OUR PROTECTOR, ST. PHELIOS.
I THOUGHT IT WAS IN ALL OF OUR BEST INTERESTS TO STRENGTHEN OUR TIES TO WHAT'S LEFT OF HIS LINE. MAYBE HE WAS JUST BEING STUBBORN, BUT...
...AT ANY RATE, I CERTAINLY DIDN'T CONSIDER YUUJEL'S FEELINGS.
OR LEENE'S, FOR THAT MATTER. OR EVEN PRINCESS ISHTAR'S.
HOW COULD I...
...HAVE BEEN SO HORRIBLE?
WHAT KIND OF A MOTHER PUSHES HER OWN CHILD TO TRY AND KILL HIMSELF? AND POOR LEENE...

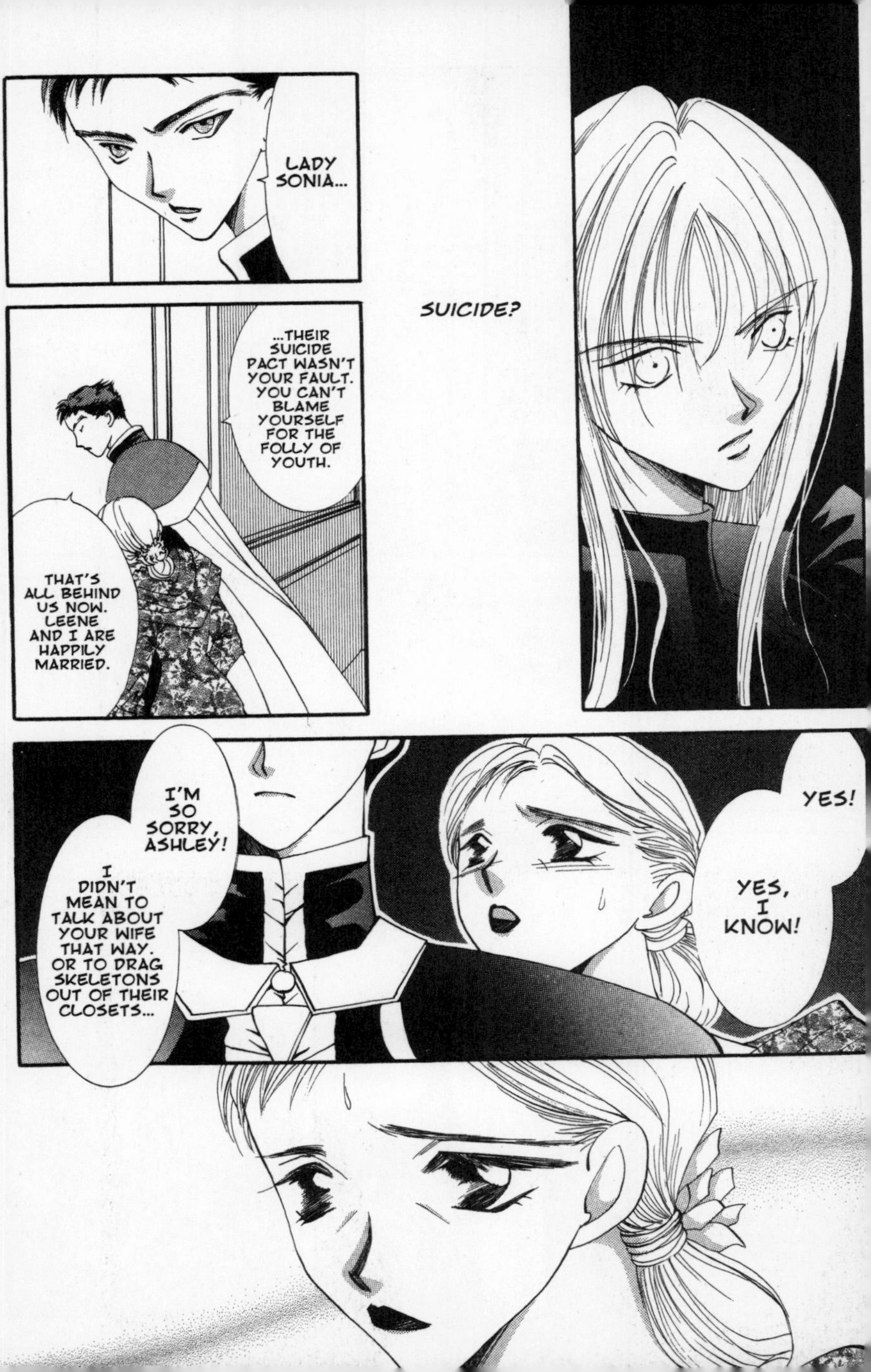
SUICIDE?
LADY SONIA...
...THEIR SUICIDE PACT WASN'T YOUR FAULT. YOU CAN'T BLAME YOURSELF FOR THE FOLLY OF YOUTH.
THAT'S ALL BEHIND US NOW. LEENE AND I ARE HAPPILY MARRIED.
YES!
YES, I KNOW!
I'M SO SORRY, ASHLEY!
I DIDN'T MEAN TO TALK ABOUT YOUR WIFE THAT WAY. OR TO DRAG SKELETONS OUT OF THEIR CLOSETS...

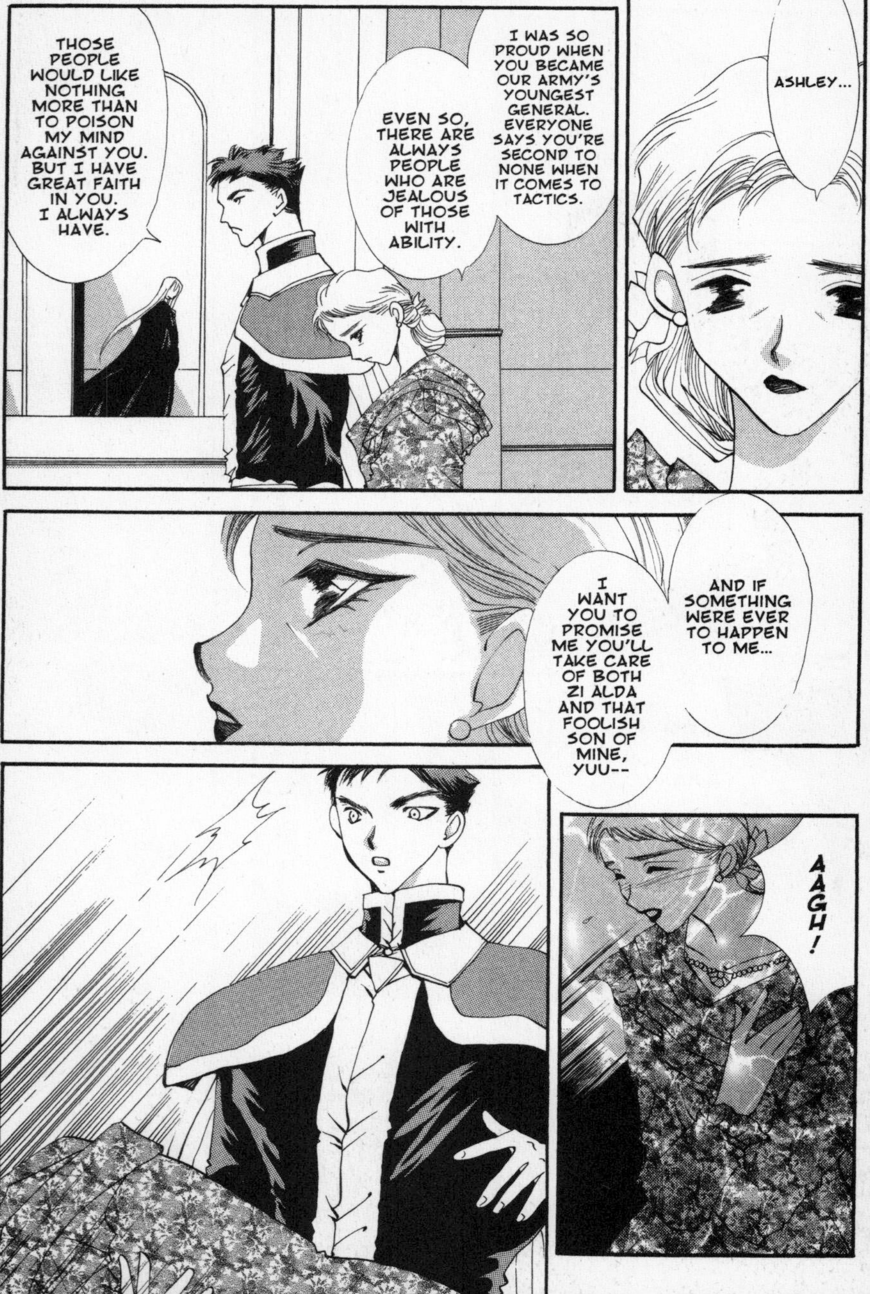
ASHLEY...
I WAS SO PROUD WHEN YOU BECAME OUR ARMY'S YOUNGEST GENERAL. EVERYONE SAYS YOU'RE SECOND TO NONE WHEN IT COMES TO TACTICS.
EVEN SO, THERE ARE ALWAYS PEOPLE WHO ARE JEALOUS OF THOSE WITH ABILITY.
THOSE PEOPLE WOULD LIKE NOTHING MORE THAN TO POISON MY MIND AGAINST YOU. BUT I HAVE GREAT FAITH IN YOU. I ALWAYS HAVE.
AND IF SOMETHING WERE EVER TO HAPPEN TO ME...
I WANT YOU TO PROMISE ME YOU'LL TAKE CARE OF BOTH ZI ALDA AND THAT FOOLISH SON OF MINE, YUU--
AAGH!

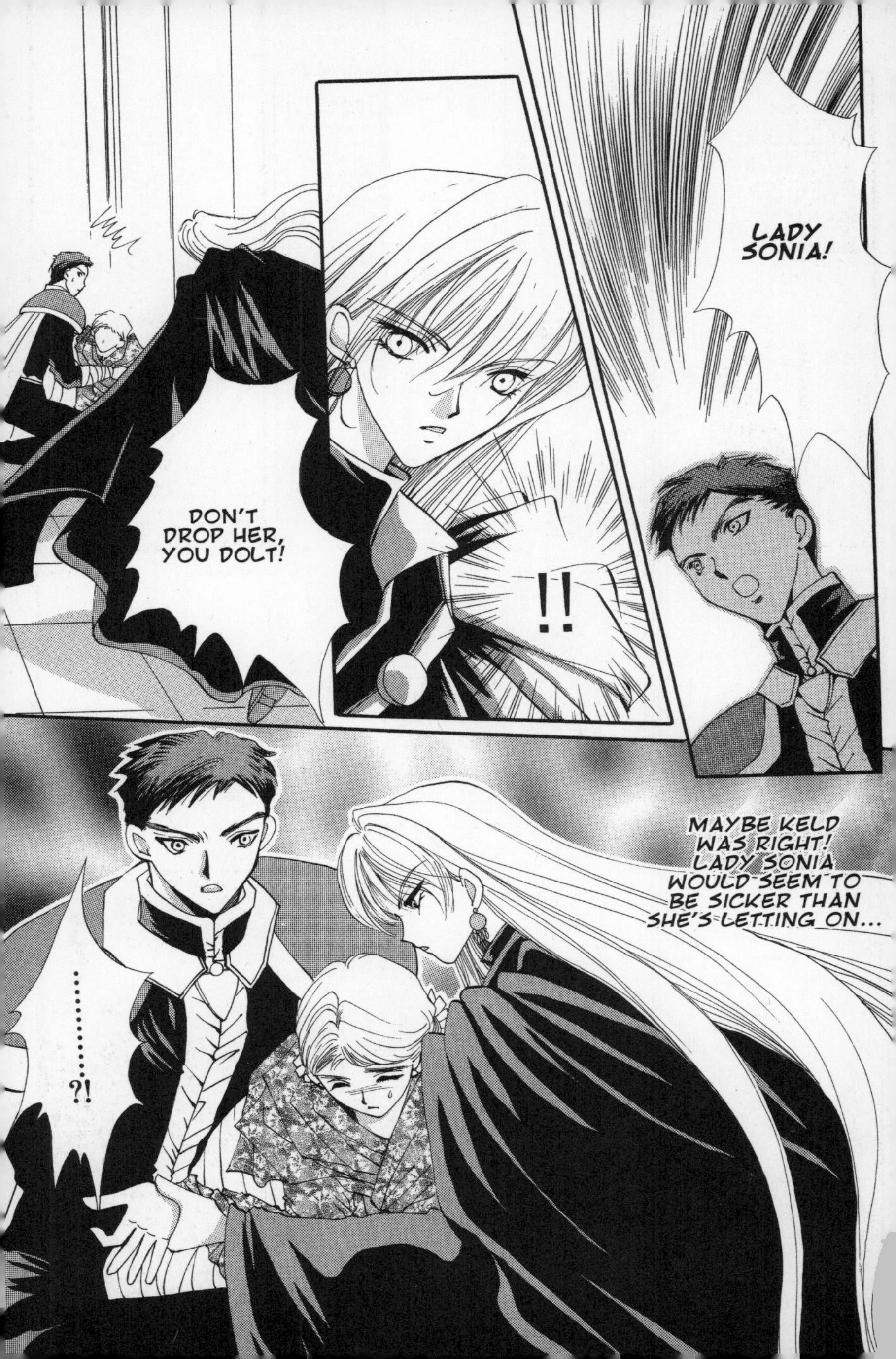
LADY SONIA!
!!
DON'T DROP HER, YOU DOLT!
MAYBE KELD WAS RIGHT! LADY SONIA WOULD SEEM TO BE SICKER THAN SHE'S LETTING ON...
......?!

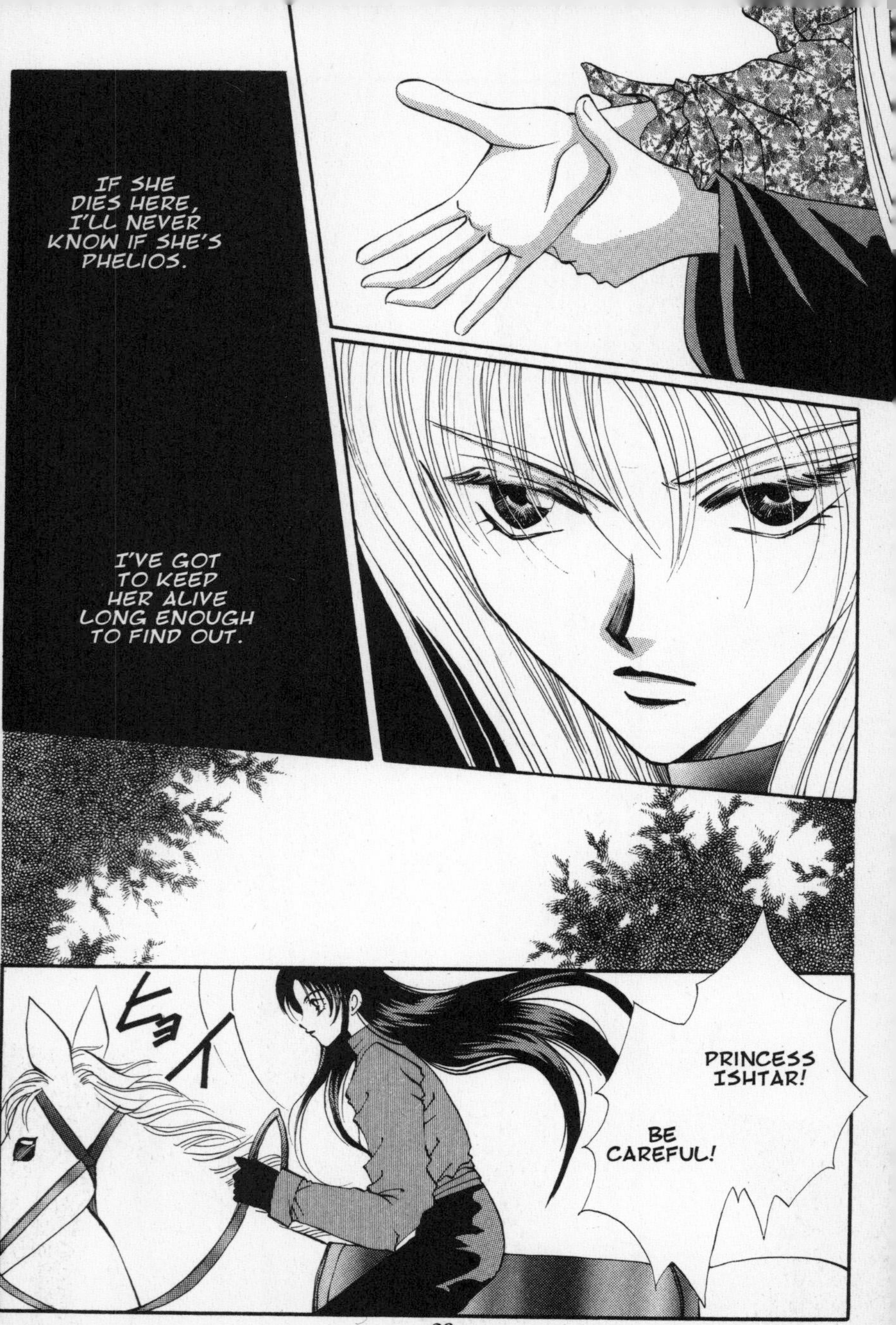
IF SHE DIES HERE, I'LL NEVER KNOW IF SHE'S PHELIOS.
I'VE GOT TO KEEP HER ALIVE LONG ENOUGH TO FIND OUT.
PRINCESS ISHTAR!
BE CAREFUL!
ヒョイ

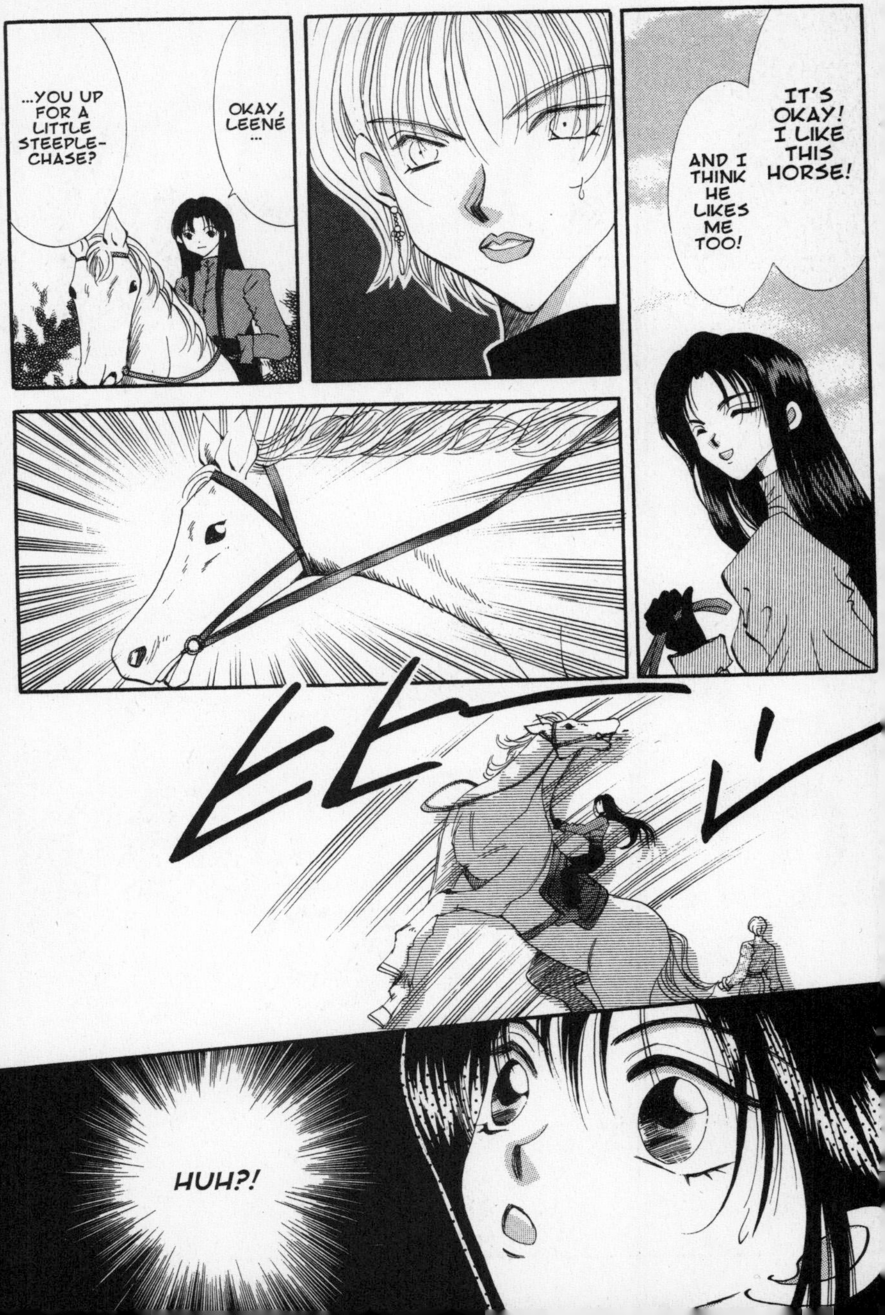
IT'S OKAY! I LIKE THIS HORSE!
AND I THINK HE LIKES ME TOO!
OKAY, LEENÉ ...
...YOU UP FOR A LITTLE STEEPLE-CHASE?
HUH?!

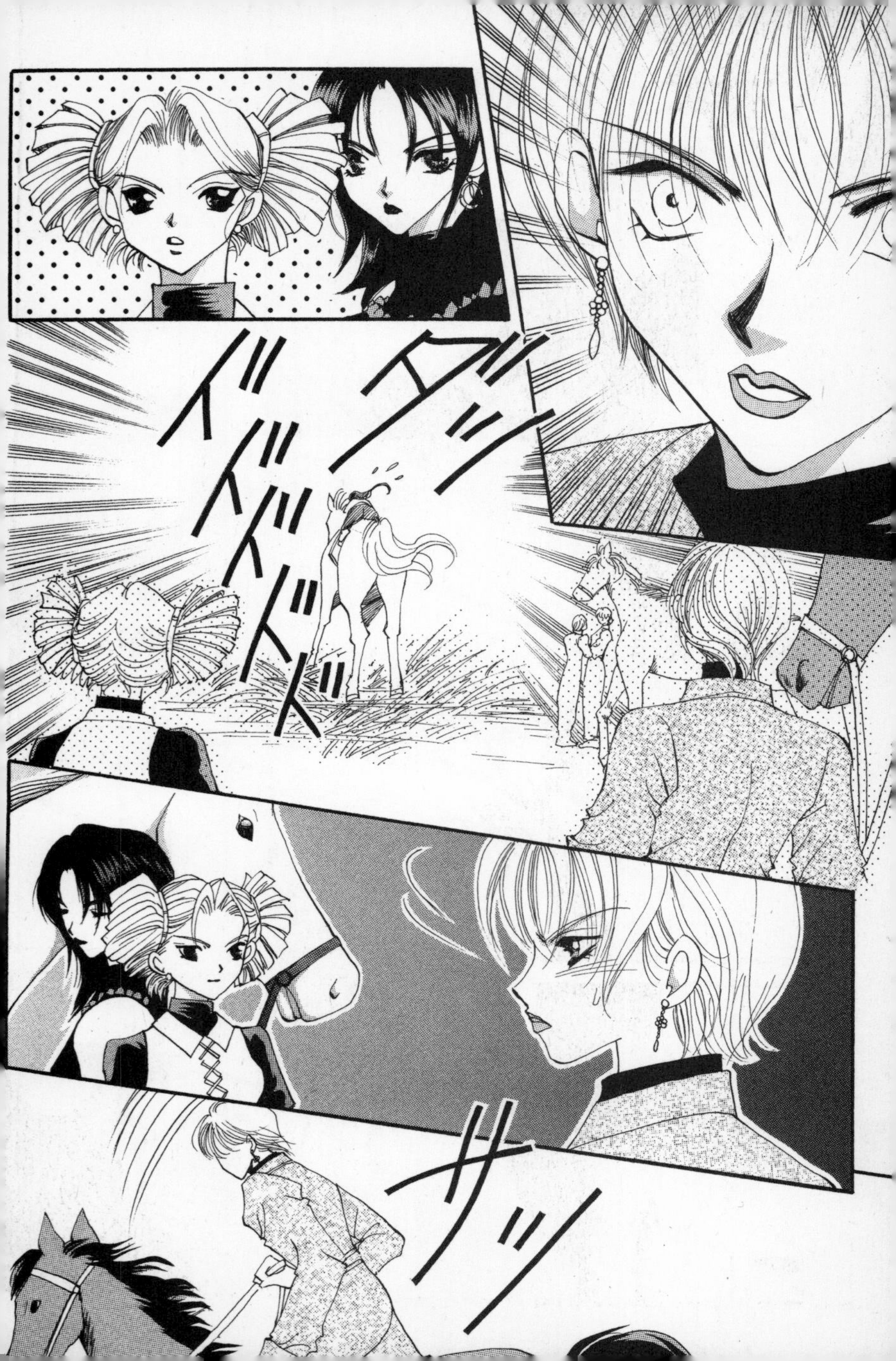
ダッ
ドドドドド
ザッ

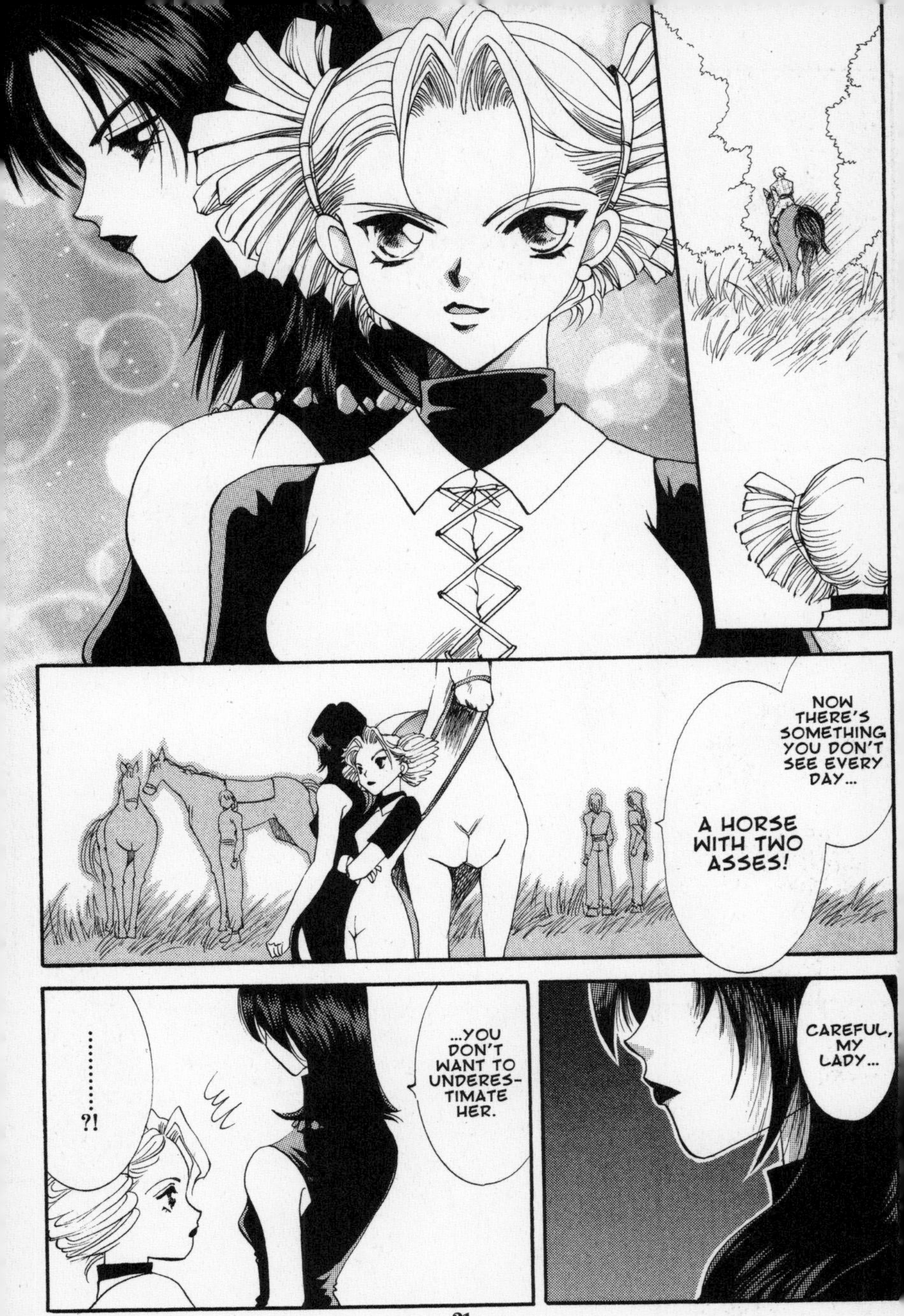
NOW THERE'S SOMETHING YOU DON'T SEE EVERY DAY...
A HORSE WITH TWO ASSES!
CAREFUL, MY LADY...
...YOU DON'T WANT TO UNDERES-TIMATE HER.
....
?!

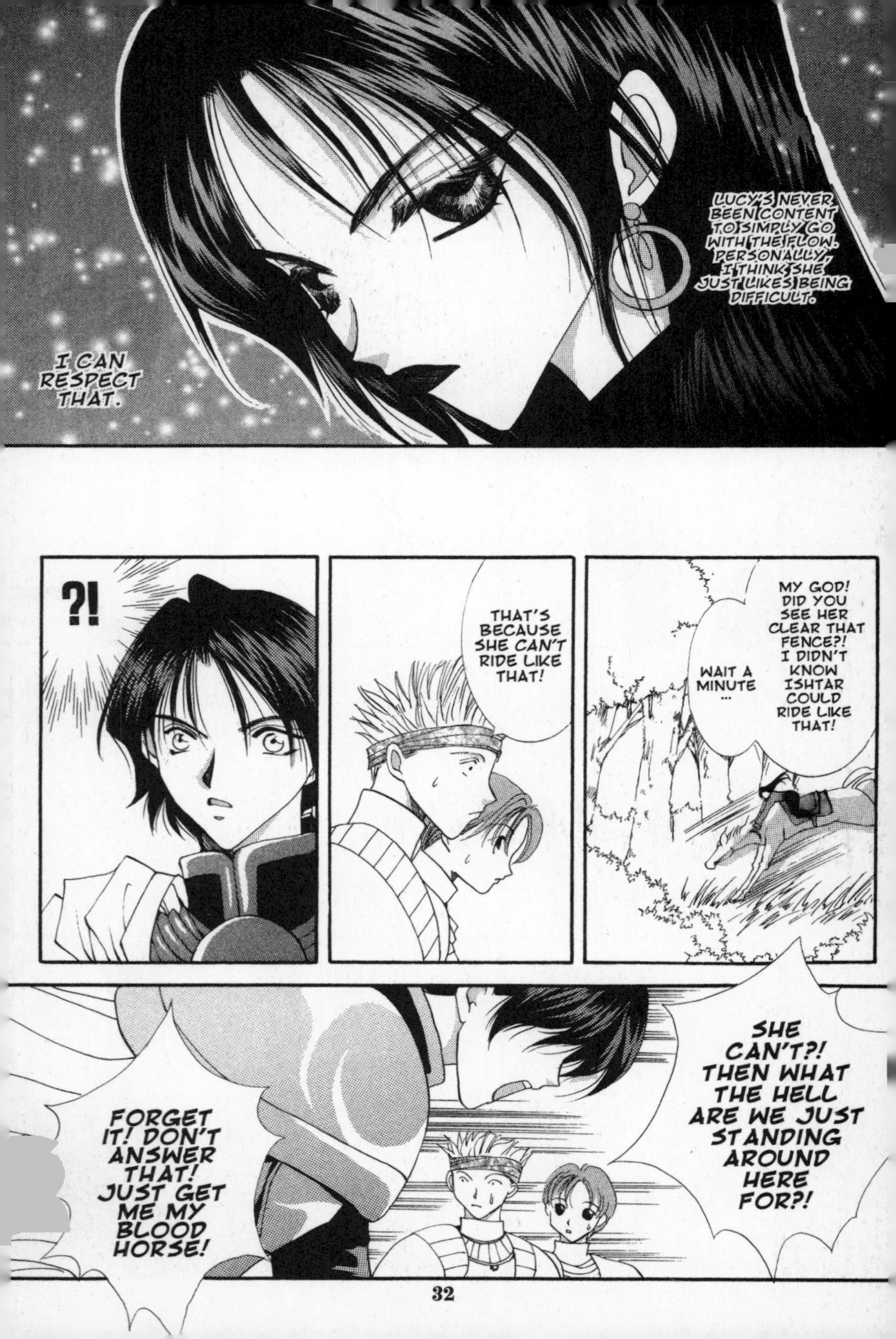
LUCY'S NEVER BEEN CONTENT TO SIMPLY GO WITH THE FLOW. PERSONALLY, I THINK SHE JUST LIKES BEING DIFFICULT.
I CAN RESPECT THAT.
MY GOD! DID YOU SEE HER CLEAR THAT FENCE?! I DIDN'T KNOW ISHTAR COULD RIDE LIKE THAT!
WAIT A MINUTE ...
THAT'S BECAUSE SHE CAN'T RIDE LIKE THAT!
?!
SHE CAN'T?! THEN WHAT THE HELL ARE WE JUST STANDING AROUND HERE FOR?!
FORGET IT! DON'T ANSWER THAT! JUST GET ME MY BLOOD HORSE!

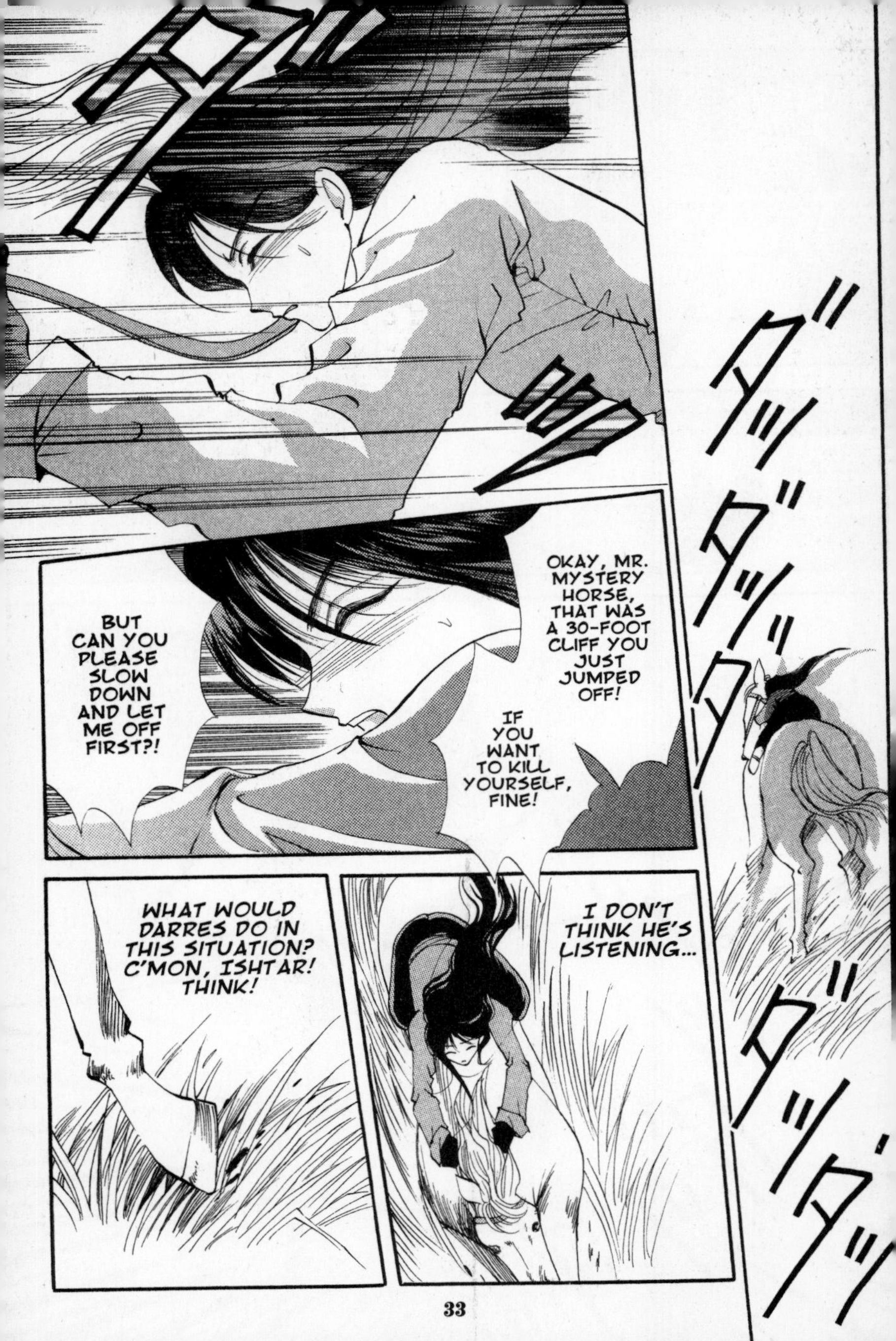
OKAY, MR. MYSTERY HORSE, THAT WAS A 30-FOOT CLIFF YOU JUST JUMPED OFF!
IF YOU WANT TO KILL YOURSELF, FINE!
BUT CAN YOU PLEASE SLOW DOWN AND LET ME OFF FIRST?!
I DON'T THINK HE'S LISTENING...
WHAT WOULD DARRES DO IN THIS SITUATION? C'MON, ISHTAR! THINK!

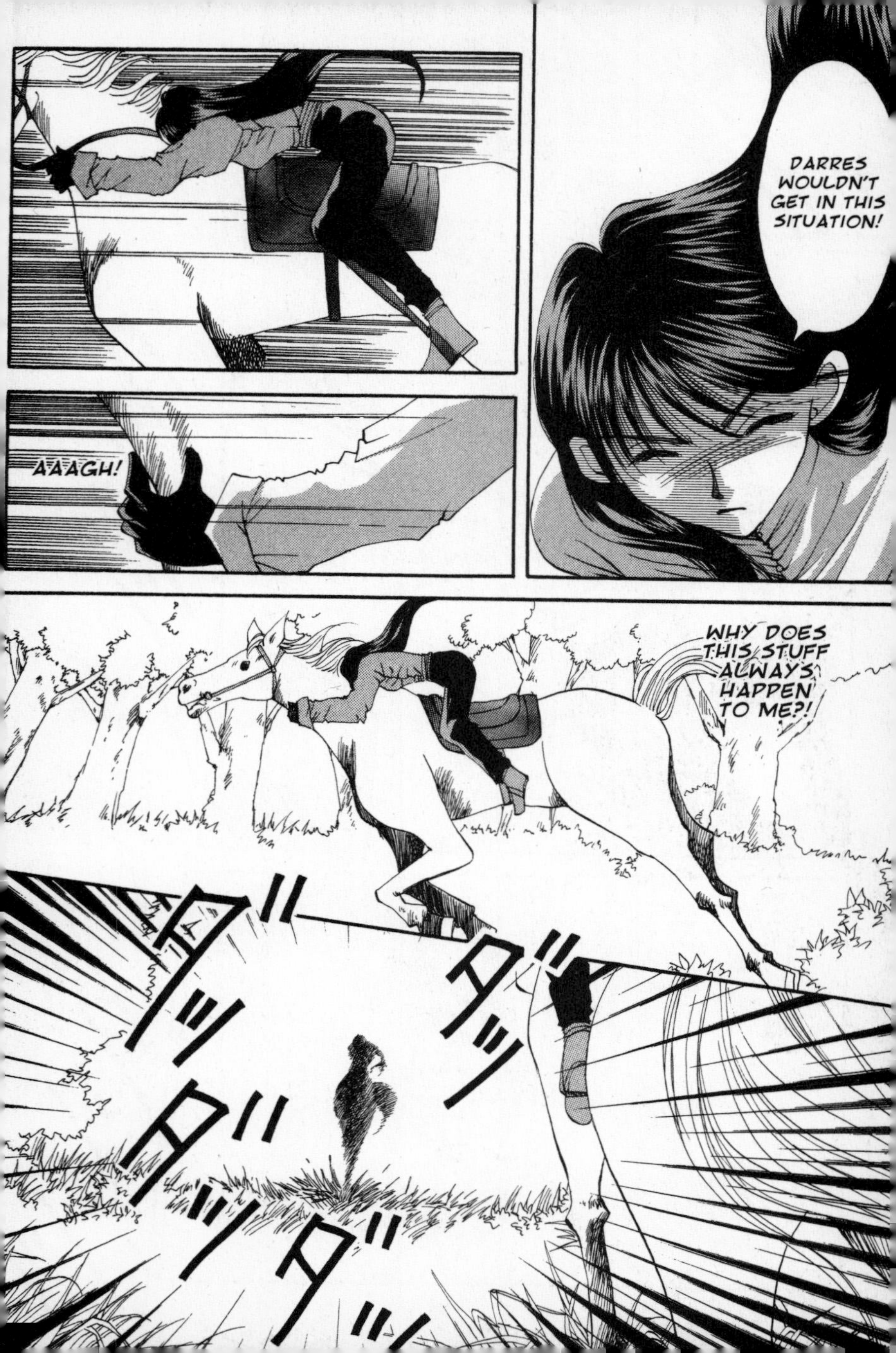
DARRES WOULDN'T GET IN THIS SITUATION!
AAAGH!
WHY DOES THIS STUFF ALWAYS HAPPEN TO ME?!
ダッ
ダッ
ダッ
ダッ

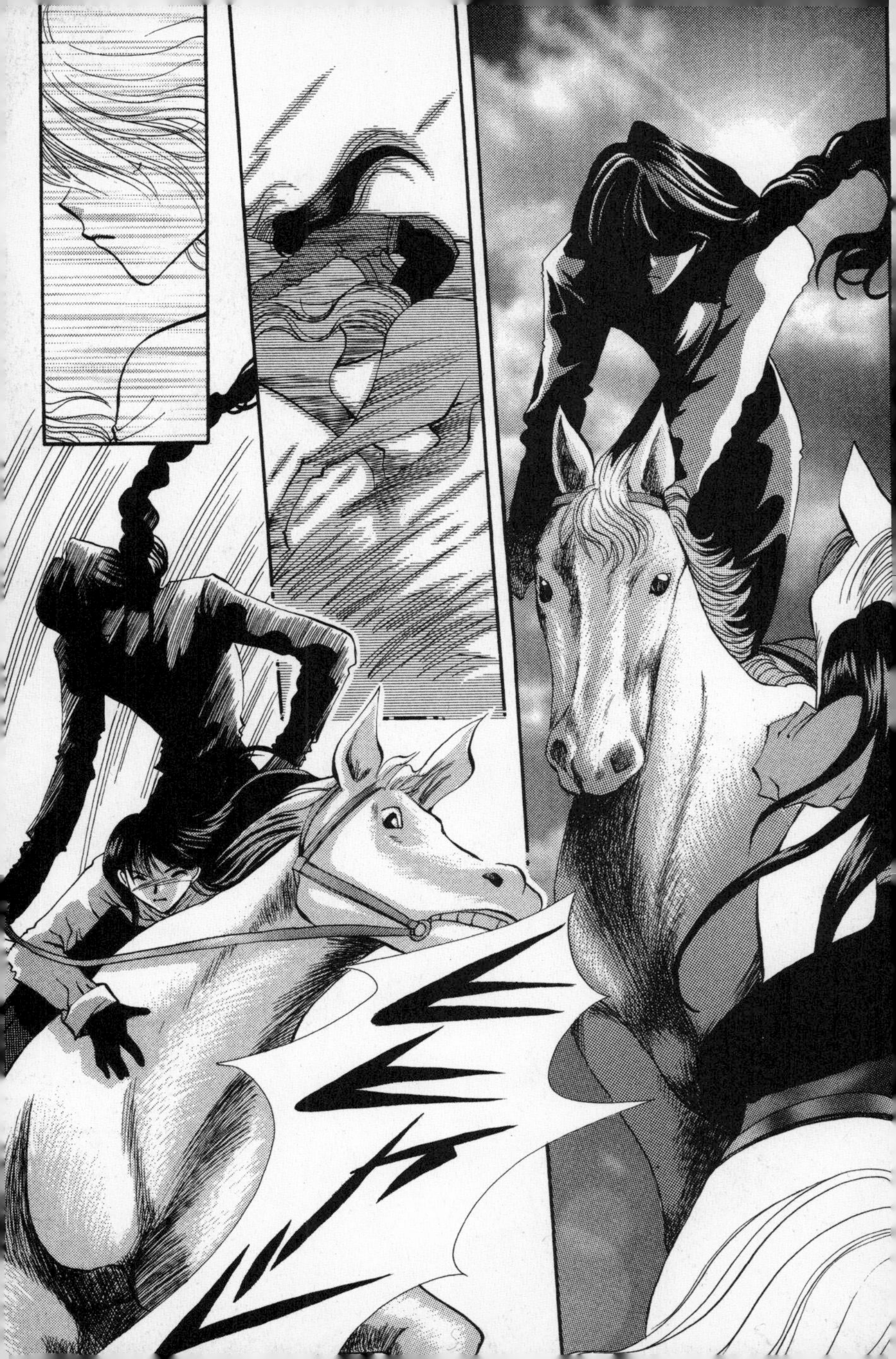

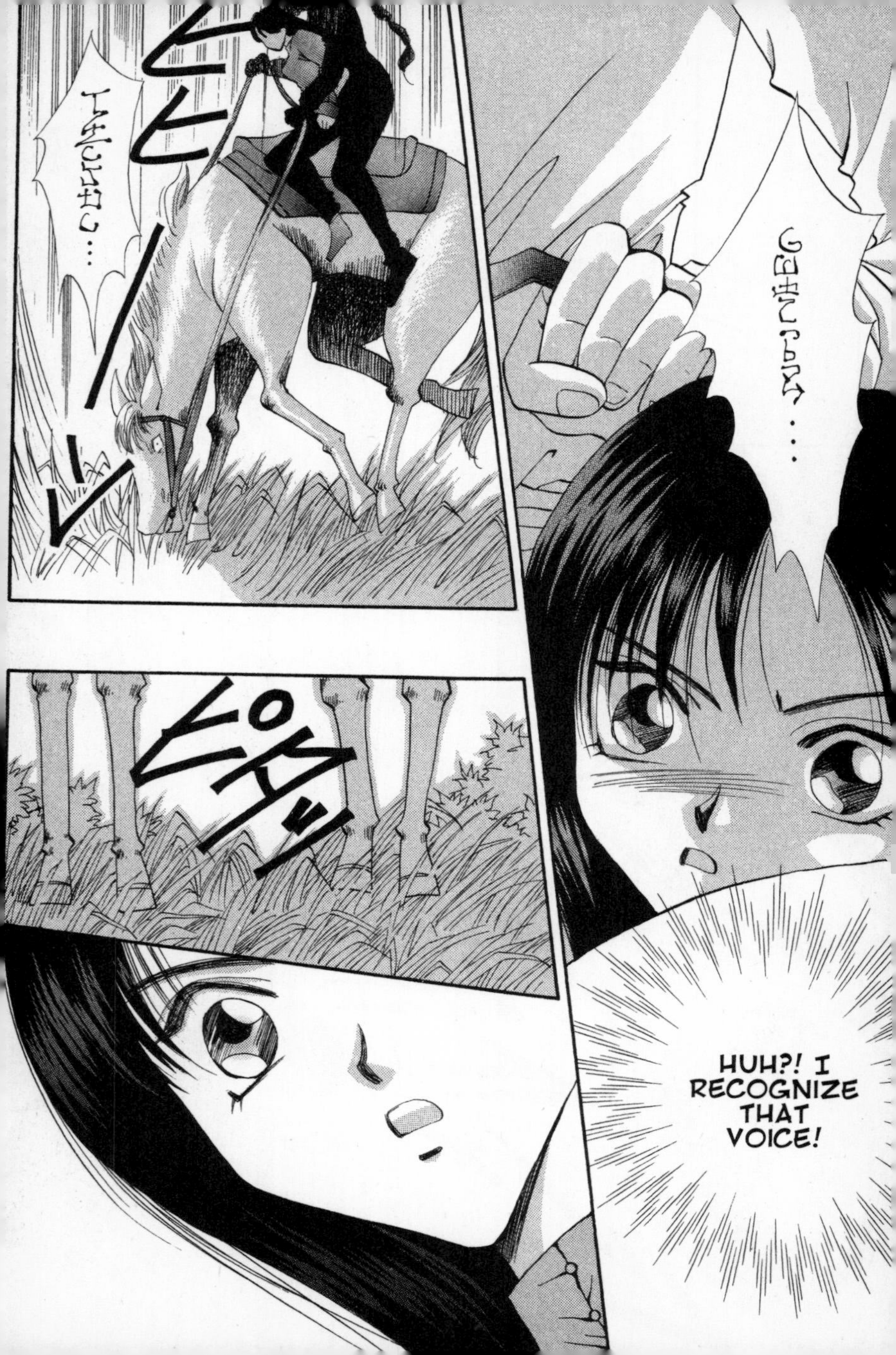
HUH?! I RECOGNIZE THAT VOICE!

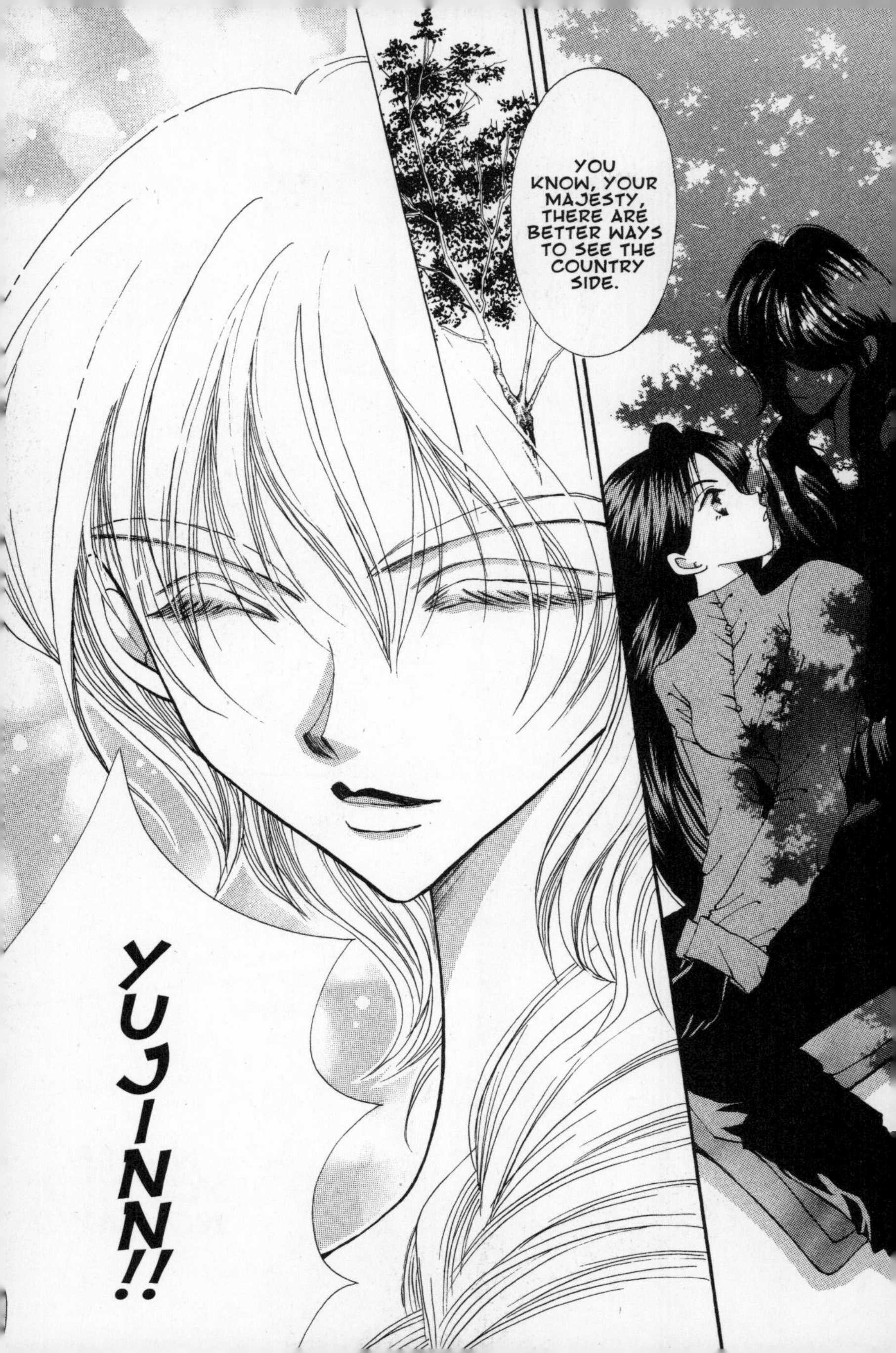
YOU KNOW, YOUR MAJESTY, THERE ARE BETTER WAYS TO SEE THE COUNTRY SIDE.
YUJINN!!

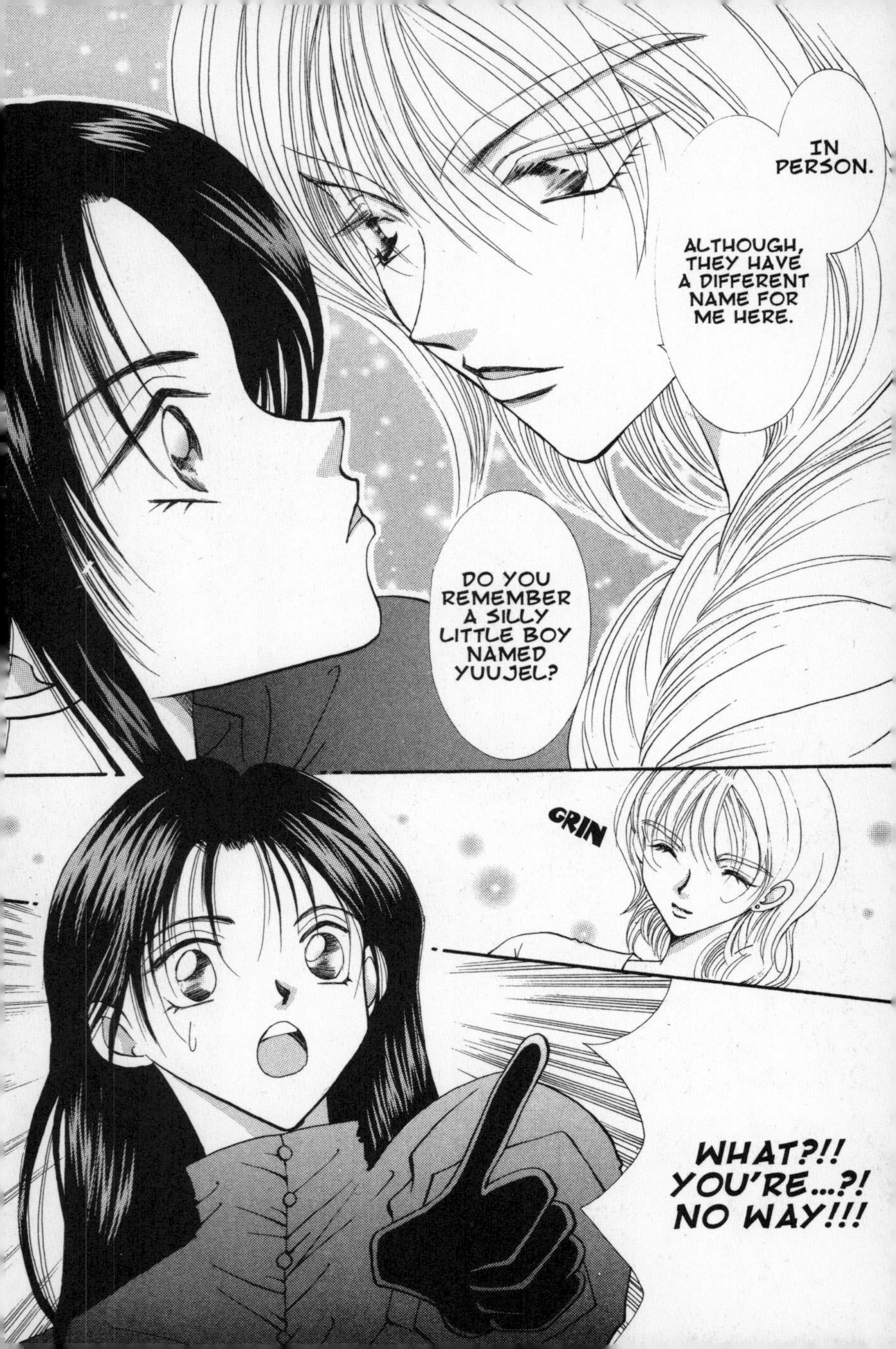
IN PERSON.
ALTHOUGH, THEY HAVE A DIFFERENT NAME FOR ME HERE.
DO YOU REMEMBER A SILLY LITTLE BOY NAMED YUUJEL?
GRIN
WHAT?!! YOU'RE...?! NO WAY!!!

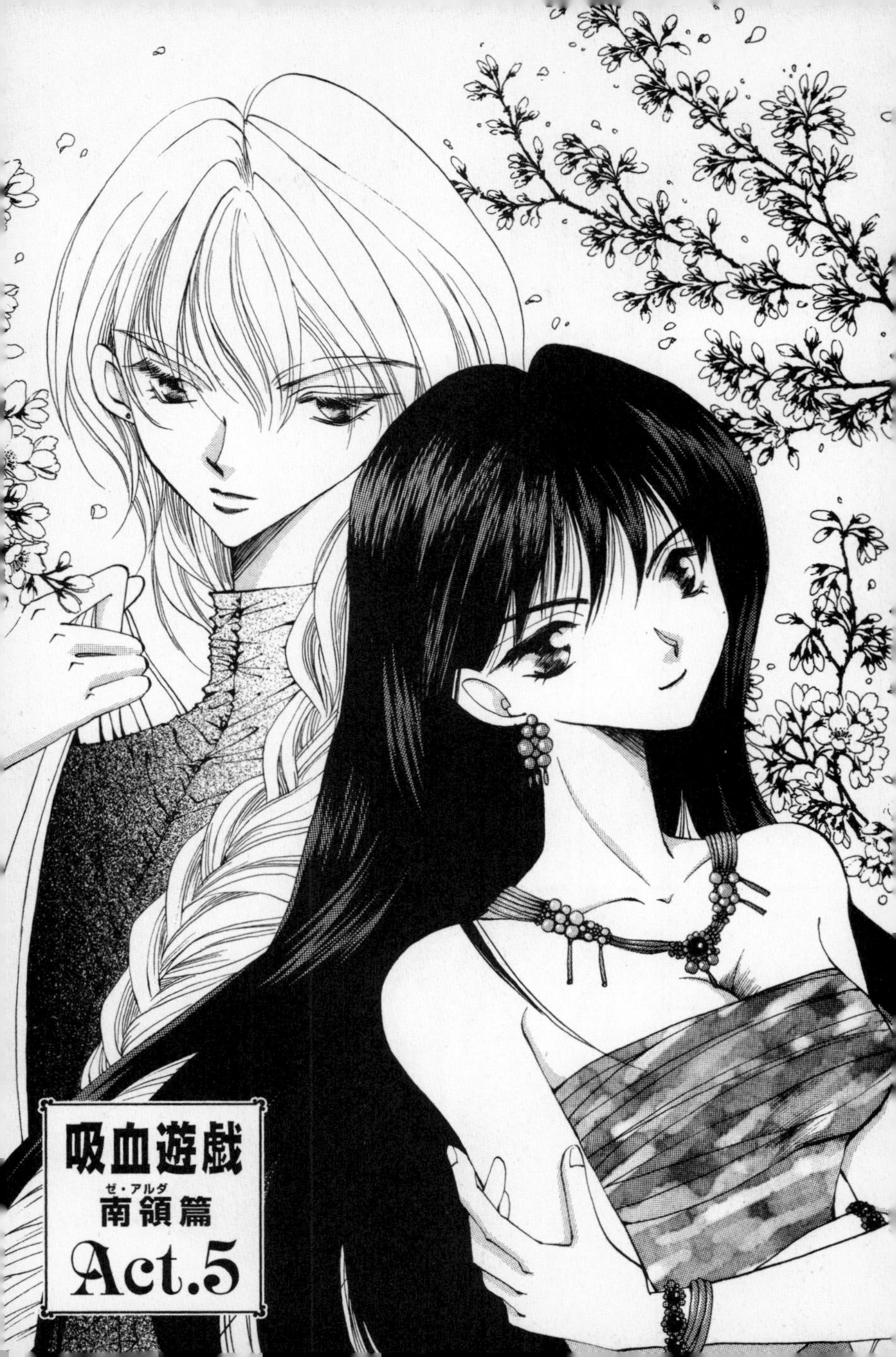
吸血遊戯
南領篇（ゼ・アルダ）
Act.5

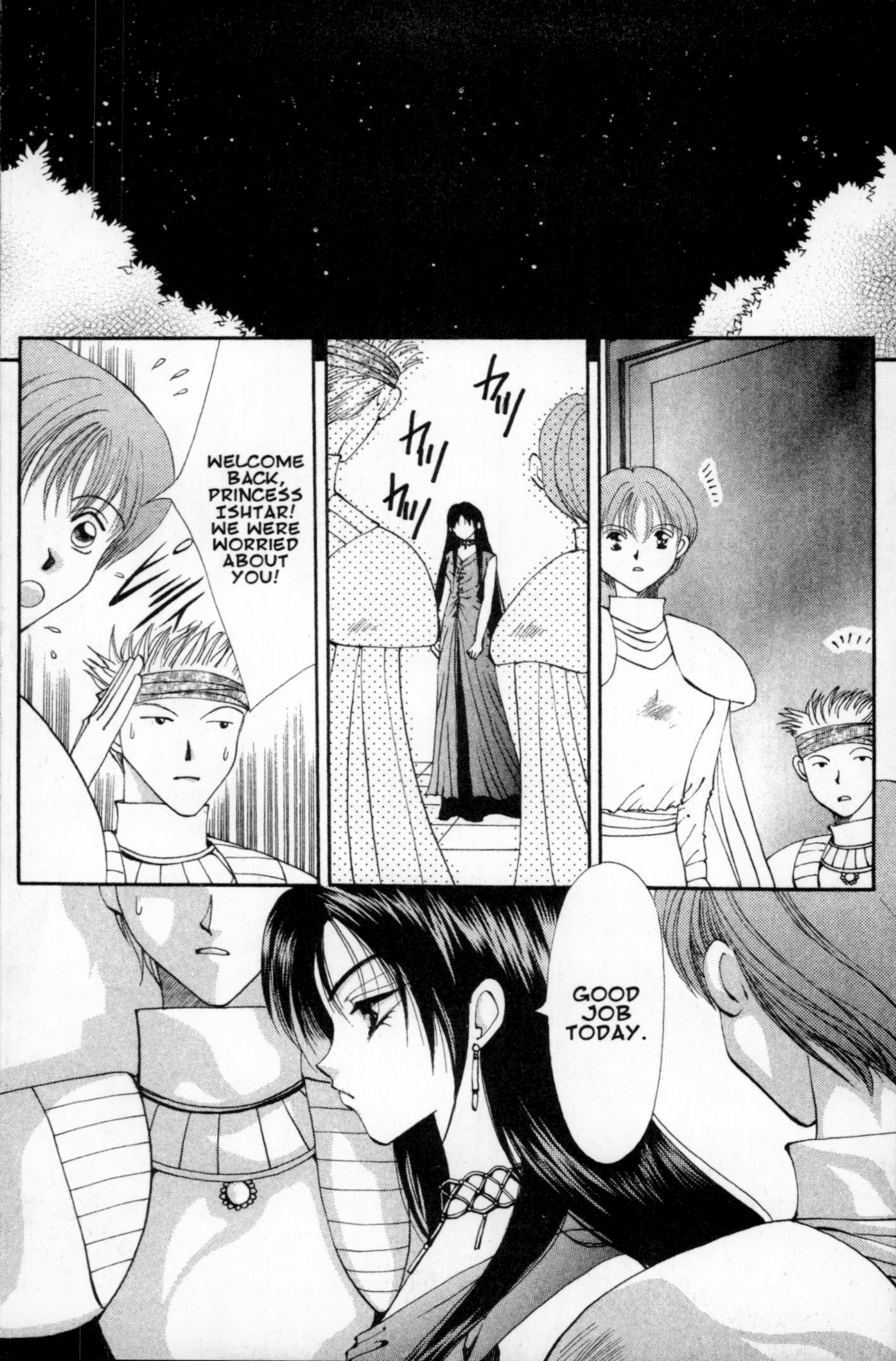
カッ
カッ
カッ
WELCOME BACK, PRINCESS ISHTAR! WE WERE WORRIED ABOUT YOU!
GOOD JOB TODAY.

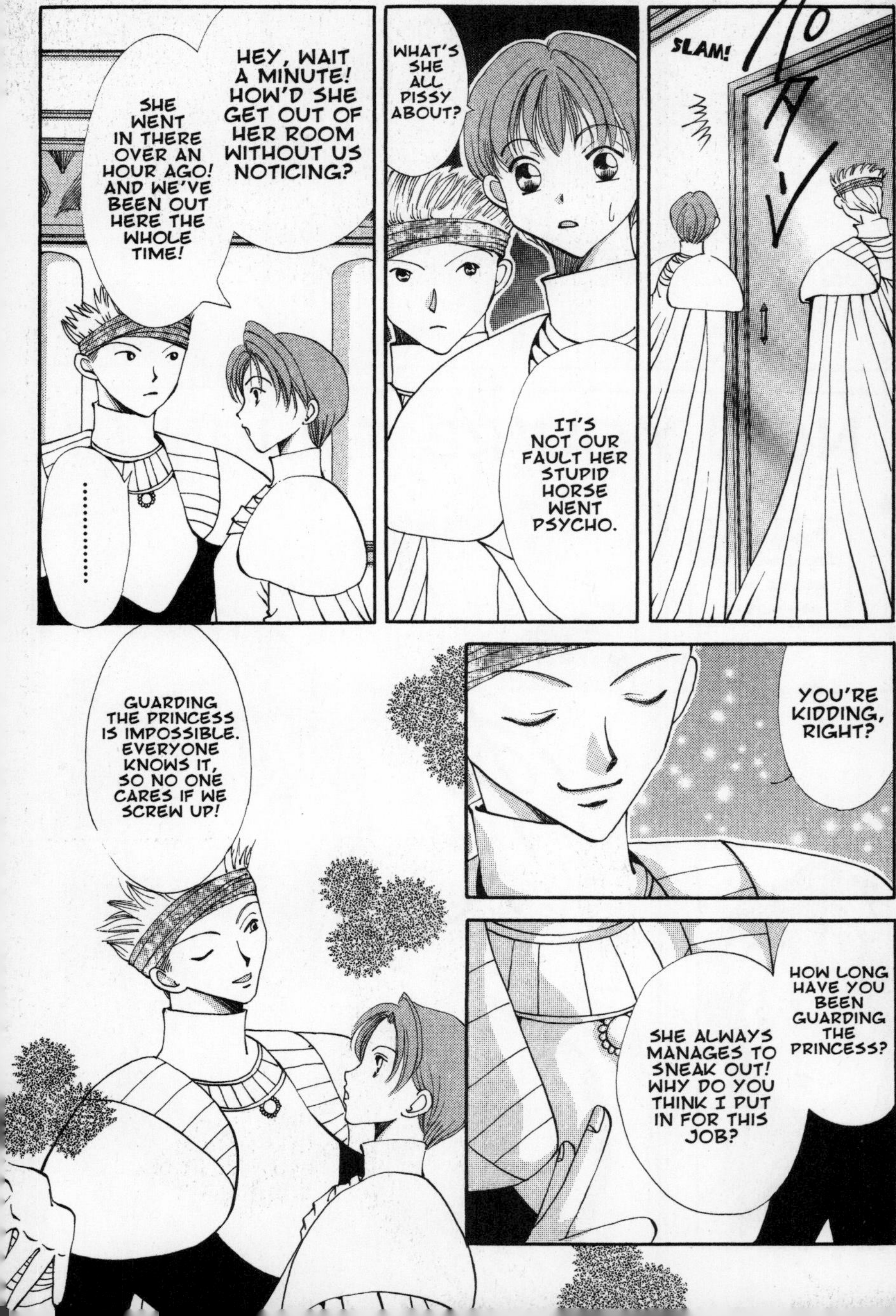
SLAM!
WHAT'S SHE ALL PISSY ABOUT?
IT'S NOT OUR FAULT HER STUPID HORSE WENT PSYCHO.
HEY, WAIT A MINUTE! HOW'D SHE GET OUT OF HER ROOM WITHOUT US NOTICING?
SHE WENT IN THERE OVER AN HOUR AGO! AND WE'VE BEEN OUT HERE THE WHOLE TIME!
....
YOU'RE KIDDING, RIGHT?
HOW LONG HAVE YOU BEEN GUARDING THE PRINCESS?
SHE ALWAYS MANAGES TO SNEAK OUT! WHY DO YOU THINK I PUT IN FOR THIS JOB?
GUARDING THE PRINCESS IS IMPOSSIBLE. EVERYONE KNOWS IT, SO NO ONE CARES IF WE SCREW UP!

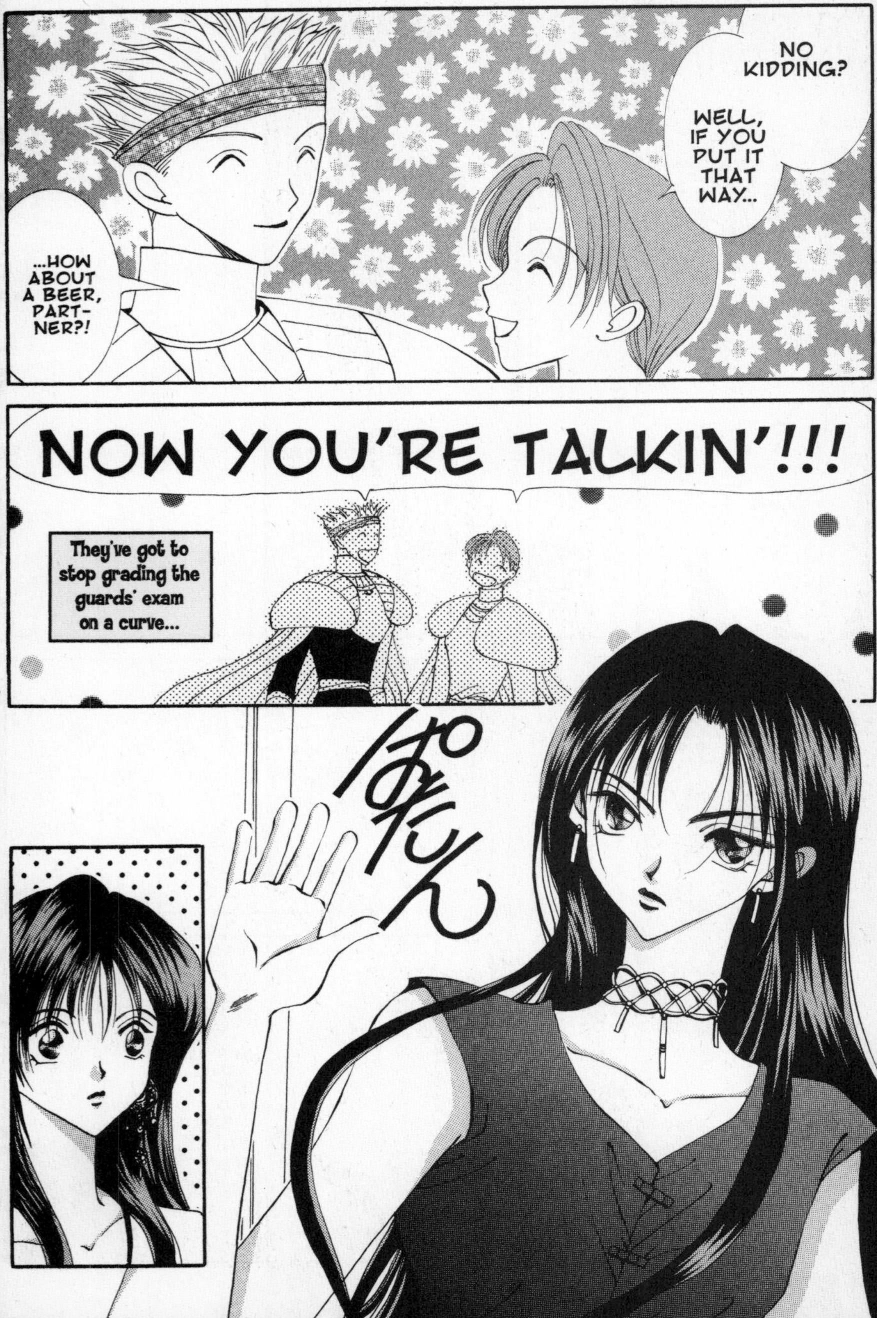
NO KIDDING?
WELL, IF YOU PUT IT THAT WAY...
...HOW ABOUT A BEER, PARTNER?!
NOW YOU'RE TALKIN'!!!
They've got to stop grading the guards' exam on a curve...
ぱたん

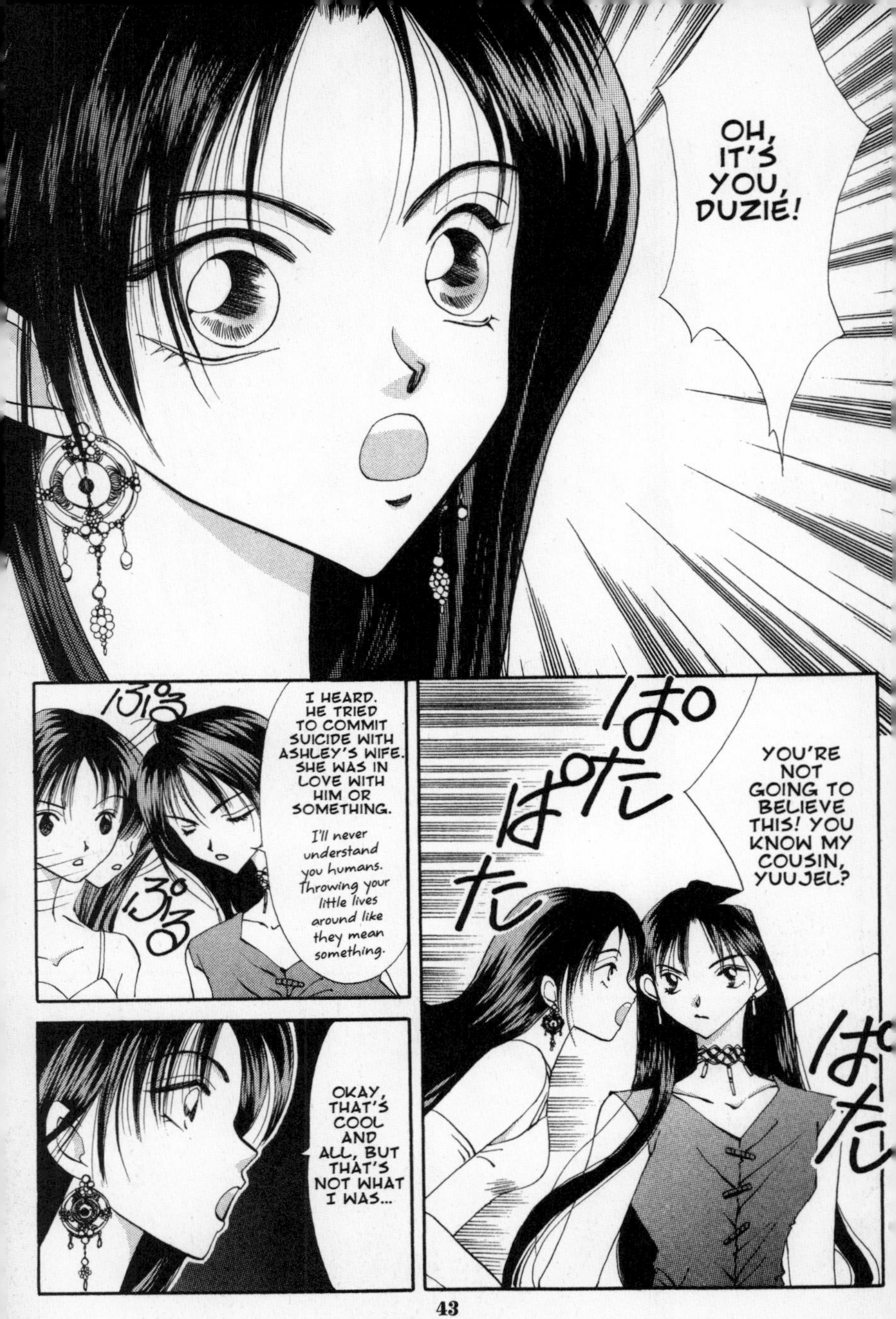
OH, IT'S YOU, DUZIÉ!
ぱたぱた
YOU'RE NOT GOING TO BELIEVE THIS! YOU KNOW MY COUSIN, YUUJEL?
ぱた
ぷる ぷる
I HEARD. HE TRIED TO COMMIT SUICIDE WITH ASHLEY'S WIFE. SHE WAS IN LOVE WITH HIM OR SOMETHING.
I'll never understand you humans. Throwing your little lives around like they mean something.
OKAY, THAT'S COOL AND ALL, BUT THAT'S NOT WHAT I WAS...

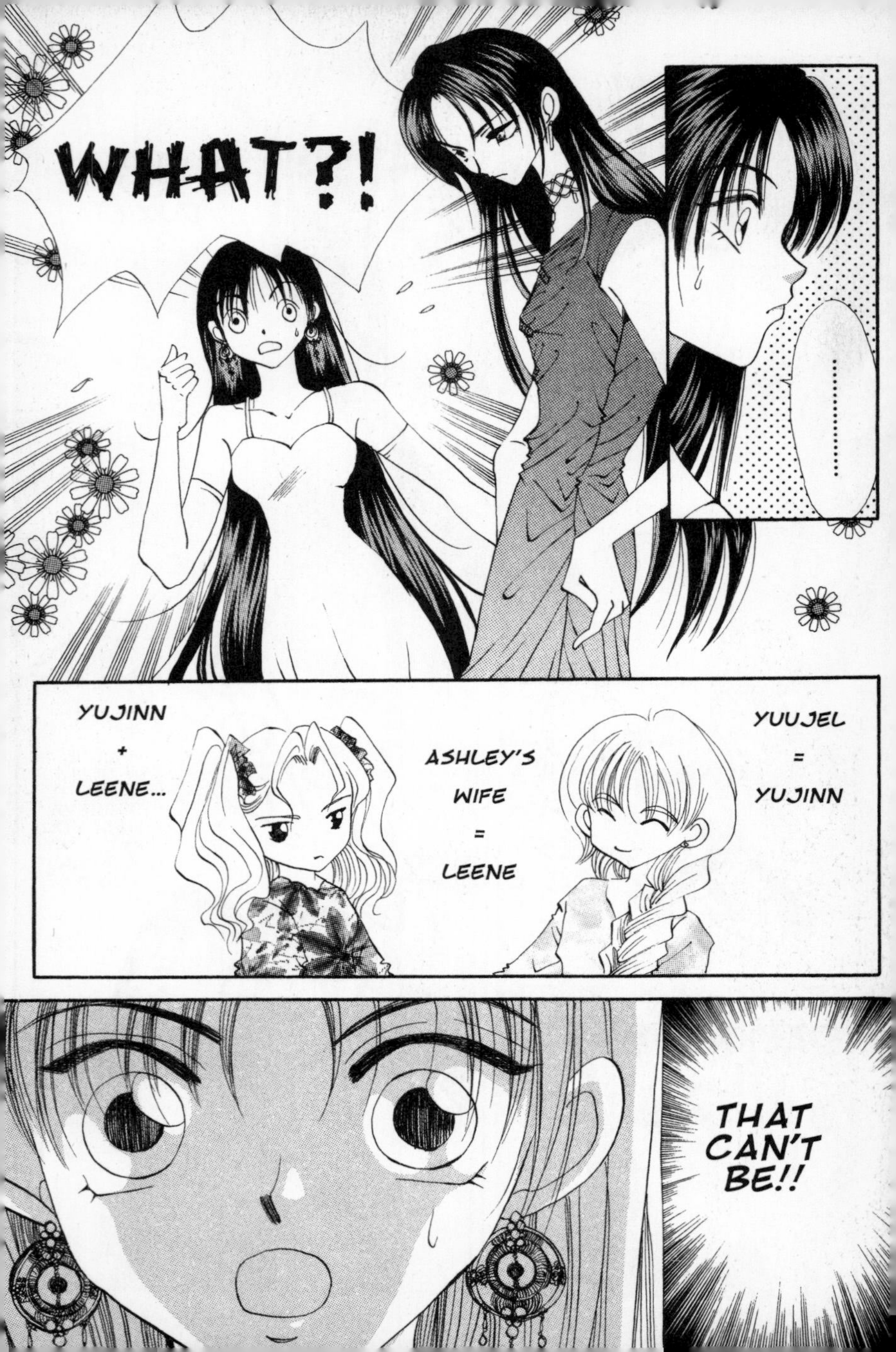
......
WHAT?!
YUUJEL = YUJINN
ASHLEY'S WIFE = LEENE
YUJINN + LEENE...
THAT CAN'T BE!!

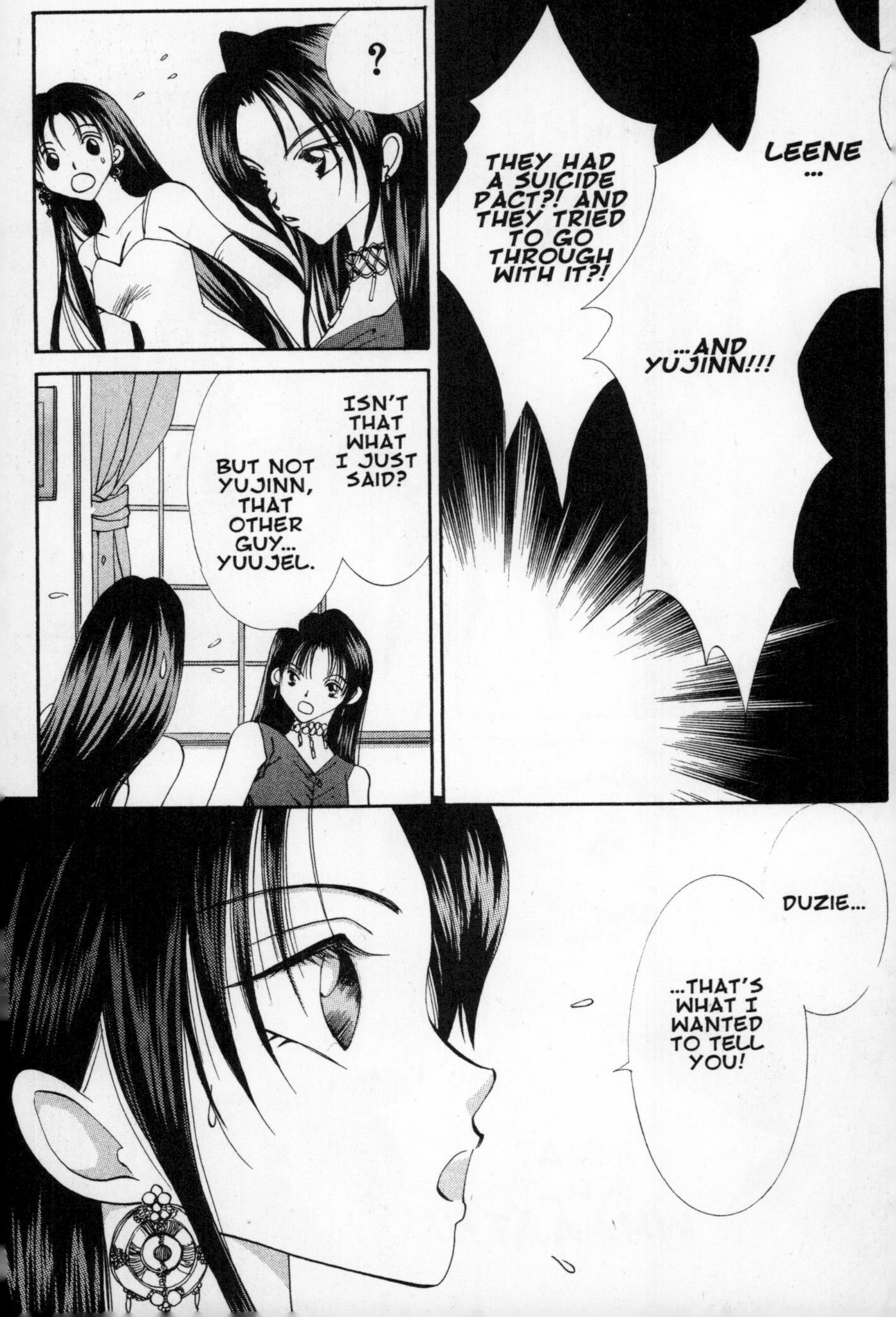
LEENE ...
THEY HAD A SUICIDE PACT?! AND THEY TRIED TO GO THROUGH WITH IT?!
...AND YUJINN!!!
?
ISN'T THAT WHAT I JUST SAID?
BUT NOT YUJINN, THAT OTHER GUY... YUUJEL.
DUZIE...
...THAT'S WHAT I WANTED TO TELL YOU!

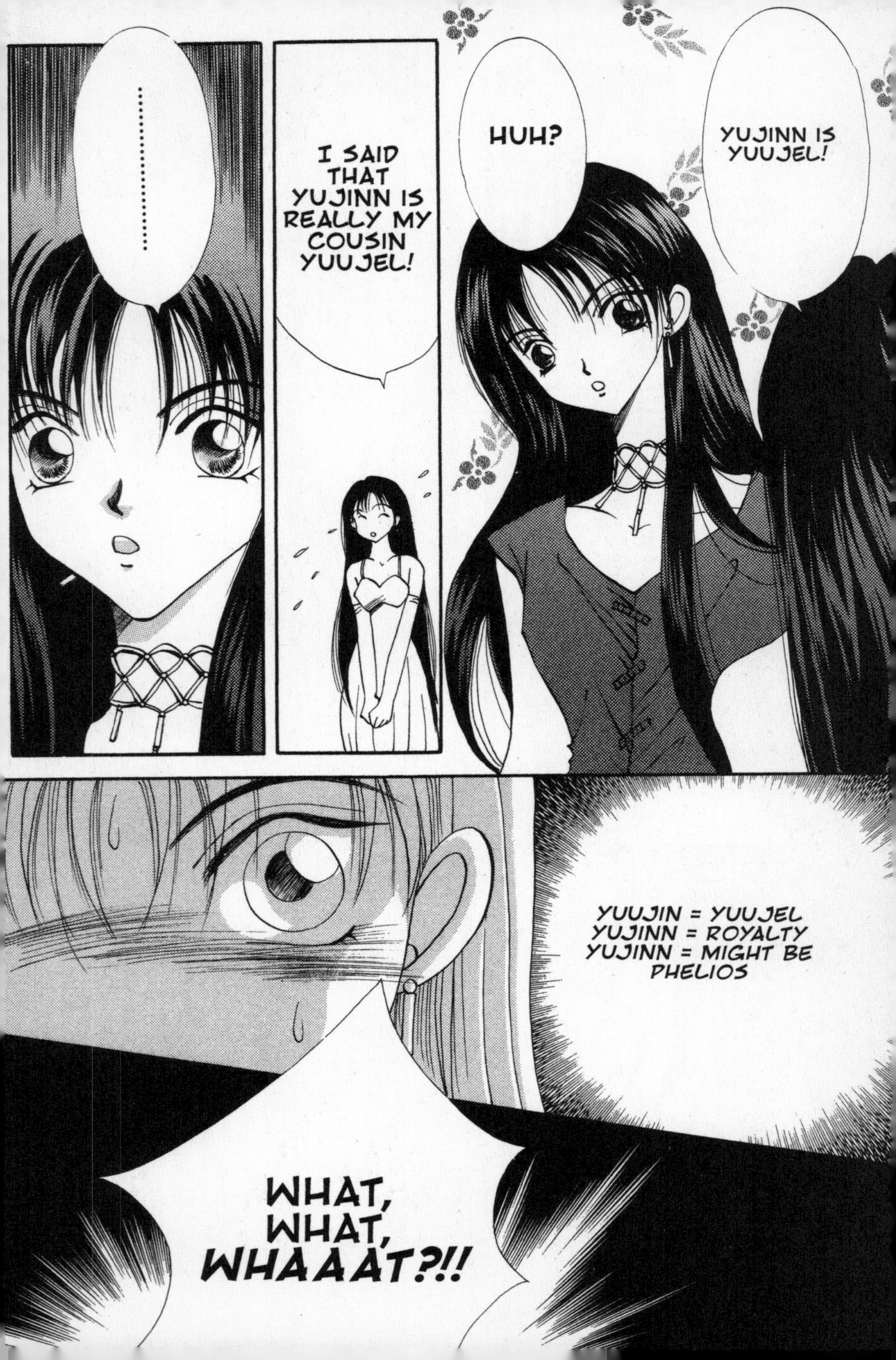
YUJINN IS YUUJEL!
HUH?
I SAID THAT YUJINN IS REALLY MY COUSIN YUUJEL!
......
YUUJIN = YUUJEL
YUJINN = ROYALTY
YUJINN = MIGHT BE PHELIOS
WHAT, WHAT, WHAAAT?!!

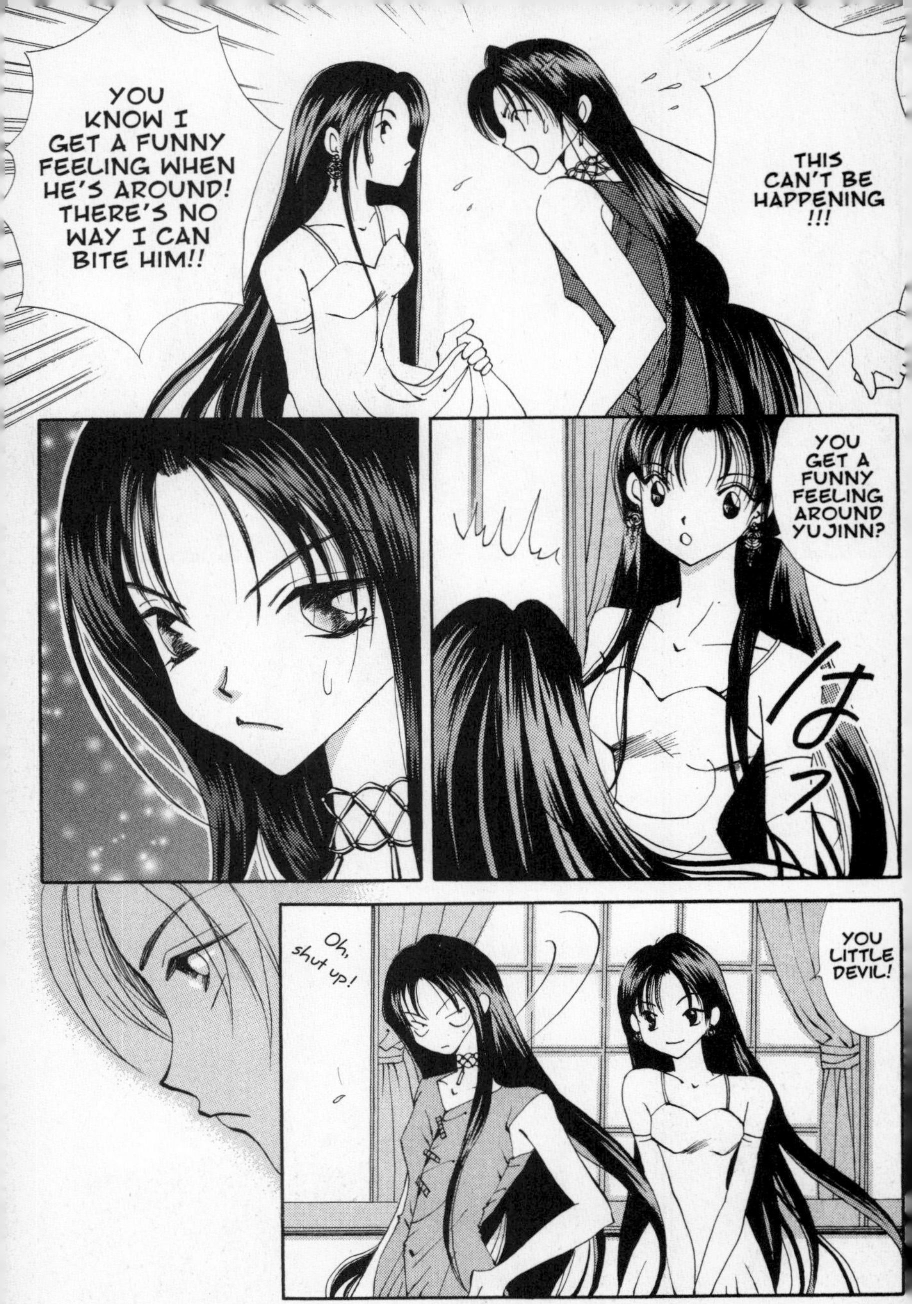
THIS CAN'T BE HAPPENING!!!
YOU KNOW I GET A FUNNY FEELING WHEN HE'S AROUND! THERE'S NO WAY I CAN BITE HIM!!
YOU GET A FUNNY FEELING AROUND YUJINN?
はっ
YOU LITTLE DEVIL!
Oh, shut up!

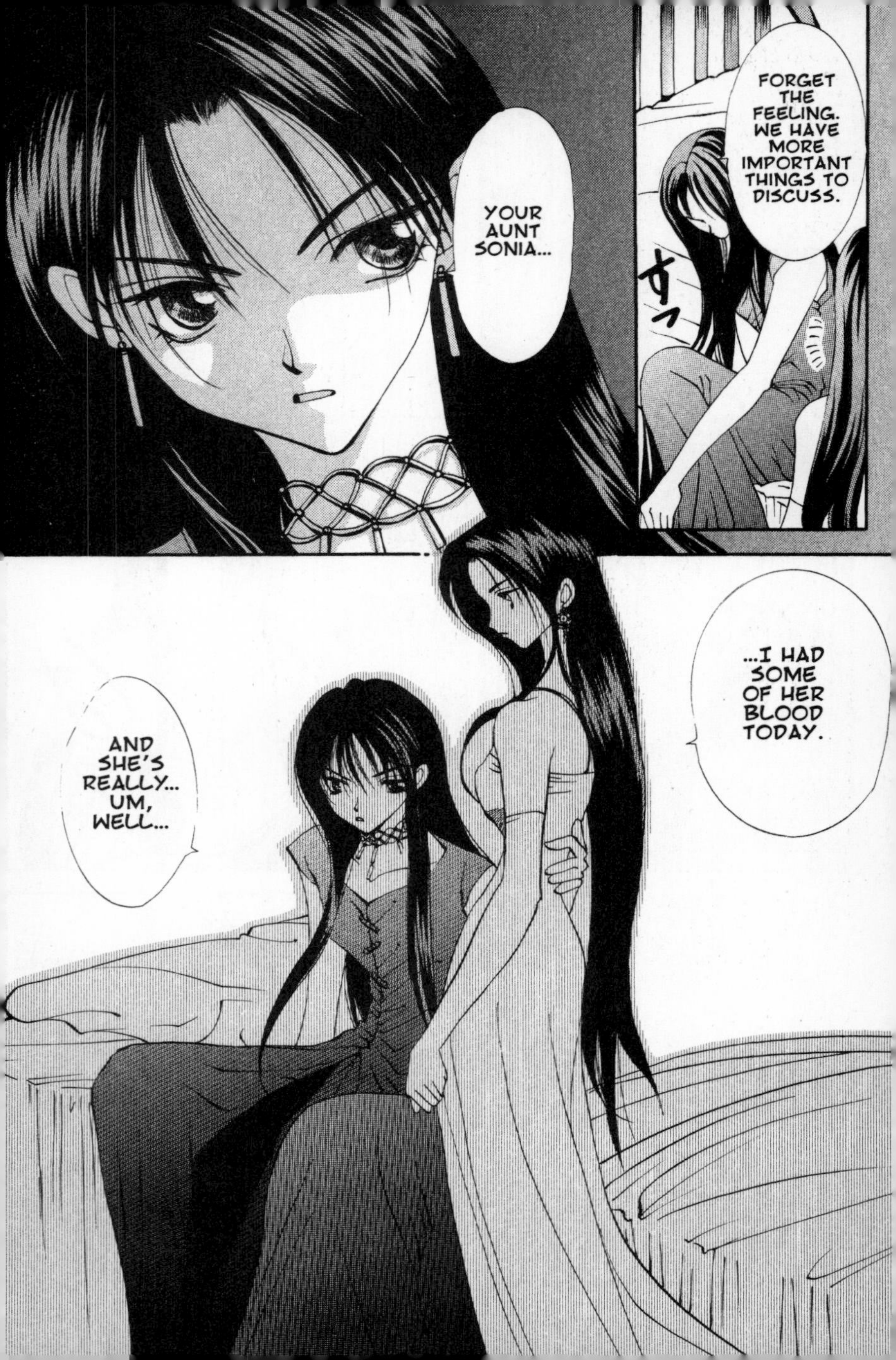
FORGET THE FEELING. WE HAVE MORE IMPORTANT THINGS TO DISCUSS.
すっ
YOUR AUNT SONIA...
...I HAD SOME OF HER BLOOD TODAY.
AND SHE'S REALLY... UM, WELL...

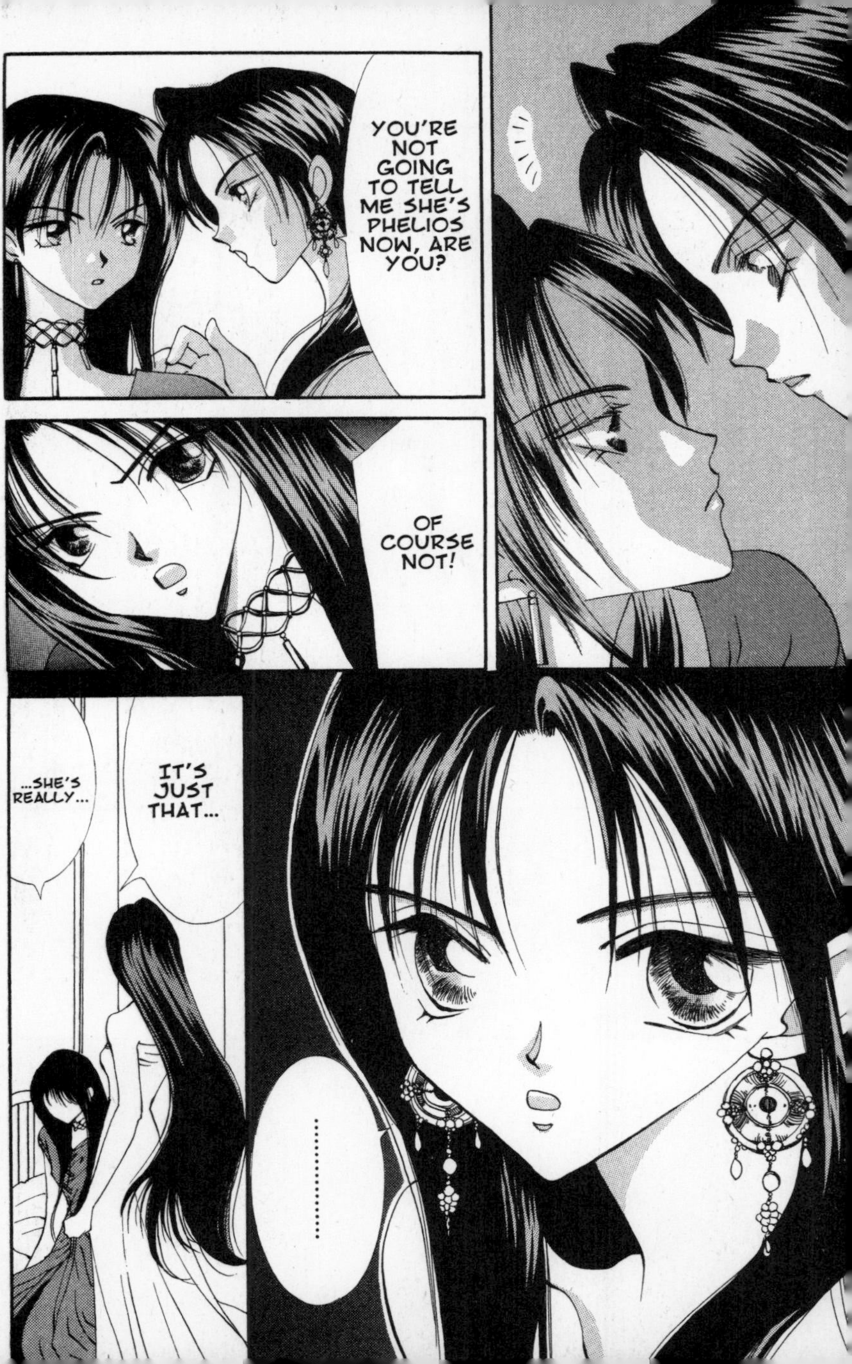
YOU'RE NOT GOING TO TELL ME SHE'S PHELIOS NOW, ARE YOU?
OF COURSE NOT!
....
IT'S JUST THAT...
...SHE'S REALLY...

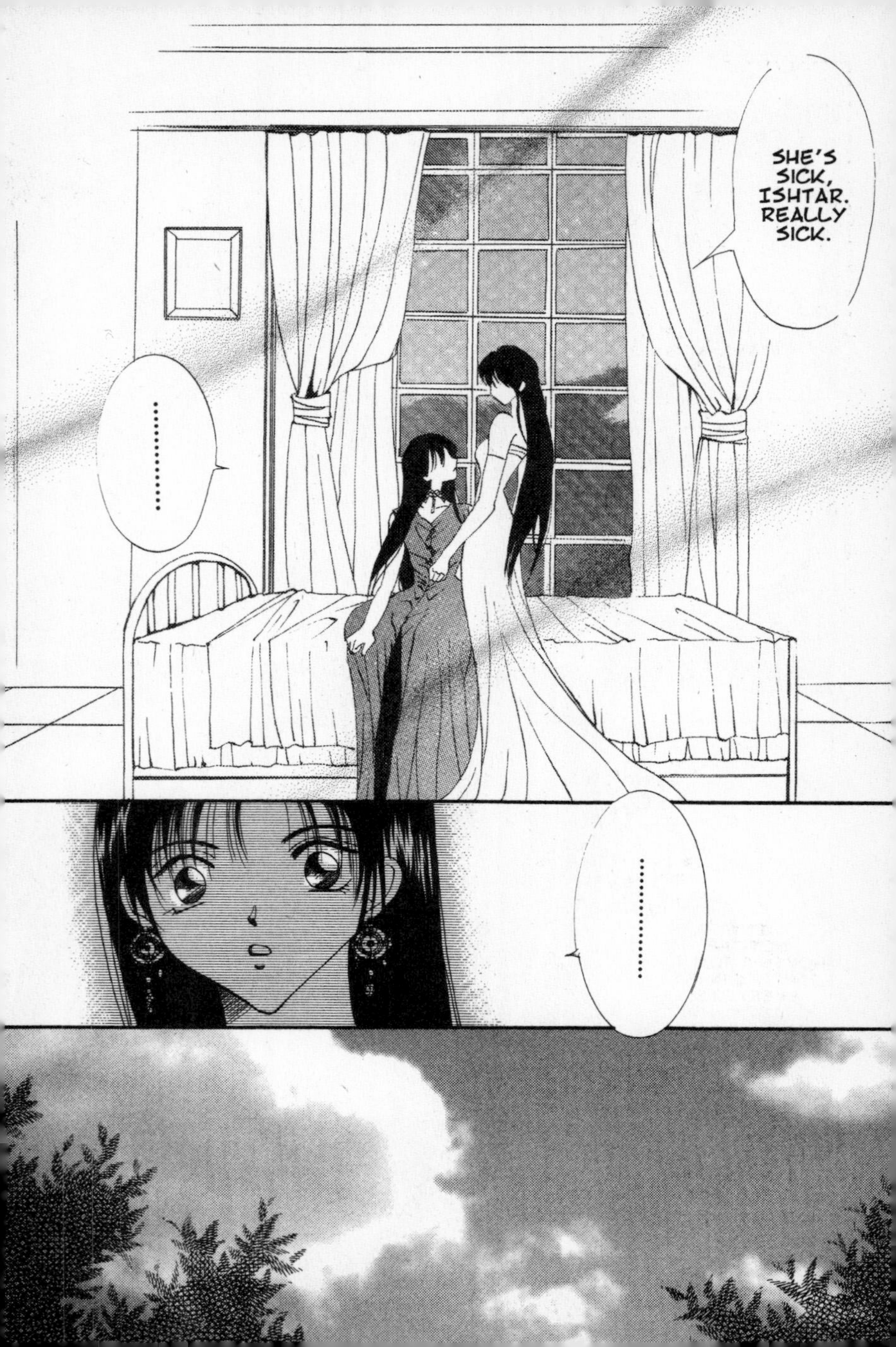
SHE'S SICK, ISHTAR. REALLY SICK.
....
....

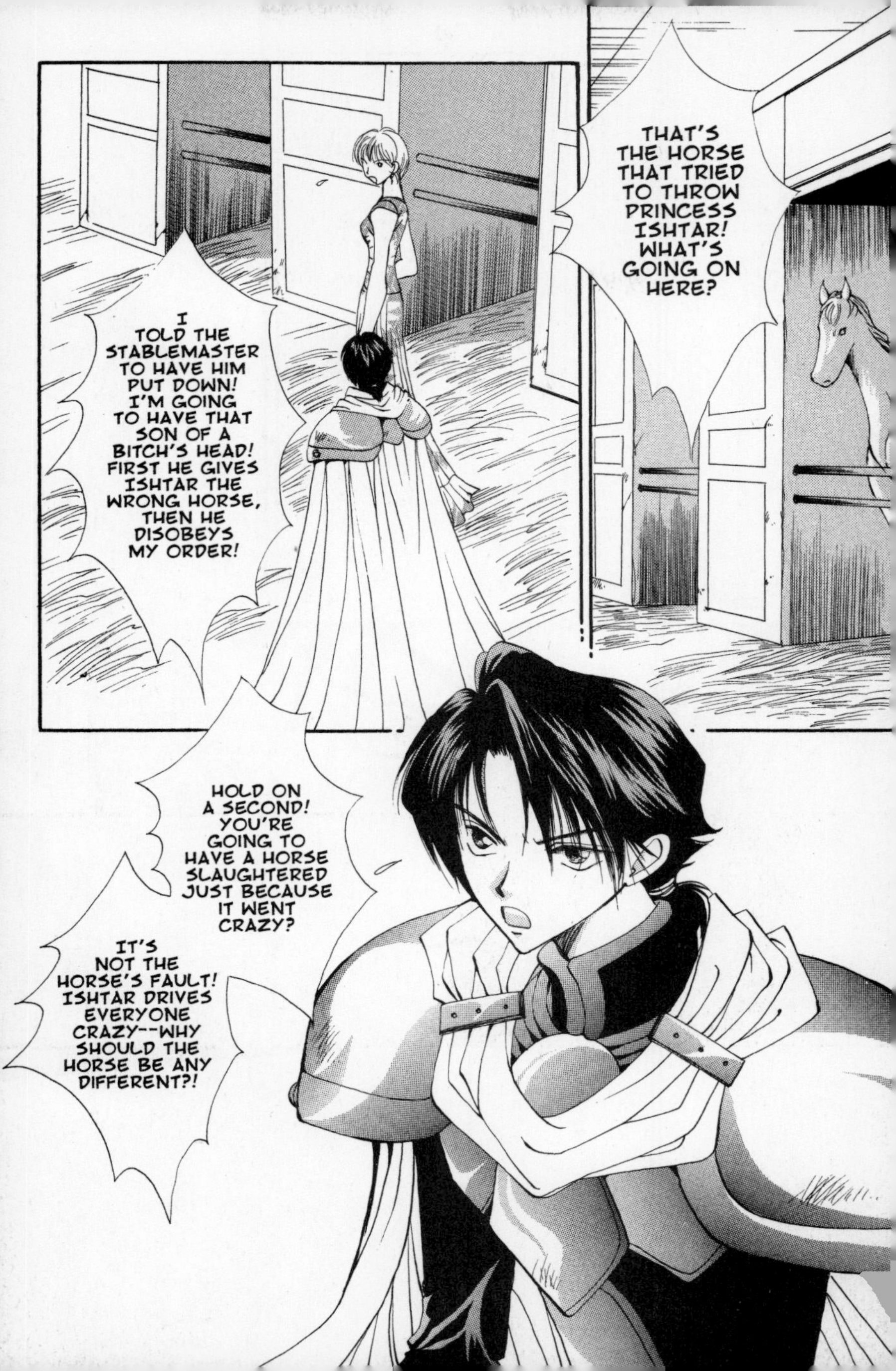
THAT'S THE HORSE THAT TRIED TO THROW PRINCESS ISHTAR! WHAT'S GOING ON HERE?
I TOLD THE STABLEMASTER TO HAVE HIM PUT DOWN! I'M GOING TO HAVE THAT SON OF A BITCH'S HEAD! FIRST HE GIVES ISHTAR THE WRONG HORSE, THEN HE DISOBEYS MY ORDER!
HOLD ON A SECOND! YOU'RE GOING TO HAVE A HORSE SLAUGHTERED JUST BECAUSE IT WENT CRAZY?
IT'S NOT THE HORSE'S FAULT! ISHTAR DRIVES EVERYONE CRAZY--WHY SHOULD THE HORSE BE ANY DIFFERENT?!

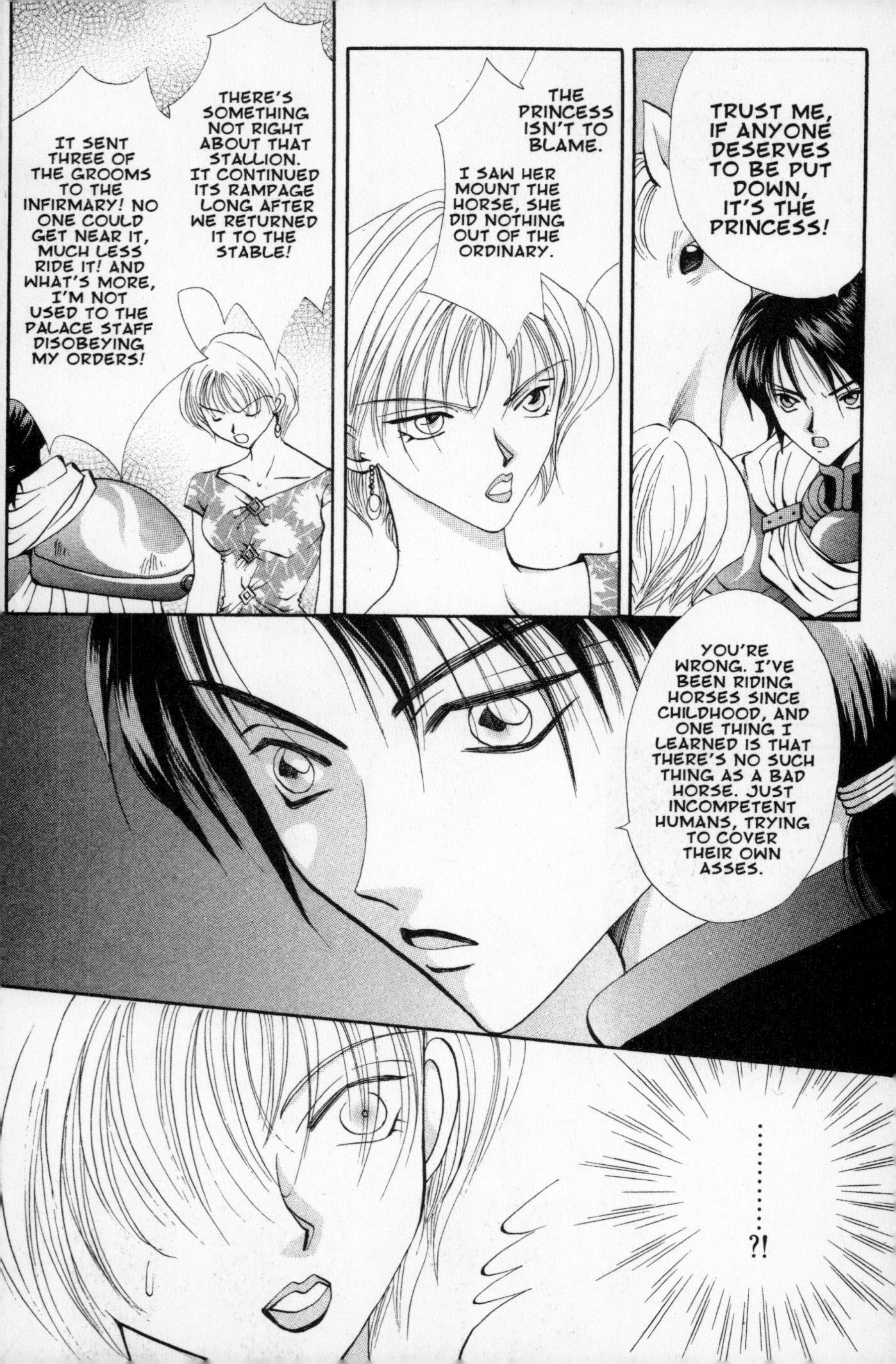
TRUST ME, IF ANYONE DESERVES TO BE PUT DOWN, IT'S THE PRINCESS!
THE PRINCESS ISN'T TO BLAME.
I SAW HER MOUNT THE HORSE, SHE DID NOTHING OUT OF THE ORDINARY.
THERE'S SOMETHING NOT RIGHT ABOUT THAT STALLION. IT CONTINUED ITS RAMPAGE LONG AFTER WE RETURNED IT TO THE STABLE!
IT SENT THREE OF THE GROOMS TO THE INFIRMARY! NO ONE COULD GET NEAR IT, MUCH LESS RIDE IT! AND WHAT'S MORE, I'M NOT USED TO THE PALACE STAFF DISOBEYING MY ORDERS!
YOU'RE WRONG. I'VE BEEN RIDING HORSES SINCE CHILDHOOD, AND ONE THING I LEARNED IS THAT THERE'S NO SUCH THING AS A BAD HORSE. JUST INCOMPETENT HUMANS, TRYING TO COVER THEIR OWN ASSES.
....
?!

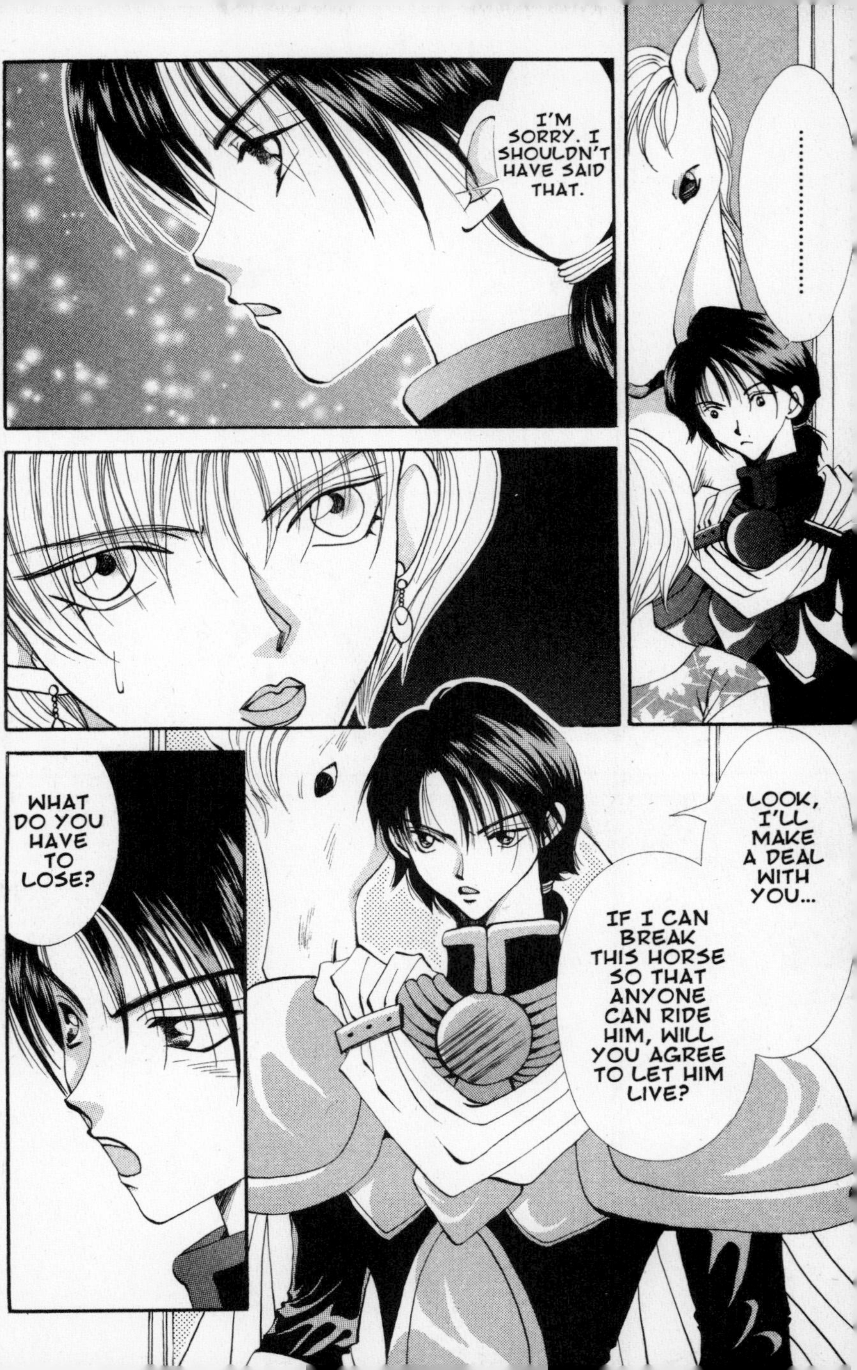
......
I'M SORRY. I SHOULDN'T HAVE SAID THAT.
LOOK, I'LL MAKE A DEAL WITH YOU...
IF I CAN BREAK THIS HORSE SO THAT ANYONE CAN RIDE HIM, WILL YOU AGREE TO LET HIM LIVE?
WHAT DO YOU HAVE TO LOSE?

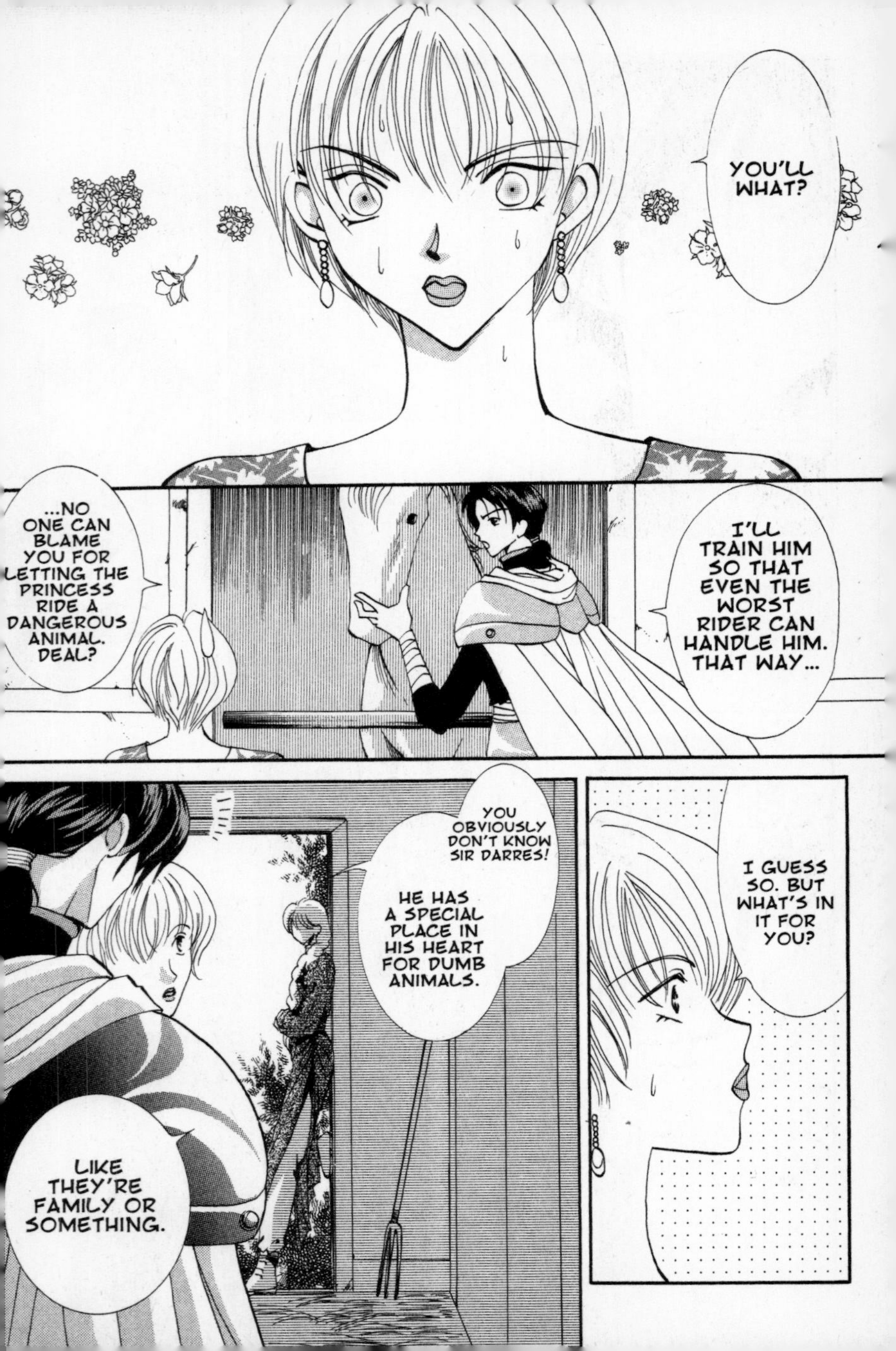
YOU'LL WHAT?
I'LL TRAIN HIM SO THAT EVEN THE WORST RIDER CAN HANDLE HIM. THAT WAY...
...NO ONE CAN BLAME YOU FOR LETTING THE PRINCESS RIDE A DANGEROUS ANIMAL. DEAL?
I GUESS SO. BUT WHAT'S IN IT FOR YOU?
YOU OBVIOUSLY DON'T KNOW SIR DARRES!
HE HAS A SPECIAL PLACE IN HIS HEART FOR DUMB ANIMALS.
LIKE THEY'RE FAMILY OR SOMETHING.

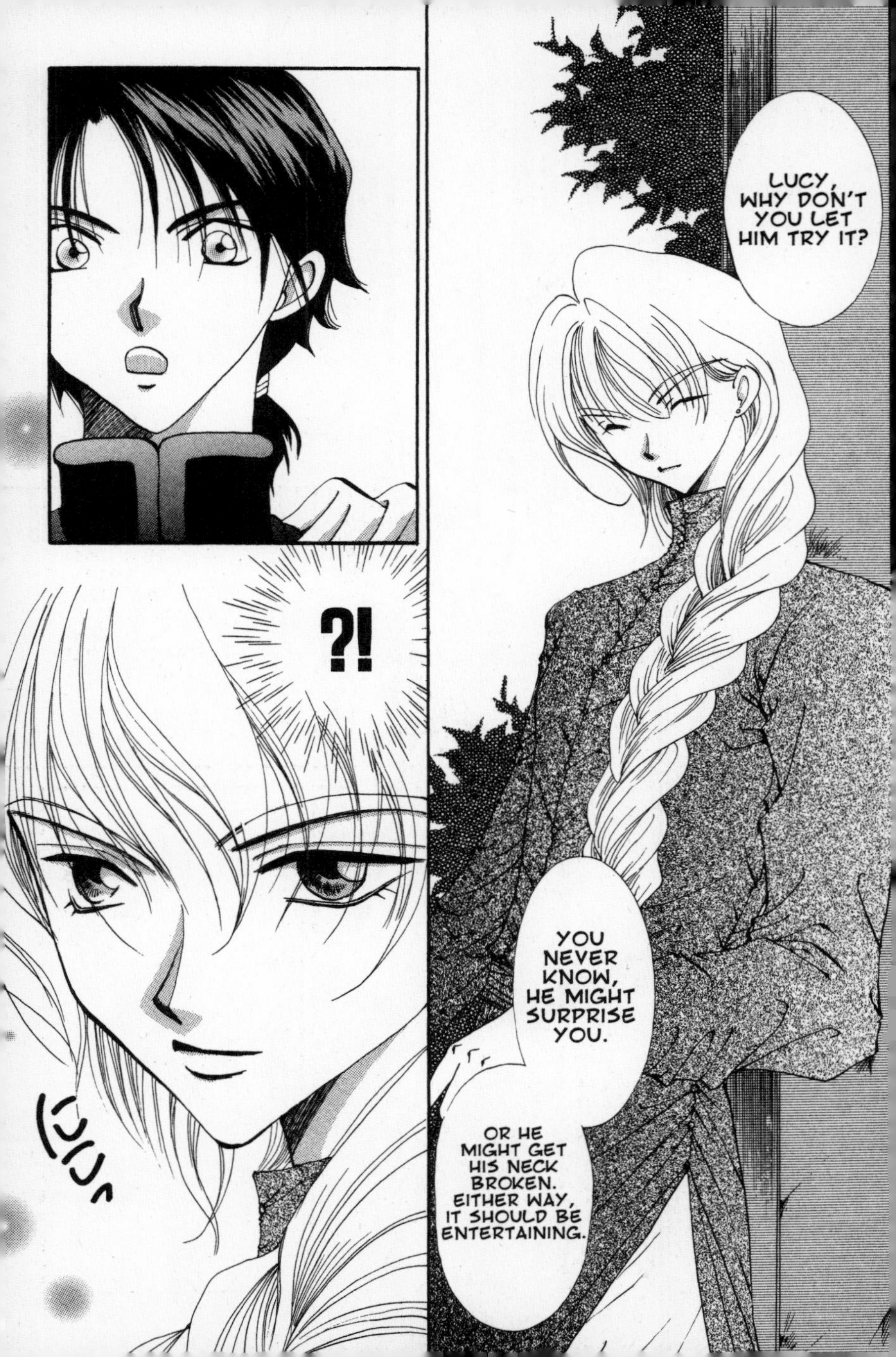
LUCY, WHY DON'T YOU LET HIM TRY IT?
YOU NEVER KNOW, HE MIGHT SURPRISE YOU.
OR HE MIGHT GET HIS NECK BROKEN. EITHER WAY, IT SHOULD BE ENTERTAINING.
?!

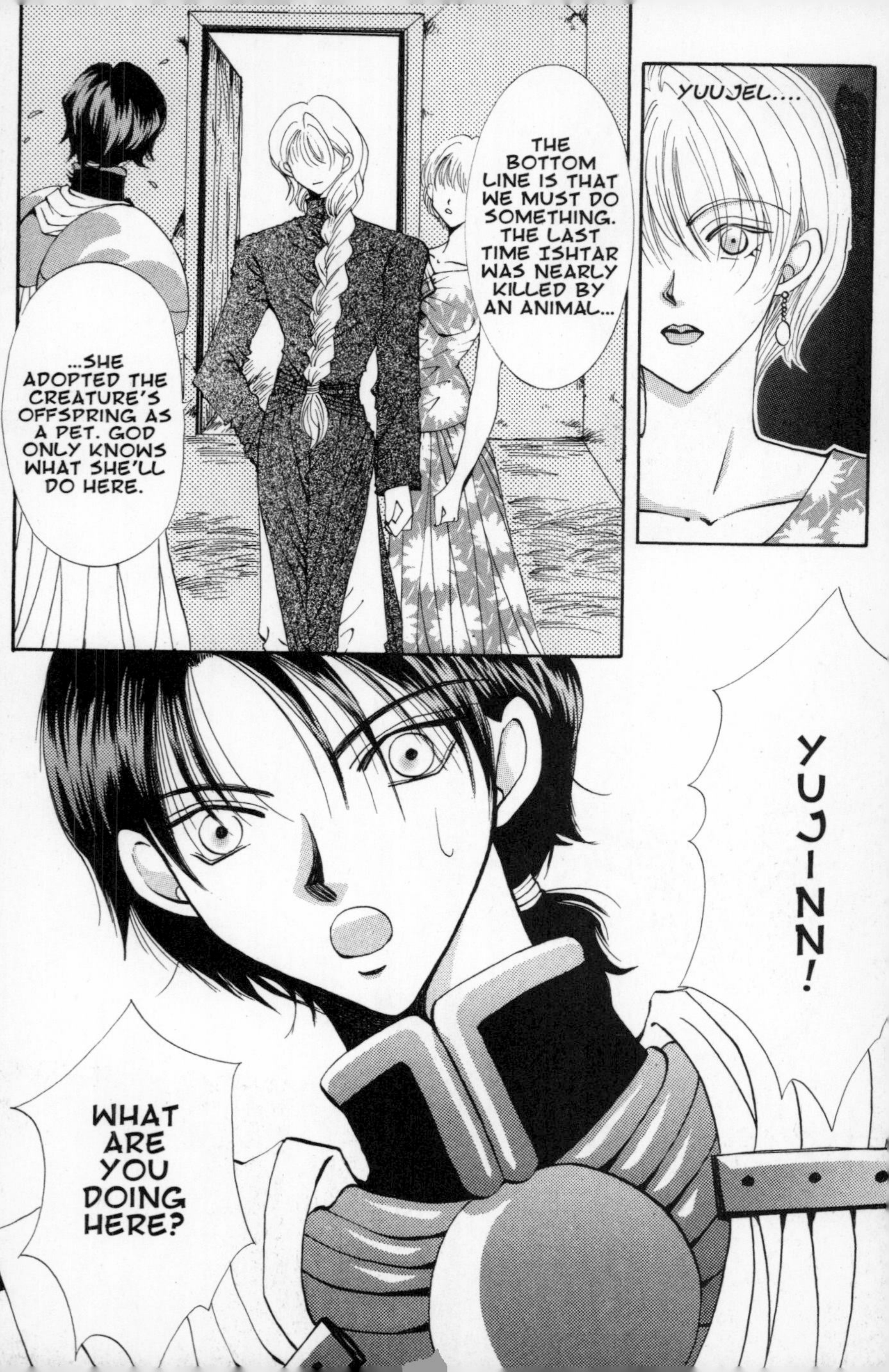
YUUJEL....
THE BOTTOM LINE IS THAT WE MUST DO SOMETHING. THE LAST TIME ISHTAR WAS NEARLY KILLED BY AN ANIMAL...
...SHE ADOPTED THE CREATURE'S OFFSPRING AS A PET. GOD ONLY KNOWS WHAT SHE'LL DO HERE.
YUJINN!
WHAT ARE YOU DOING HERE?

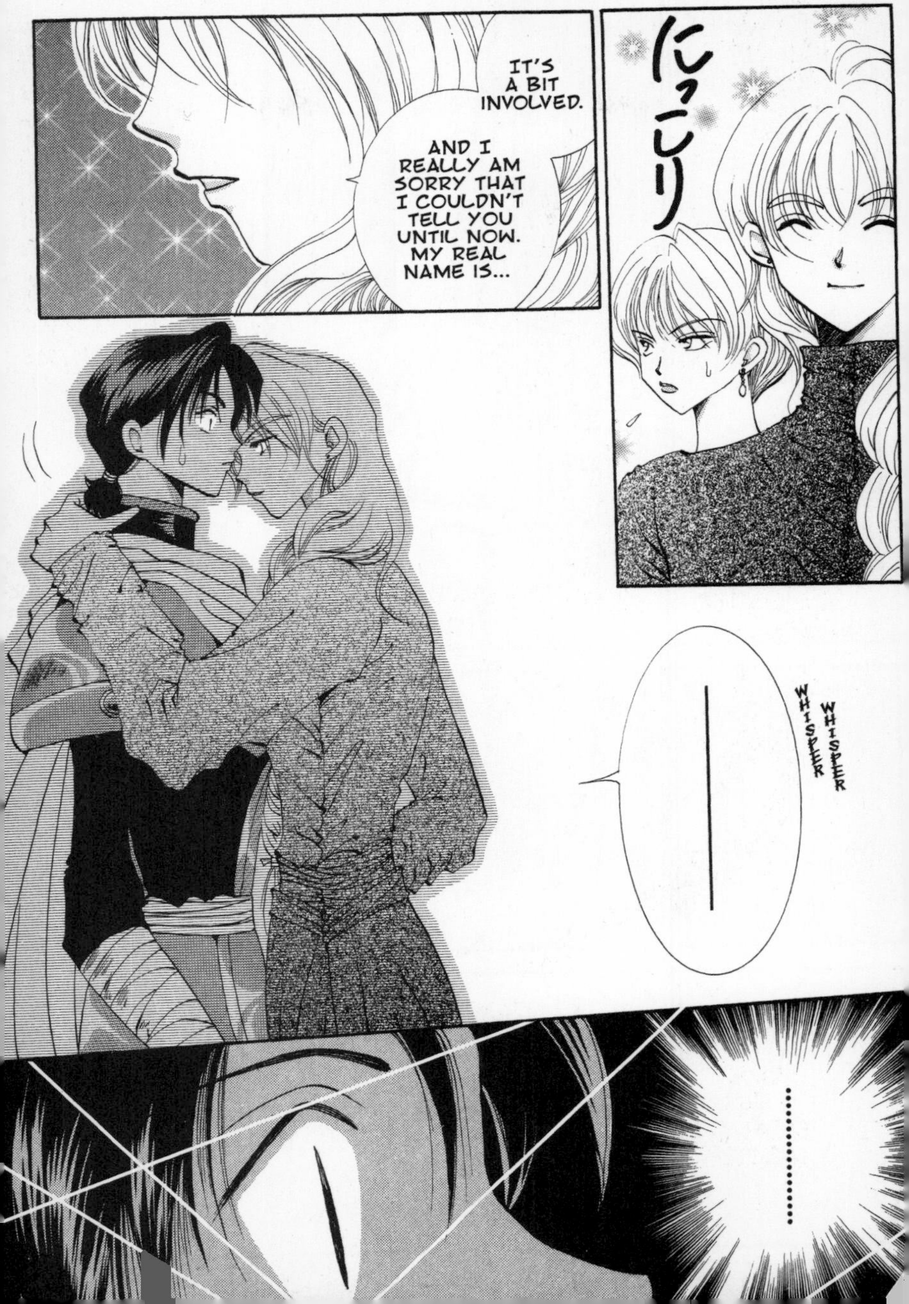
にっこり
IT'S A BIT INVOLVED.
AND I REALLY AM SORRY THAT I COULDN'T TELL YOU UNTIL NOW. MY REAL NAME IS...
WHISPER WHISPER
—
....

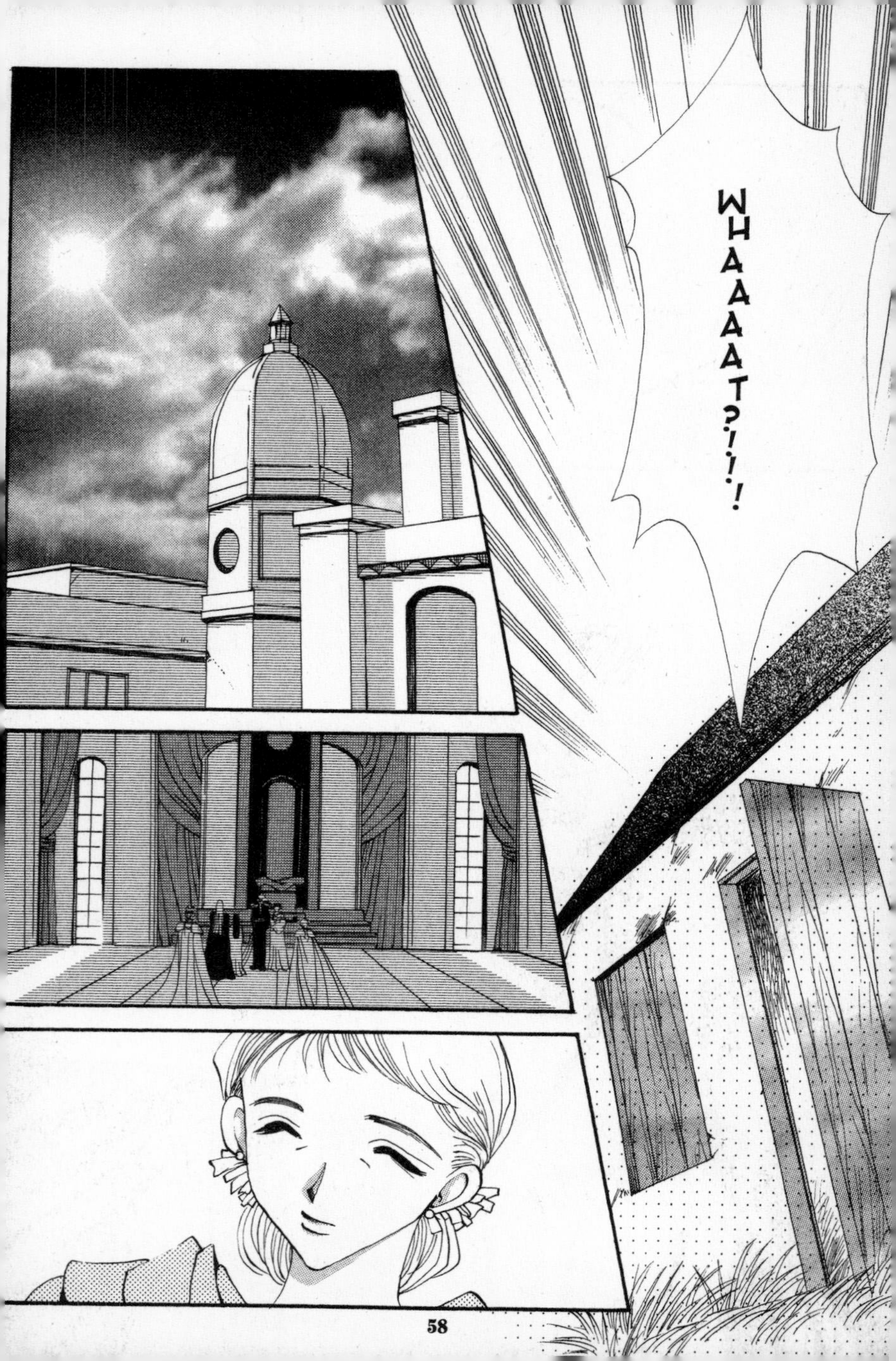
WHAAAAT?!!!

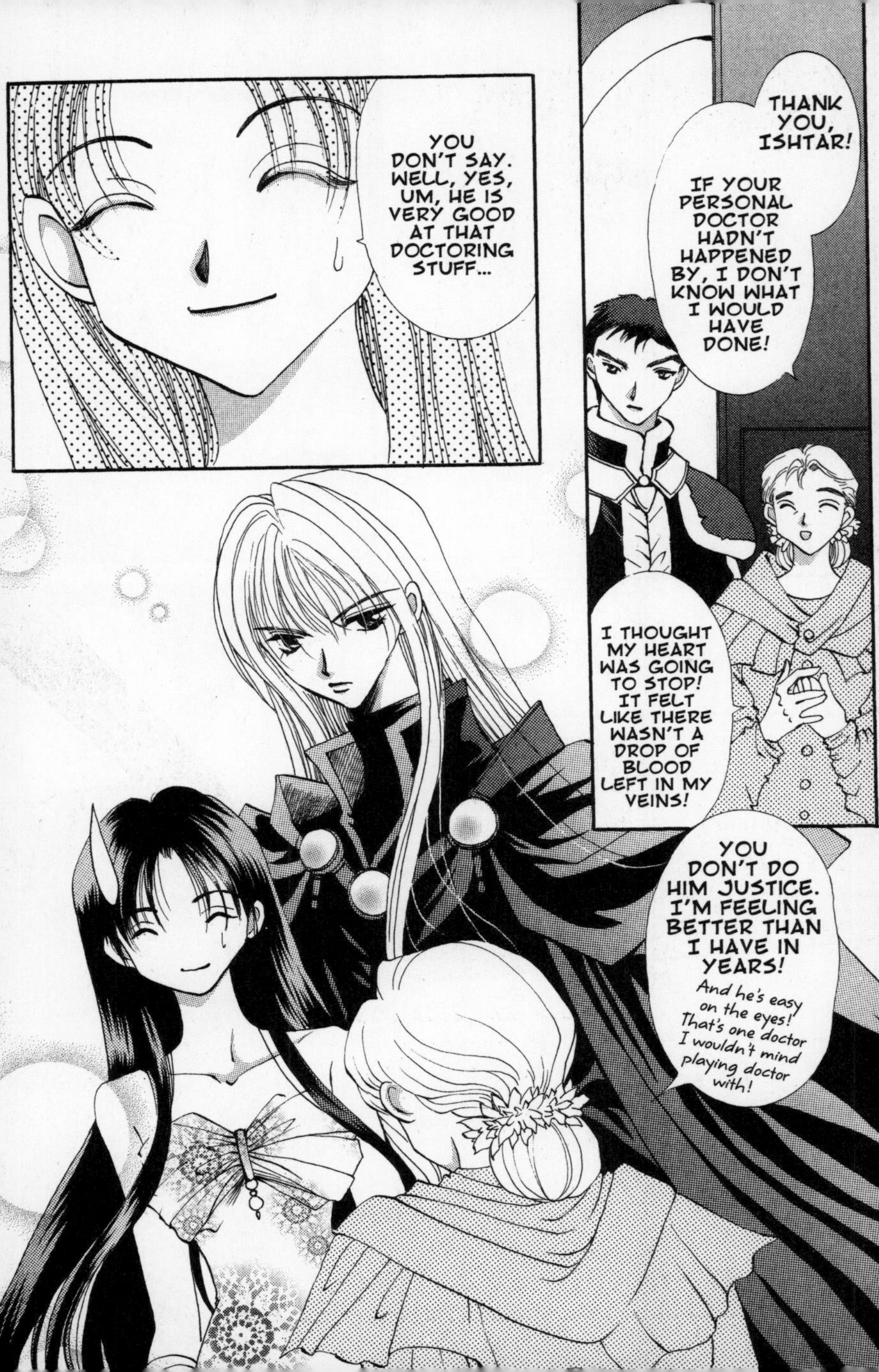
THANK YOU, ISHTAR!
IF YOUR PERSONAL DOCTOR HADN'T HAPPENED BY, I DON'T KNOW WHAT I WOULD HAVE DONE!
I THOUGHT MY HEART WAS GOING TO STOP! IT FELT LIKE THERE WASN'T A DROP OF BLOOD LEFT IN MY VEINS!
YOU DON'T SAY. WELL, YES, UM, HE IS VERY GOOD AT THAT DOCTORING STUFF...
YOU DON'T DO HIM JUSTICE. I'M FEELING BETTER THAN I HAVE IN YEARS!
And he's easy on the eyes! That's one doctor I wouldn't mind playing doctor with!

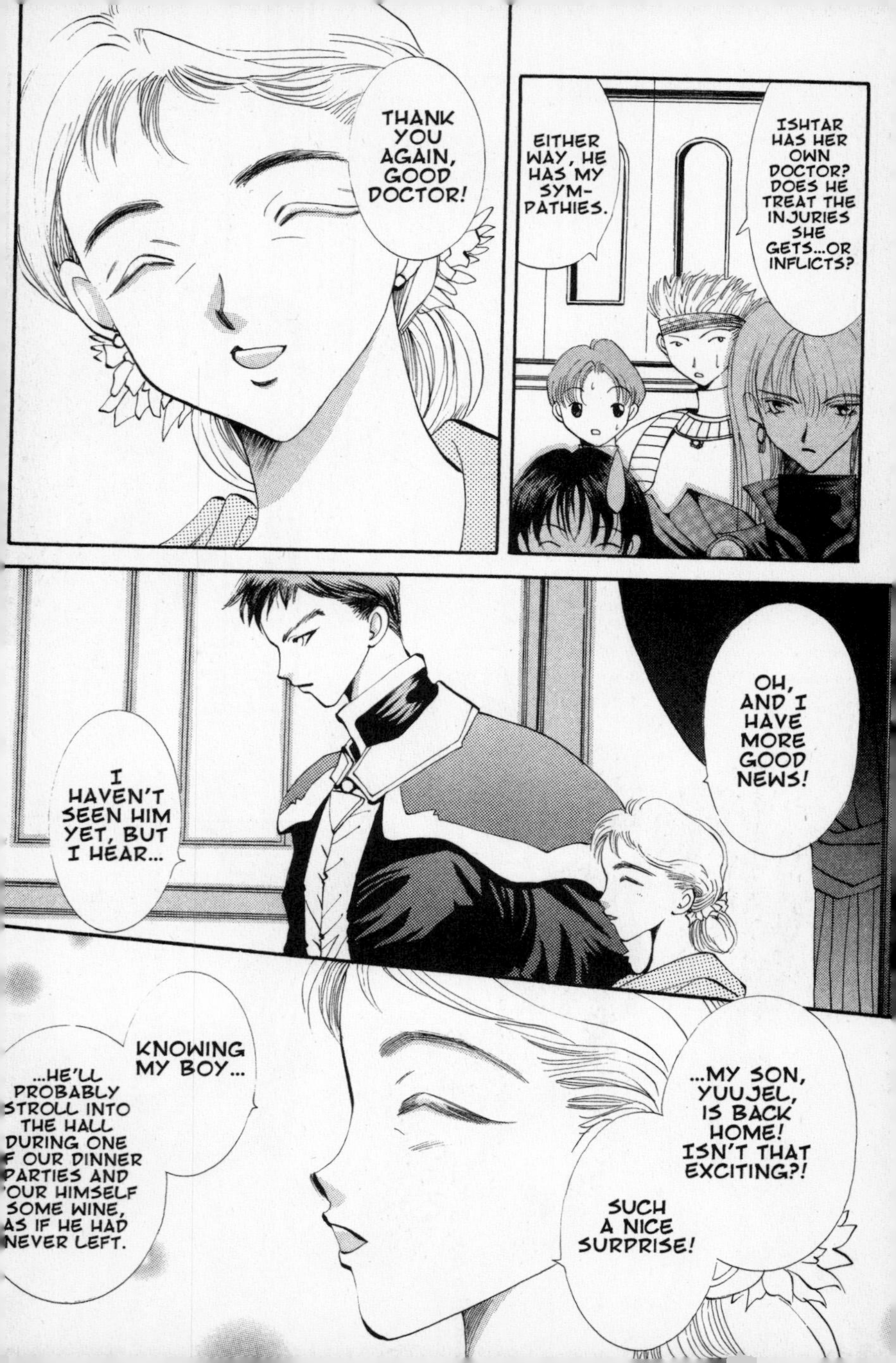
ISHTAR HAS HER OWN DOCTOR? DOES HE TREAT THE INJURIES SHE GETS...OR INFLICTS?
EITHER WAY, HE HAS MY SYM-PATHIES.
THANK YOU AGAIN, GOOD DOCTOR!
OH, AND I HAVE MORE GOOD NEWS!
I HAVEN'T SEEN HIM YET, BUT I HEAR...
...MY SON, YUUJEL, IS BACK HOME! ISN'T THAT EXCITING?!
SUCH A NICE SURPRISE!
KNOWING MY BOY...
...HE'LL PROBABLY STROLL INTO THE HALL DURING ONE F OUR DINNER PARTIES AND 'OUR HIMSELF SOME WINE, AS IF HE HAD NEVER LEFT.

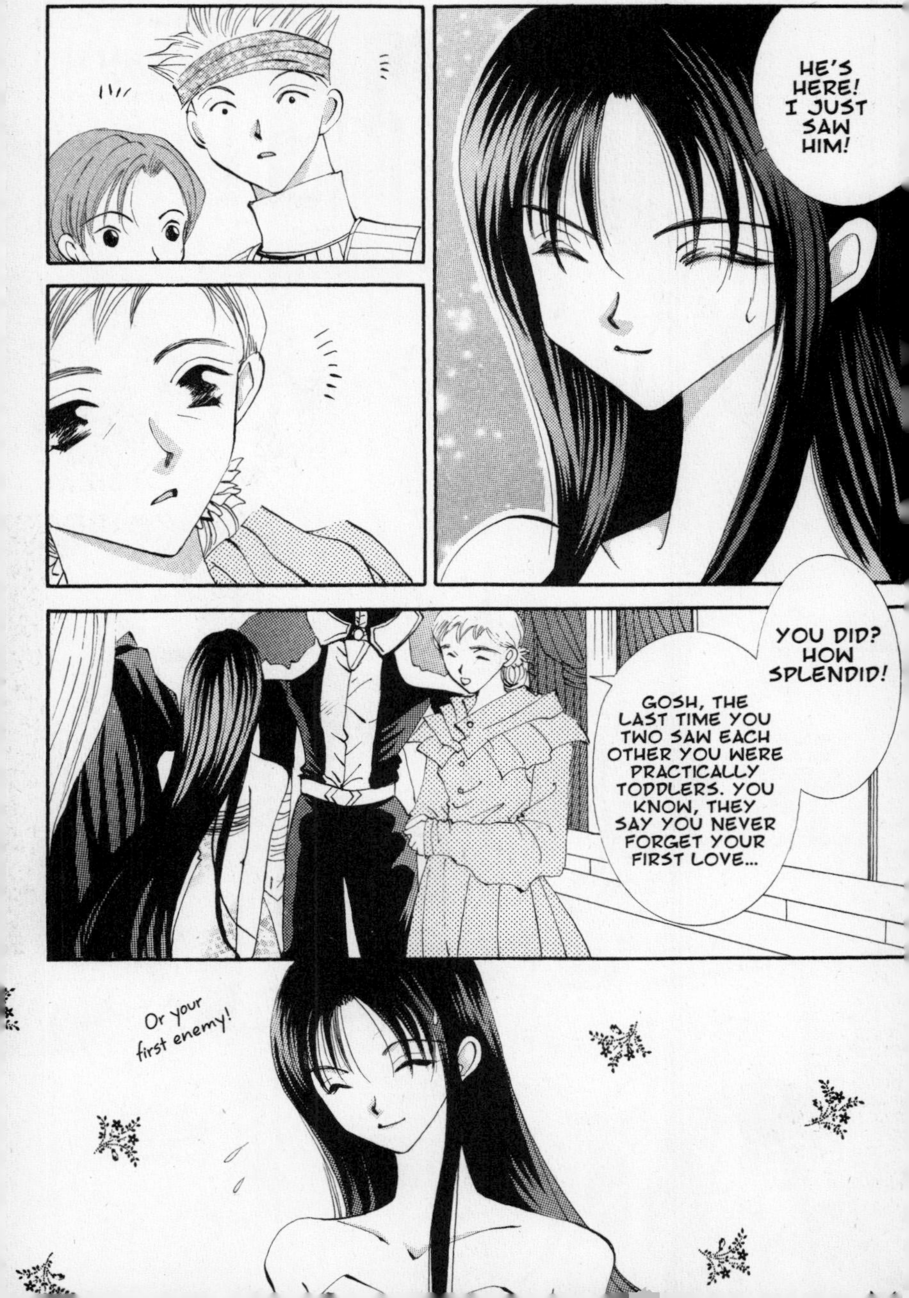
HE'S HERE! I JUST SAW HIM!
YOU DID? HOW SPLENDID!
GOSH, THE LAST TIME YOU TWO SAW EACH OTHER YOU WERE PRACTICALLY TODDLERS. YOU KNOW, THEY SAY YOU NEVER FORGET YOUR FIRST LOVE...
Or your first enemy!

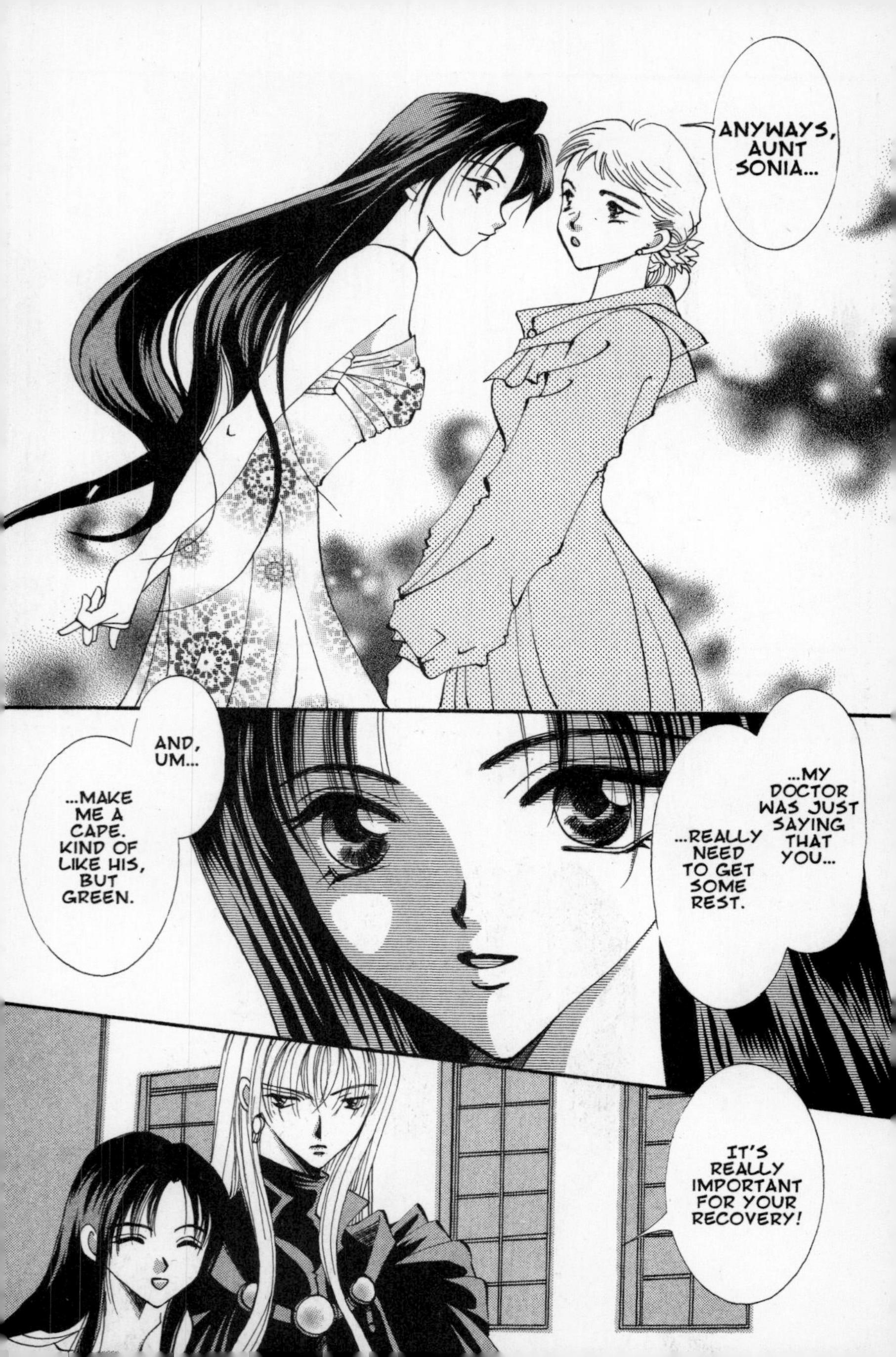
ANYWAYS, AUNT SONIA...
...MY DOCTOR WAS JUST SAYING THAT YOU...
...REALLY NEED TO GET SOME REST.
AND, UM...
...MAKE ME A CAPE. KIND OF LIKE HIS, BUT GREEN.
IT'S REALLY IMPORTANT FOR YOUR RECOVERY!

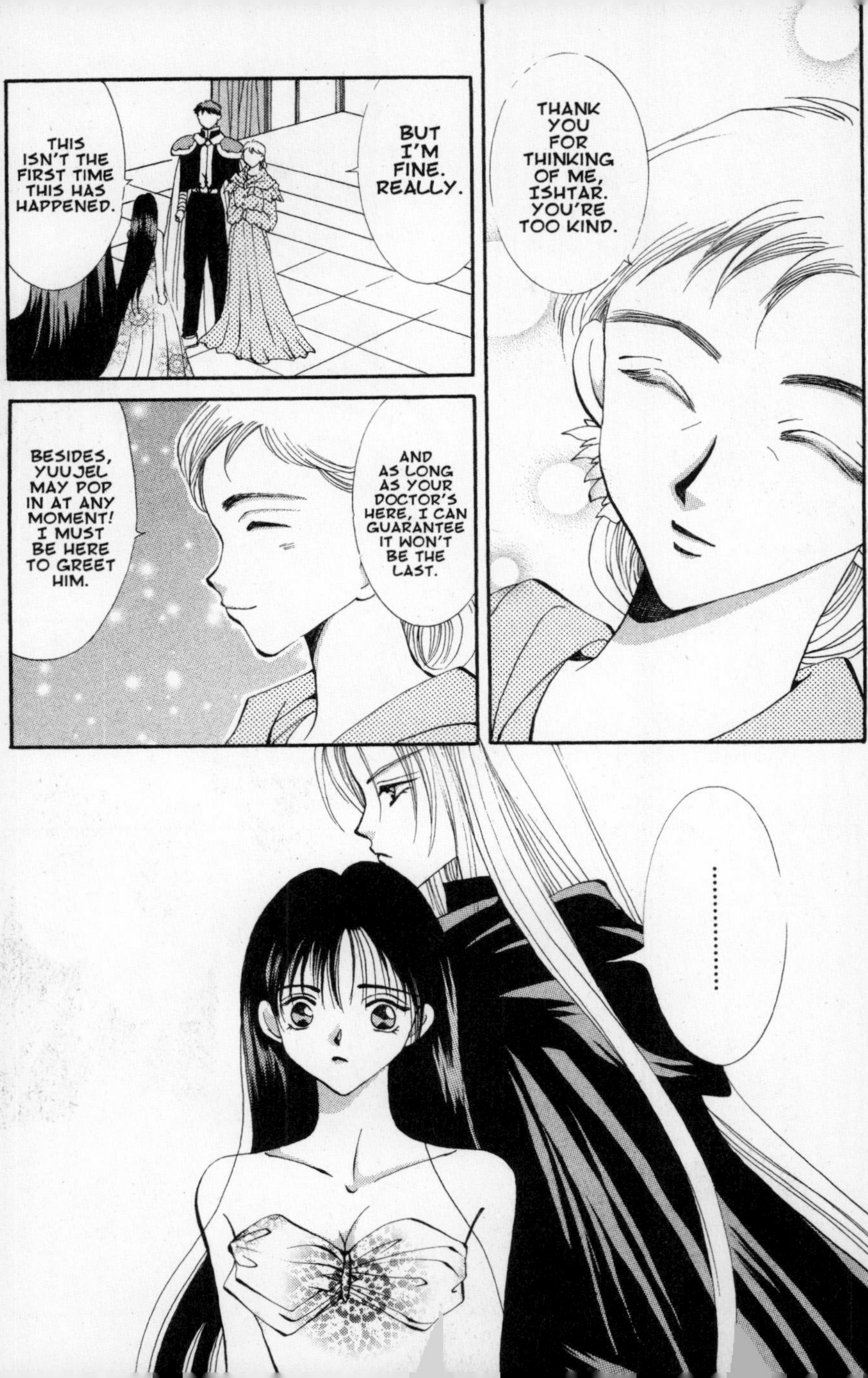
THANK YOU FOR THINKING OF ME, ISHTAR. YOU'RE TOO KIND.
BUT I'M FINE. REALLY.
THIS ISN'T THE FIRST TIME THIS HAS HAPPENED.
AND AS LONG AS YOUR DOCTOR'S HERE, I CAN GUARANTEE IT WON'T BE THE LAST.
BESIDES, YUUJEL MAY POP IN AT ANY MOMENT! I MUST BE HERE TO GREET HIM.
....

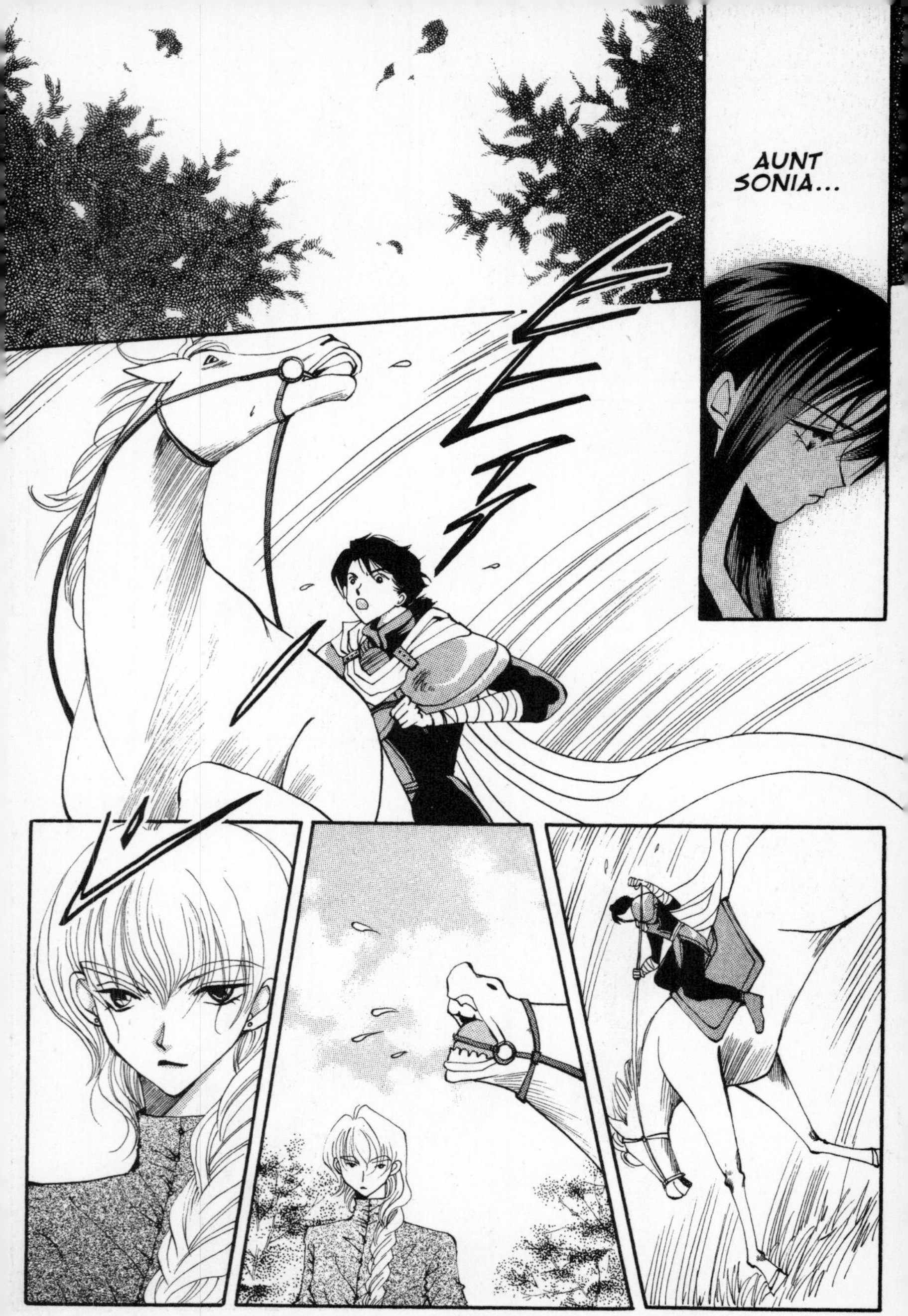
AUNT SONIA...

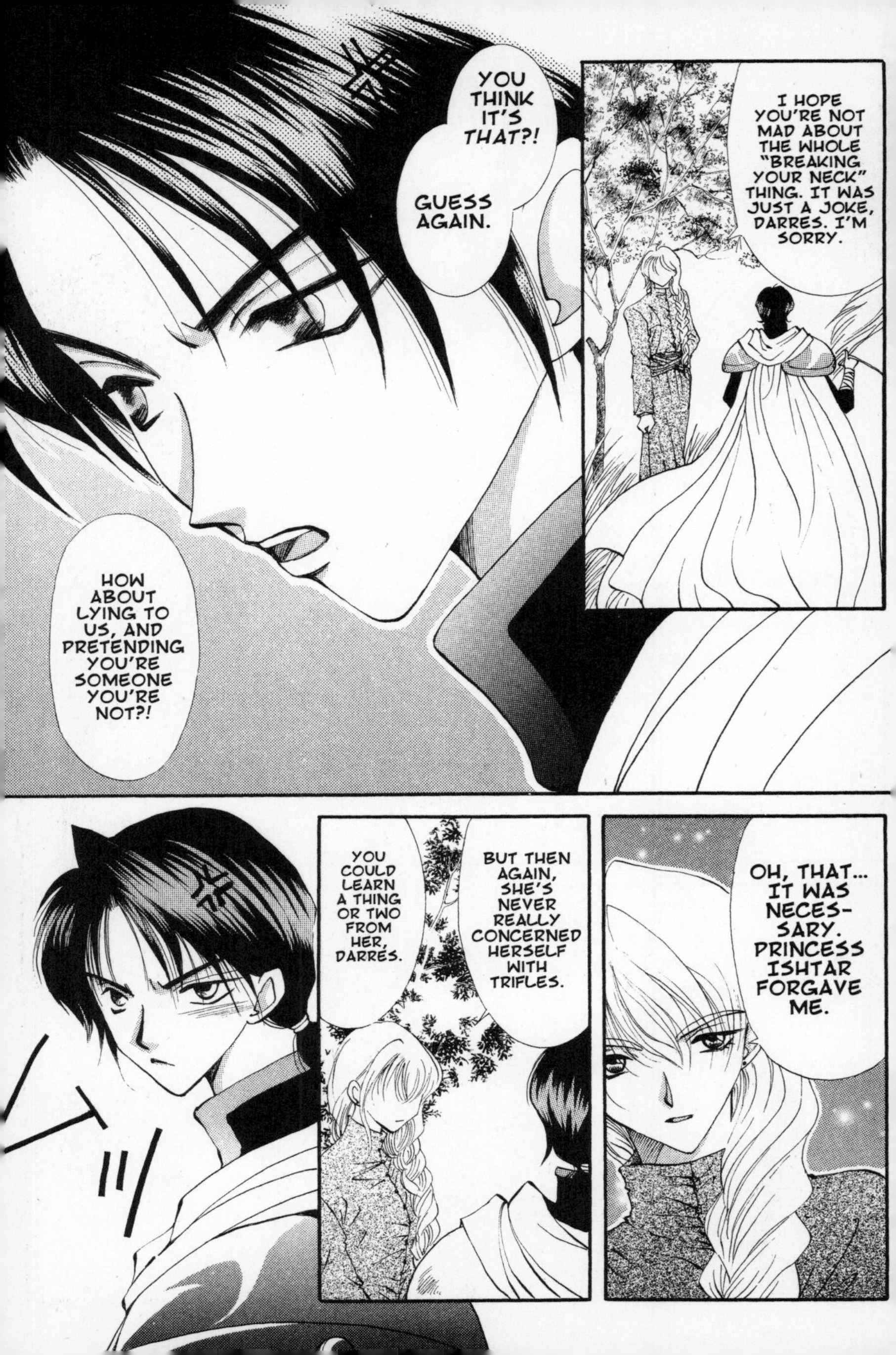
I HOPE YOU'RE NOT MAD ABOUT THE WHOLE "BREAKING YOUR NECK" THING. IT WAS JUST A JOKE, DARRES. I'M SORRY.
YOU THINK IT'S *THAT*?!
GUESS AGAIN.
HOW ABOUT LYING TO US, AND PRETENDING YOU'RE SOMEONE YOU'RE NOT?!
OH, THAT... IT WAS NECES-SARY. PRINCESS ISHTAR FORGAVE ME.
BUT THEN AGAIN, SHE'S NEVER REALLY CONCERNED HERSELF WITH TRIFLES.
YOU COULD LEARN A THING OR TWO FROM HER, DARRES.

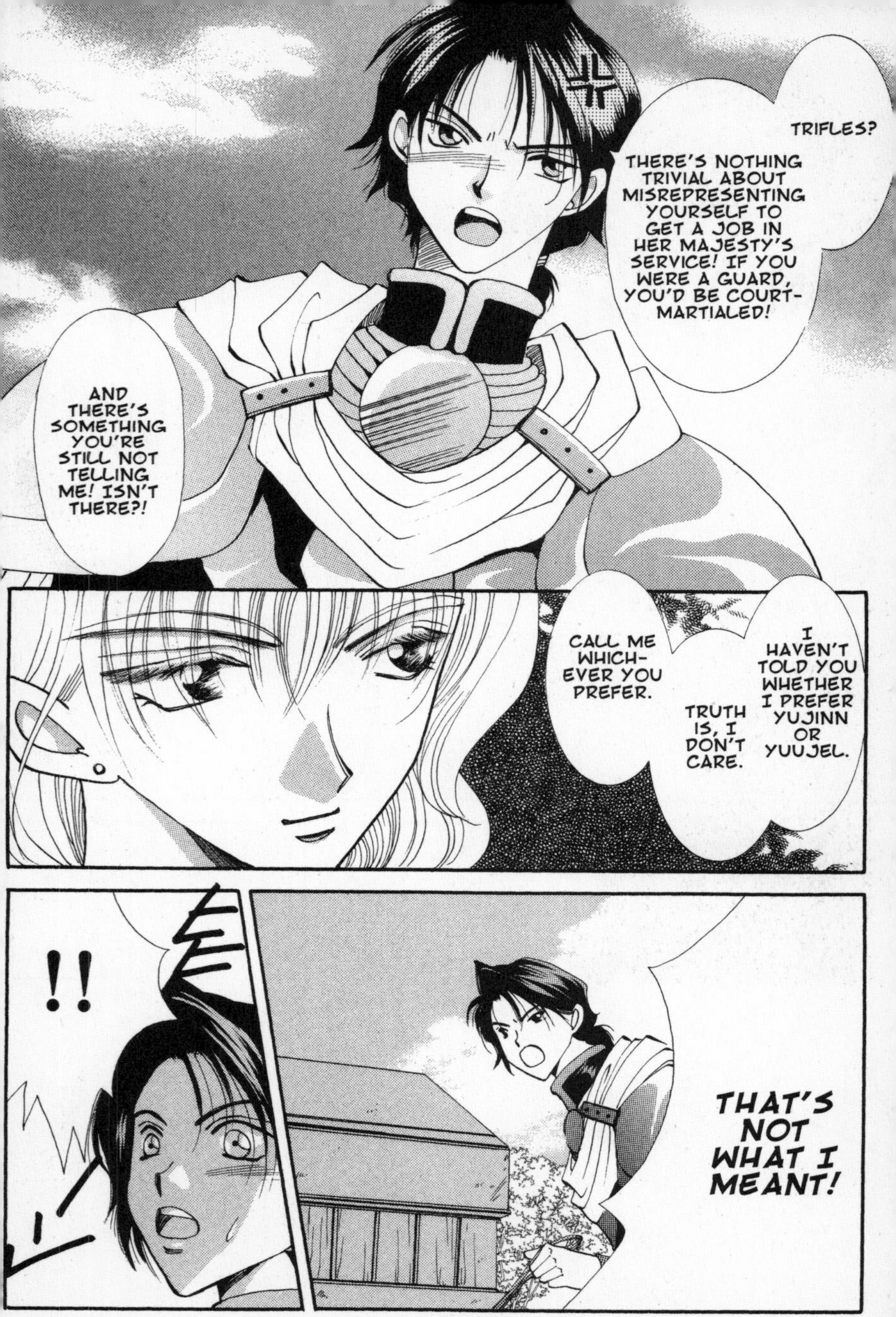
TRIFLES?
THERE'S NOTHING TRIVIAL ABOUT MISREPRESENTING YOURSELF TO GET A JOB IN HER MAJESTY'S SERVICE! IF YOU WERE A GUARD, YOU'D BE COURT-MARTIALED!
AND THERE'S SOMETHING YOU'RE STILL NOT TELLING ME! ISN'T THERE?!
I HAVEN'T TOLD YOU WHETHER I PREFER YUJINN OR YUUJEL.
TRUTH IS, I DON'T CARE.
CALL ME WHICH-EVER YOU PREFER.
THAT'S NOT WHAT I MEANT!
!!

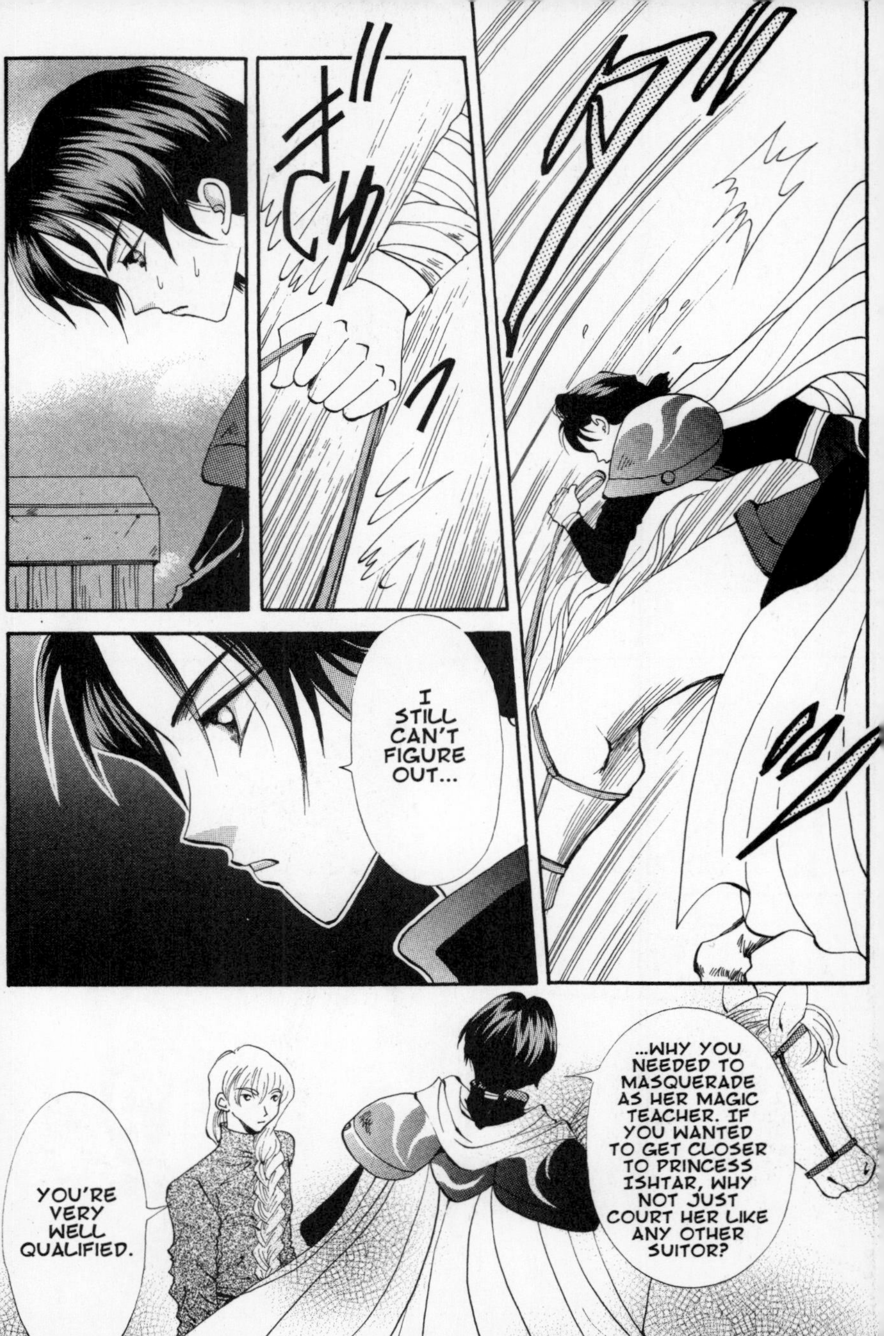

ぎゅ
I STILL CAN'T FIGURE OUT...
...WHY YOU NEEDED TO MASQUERADE AS HER MAGIC TEACHER. IF YOU WANTED TO GET CLOSER TO PRINCESS ISHTAR, WHY NOT JUST COURT HER LIKE ANY OTHER SUITOR?
YOU'RE VERY WELL QUALIFIED.

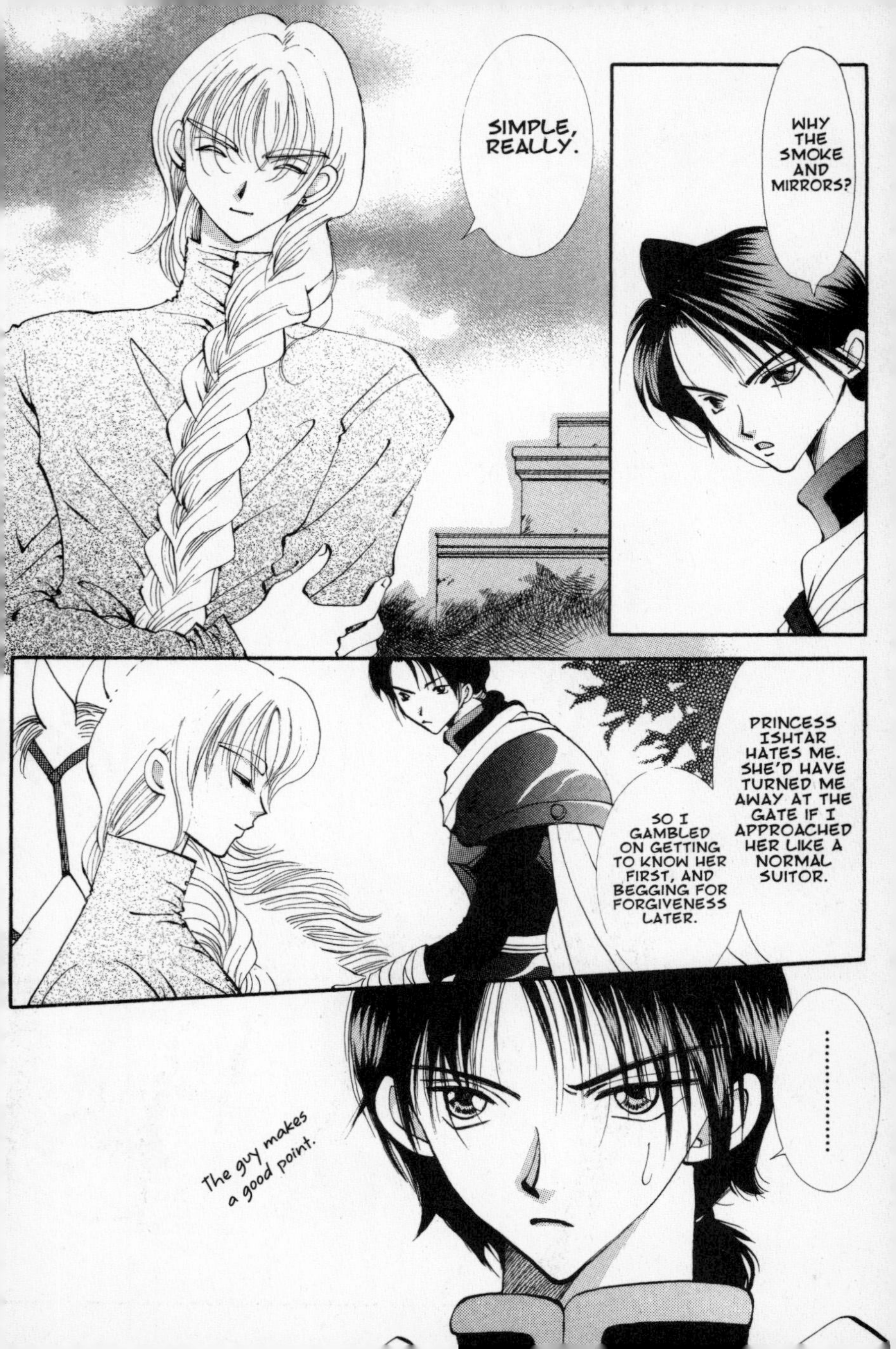
WHY THE SMOKE AND MIRRORS?
SIMPLE, REALLY.
PRINCESS ISHTAR HATES ME. SHE'D HAVE TURNED ME AWAY AT THE GATE IF I APPROACHED HER LIKE A NORMAL SUITOR.
SO I GAMBLED ON GETTING TO KNOW HER FIRST, AND BEGGING FOR FORGIVENESS LATER.
......
The guy makes a good point.

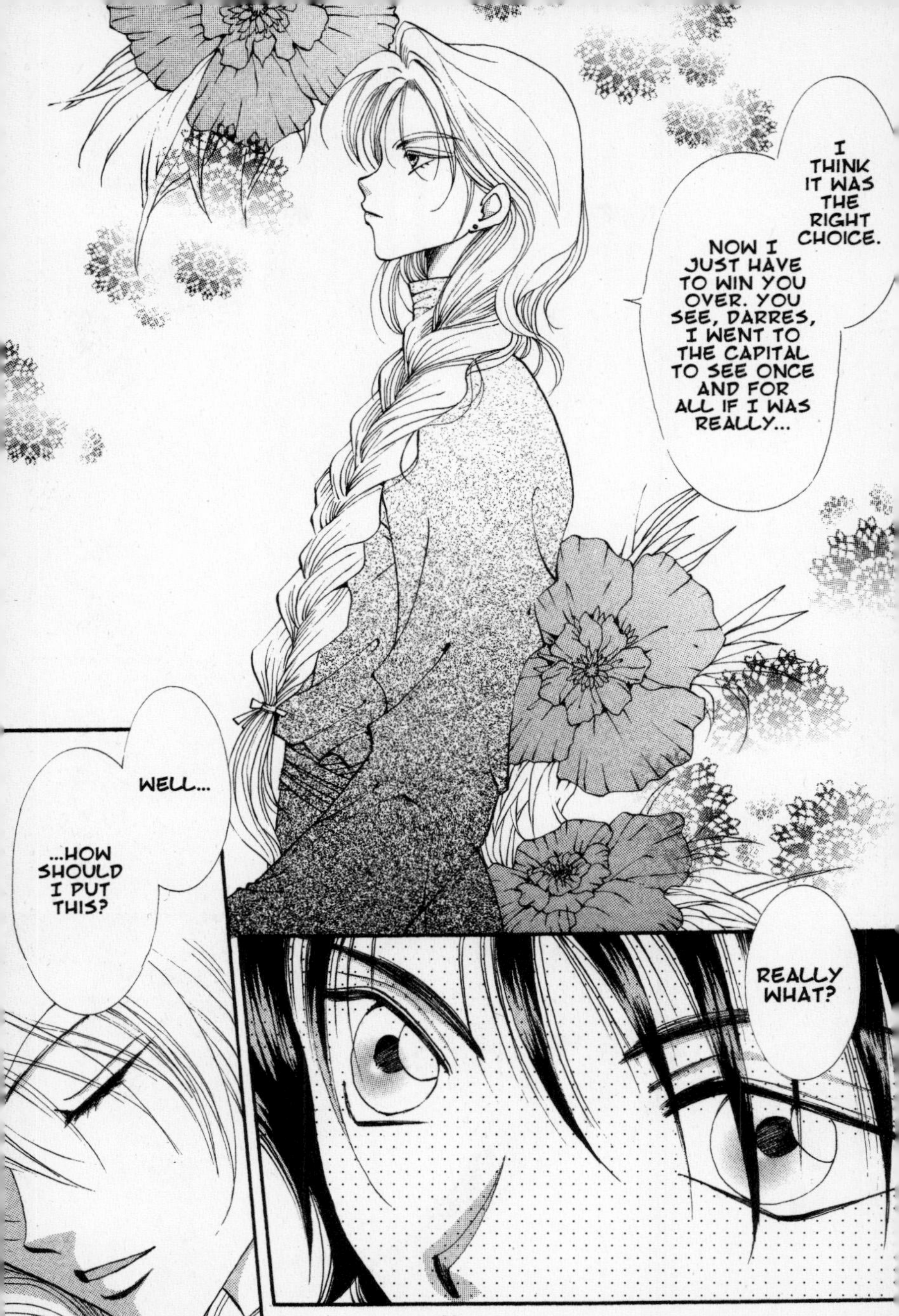
I THINK IT WAS THE RIGHT CHOICE.
NOW I JUST HAVE TO WIN YOU OVER. YOU SEE, DARRES, I WENT TO THE CAPITAL TO SEE ONCE AND FOR ALL IF I WAS REALLY...
WELL...
...HOW SHOULD I PUT THIS?
REALLY WHAT?

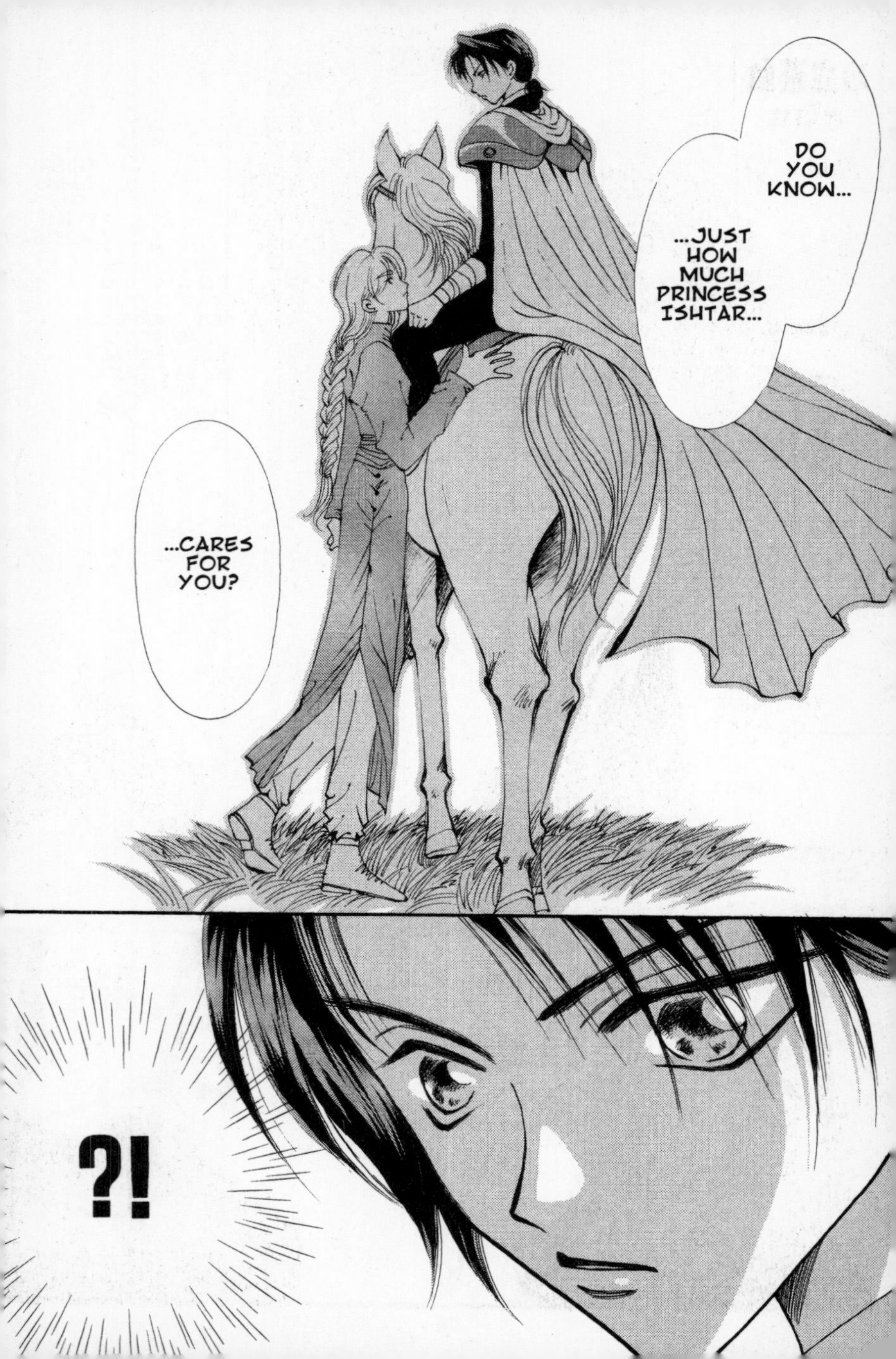
DO YOU KNOW...
...JUST HOW MUCH PRINCESS ISHTAR...
...CARES FOR YOU?
?!

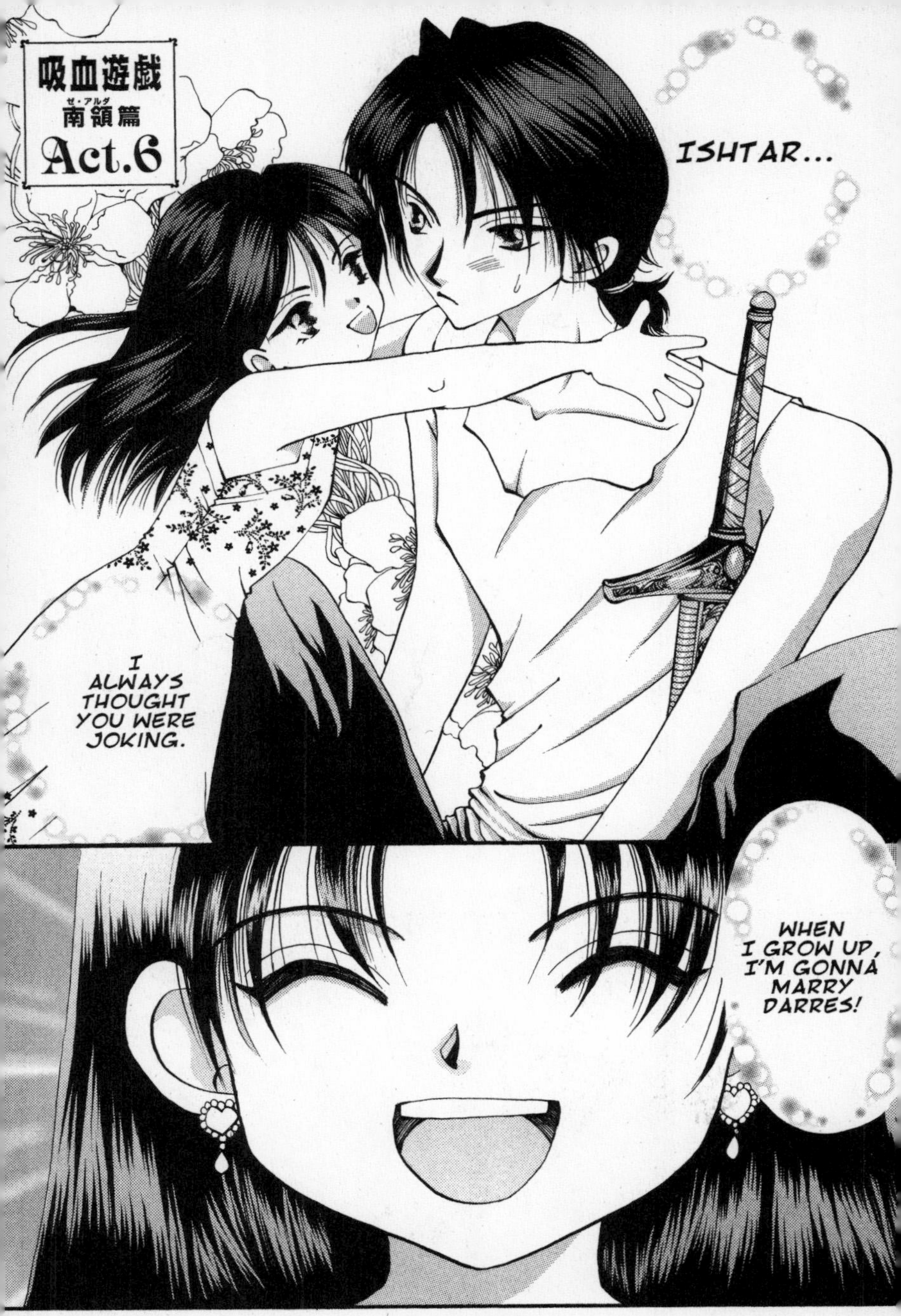
ISHTAR...
吸血遊戯
ゼ・アルダ
南領篇
Act.6
I ALWAYS THOUGHT YOU WERE JOKING.
WHEN I GROW UP, I'M GONNA MARRY DARRES!

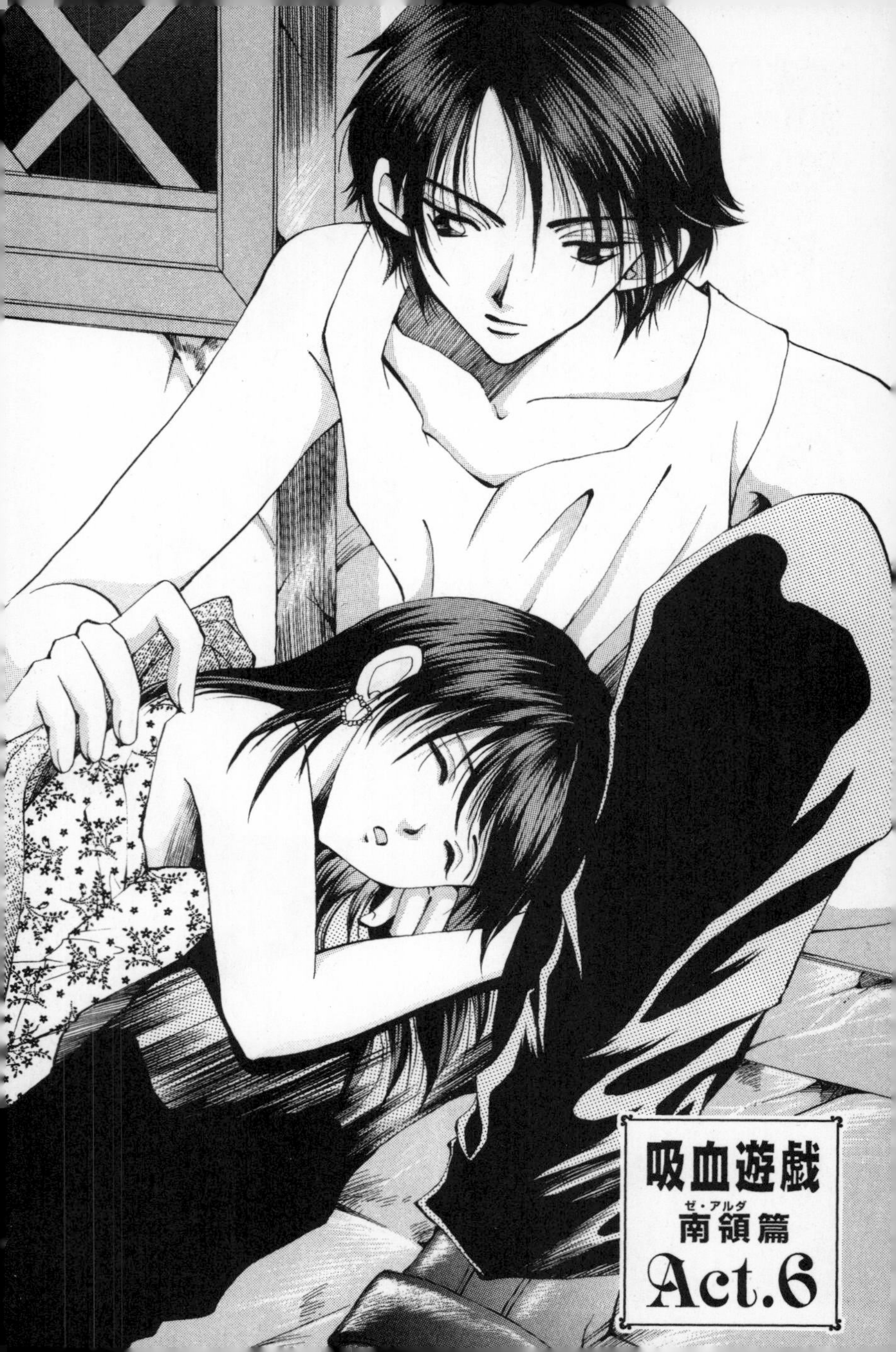
吸血遊戯
ゼ・アルダ
南領篇
Act.6

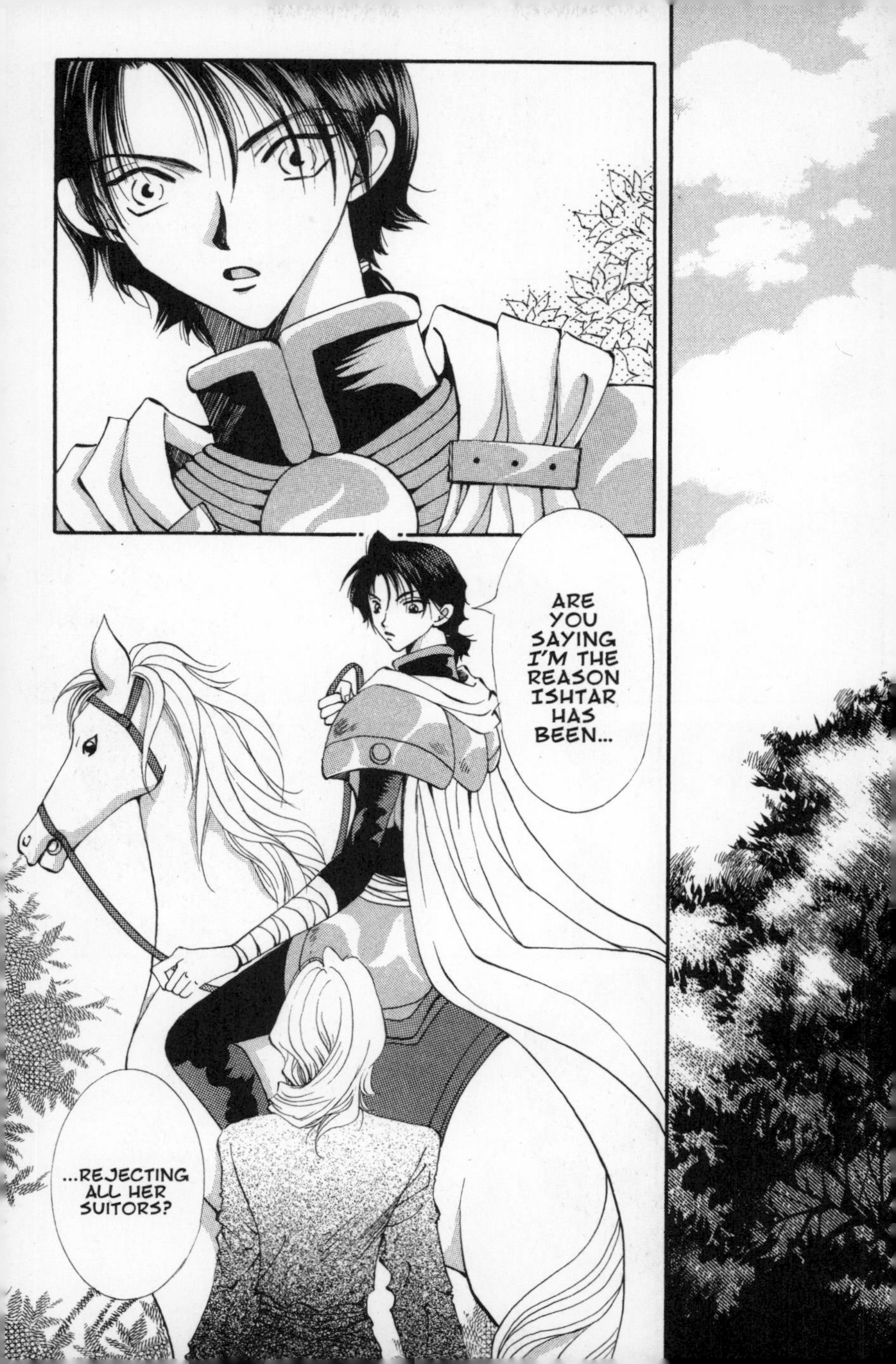
...
ARE YOU SAYING I'M THE REASON ISHTAR HAS BEEN...
...REJECTING ALL HER SUITORS?

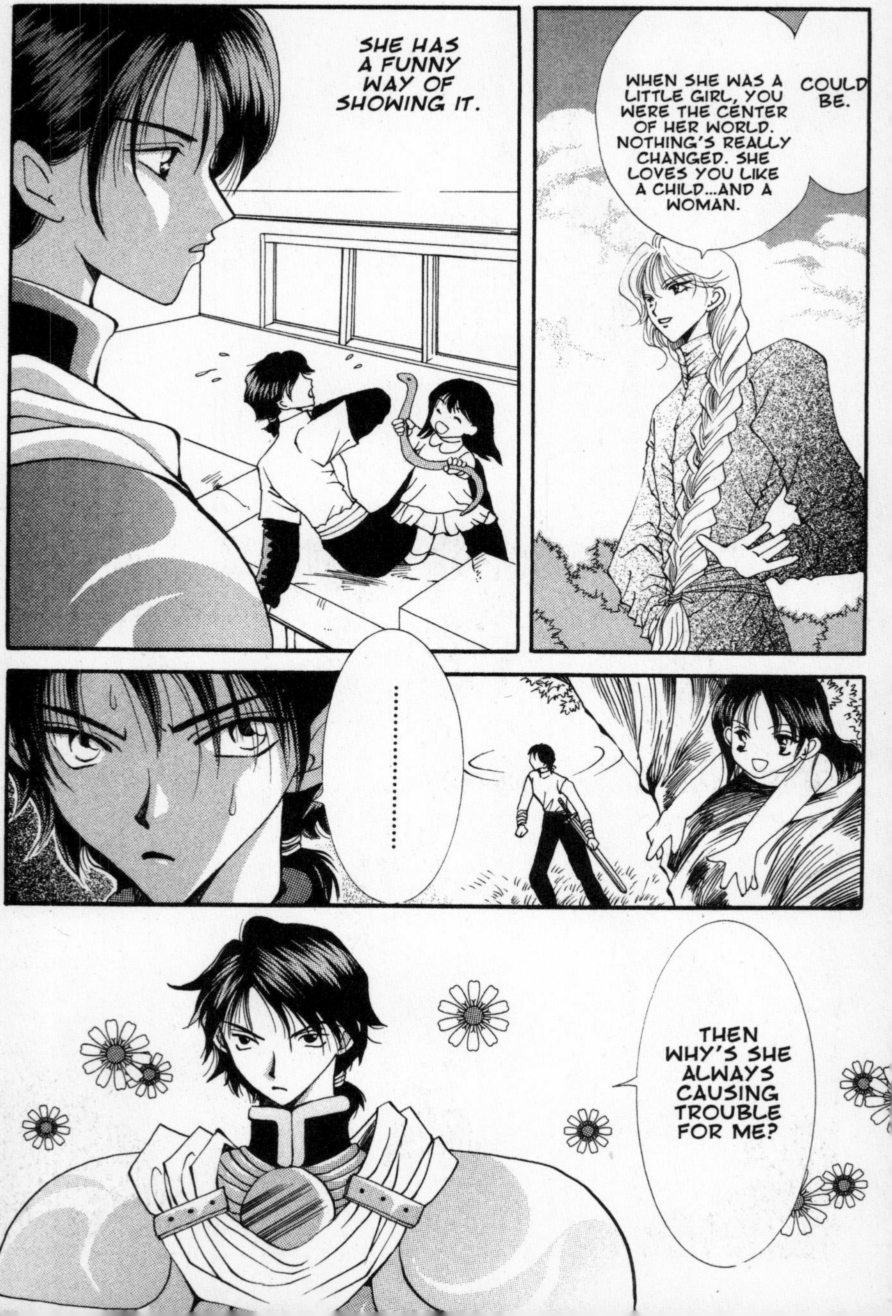
COULD BE.
WHEN SHE WAS A LITTLE GIRL, YOU WERE THE CENTER OF HER WORLD. NOTHING'S REALLY CHANGED. SHE LOVES YOU LIKE A CHILD...AND A WOMAN.
SHE HAS A FUNNY WAY OF SHOWING IT.
......
THEN WHY'S SHE ALWAYS CAUSING TROUBLE FOR ME?

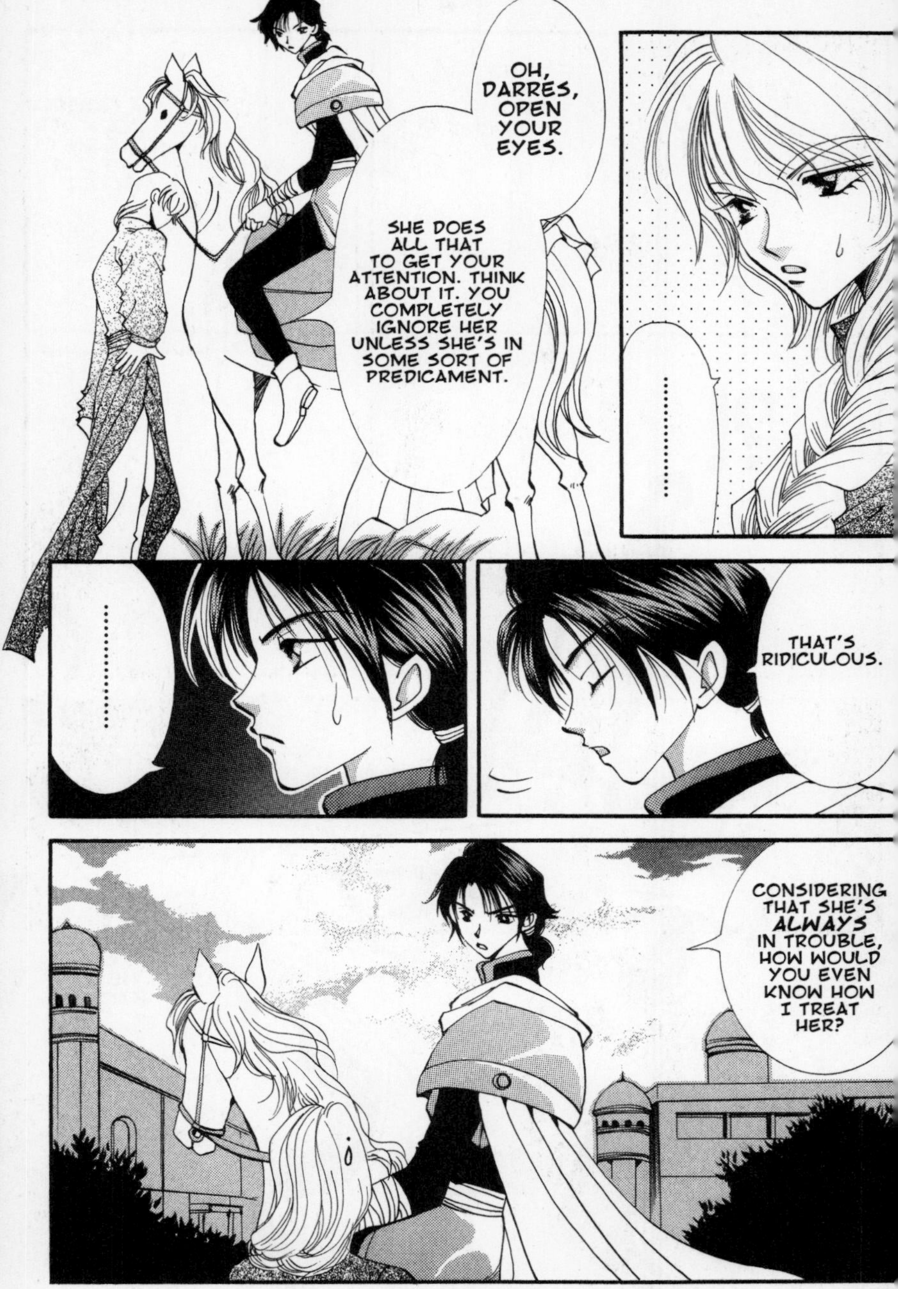
......
OH, DARRES, OPEN YOUR EYES.
SHE DOES ALL THAT TO GET YOUR ATTENTION. THINK ABOUT IT. YOU COMPLETELY IGNORE HER UNLESS SHE'S IN SOME SORT OF PREDICAMENT.
THAT'S RIDICULOUS.
......
CONSIDERING THAT SHE'S *ALWAYS* IN TROUBLE, HOW WOULD YOU EVEN KNOW HOW I TREAT HER?

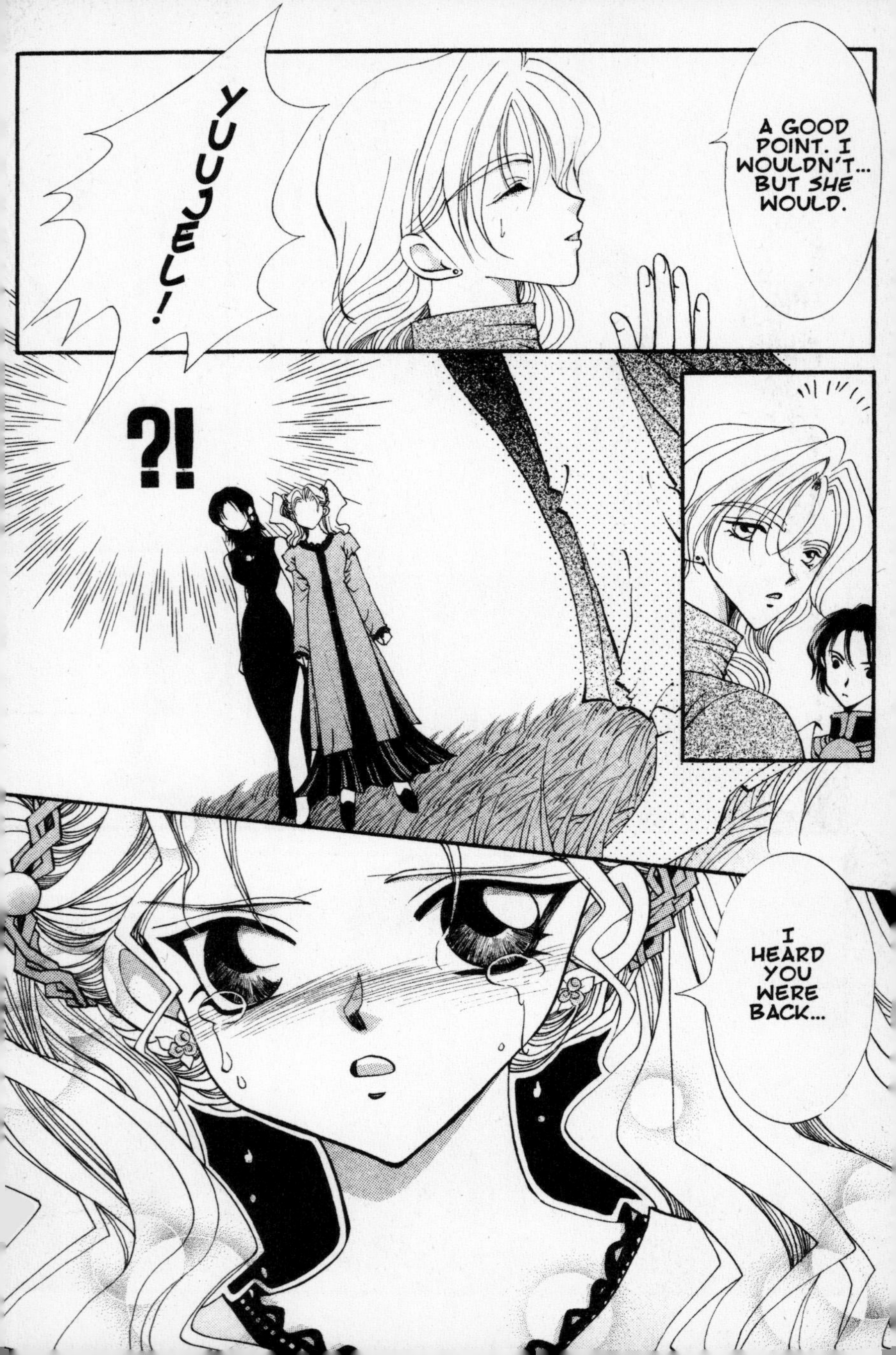

A GOOD POINT. I WOULDN'T... BUT SHE WOULD.
YUUJEL!
?!
I HEARD YOU WERE BACK...

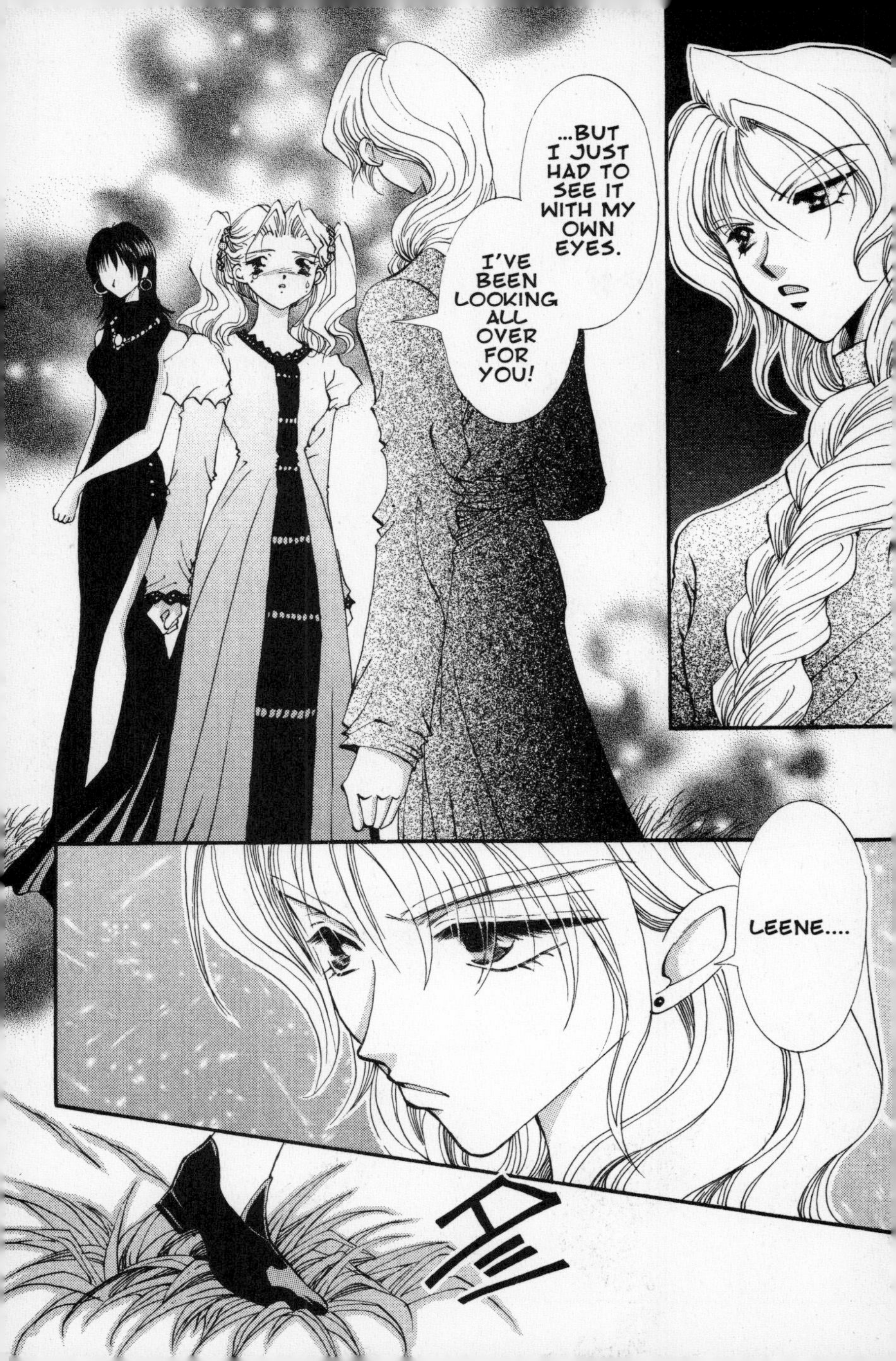
...BUT I JUST HAD TO SEE IT WITH MY OWN EYES.
I'VE BEEN LOOKING ALL OVER FOR YOU!
LEENE....

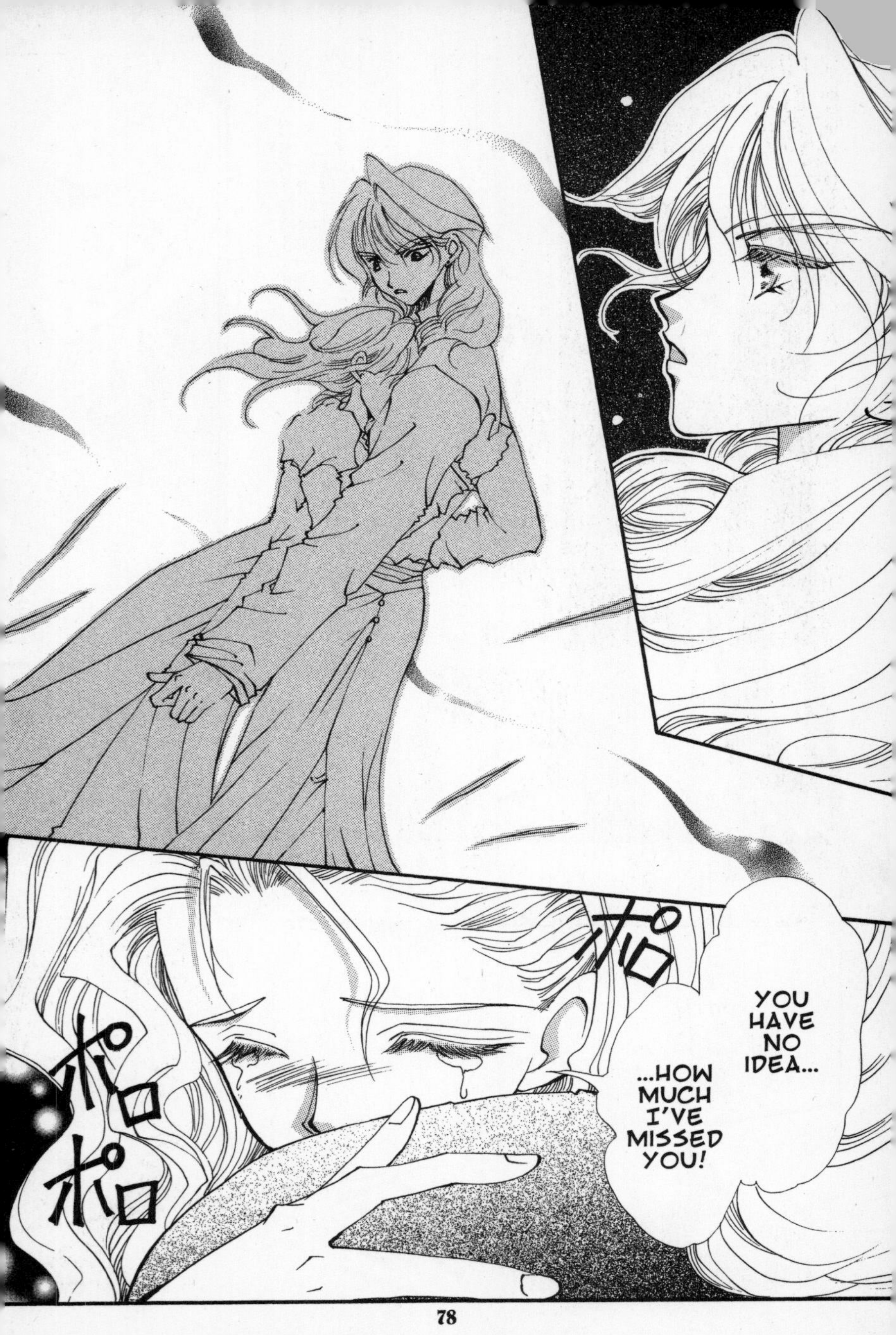
ポロ
YOU HAVE NO IDEA...
...HOW MUCH I'VE MISSED YOU!
ポロ
ポロ

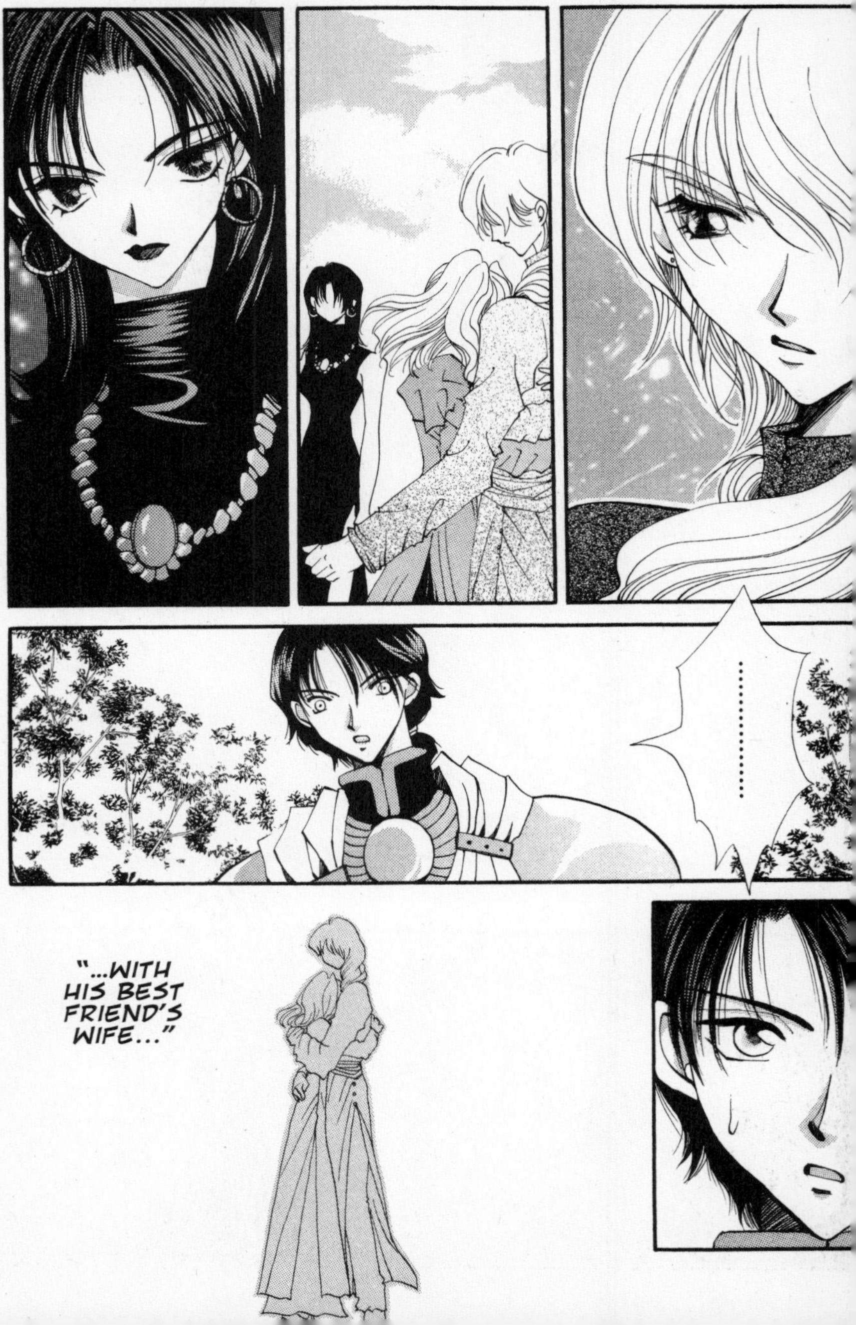
......
"...WITH HIS BEST FRIEND'S WIFE..."

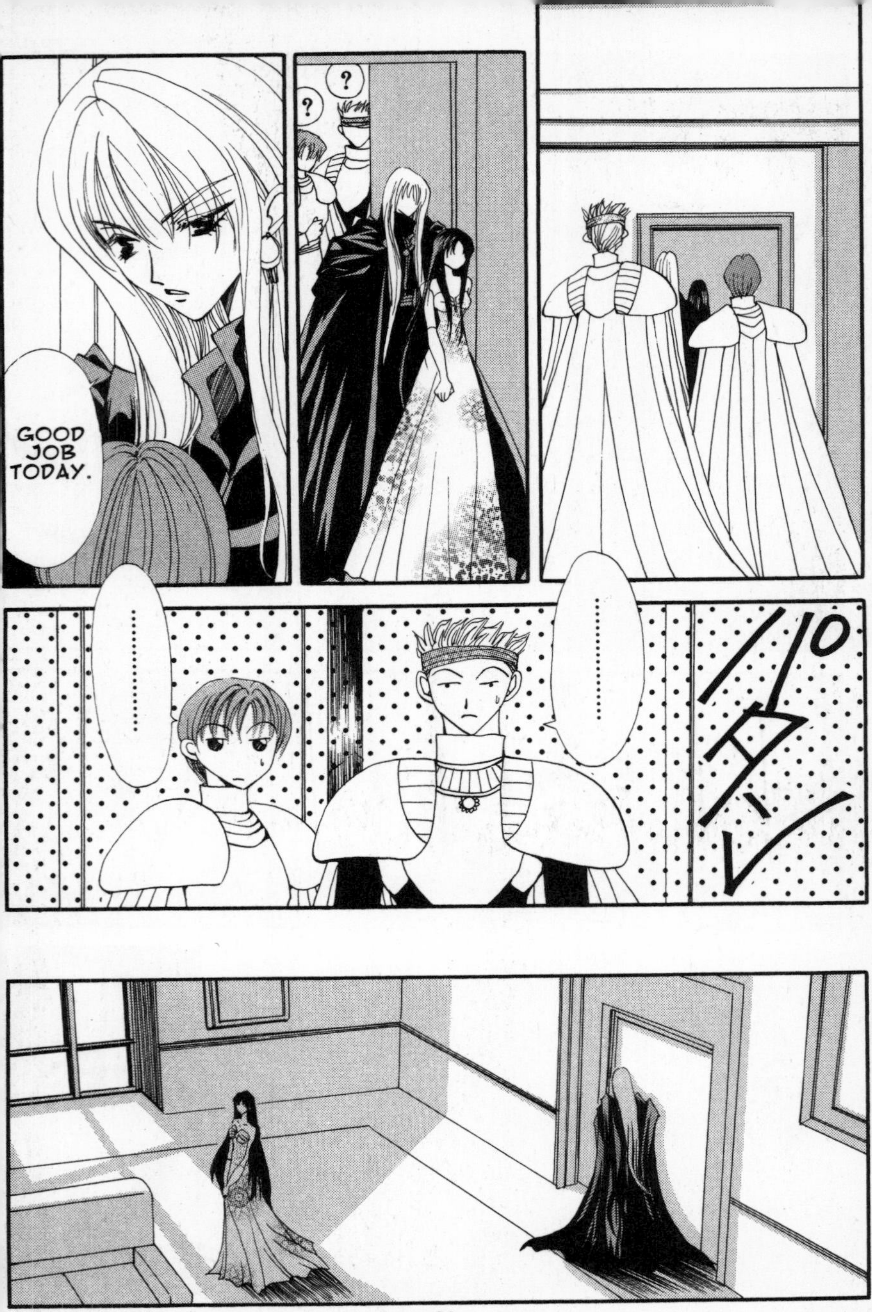
?
?
GOOD JOB TODAY.
パタン
......
......

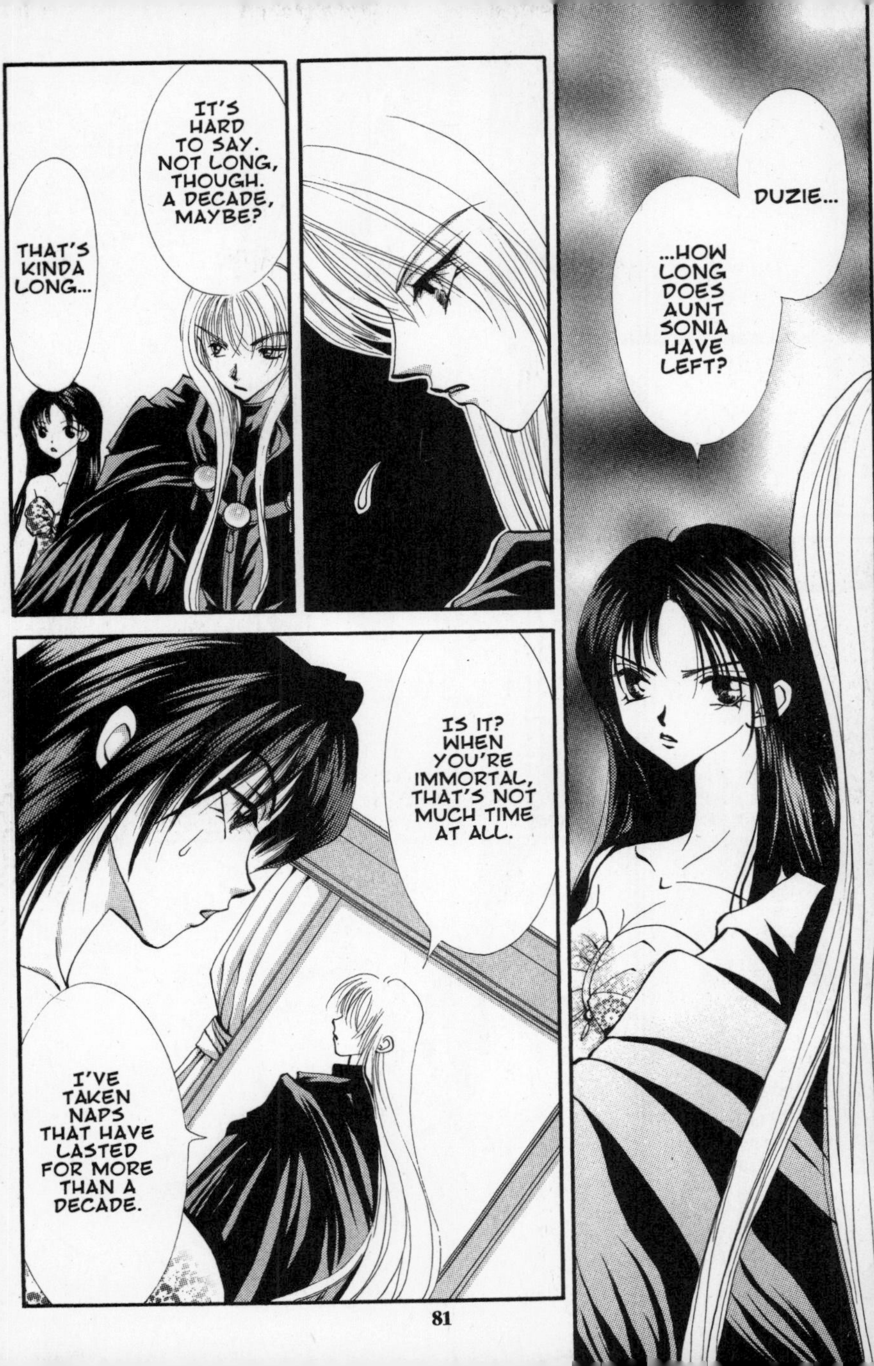
DUZIE...
...HOW LONG DOES AUNT SONIA HAVE LEFT?
IT'S HARD TO SAY. NOT LONG, THOUGH. A DECADE, MAYBE?
THAT'S KINDA LONG...
IS IT? WHEN YOU'RE IMMORTAL, THAT'S NOT MUCH TIME AT ALL.
I'VE TAKEN NAPS THAT HAVE LASTED FOR MORE THAN A DECADE.

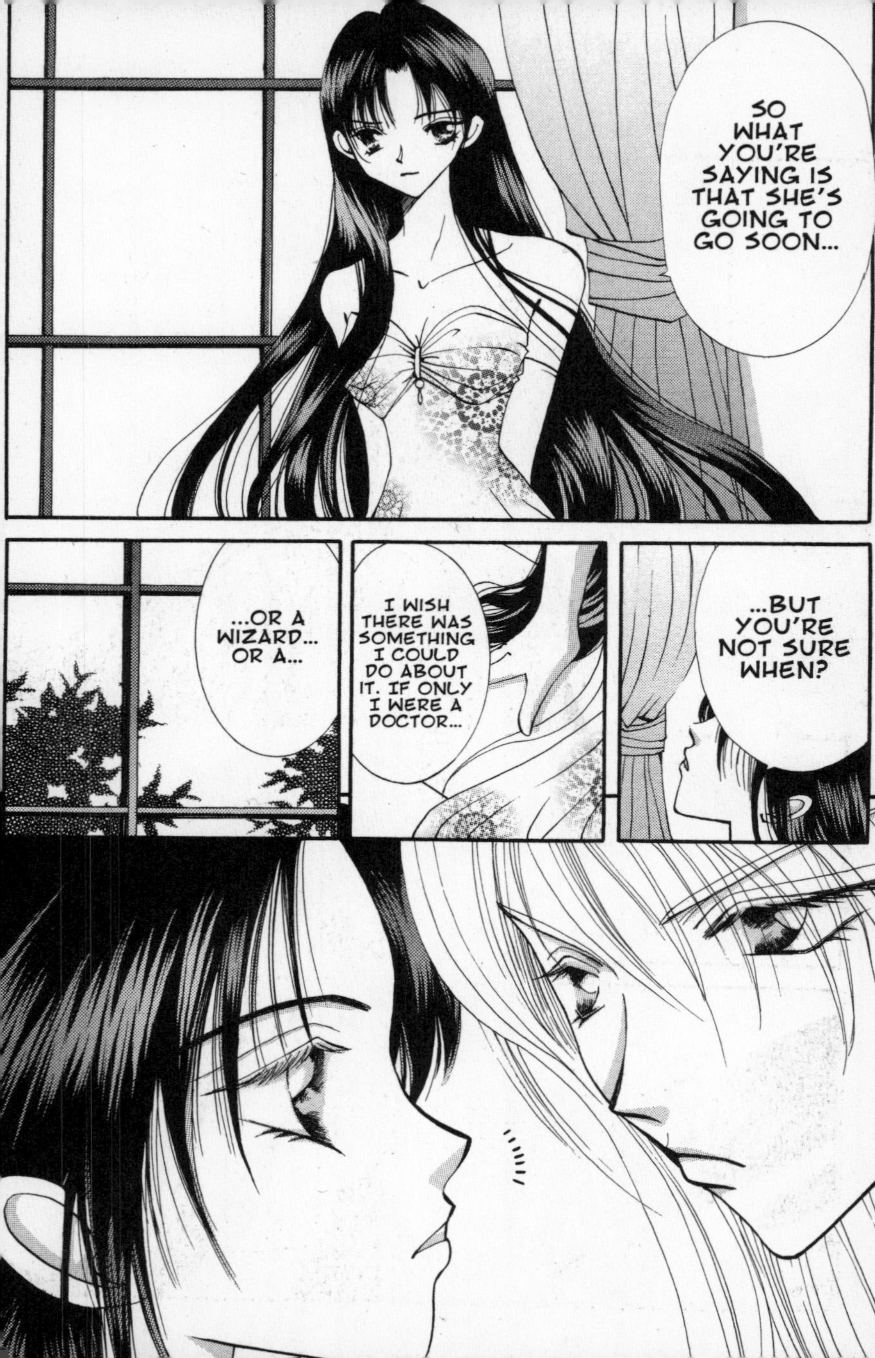
SO WHAT YOU'RE SAYING IS THAT SHE'S GOING TO GO SOON...
...BUT YOU'RE NOT SURE WHEN?
I WISH THERE WAS SOMETHING I COULD DO ABOUT IT. IF ONLY I WERE A DOCTOR...
...OR A WIZARD... OR A...

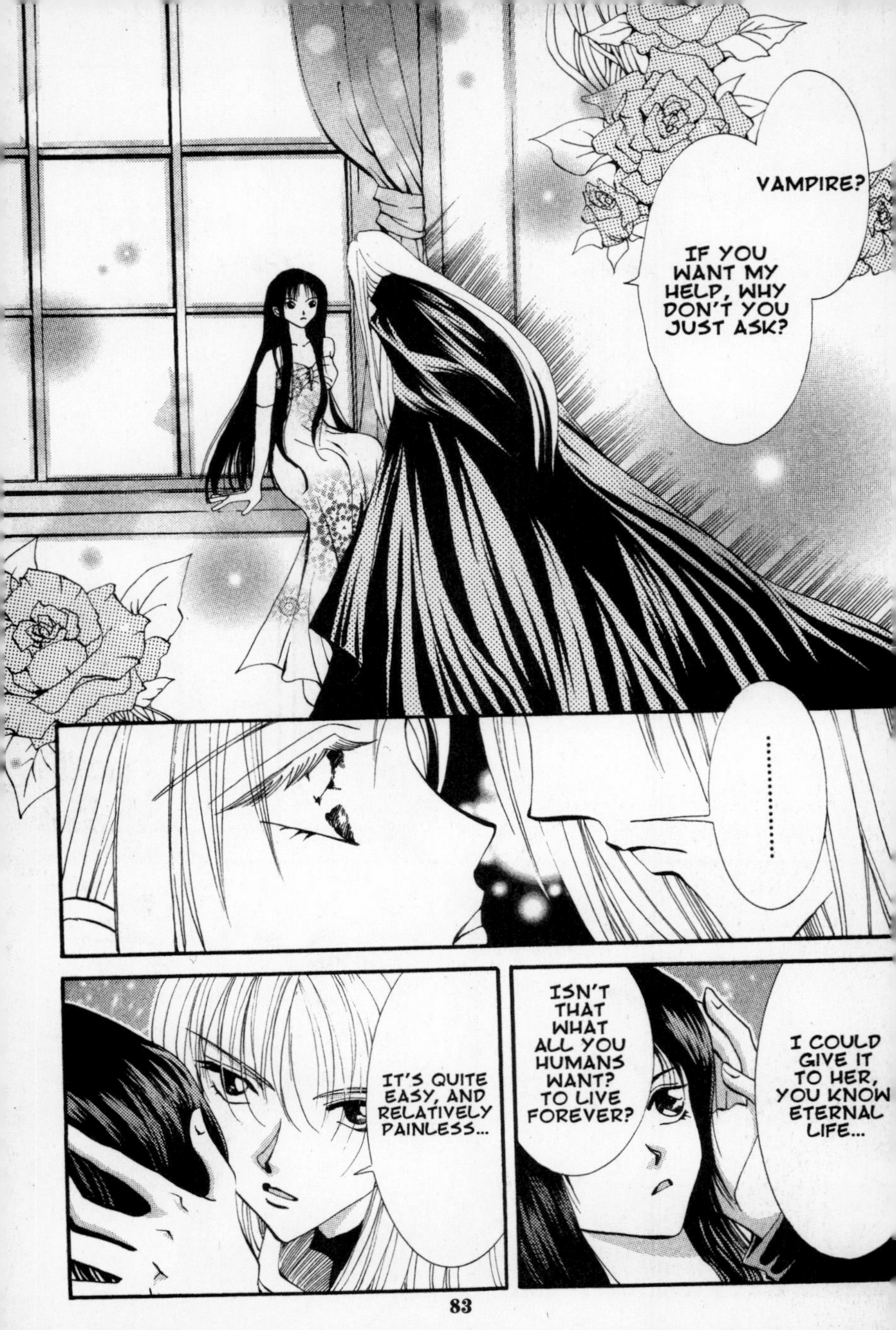
VAMPIRE?
IF YOU WANT MY HELP, WHY DON'T YOU JUST ASK?
......
I COULD GIVE IT TO HER, YOU KNOW ETERNAL LIFE...
ISN'T THAT WHAT ALL YOU HUMANS WANT? TO LIVE FOREVER?
IT'S QUITE EASY, AND RELATIVELY PAINLESS...

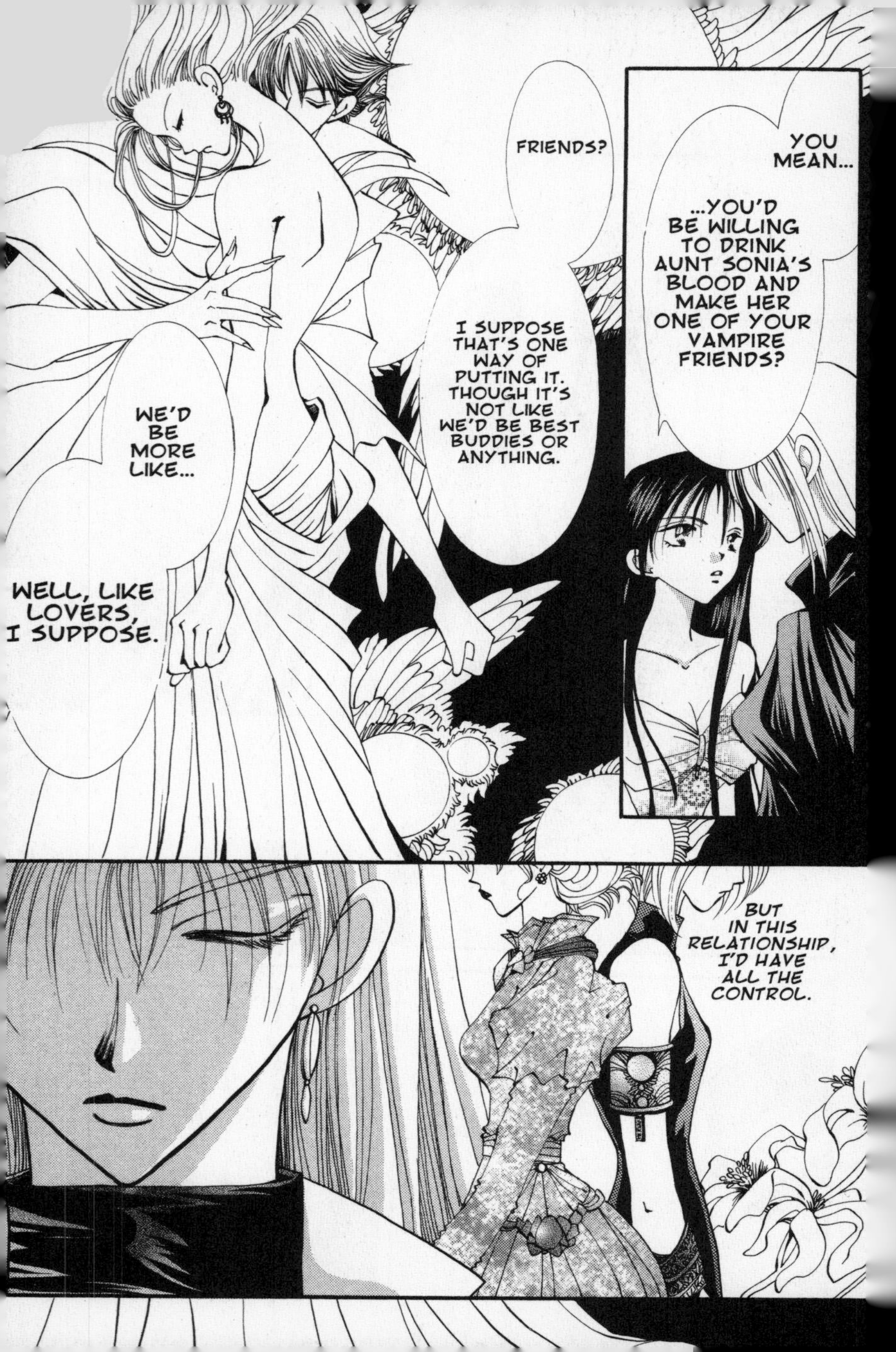
YOU MEAN...
...YOU'D BE WILLING TO DRINK AUNT SONIA'S BLOOD AND MAKE HER ONE OF YOUR VAMPIRE FRIENDS?
FRIENDS?
I SUPPOSE THAT'S ONE WAY OF PUTTING IT. THOUGH IT'S NOT LIKE WE'D BE BEST BUDDIES OR ANYTHING.
WE'D BE MORE LIKE...
WELL, LIKE LOVERS, I SUPPOSE.
BUT IN THIS RELATIONSHIP, I'D HAVE ALL THE CONTROL.

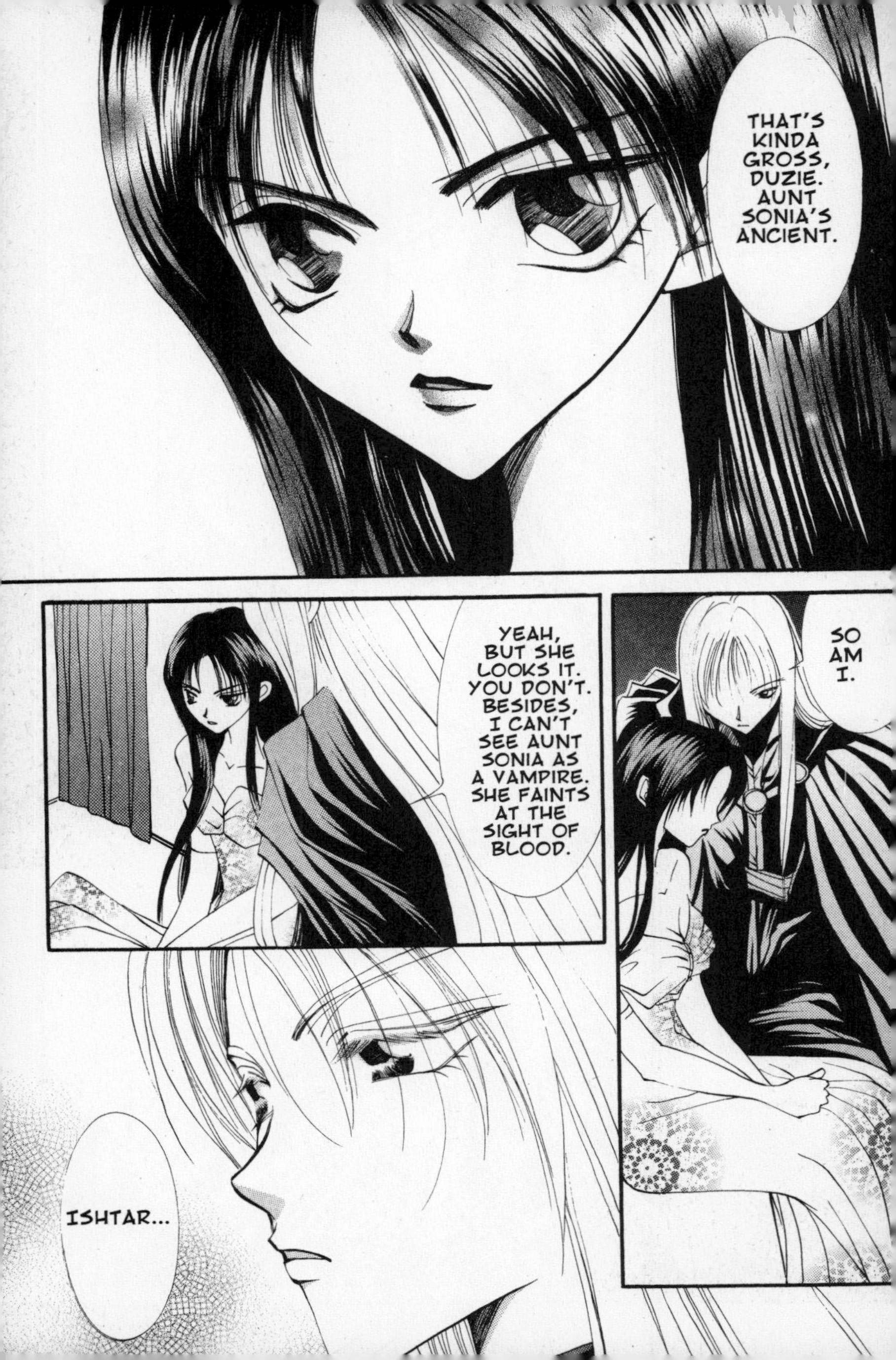
THAT'S KINDA GROSS, DUZIE. AUNT SONIA'S ANCIENT.
SO AM I.
YEAH, BUT SHE LOOKS IT. YOU DON'T. BESIDES, I CAN'T SEE AUNT SONIA AS A VAMPIRE. SHE FAINTS AT THE SIGHT OF BLOOD.
ISHTAR...

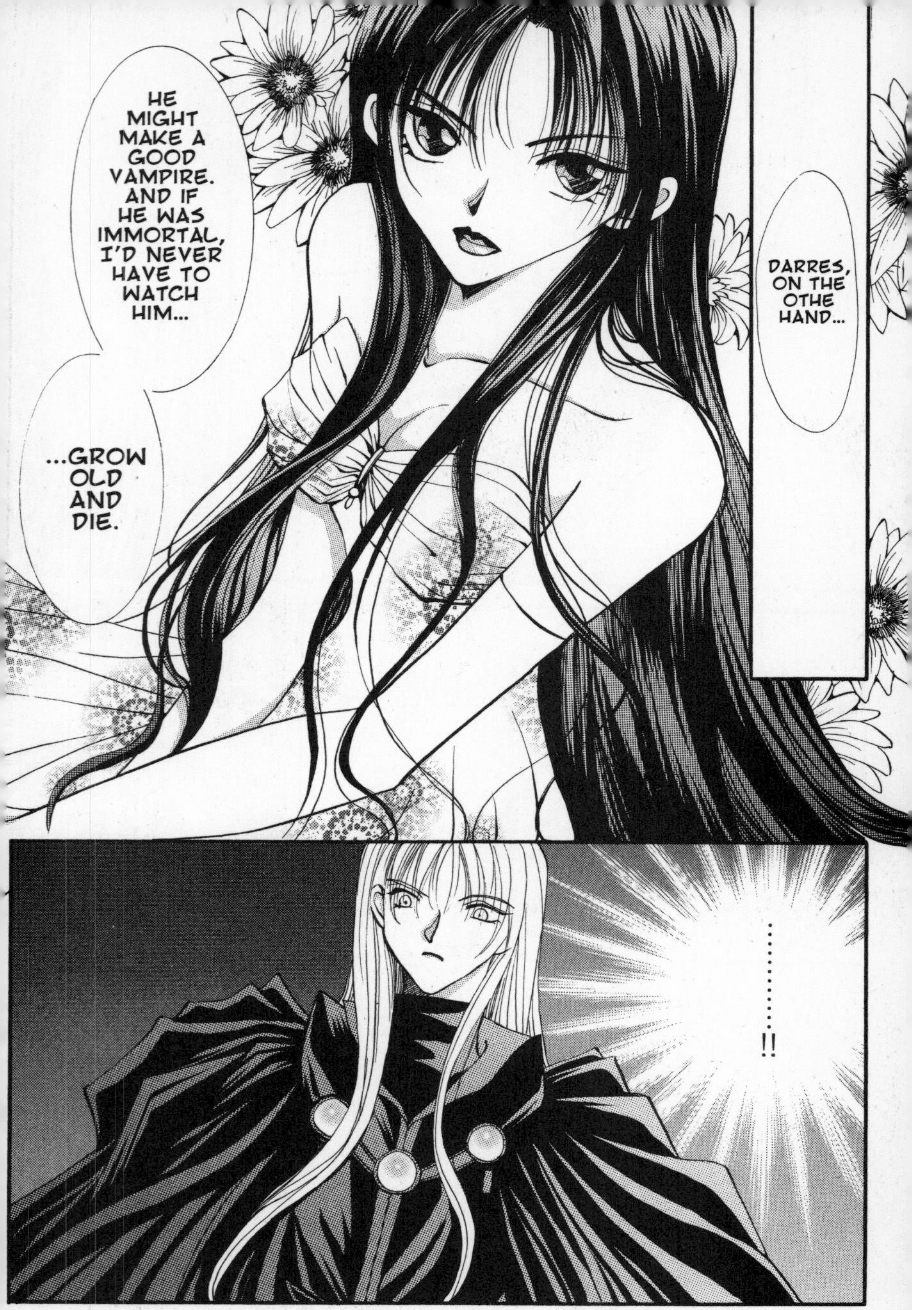
DARRES, ON THE OTHE HAND...
HE MIGHT MAKE A GOOD VAMPIRE. AND IF HE WAS IMMORTAL, I'D NEVER HAVE TO WATCH HIM...
...GROW OLD AND DIE.
.........!!

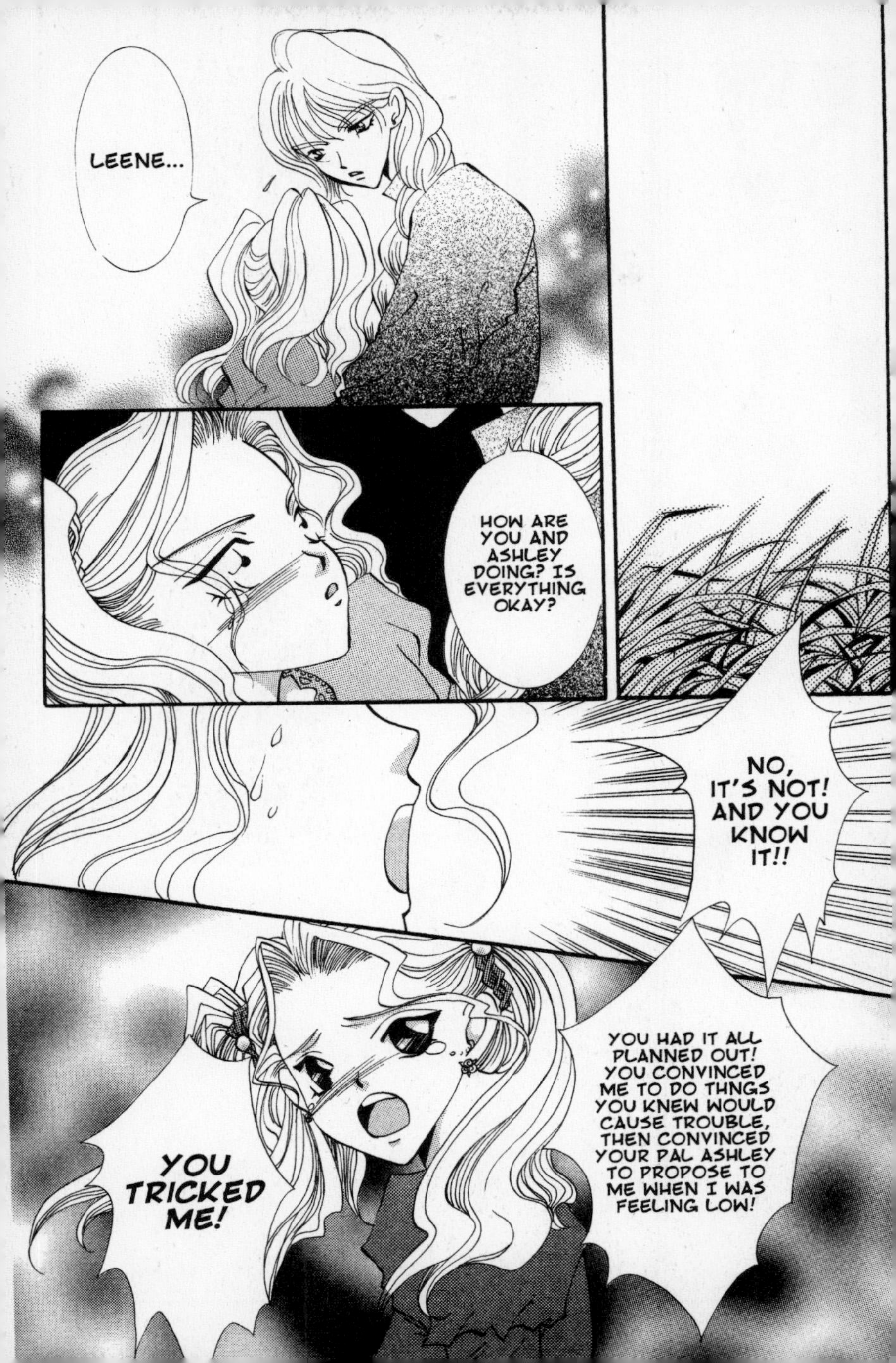
LEENE...
HOW ARE YOU AND ASHLEY DOING? IS EVERYTHING OKAY?
NO, IT'S NOT! AND YOU KNOW IT!!
YOU HAD IT ALL PLANNED OUT! YOU CONVINCED ME TO DO THNGS YOU KNEW WOULD CAUSE TROUBLE, THEN CONVINCED YOUR PAL ASHLEY TO PROPOSE TO ME WHEN I WAS FEELING LOW!
YOU TRICKED ME!

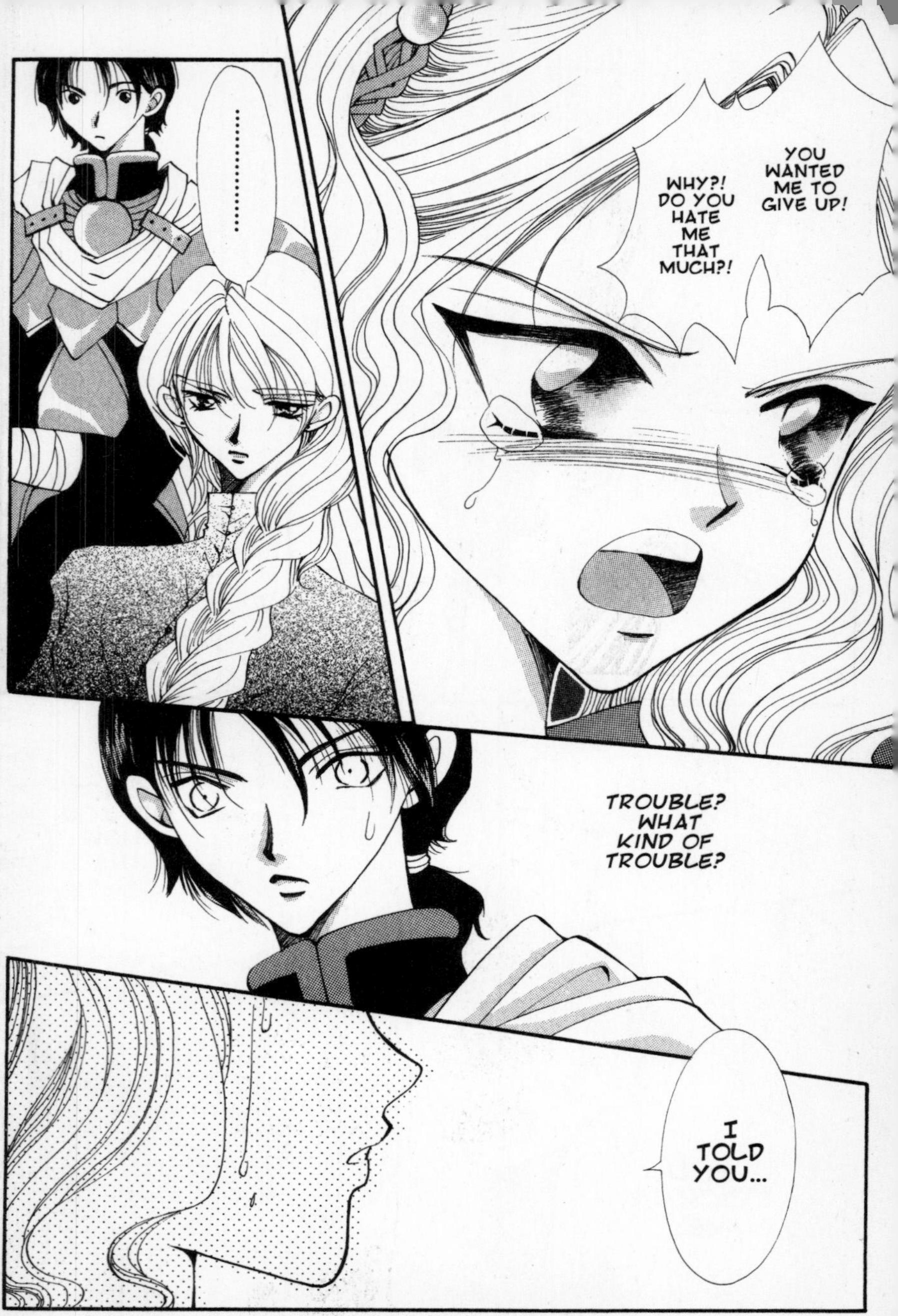
YOU WANTED ME TO GIVE UP!
WHY?! DO YOU HATE ME THAT MUCH?!
......
TROUBLE? WHAT KIND OF TROUBLE?
I TOLD YOU...

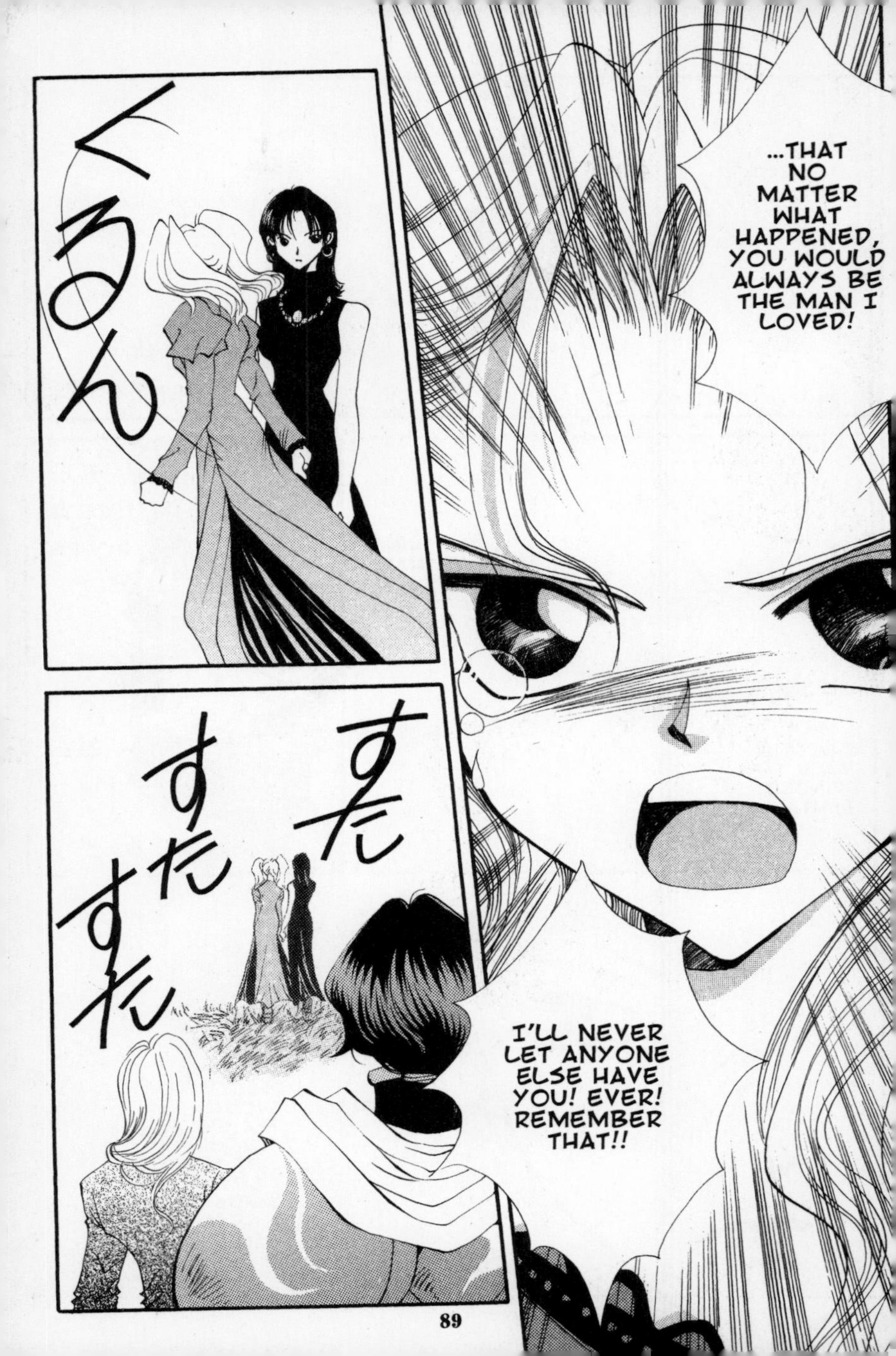
...THAT NO MATTER WHAT HAPPENED, YOU WOULD ALWAYS BE THE MAN I LOVED!
I'LL NEVER LET ANYONE ELSE HAVE YOU! EVER! REMEMBER THAT!!
くるん
すた
すた
すた

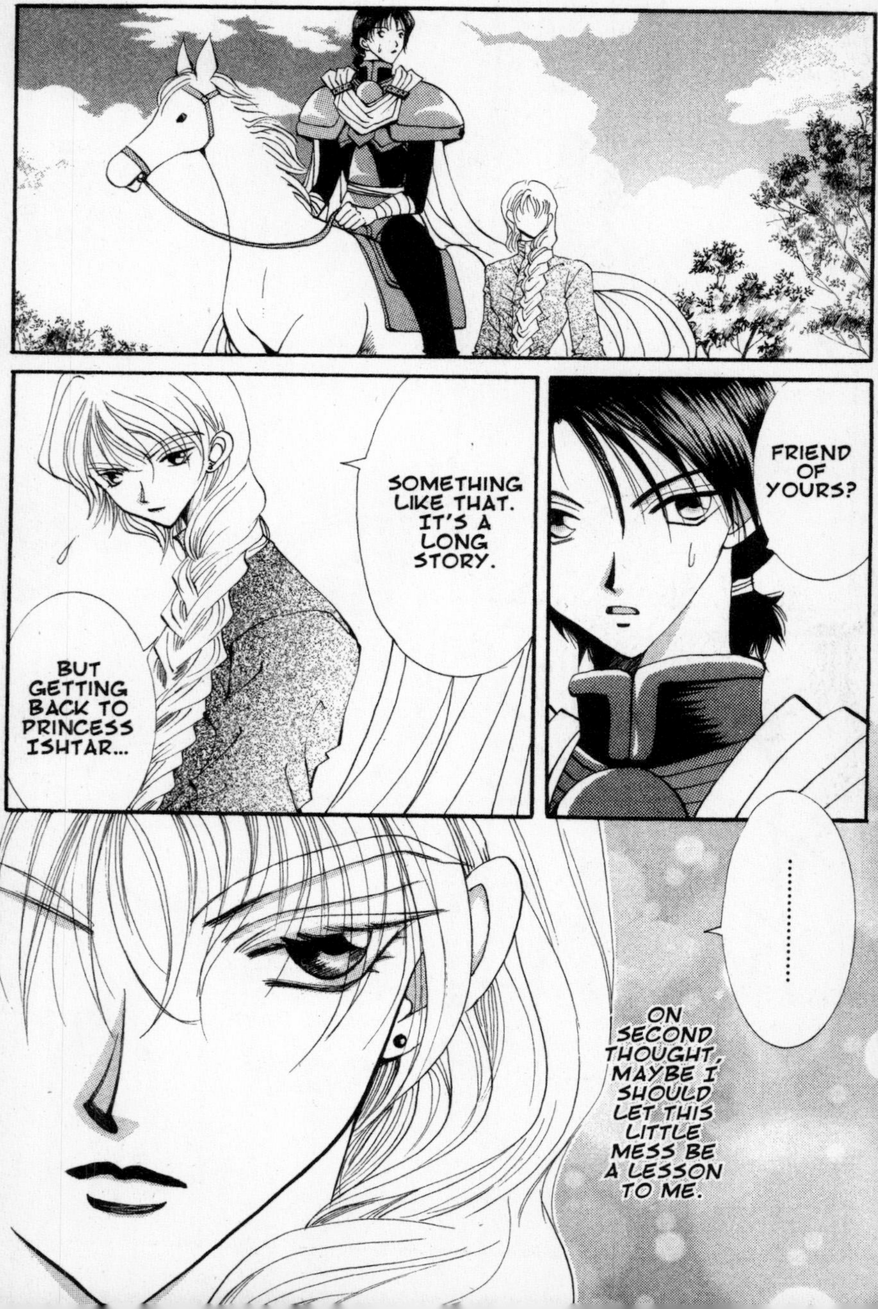
FRIEND OF YOURS?
SOMETHING LIKE THAT. IT'S A LONG STORY.
BUT GETTING BACK TO PRINCESS ISHTAR...
....
ON SECOND THOUGHT, MAYBE I SHOULD LET THIS LITTLE MESS BE A LESSON TO ME.

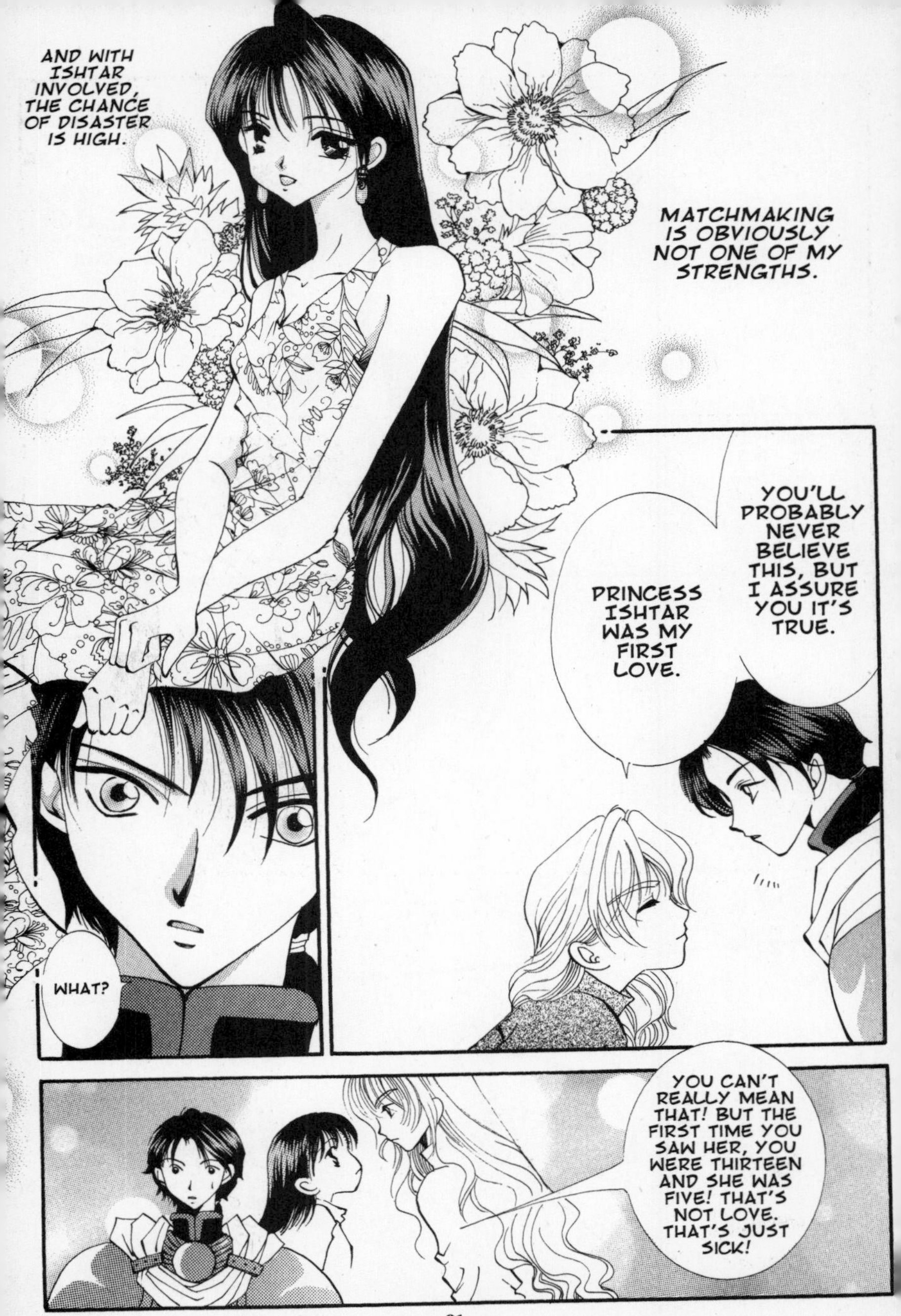
AND WITH ISHTAR INVOLVED, THE CHANCE OF DISASTER IS HIGH.
MATCHMAKING IS OBVIOUSLY NOT ONE OF MY STRENGTHS.
YOU'LL PROBABLY NEVER BELIEVE THIS, BUT I ASSURE YOU IT'S TRUE.
PRINCESS ISHTAR WAS MY FIRST LOVE.
WHAT?
YOU CAN'T REALLY MEAN THAT! BUT THE FIRST TIME YOU SAW HER, YOU WERE THIRTEEN AND SHE WAS FIVE! THAT'S NOT LOVE. THAT'S JUST SICK!

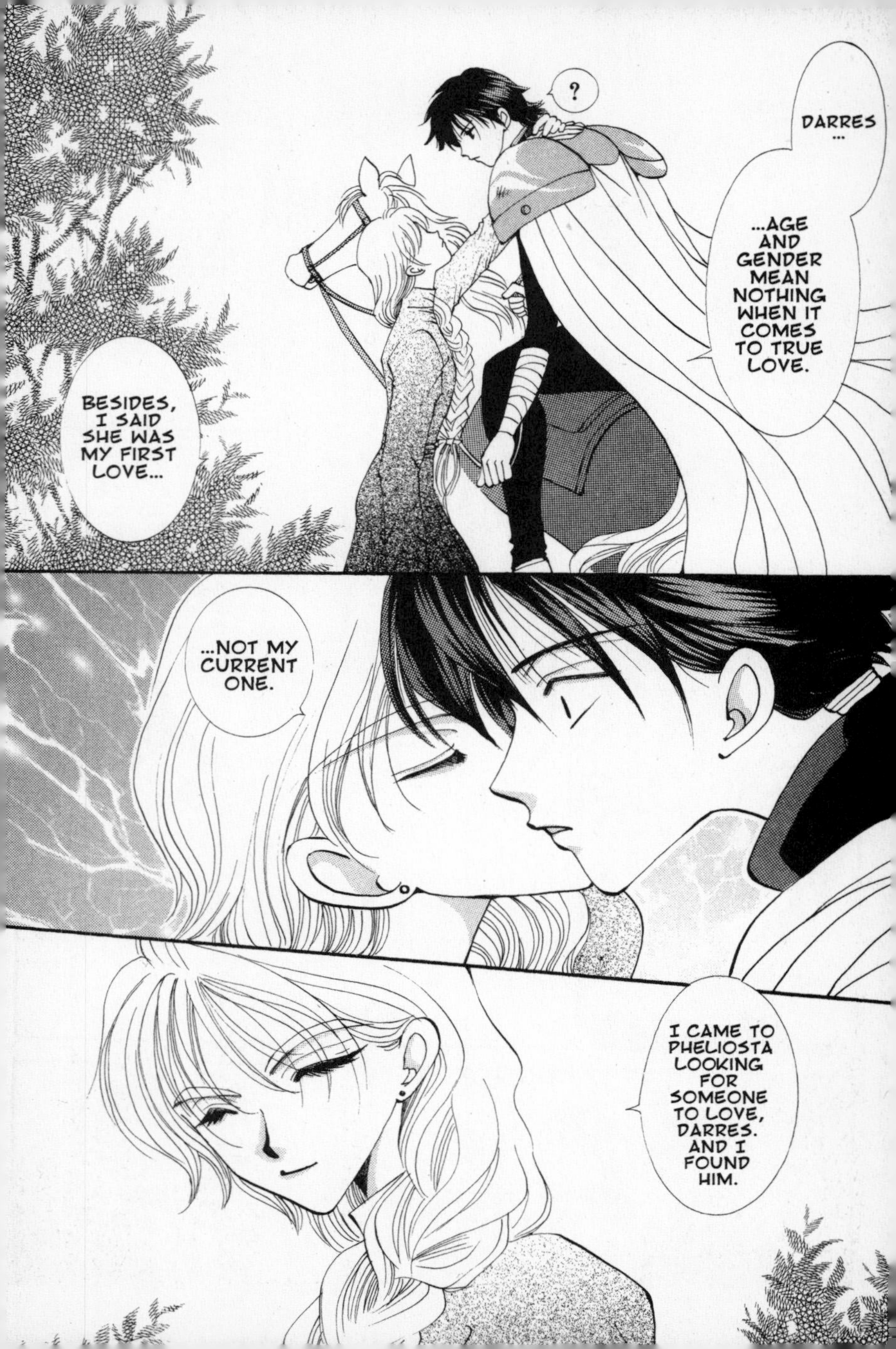
DARRES...
?
...AGE AND GENDER MEAN NOTHING WHEN IT COMES TO TRUE LOVE.
BESIDES, I SAID SHE WAS MY FIRST LOVE...
...NOT MY CURRENT ONE.
I CAME TO PHELIOSTA LOOKING FOR SOMEONE TO LOVE, DARRES. AND I FOUND HIM.

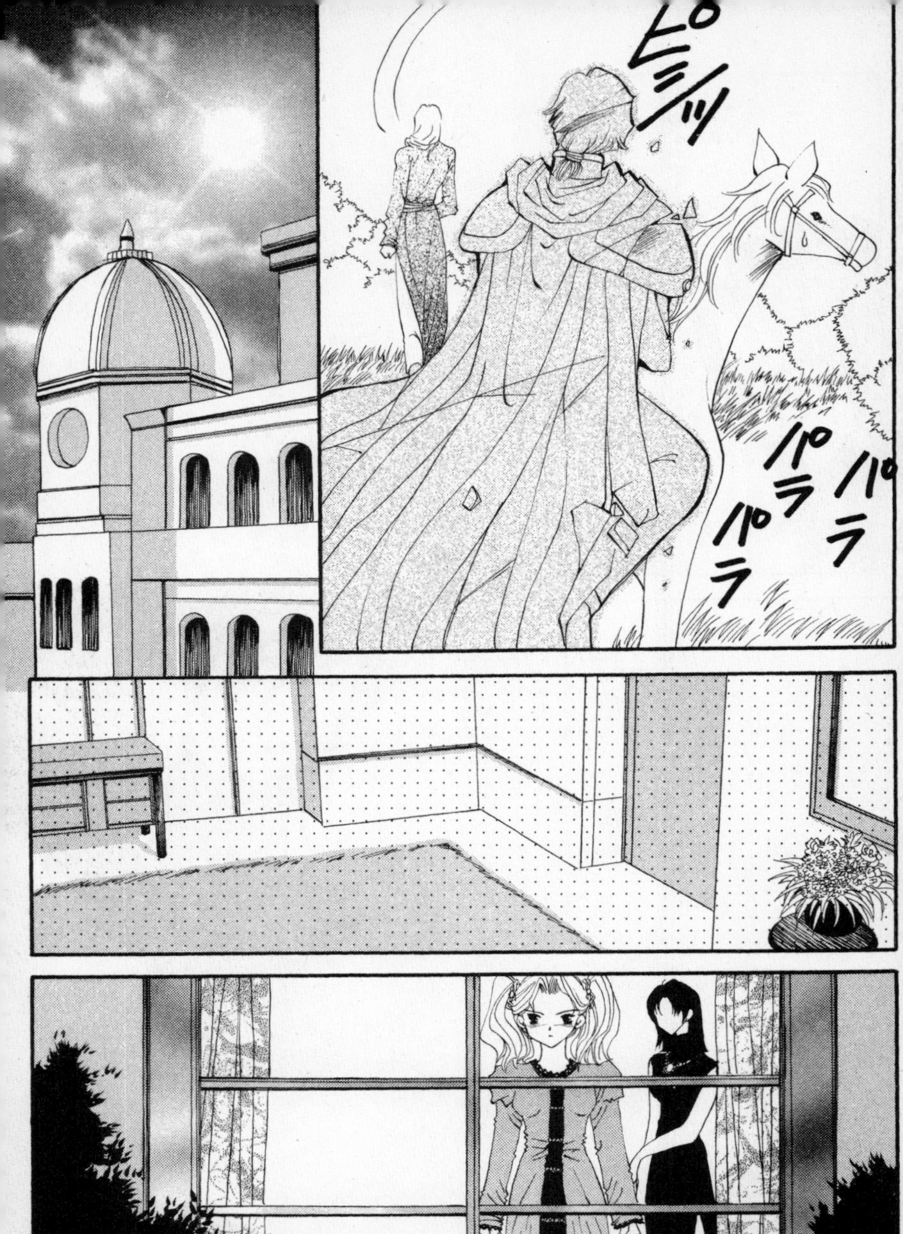
ピシッ
パラパラパラ

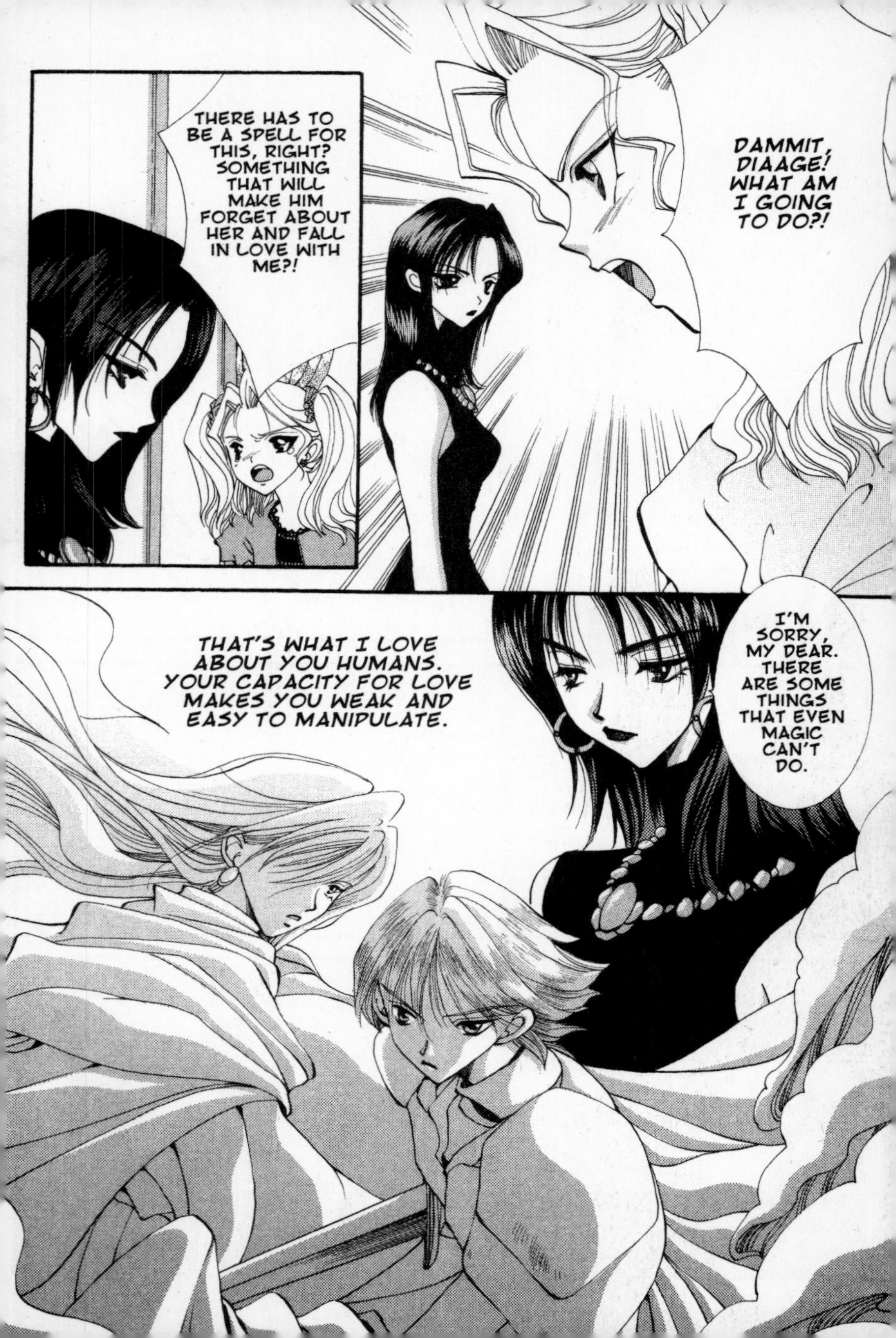
DAMMIT, DIAAGE! WHAT AM I GOING TO DO?!
THERE HAS TO BE A SPELL FOR THIS, RIGHT? SOMETHING THAT WILL MAKE HIM FORGET ABOUT HER AND FALL IN LOVE WITH ME?!
I'M SORRY, MY DEAR. THERE ARE SOME THINGS THAT EVEN MAGIC CAN'T DO.
THAT'S WHAT I LOVE ABOUT YOU HUMANS. YOUR CAPACITY FOR LOVE MAKES YOU WEAK AND EASY TO MANIPULATE.

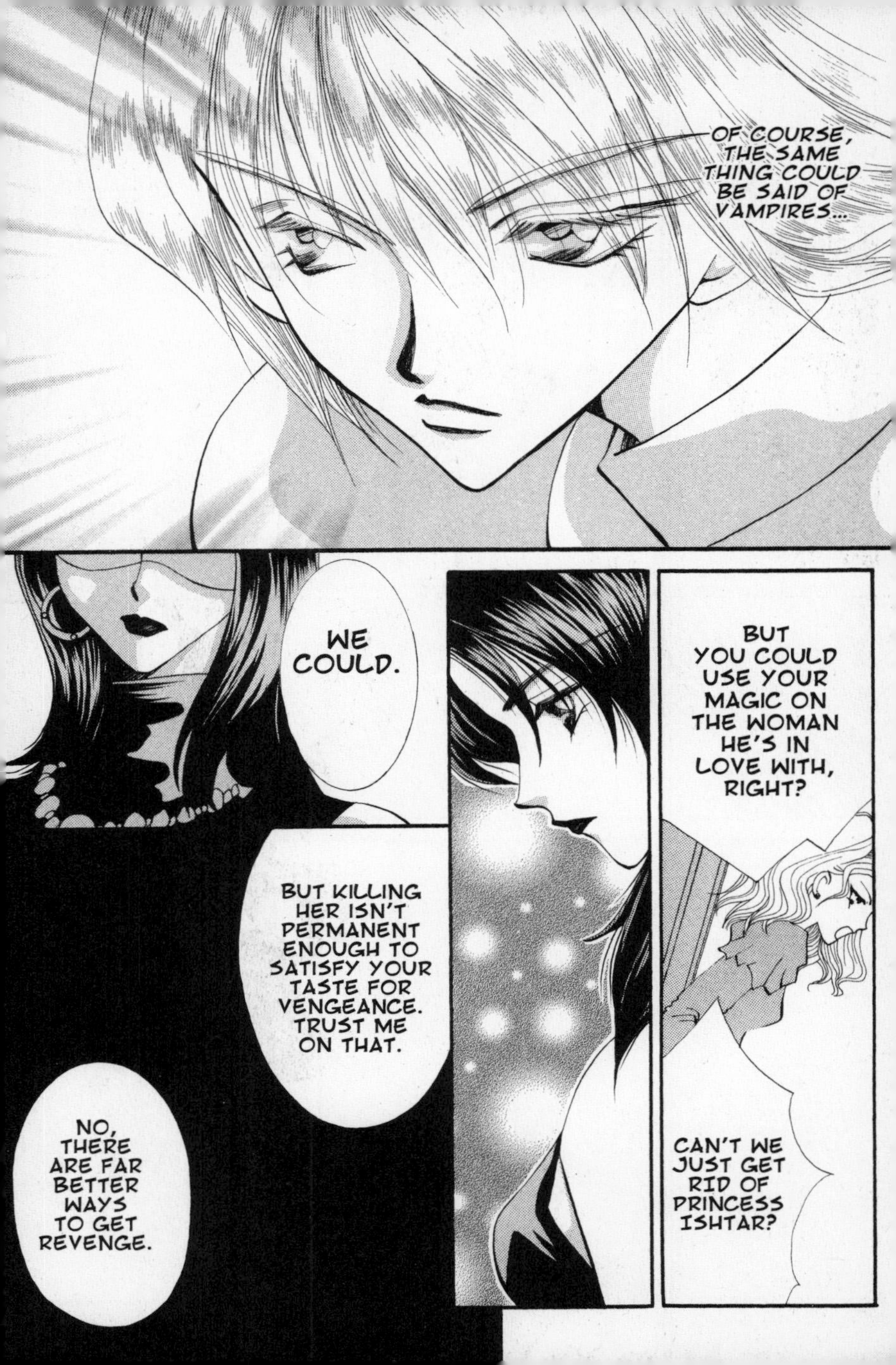
OF COURSE, THE SAME THING COULD BE SAID OF VAMPIRES...
BUT YOU COULD USE YOUR MAGIC ON THE WOMAN HE'S IN LOVE WITH, RIGHT?
CAN'T WE JUST GET RID OF PRINCESS ISHTAR?
WE COULD.
BUT KILLING HER ISN'T PERMANENT ENOUGH TO SATISFY YOUR TASTE FOR VENGEANCE. TRUST ME ON THAT.
NO, THERE ARE FAR BETTER WAYS TO GET REVENGE.

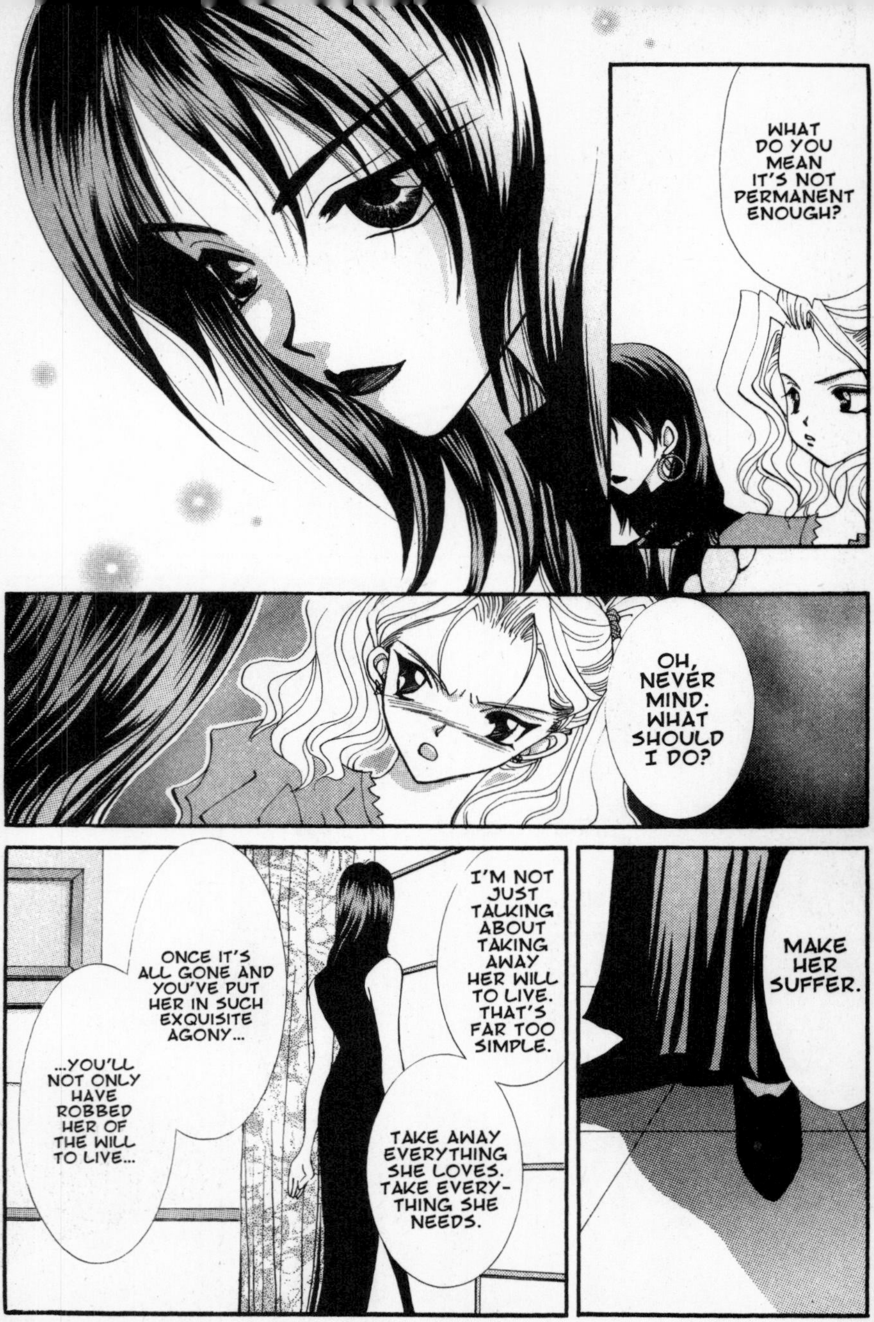
WHAT DO YOU MEAN IT'S NOT PERMANENT ENOUGH?
OH, NEVER MIND. WHAT SHOULD I DO?
MAKE HER SUFFER.
I'M NOT JUST TALKING ABOUT TAKING AWAY HER WILL TO LIVE. THAT'S FAR TOO SIMPLE.
TAKE AWAY EVERYTHING SHE LOVES. TAKE EVERY-THING SHE NEEDS.
ONCE IT'S ALL GONE AND YOU'VE PUT HER IN SUCH EXQUISITE AGONY...
...YOU'LL NOT ONLY HAVE ROBBED HER OF THE WILL TO LIVE...

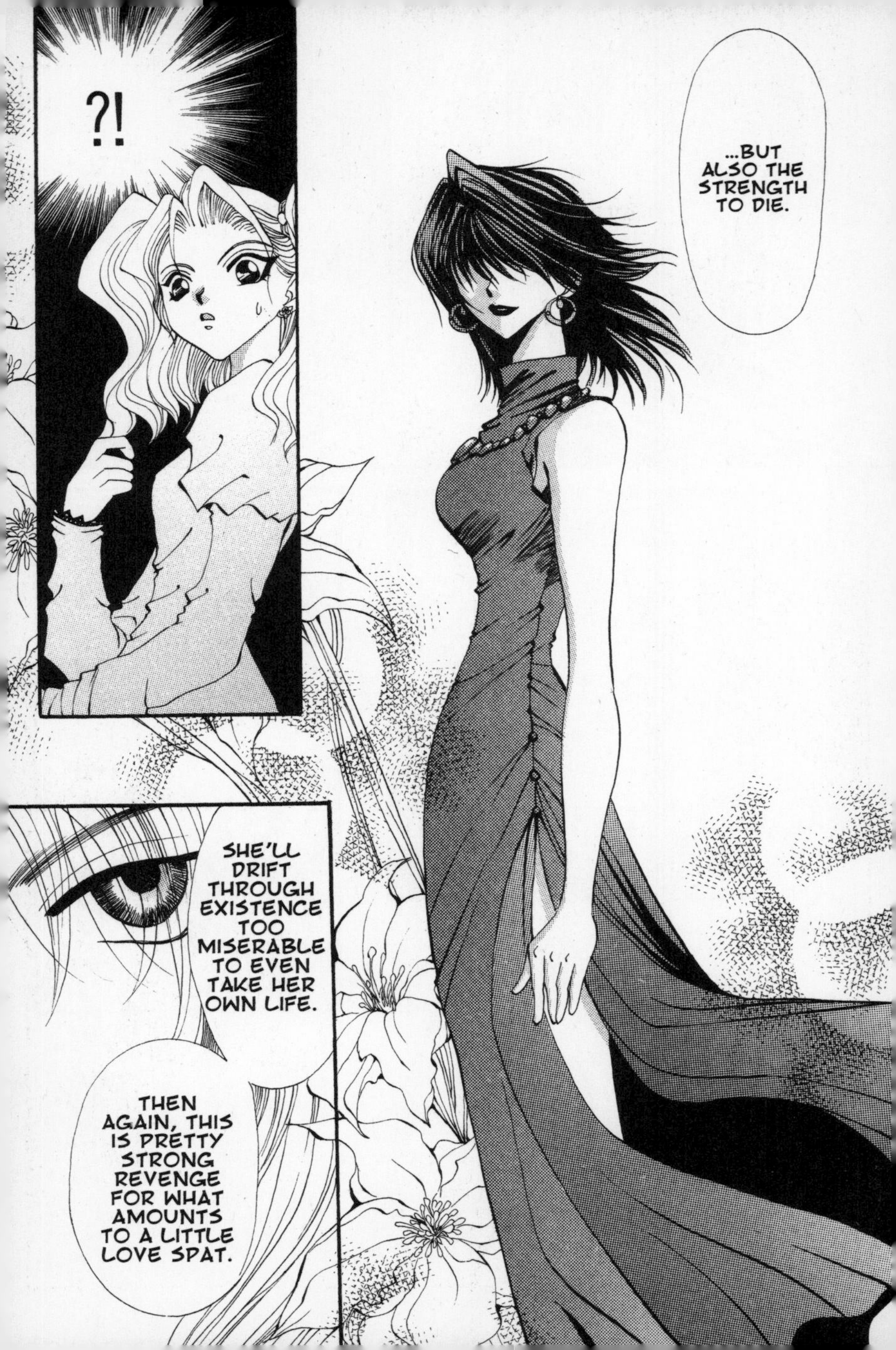
...BUT ALSO THE STRENGTH TO DIE.
?!
SHE'LL DRIFT THROUGH EXISTENCE TOO MISERABLE TO EVEN TAKE HER OWN LIFE.
THEN AGAIN, THIS IS PRETTY STRONG REVENGE FOR WHAT AMOUNTS TO A LITTLE LOVE SPAT.

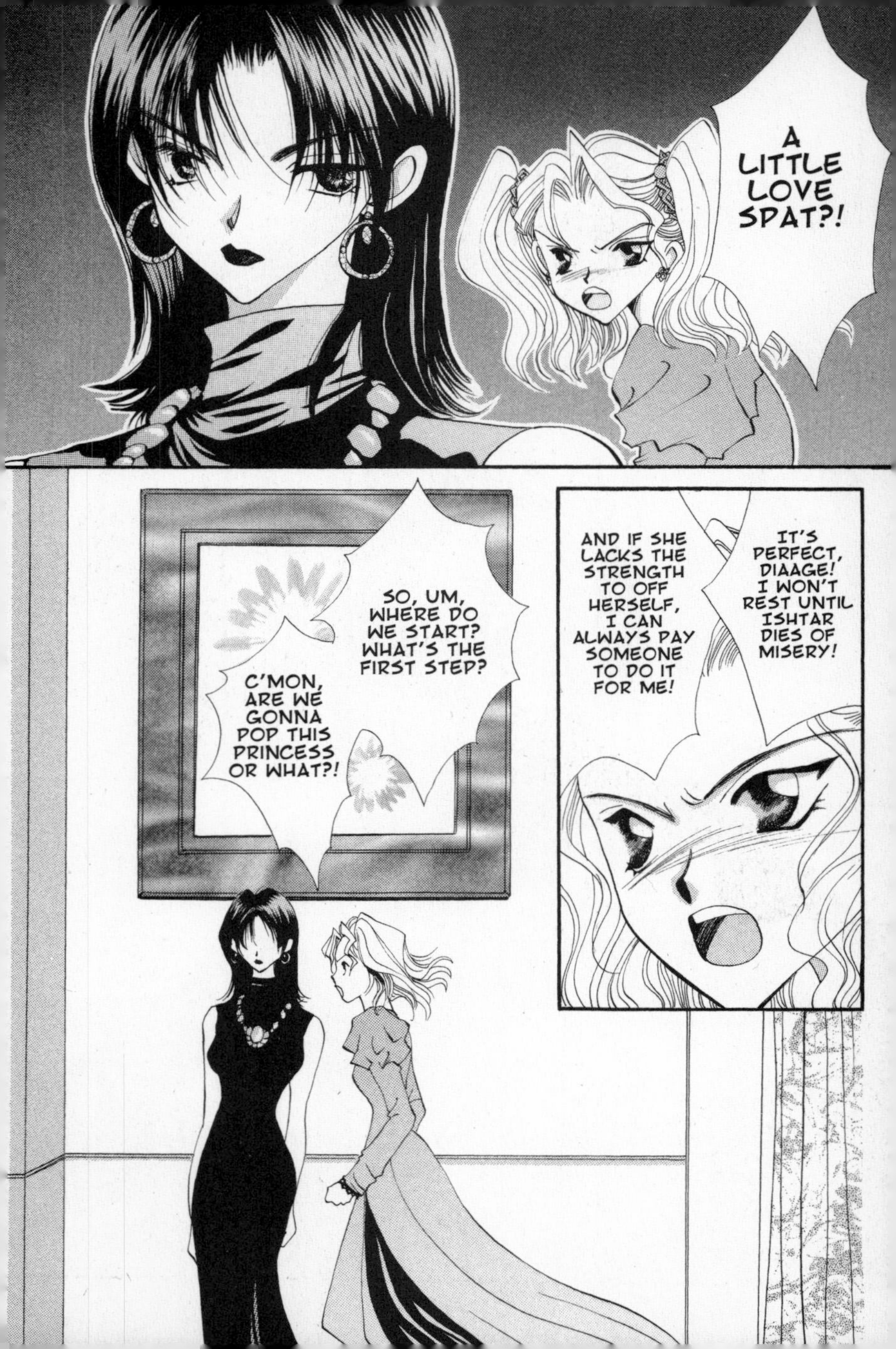
A LITTLE LOVE SPAT?!
IT'S PERFECT, DIAAGE! I WON'T REST UNTIL ISHTAR DIES OF MISERY!
AND IF SHE LACKS THE STRENGTH TO OFF HERSELF, I CAN ALWAYS PAY SOMEONE TO DO IT FOR ME!
SO, UM, WHERE DO WE START? WHAT'S THE FIRST STEP?
C'MON, ARE WE GONNA POP THIS PRINCESS OR WHAT?!

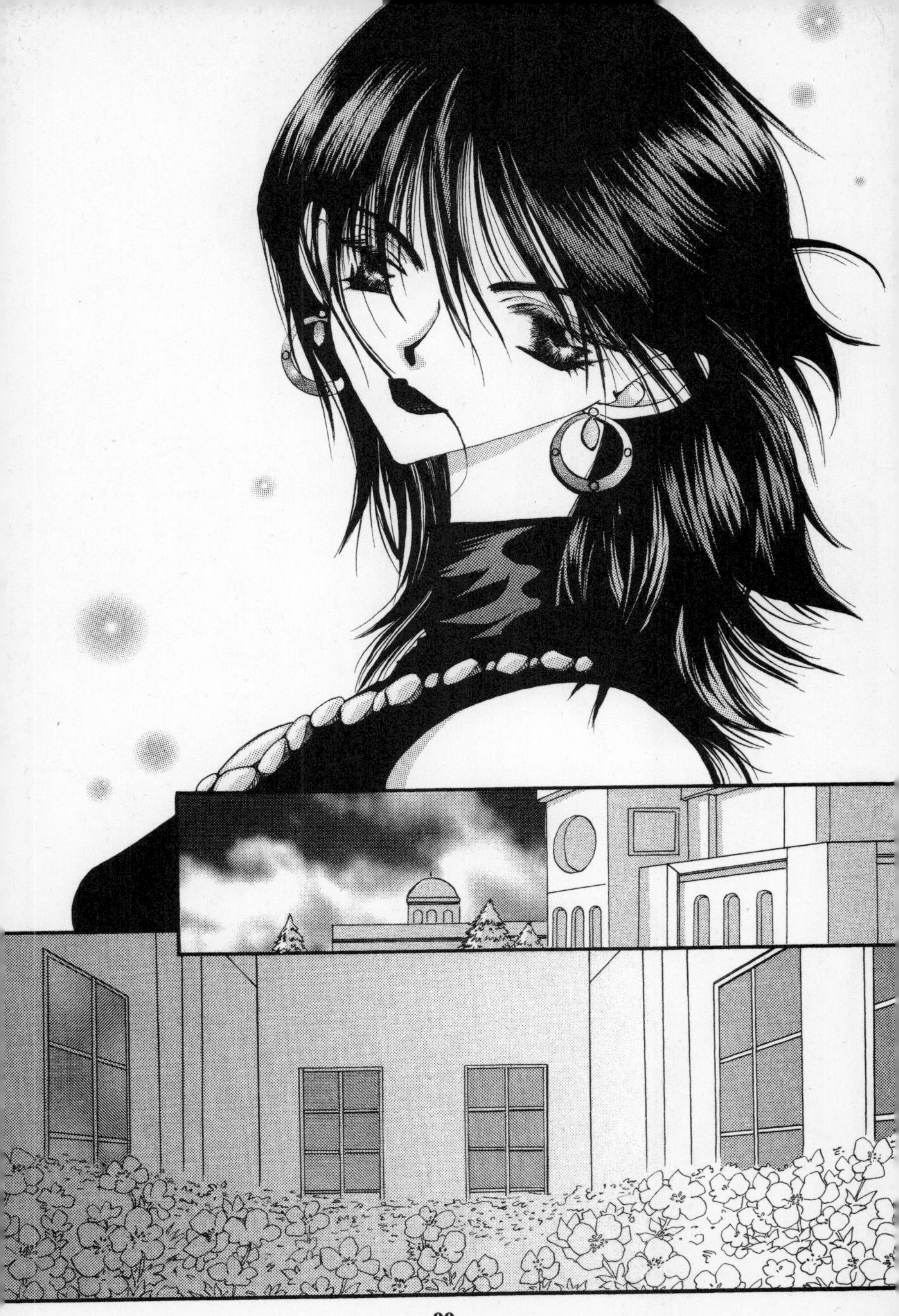

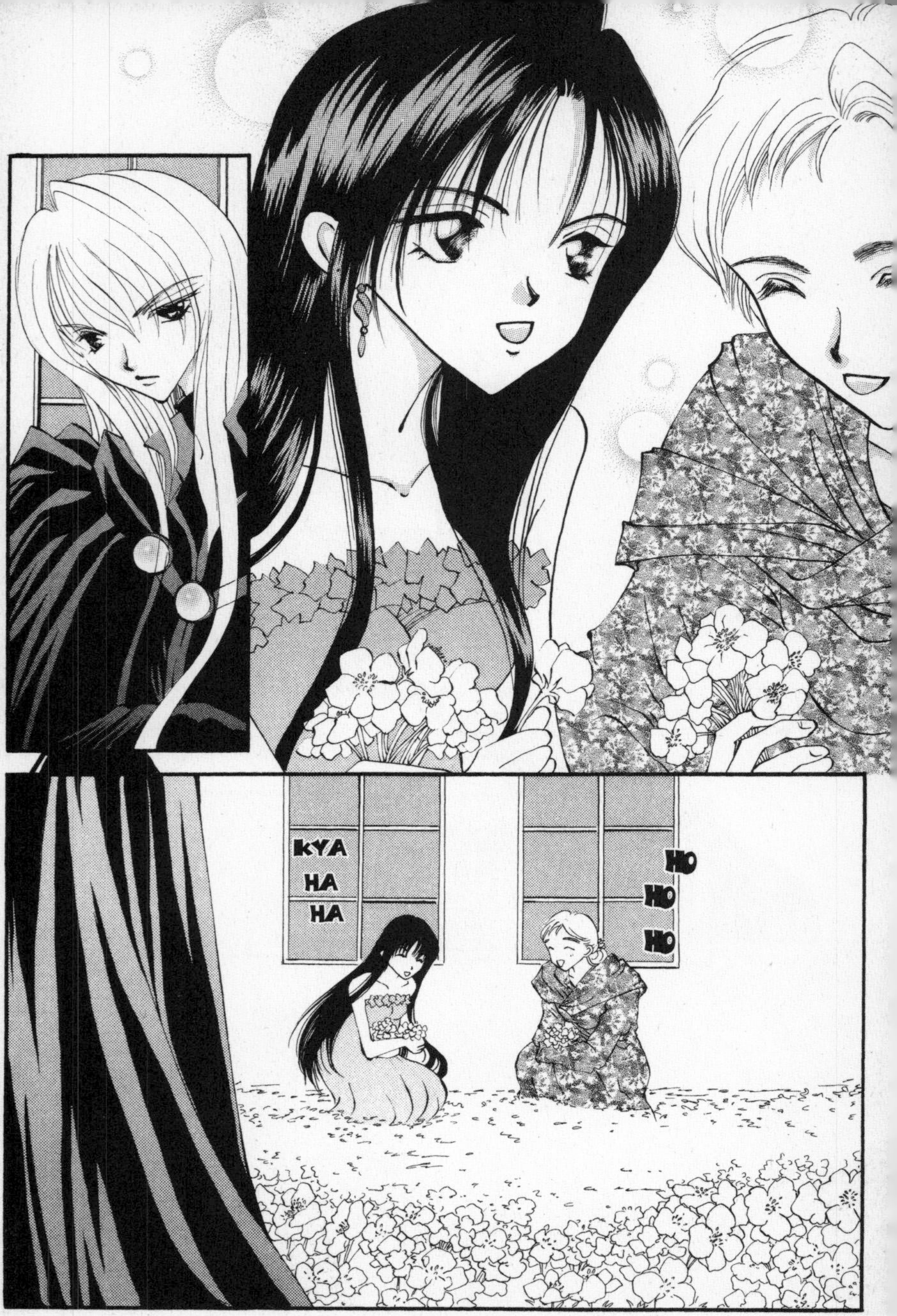
HO HO HO
KYA HA HA

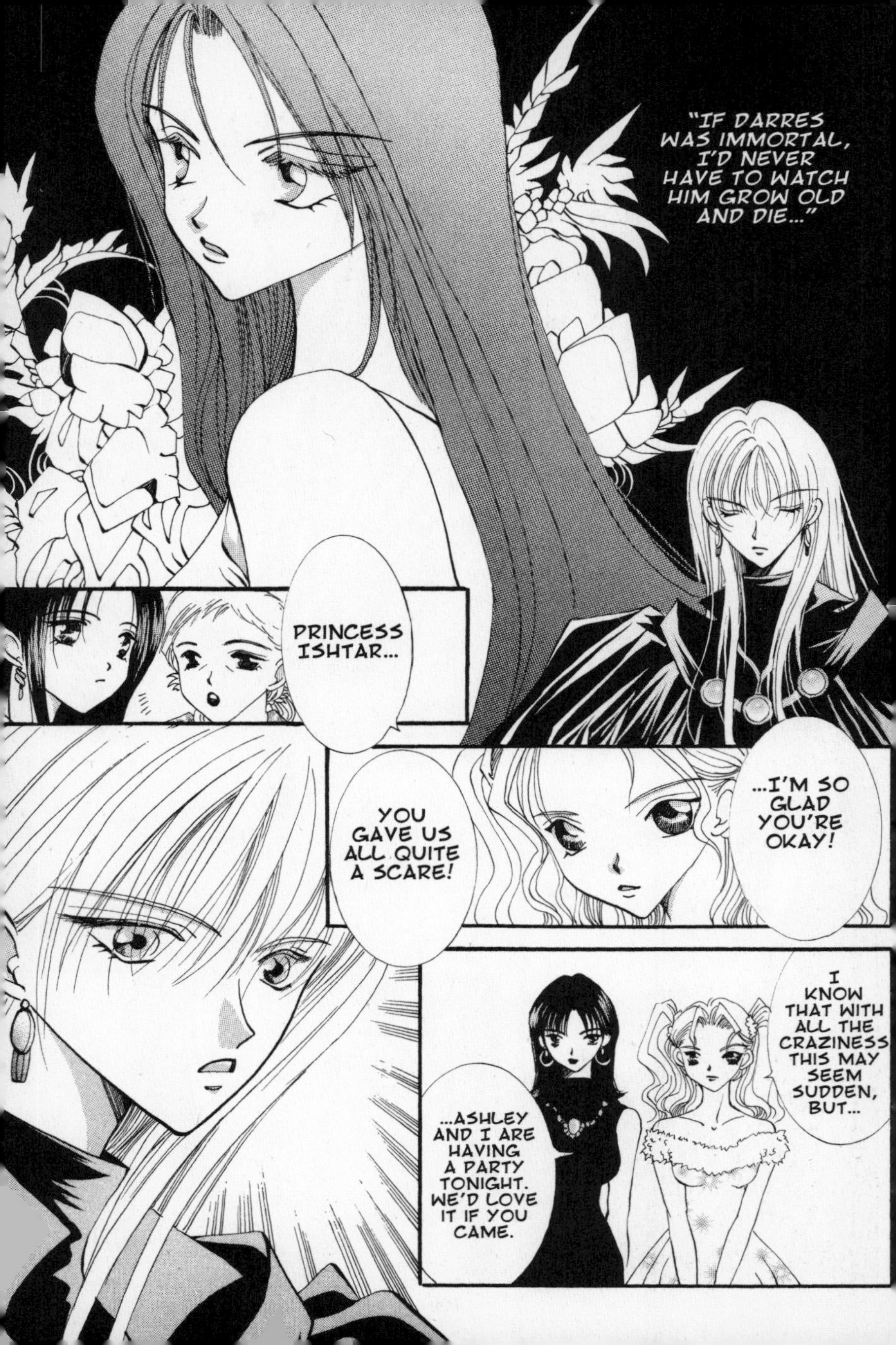
"IF DARRES WAS IMMORTAL, I'D NEVER HAVE TO WATCH HIM GROW OLD AND DIE..."
PRINCESS ISHTAR...
...I'M SO GLAD YOU'RE OKAY!
YOU GAVE US ALL QUITE A SCARE!
I KNOW THAT WITH ALL THE CRAZINESS THIS MAY SEEM SUDDEN, BUT...
...ASHLEY AND I ARE HAVING A PARTY TONIGHT. WE'D LOVE IT IF YOU CAME.

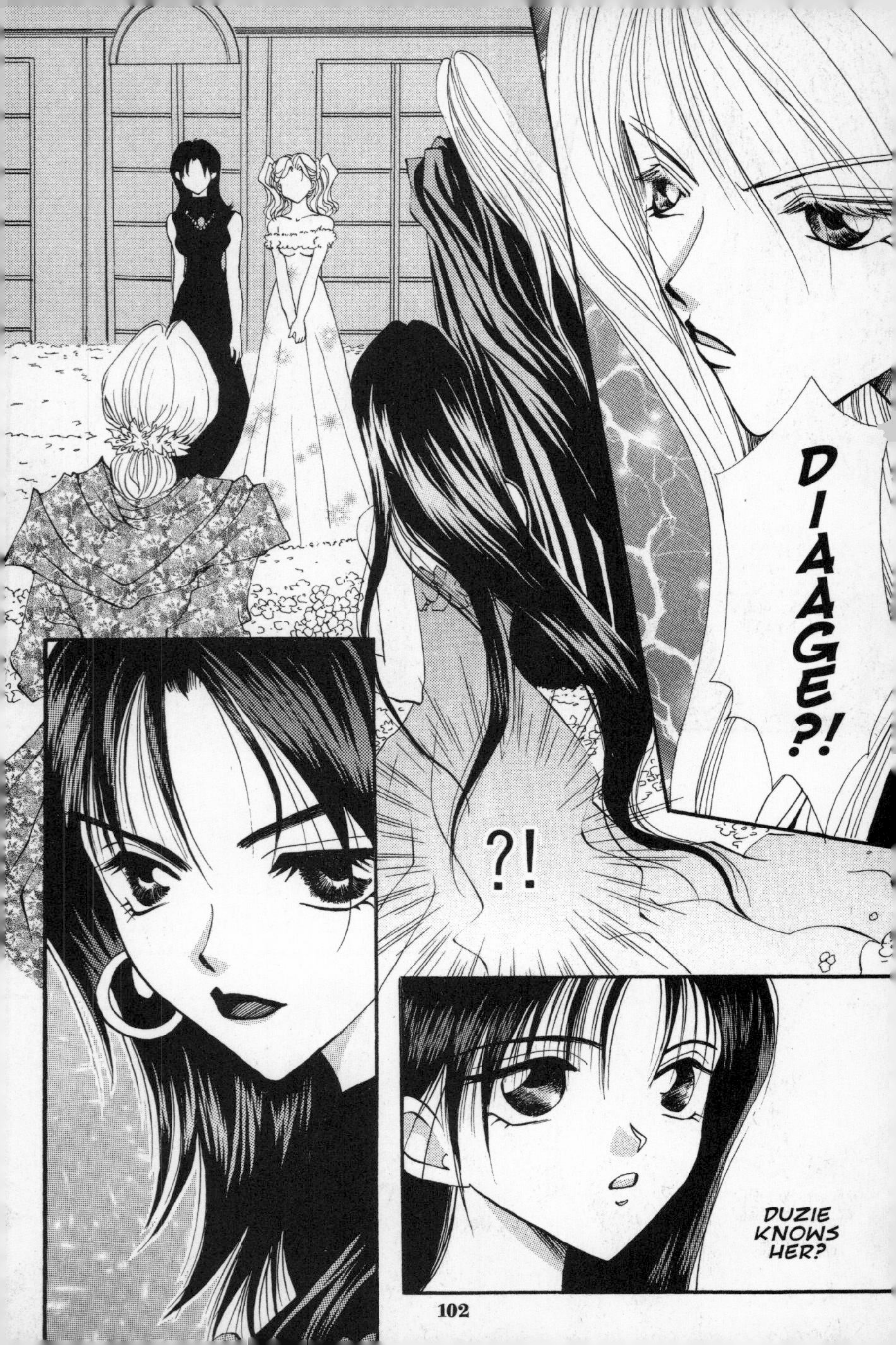
DIAAGE?!
?!
DUZIE KNOWS HER?

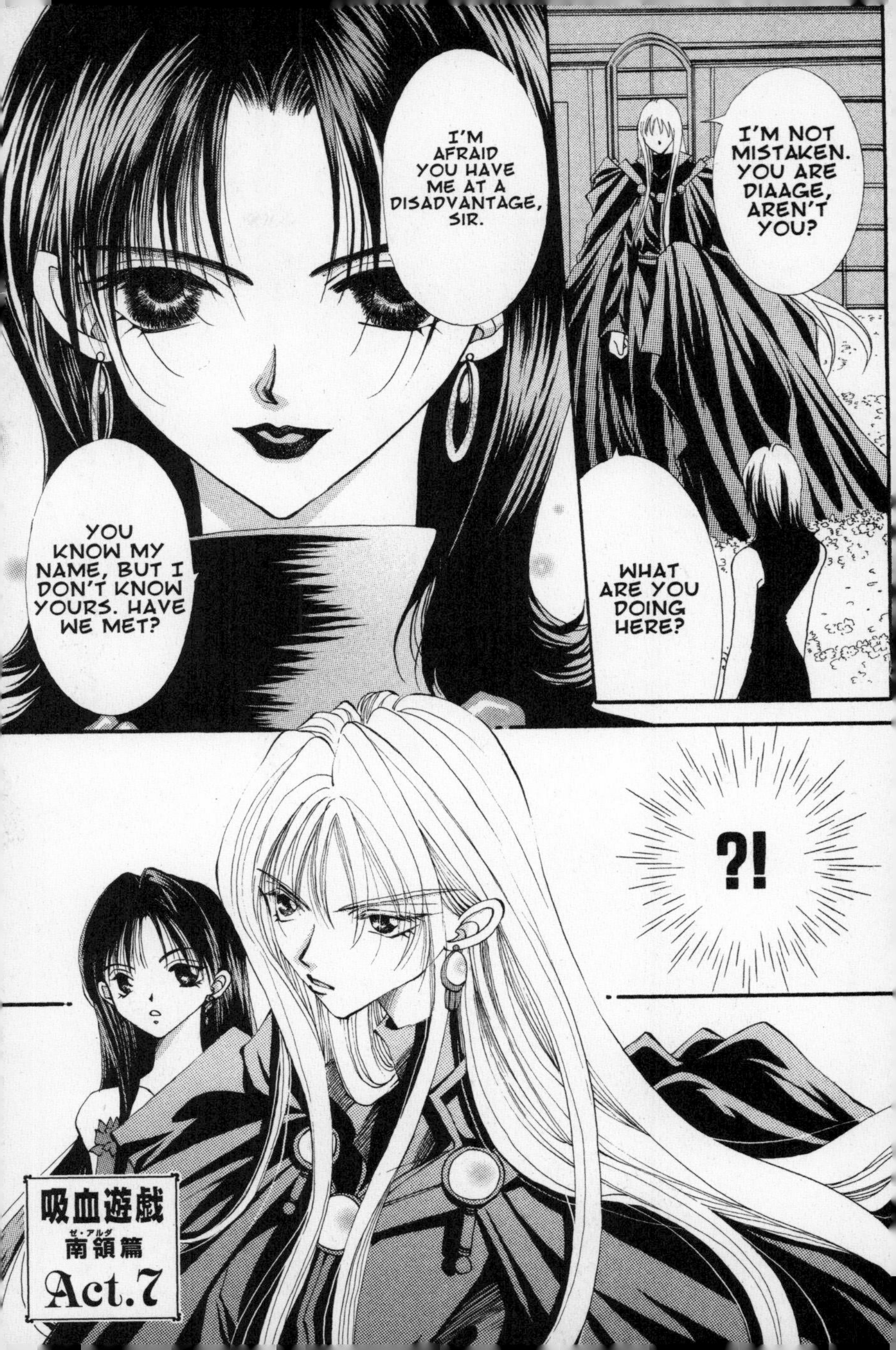
I'M NOT MISTAKEN. YOU ARE DIAAGE, AREN'T YOU?
WHAT ARE YOU DOING HERE?
I'M AFRAID YOU HAVE ME AT A DISADVANTAGE, SIR.
YOU KNOW MY NAME, BUT I DON'T KNOW YOURS. HAVE WE MET?
?!
吸血遊戯
南領篇
ゼ・アルダ
Act.7

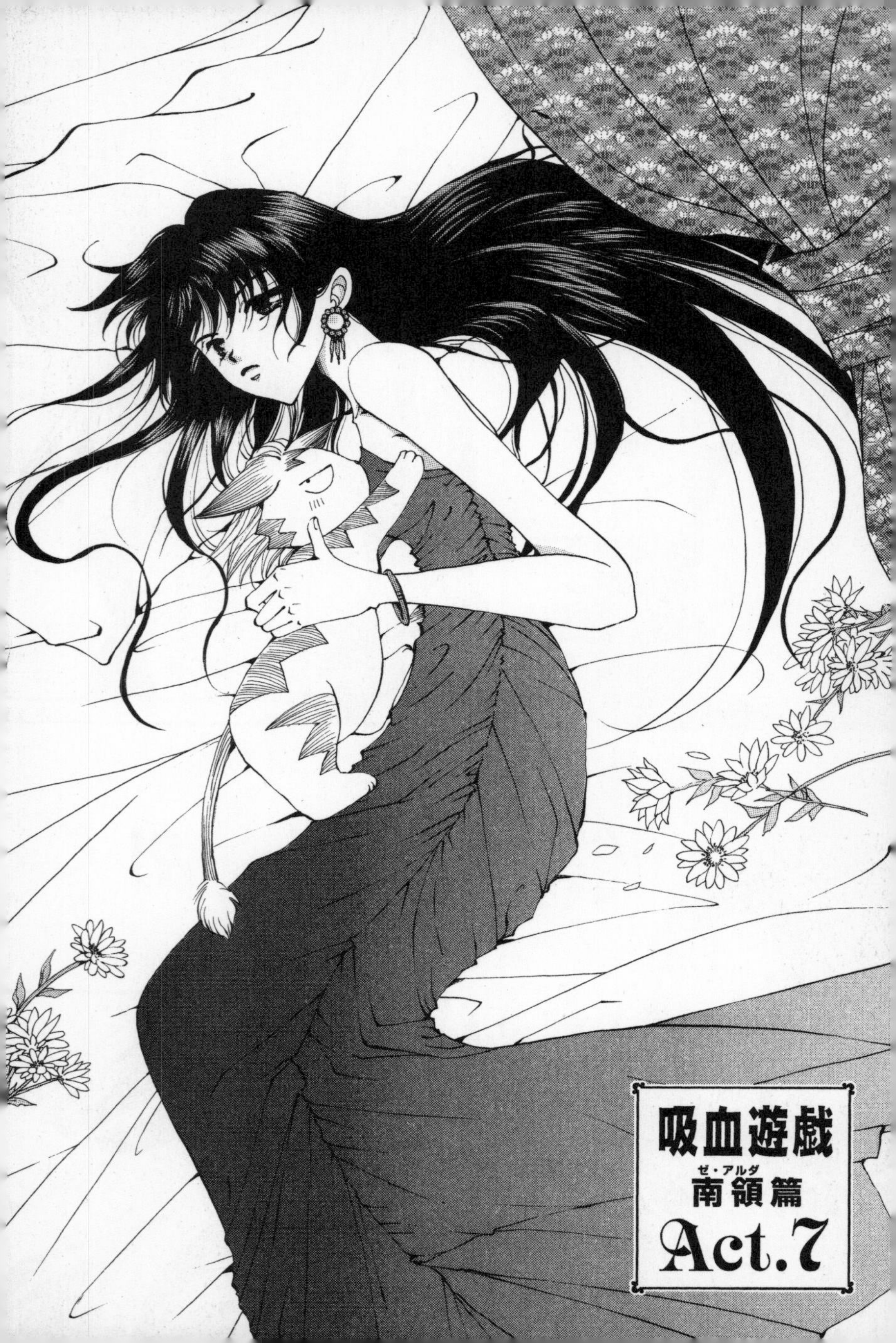
吸血遊戯
ゼ・アルダ
南領篇
Act.7

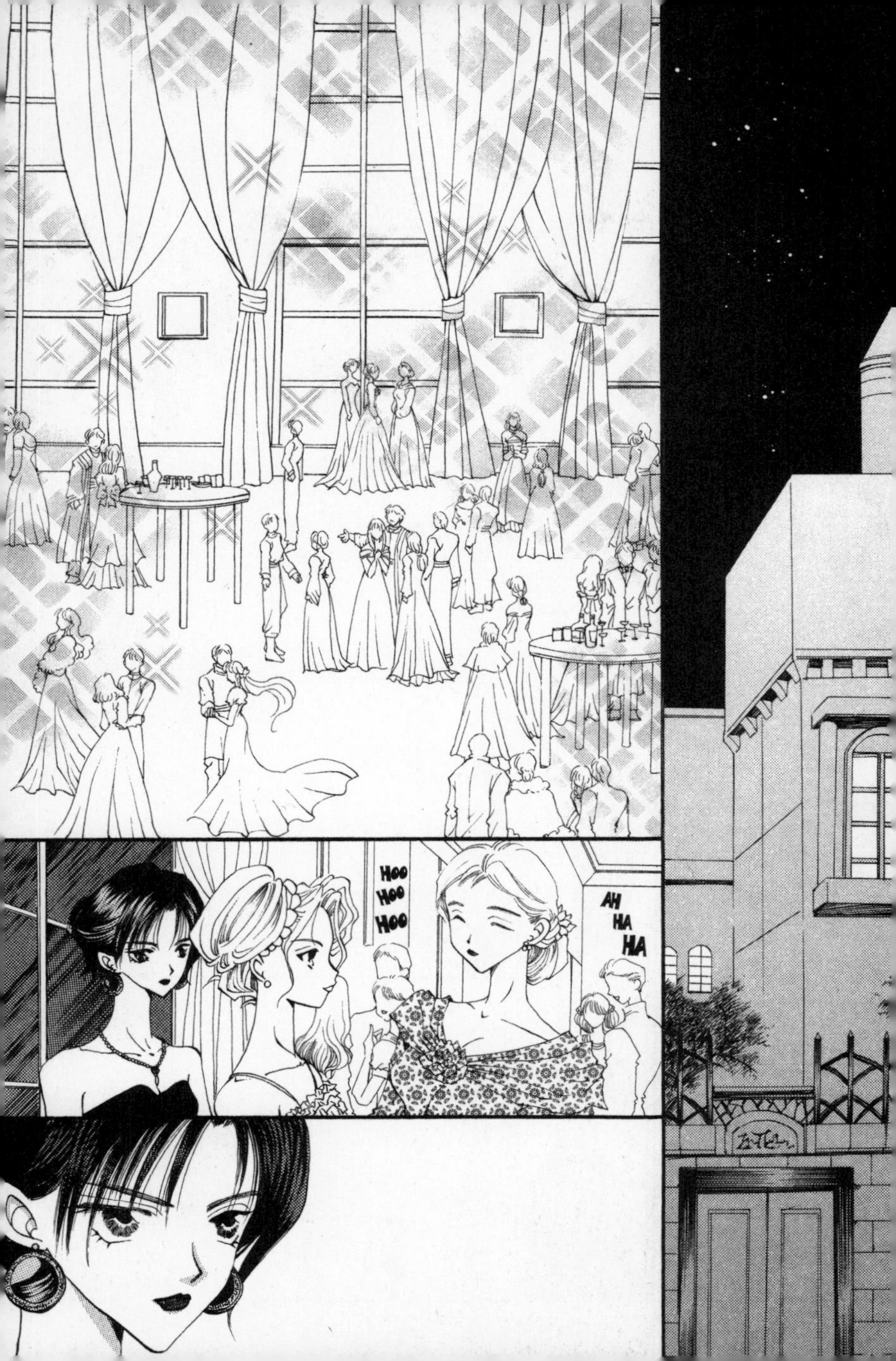
AH HA HA
HOO HOO HOO

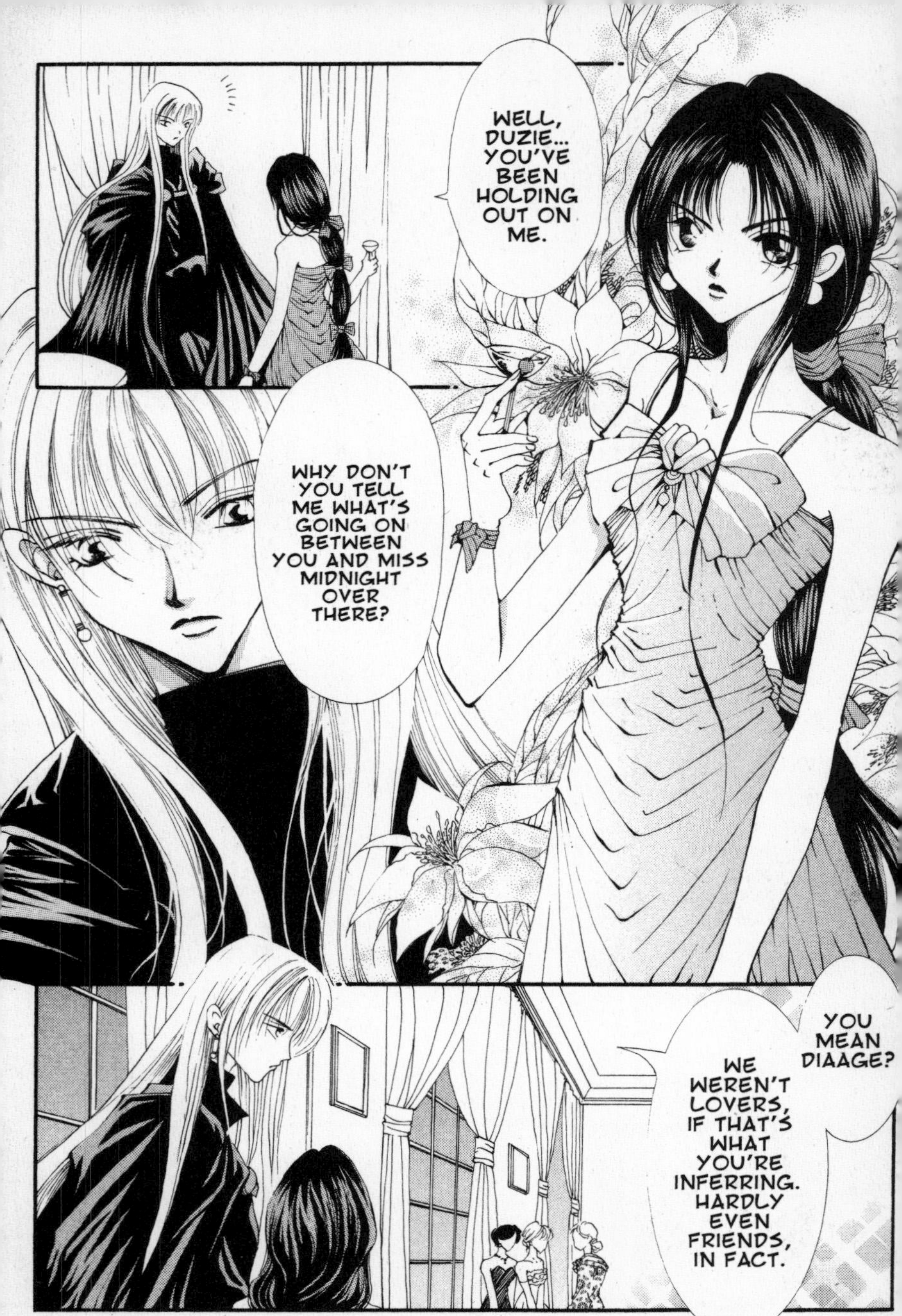
WELL, DUZIE... YOU'VE BEEN HOLDING OUT ON ME.
WHY DON'T YOU TELL ME WHAT'S GOING ON BETWEEN YOU AND MISS MIDNIGHT OVER THERE?
YOU MEAN DIAAGE?
WE WEREN'T LOVERS, IF THAT'S WHAT YOU'RE INFERRING. HARDLY EVEN FRIENDS, IN FACT.

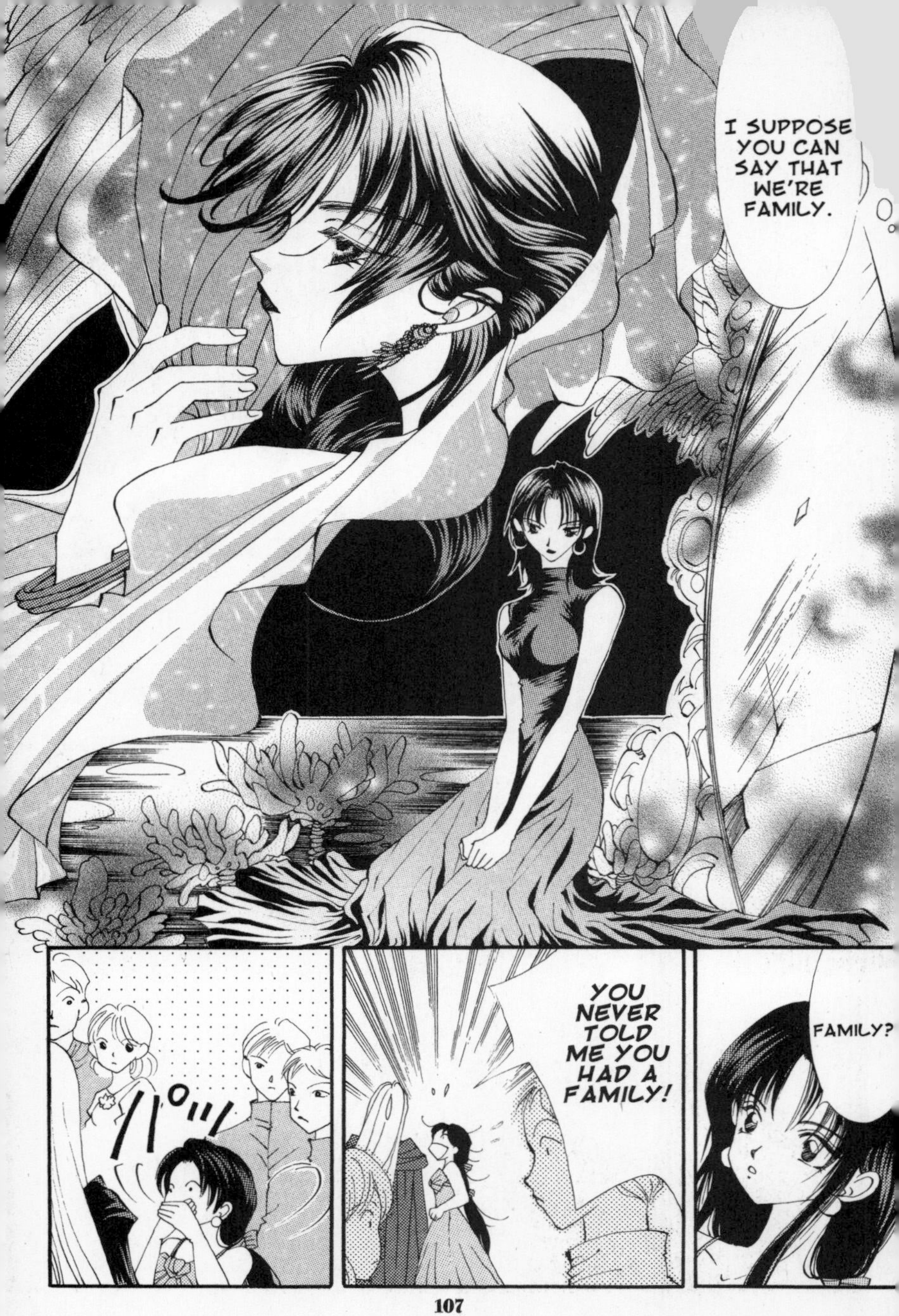
I SUPPOSE YOU CAN SAY THAT WE'RE FAMILY.
FAMILY?
YOU NEVER TOLD ME YOU HAD A FAMILY!

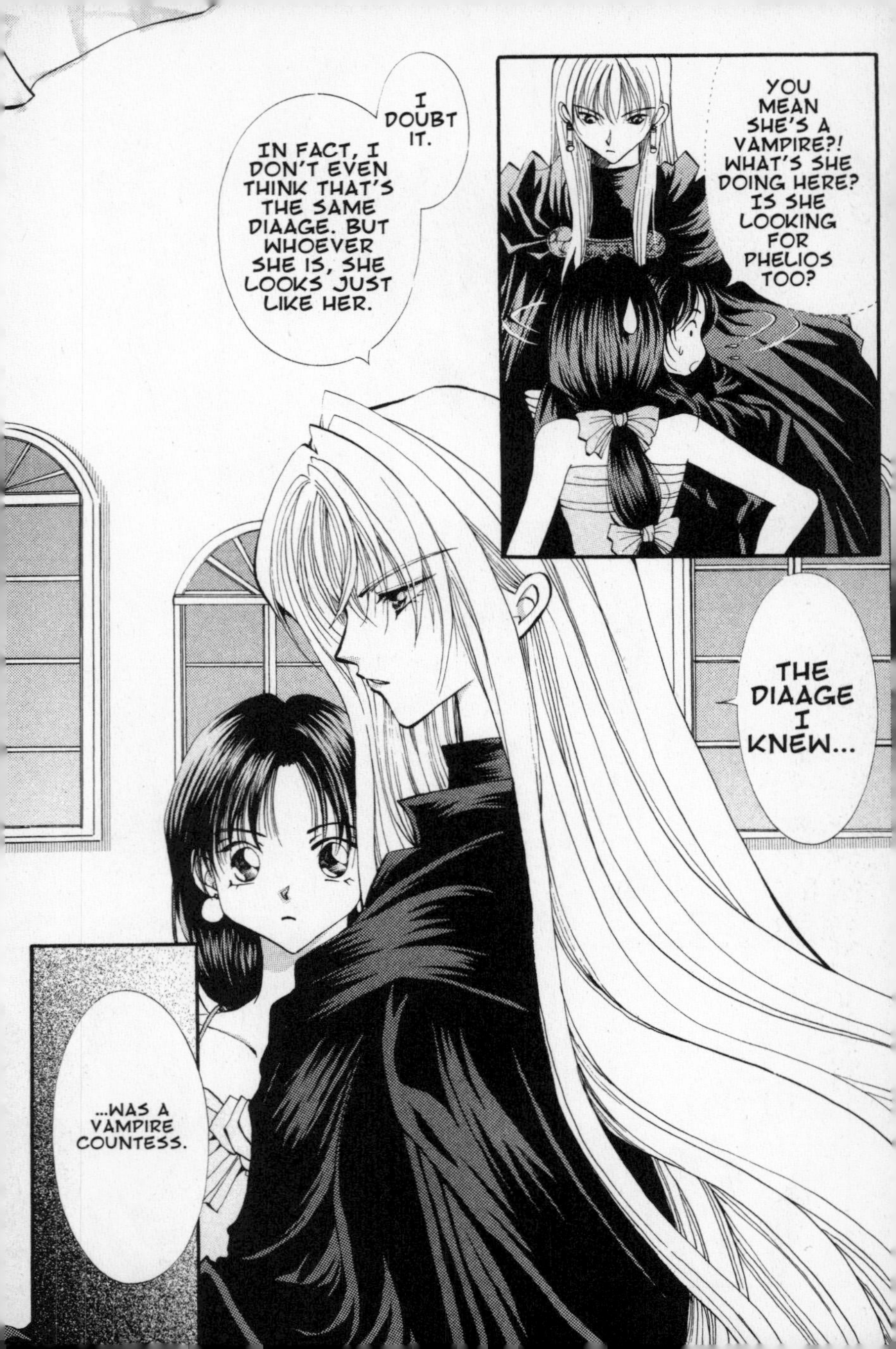
YOU MEAN SHE'S A VAMPIRE?! WHAT'S SHE DOING HERE? IS SHE LOOKING FOR PHELIOS TOO?
I DOUBT IT.
IN FACT, I DON'T EVEN THINK THAT'S THE SAME DIAAGE. BUT WHOEVER SHE IS, SHE LOOKS JUST LIKE HER.
THE DIAAGE I KNEW...
...WAS A VAMPIRE COUNTESS.

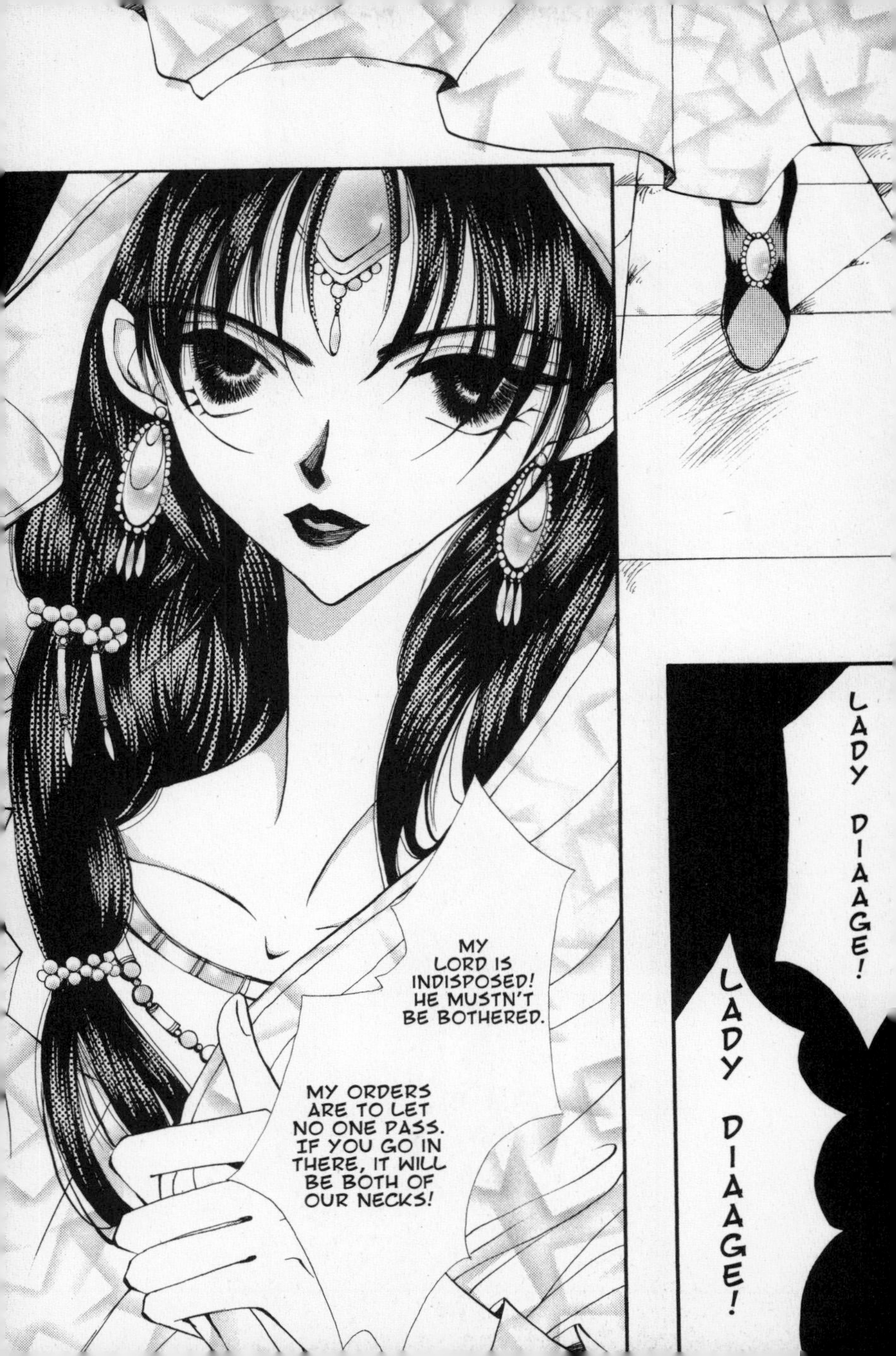
LADY DIAAGE!
LADY DIAAGE!
MY LORD IS INDISPOSED! HE MUSTN'T BE BOTHERED.
MY ORDERS ARE TO LET NO ONE PASS. IF YOU GO IN THERE, IT WILL BE BOTH OF OUR NECKS!

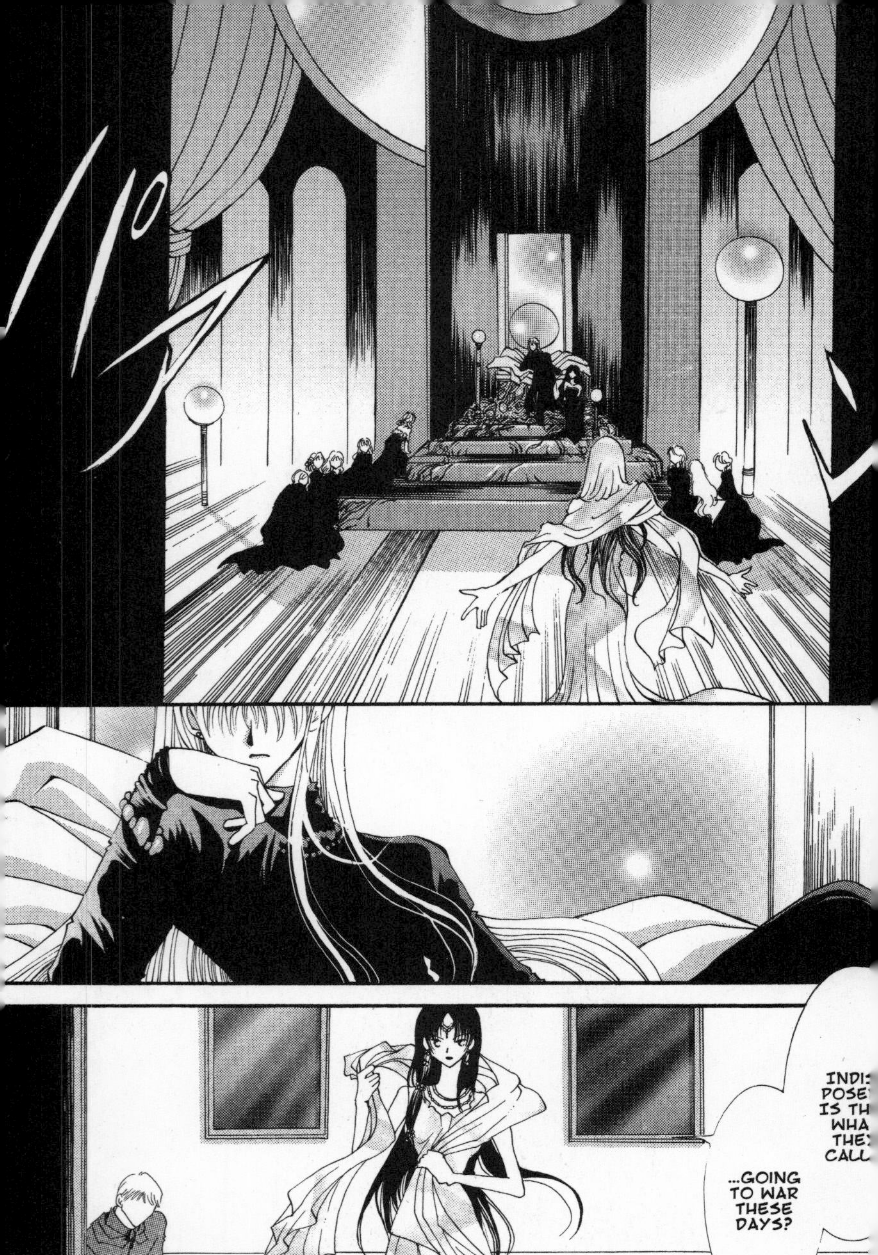
INDI POSE IS TH WHA THE CALL
...GOING TO WAR THESE DAYS?

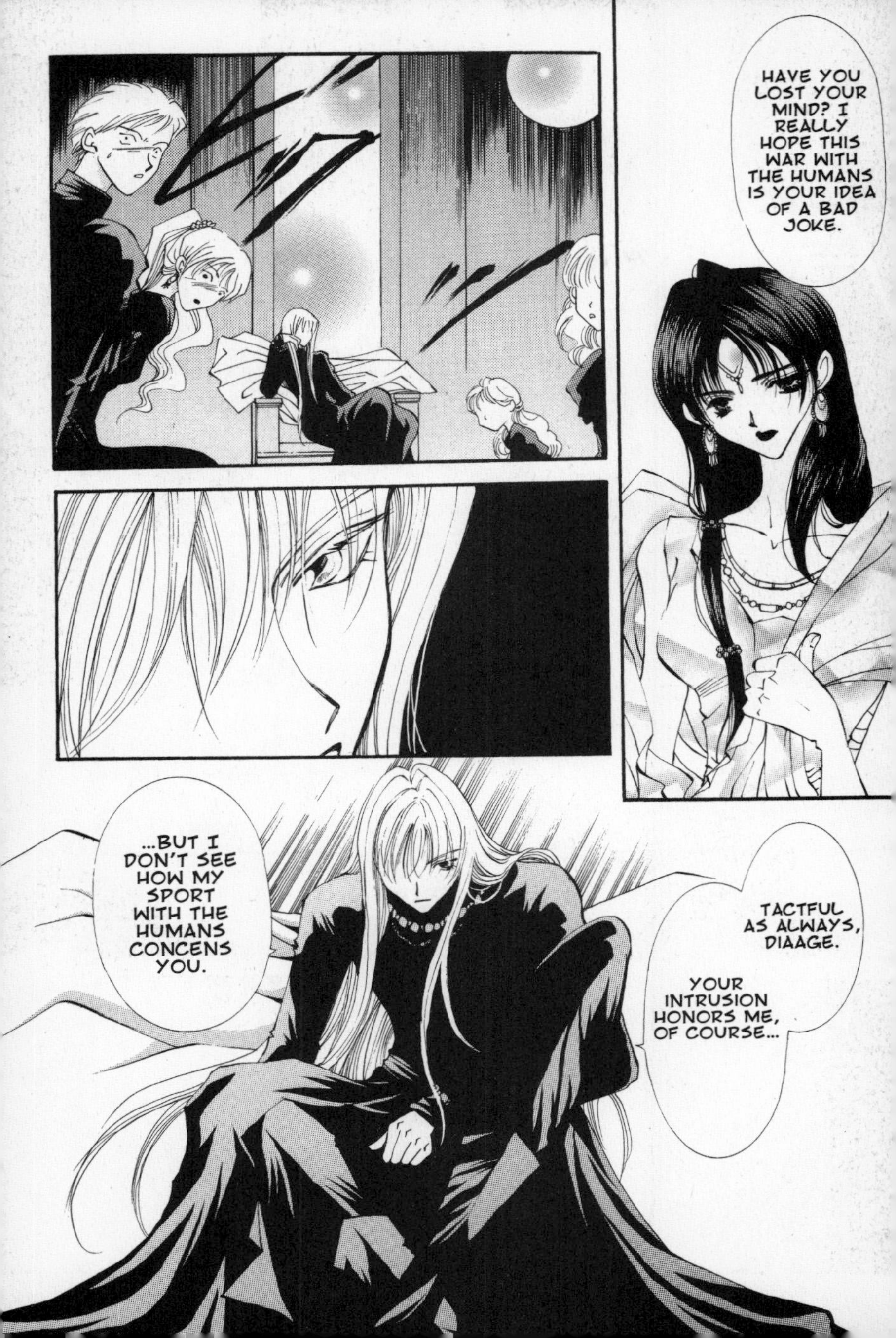
HAVE YOU LOST YOUR MIND? I REALLY HOPE THIS WAR WITH THE HUMANS IS YOUR IDEA OF A BAD JOKE.
TACTFUL AS ALWAYS, DIAAGE.
YOUR INTRUSION HONORS ME, OF COURSE...
...BUT I DON'T SEE HOW MY SPORT WITH THE HUMANS CONCENS YOU.

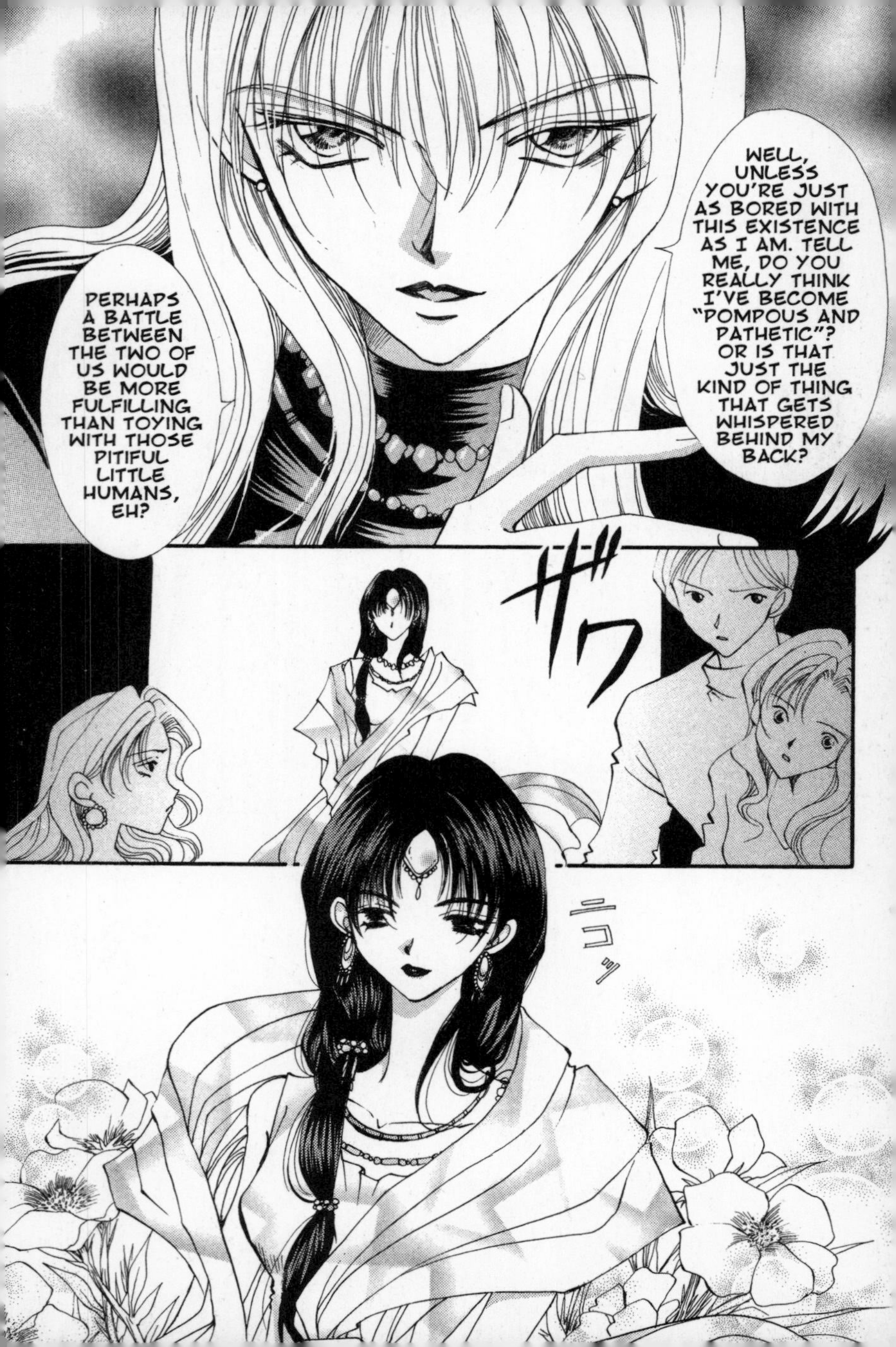
WELL, UNLESS YOU'RE JUST AS BORED WITH THIS EXISTENCE AS I AM. TELL ME, DO YOU REALLY THINK I'VE BECOME "POMPOUS AND PATHETIC"? OR IS THAT JUST THE KIND OF THING THAT GETS WHISPERED BEHIND MY BACK?
PERHAPS A BATTLE BETWEEN THE TWO OF US WOULD BE MORE FULFILLING THAN TOYING WITH THOSE PITIFUL LITTLE HUMANS, EH?
ザワ
ニコッ

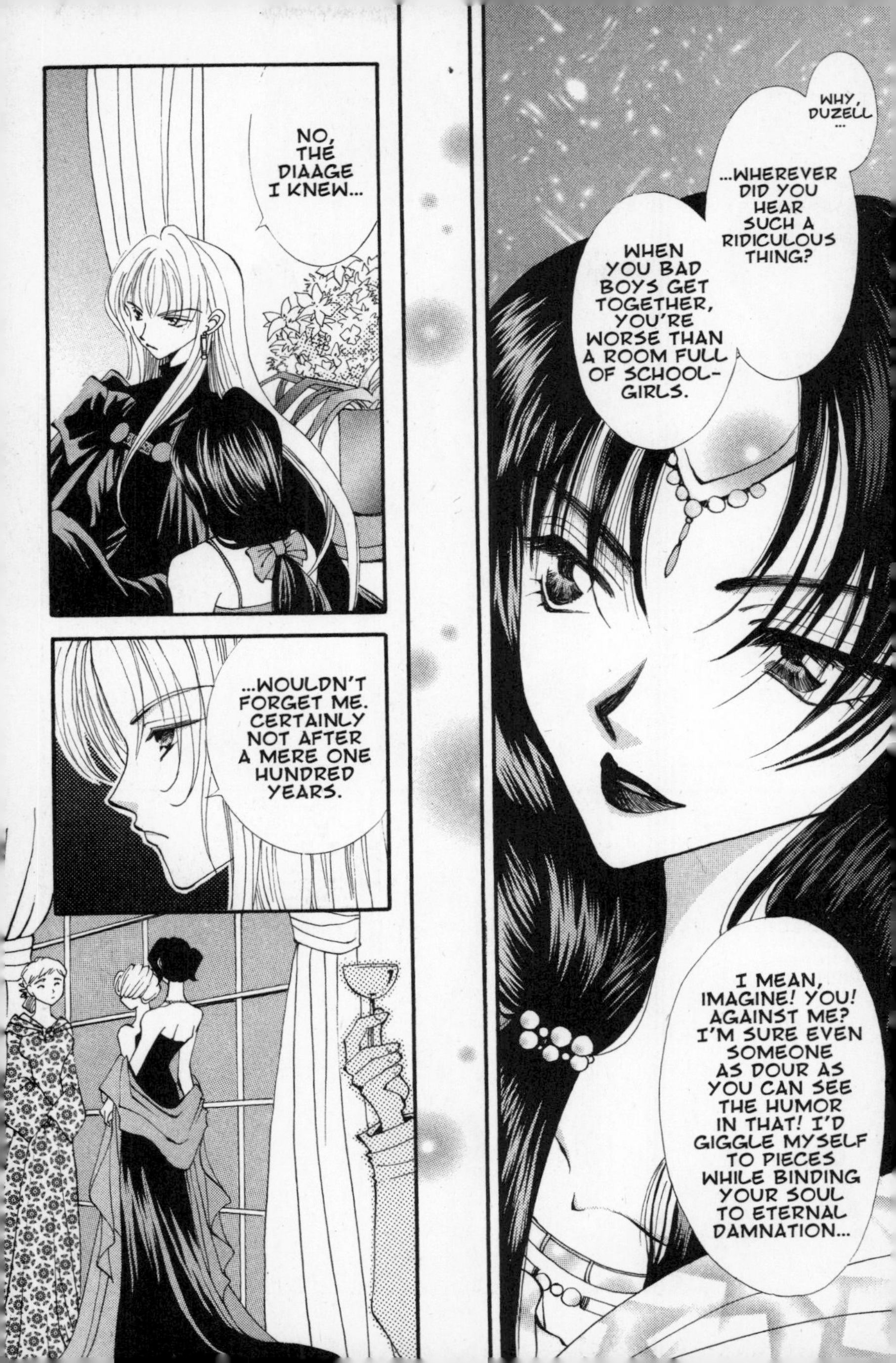
WHY, DUZELL...
...WHEREVER DID YOU HEAR SUCH A RIDICULOUS THING?
WHEN YOU BAD BOYS GET TOGETHER, YOU'RE WORSE THAN A ROOM FULL OF SCHOOL-GIRLS.
I MEAN, IMAGINE! YOU! AGAINST ME? I'M SURE EVEN SOMEONE AS DOUR AS YOU CAN SEE THE HUMOR IN THAT! I'D GIGGLE MYSELF TO PIECES WHILE BINDING YOUR SOUL TO ETERNAL DAMNATION...
NO, THE DIAAGE I KNEW...
...WOULDN'T FORGET ME. CERTAINLY NOT AFTER A MERE ONE HUNDRED YEARS.

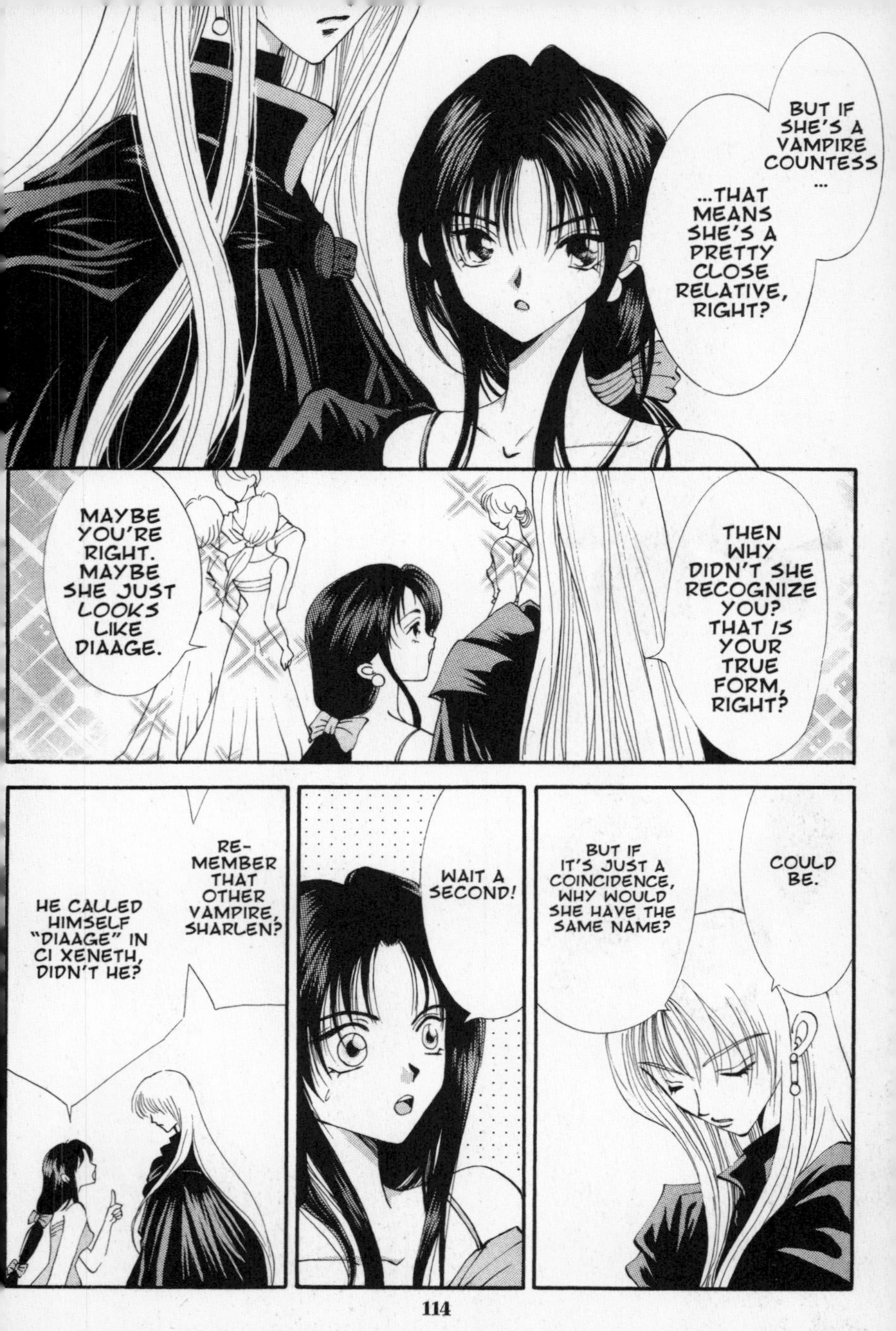
BUT IF SHE'S A VAMPIRE COUNTESS ...
...THAT MEANS SHE'S A PRETTY CLOSE RELATIVE, RIGHT?
THEN WHY DIDN'T SHE RECOGNIZE YOU? THAT IS YOUR TRUE FORM, RIGHT?
MAYBE YOU'RE RIGHT. MAYBE SHE JUST LOOKS LIKE DIAAGE.
COULD BE.
BUT IF IT'S JUST A COINCIDENCE, WHY WOULD SHE HAVE THE SAME NAME?
WAIT A SECOND!
RE-MEMBER THAT OTHER VAMPIRE, SHARLEN?
HE CALLED HIMSELF "DIAAGE" IN CI XENETH, DIDN'T HE?

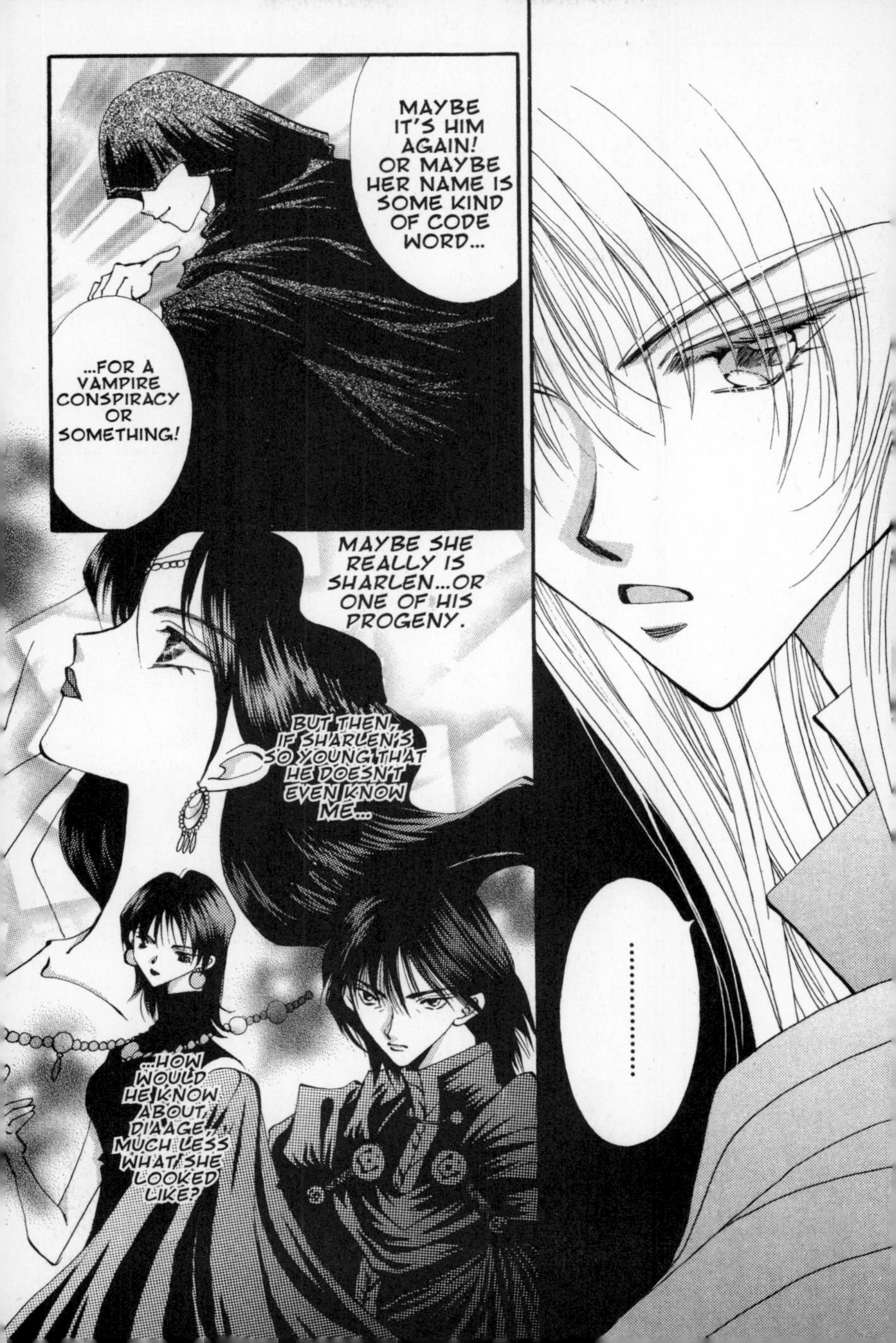
....
MAYBE IT'S HIM AGAIN! OR MAYBE HER NAME IS SOME KIND OF CODE WORD...
...FOR A VAMPIRE CONSPIRACY OR SOMETHING!
MAYBE SHE REALLY IS SHARLEN...OR ONE OF HIS PROGENY.
BUT THEN, IF SHARLEN'S SO YOUNG THAT HE DOESN'T EVEN KNOW ME...
...HOW WOULD HE KNOW ABOUT DIAAGE, MUCH LESS WHAT SHE LOOKED LIKE?

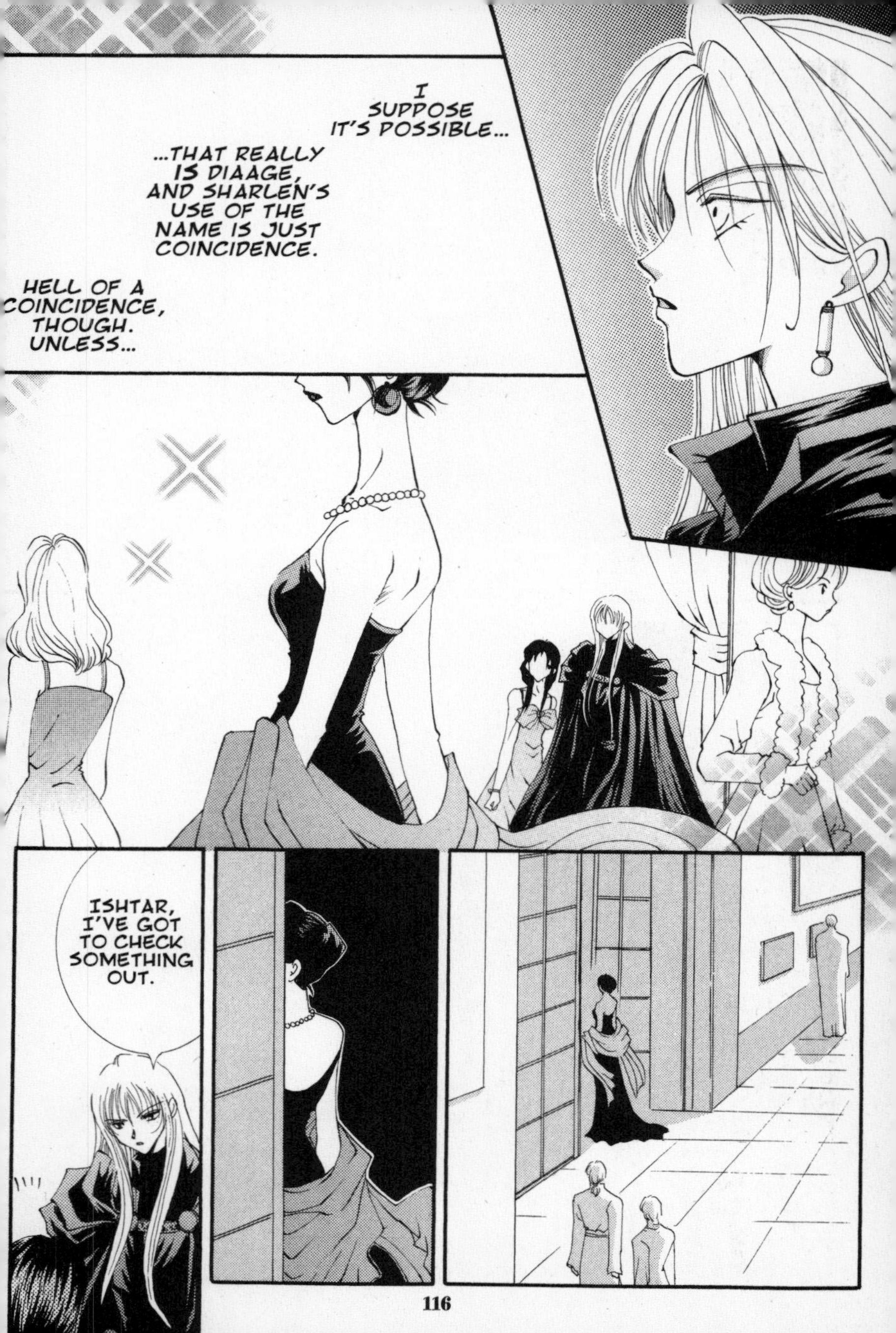
I SUPPOSE IT'S POSSIBLE...
...THAT REALLY IS DIAAGE, AND SHARLEN'S USE OF THE NAME IS JUST COINCIDENCE.
HELL OF A COINCIDENCE, THOUGH. UNLESS...
ISHTAR, I'VE GOT TO CHECK SOMETHING OUT.

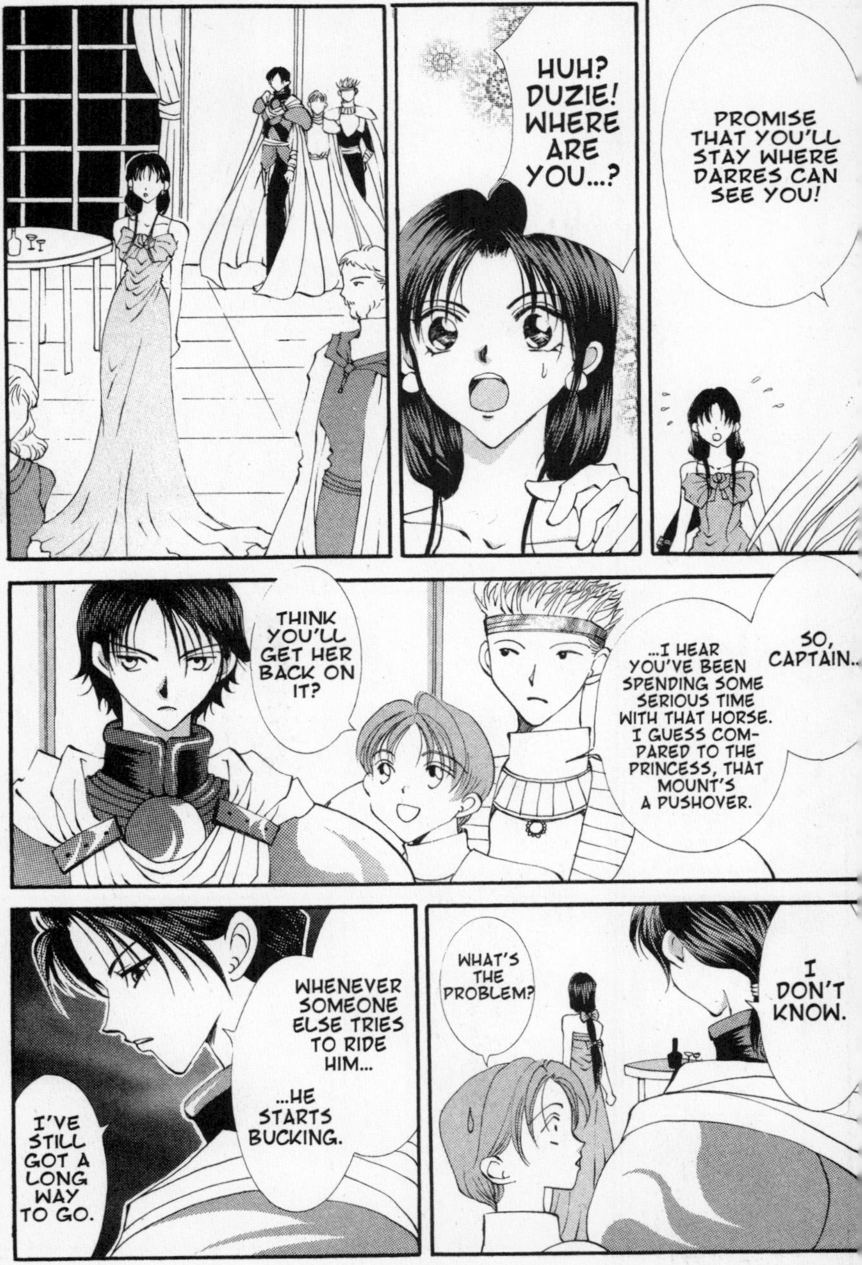
PROMISE THAT YOU'LL STAY WHERE DARRES CAN SEE YOU!
HUH? DUZIE! WHERE ARE YOU...?
SO, CAPTAIN...
...I HEAR YOU'VE BEEN SPENDING SOME SERIOUS TIME WITH THAT HORSE. I GUESS COM-PARED TO THE PRINCESS, THAT MOUNT'S A PUSHOVER.
THINK YOU'LL GET HER BACK ON IT?
I DON'T KNOW.
WHAT'S THE PROBLEM?
WHENEVER SOMEONE ELSE TRIES TO RIDE HIM...
...HE STARTS BUCKING.
I'VE STILL GOT A LONG WAY TO GO.

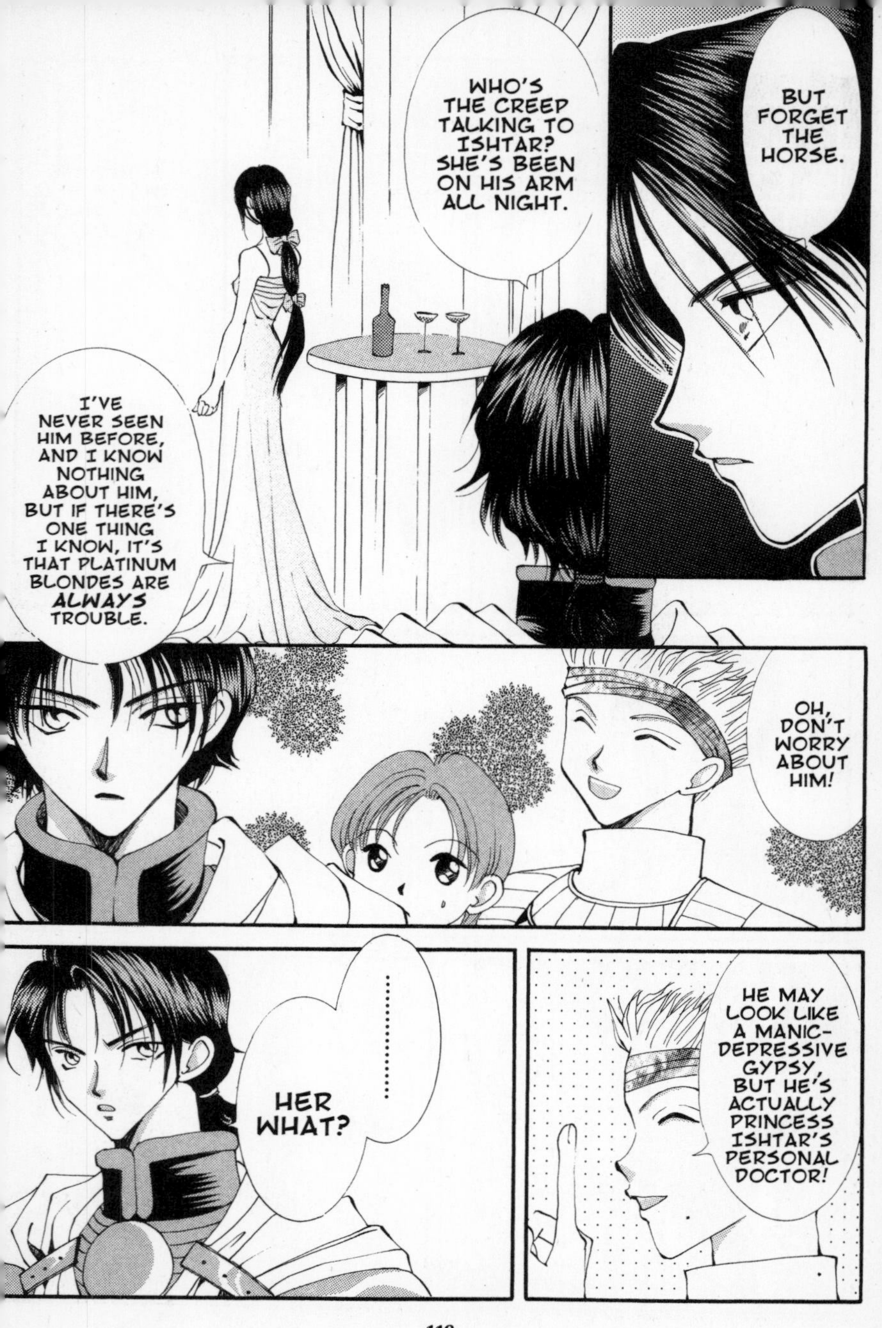
BUT FORGET THE HORSE.
WHO'S THE CREEP TALKING TO ISHTAR? SHE'S BEEN ON HIS ARM ALL NIGHT.
I'VE NEVER SEEN HIM BEFORE, AND I KNOW NOTHING ABOUT HIM, BUT IF THERE'S ONE THING I KNOW, IT'S THAT PLATINUM BLONDES ARE *ALWAYS* TROUBLE.
OH, DON'T WORRY ABOUT HIM!
HE MAY LOOK LIKE A MANIC-DEPRESSIVE GYPSY, BUT HE'S ACTUALLY PRINCESS ISHTAR'S PERSONAL DOCTOR!
....
HER WHAT?

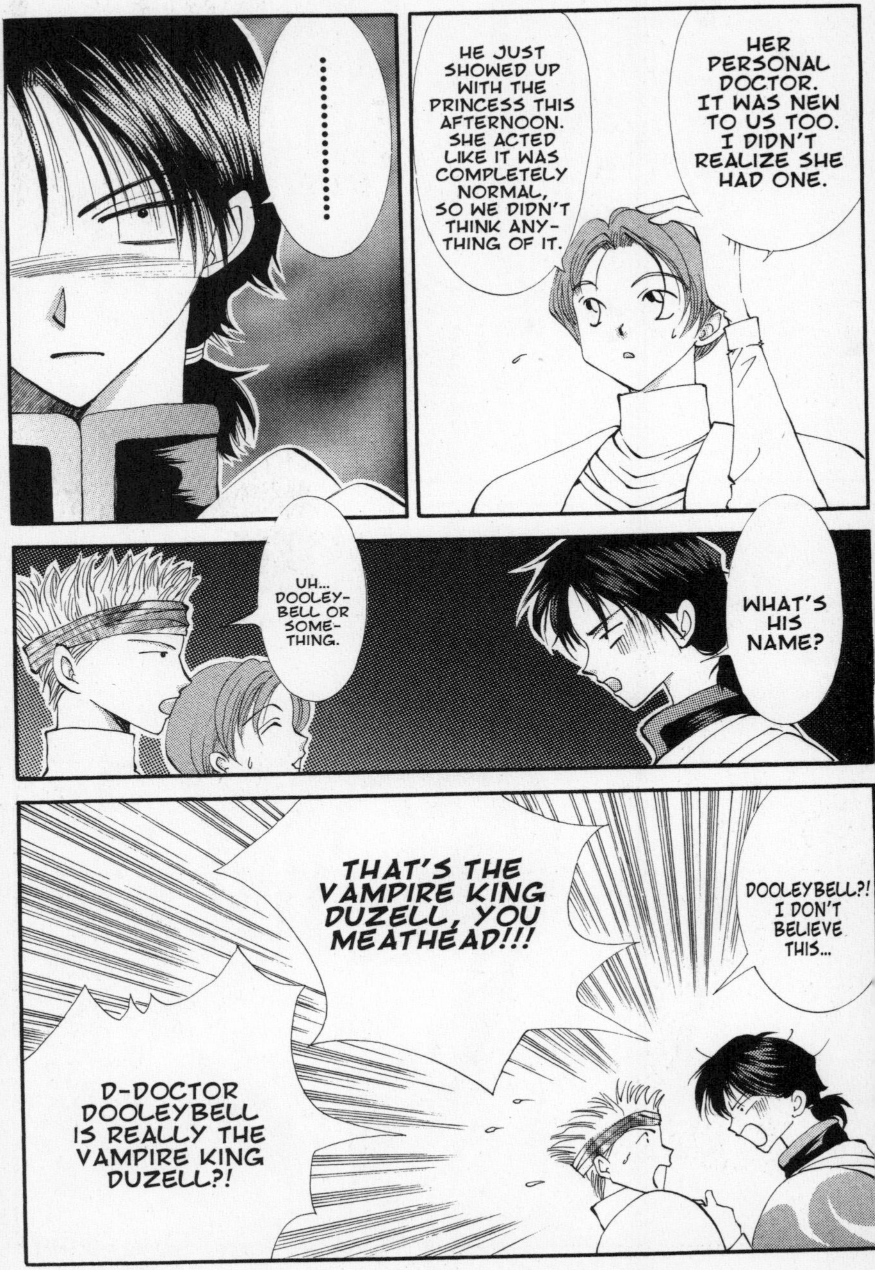
HER PERSONAL DOCTOR. IT WAS NEW TO US TOO. I DIDN'T REALIZE SHE HAD ONE.
HE JUST SHOWED UP WITH THE PRINCESS THIS AFTERNOON. SHE ACTED LIKE IT WAS COMPLETELY NORMAL, SO WE DIDN'T THINK ANY-THING OF IT.
....
WHAT'S HIS NAME?
UH... DOOLEY-BELL OR SOME-THING.
DOOLEYBELL?! I DON'T BELIEVE THIS...
THAT'S THE VAMPIRE KING DUZELL, YOU MEATHEAD!!!
D-DOCTOR DOOLEYBELL IS REALLY THE VAMPIRE KING DUZELL?!

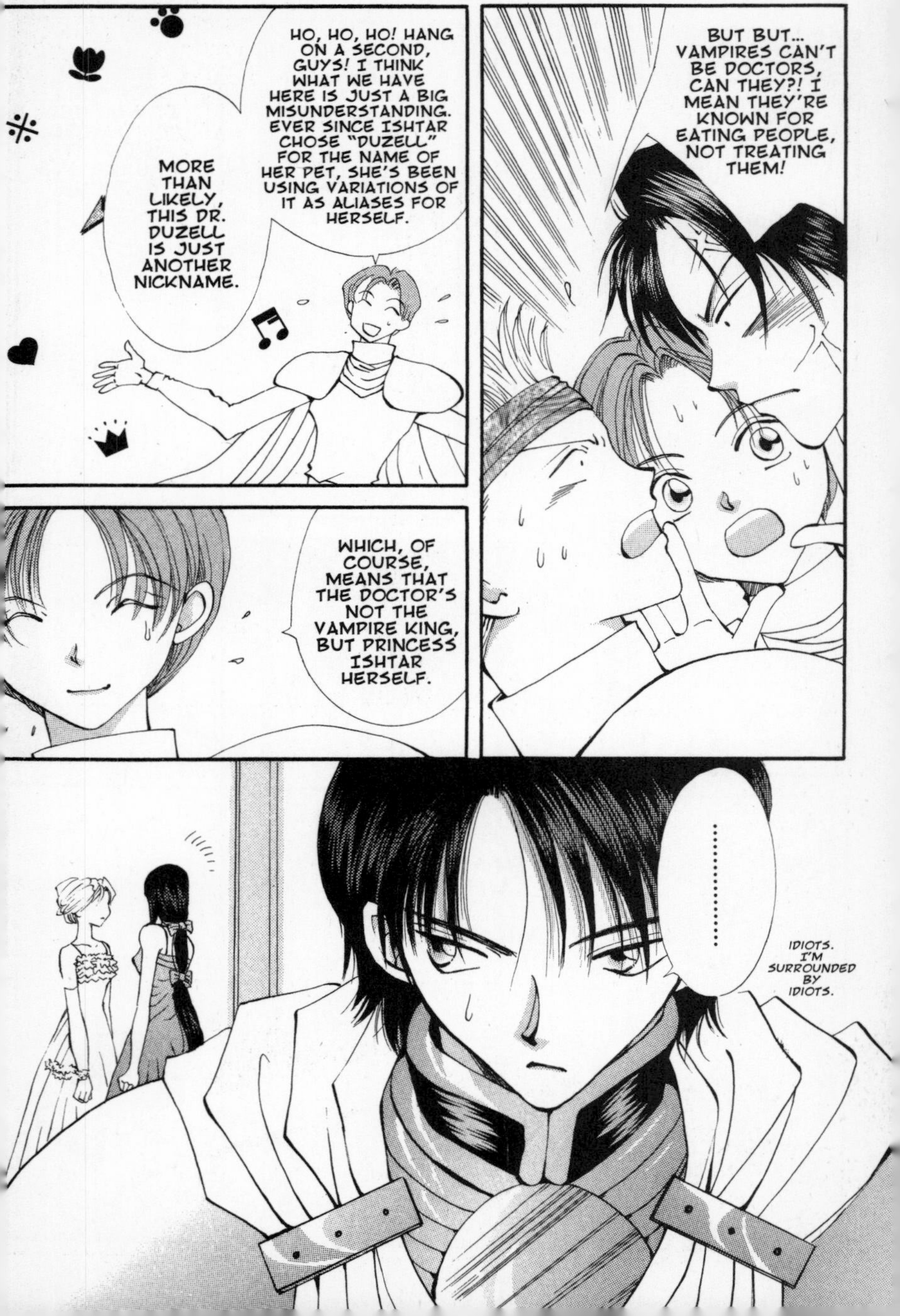
BUT BUT... VAMPIRES CAN'T BE DOCTORS, CAN THEY?! I MEAN THEY'RE KNOWN FOR EATING PEOPLE, NOT TREATING THEM!
HO, HO, HO! HANG ON A SECOND, GUYS! I THINK WHAT WE HAVE HERE IS JUST A BIG MISUNDERSTANDING. EVER SINCE ISHTAR CHOSE "DUZELL" FOR THE NAME OF HER PET, SHE'S BEEN USING VARIATIONS OF IT AS ALIASES FOR HERSELF.
MORE THAN LIKELY, THIS DR. DUZELL IS JUST ANOTHER NICKNAME.
WHICH, OF COURSE, MEANS THAT THE DOCTOR'S NOT THE VAMPIRE KING, BUT PRINCESS ISHTAR HERSELF.
......
IDIOTS. I'M SURROUNDED BY IDIOTS.

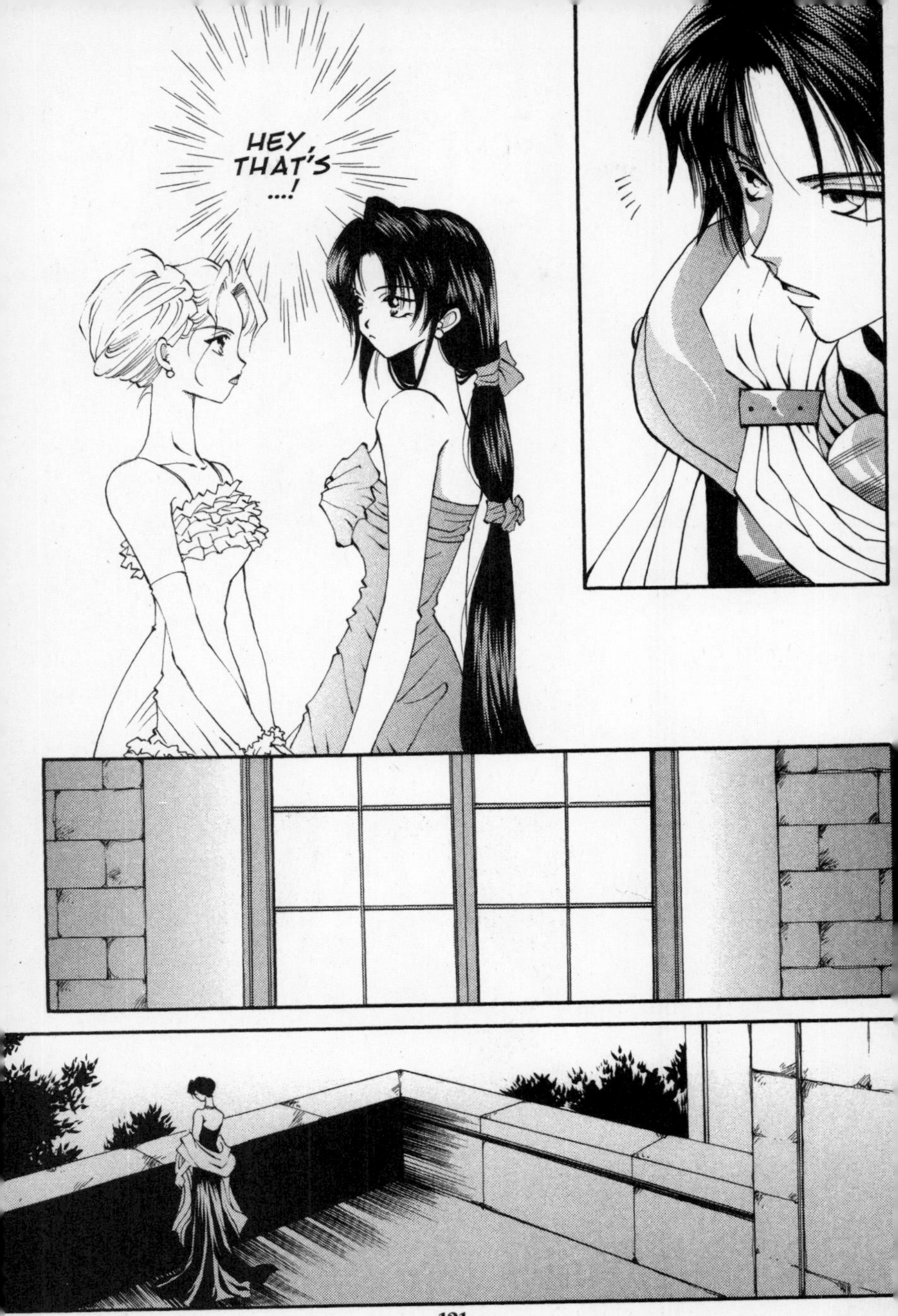
HEY, THAT'S ...!

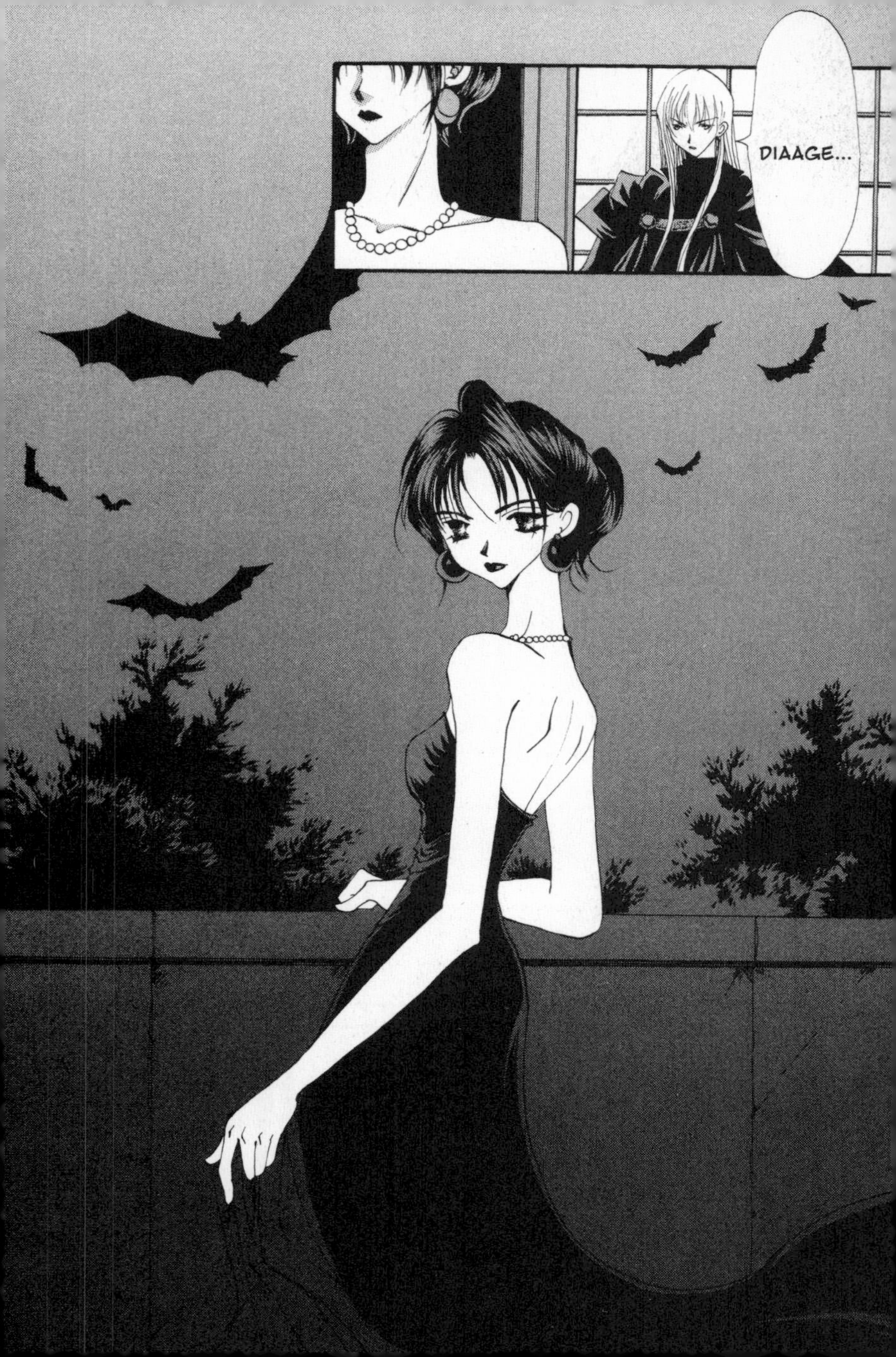
DIAAGE...

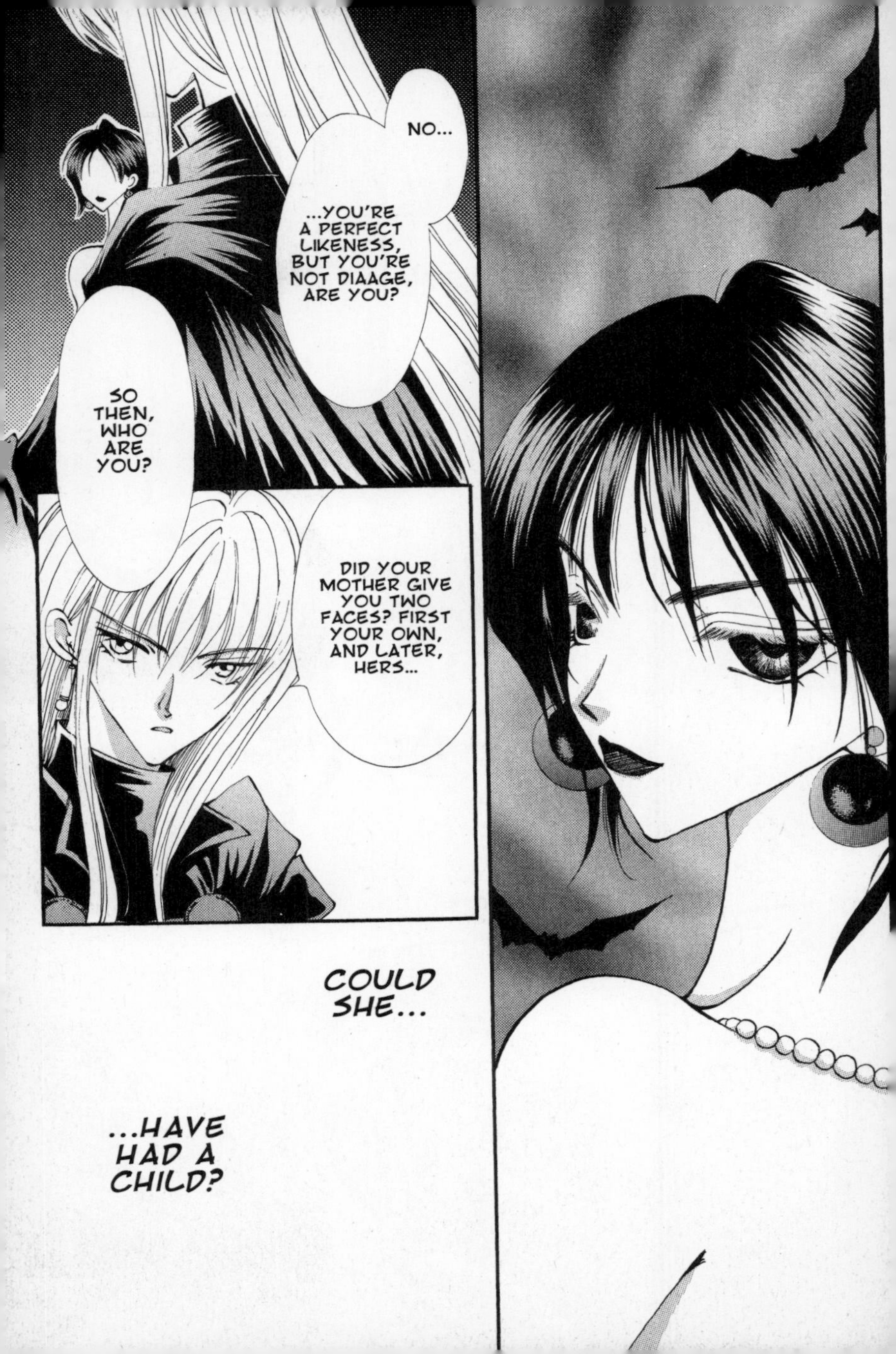
NO...
...YOU'RE A PERFECT LIKENESS, BUT YOU'RE NOT DIAAGE, ARE YOU?
SO THEN, WHO ARE YOU?
DID YOUR MOTHER GIVE YOU TWO FACES? FIRST YOUR OWN, AND LATER, HERS...
COULD SHE...
...HAVE HAD A CHILD?

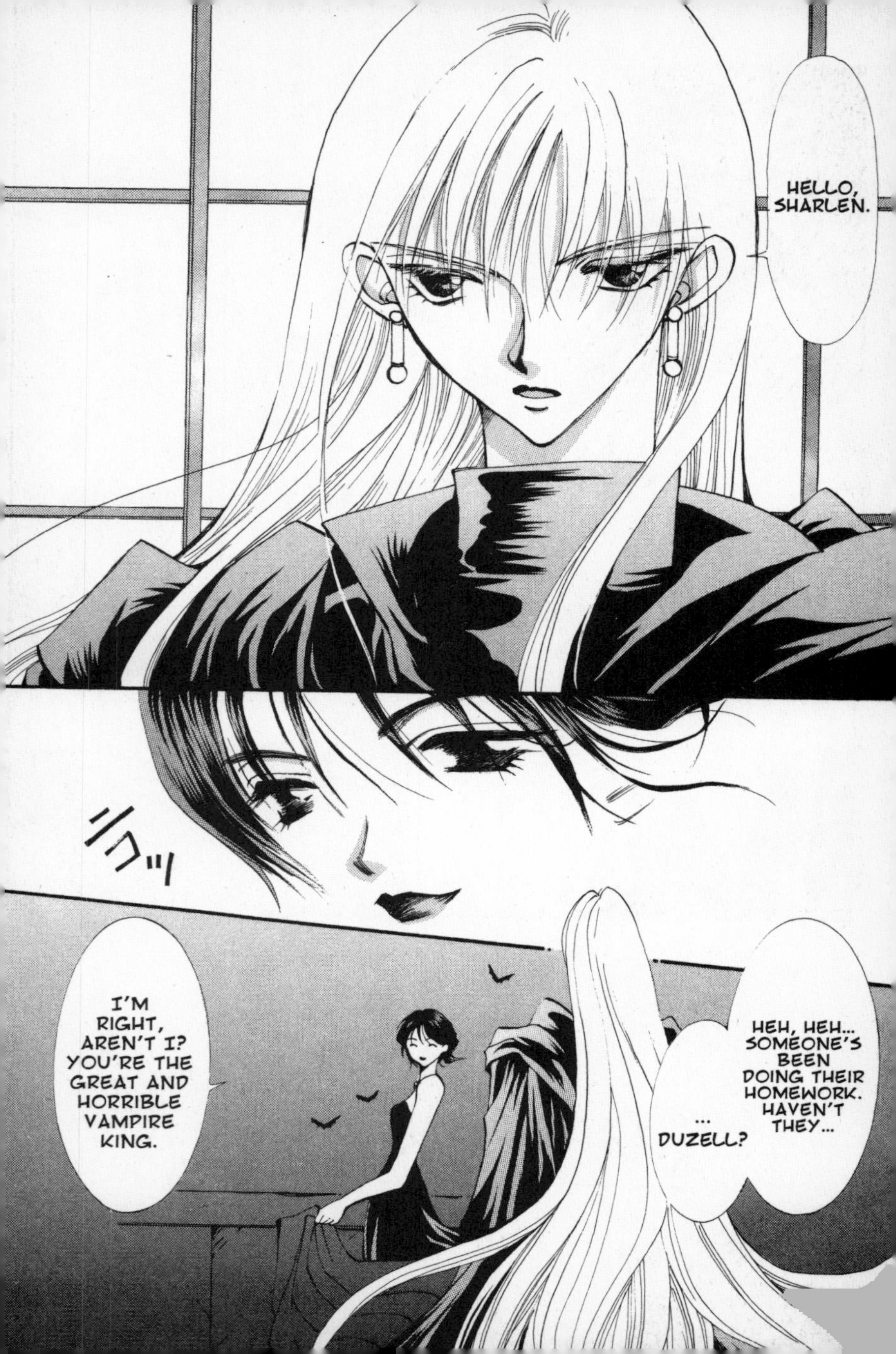
HELLO, SHARLEN.
HEH, HEH... SOMEONE'S BEEN DOING THEIR HOMEWORK. HAVEN'T THEY...
... DUZELL?
I'M RIGHT, AREN'T I? YOU'RE THE GREAT AND HORRIBLE VAMPIRE KING.

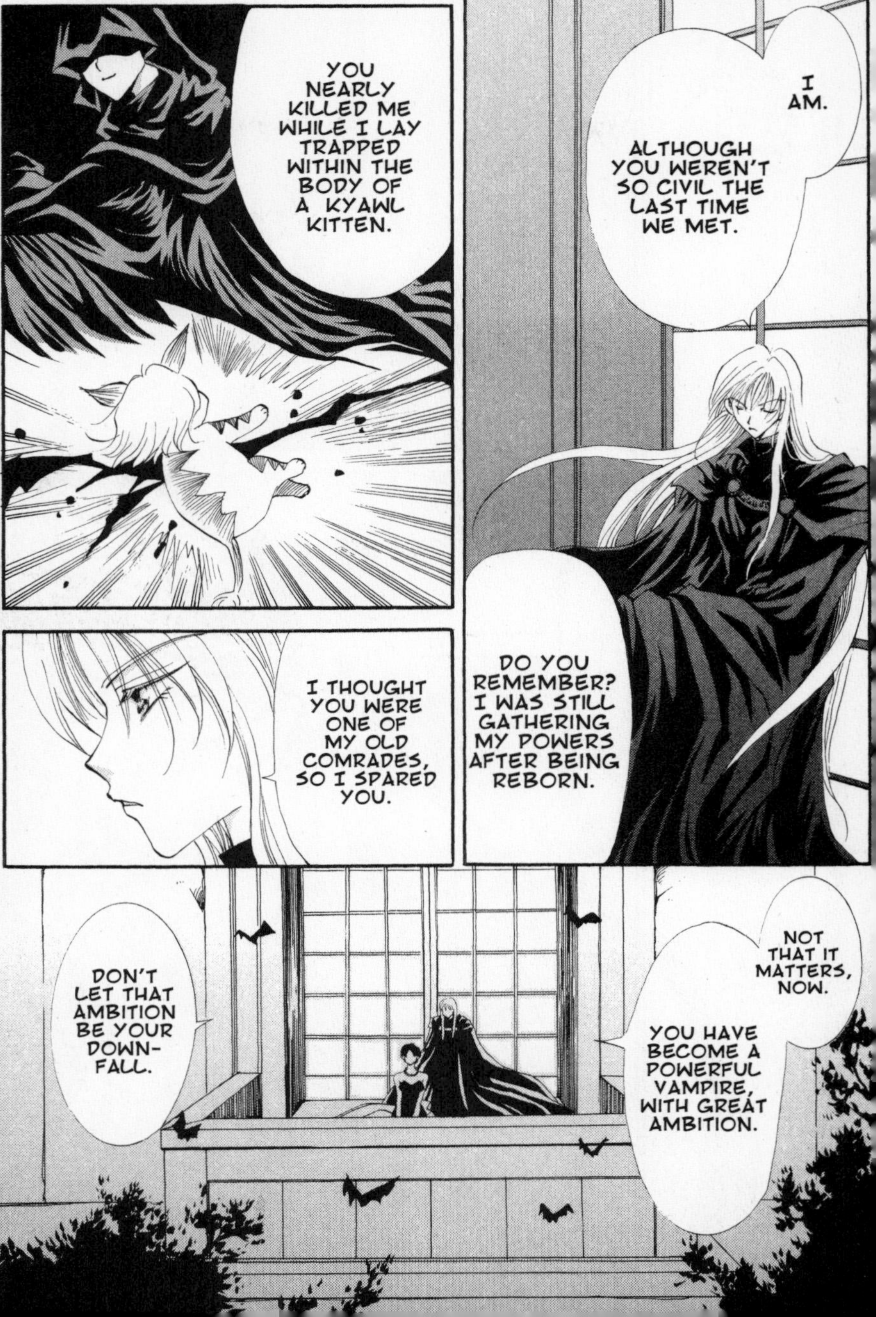
I AM.
ALTHOUGH YOU WEREN'T SO CIVIL THE LAST TIME WE MET.
DO YOU REMEMBER? I WAS STILL GATHERING MY POWERS AFTER BEING REBORN.
YOU NEARLY KILLED ME WHILE I LAY TRAPPED WITHIN THE BODY OF A KYAWL KITTEN.
I THOUGHT YOU WERE ONE OF MY OLD COMRADES, SO I SPARED YOU.
NOT THAT IT MATTERS, NOW.
YOU HAVE BECOME A POWERFUL VAMPIRE, WITH GREAT AMBITION.
DON'T LET THAT AMBITION BE YOUR DOWN-FALL.

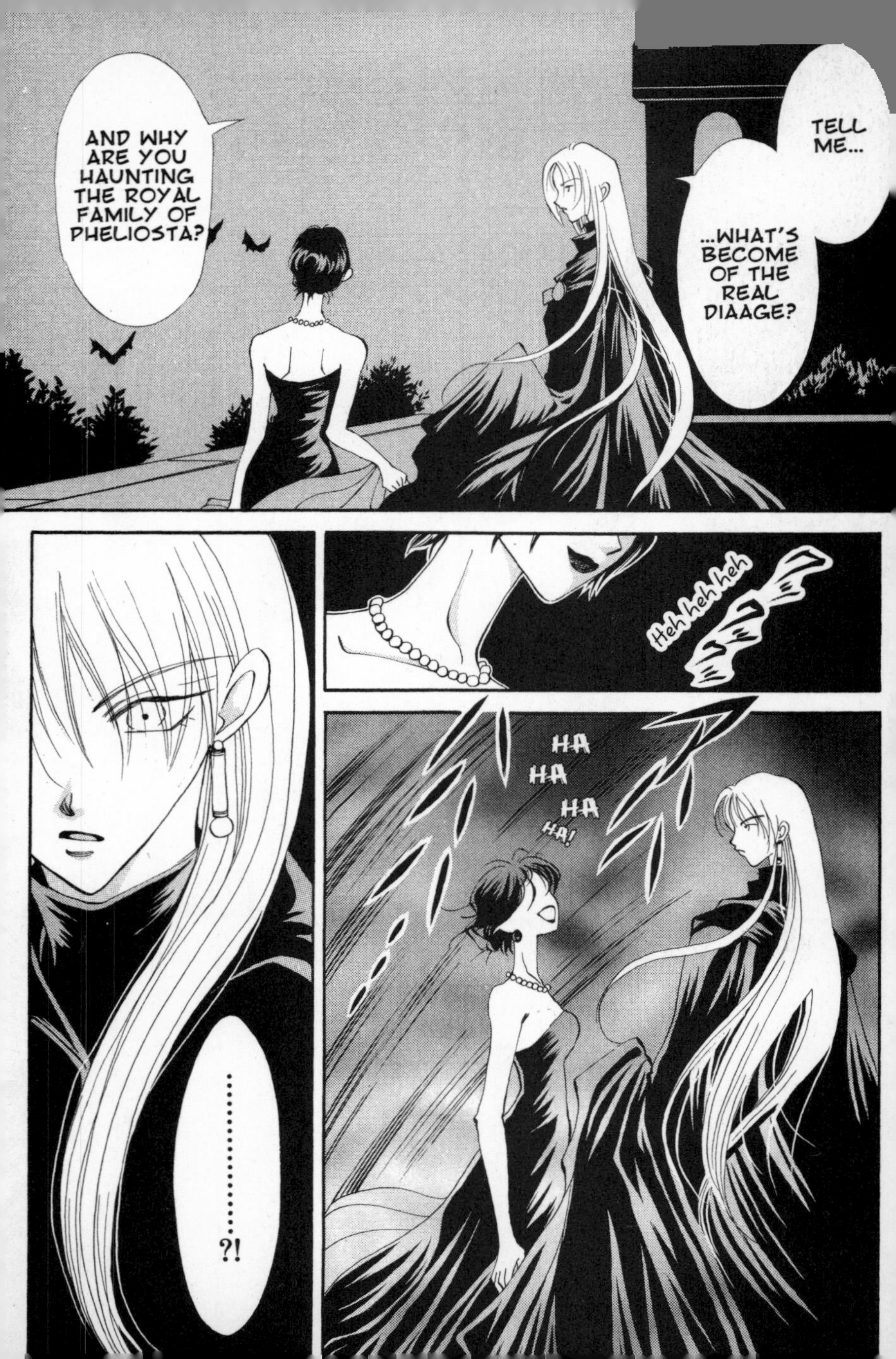
TELL ME...
...WHAT'S BECOME OF THE REAL DIAAGE?
AND WHY ARE YOU HAUNTING THE ROYAL FAMILY OF PHELIOSTA?
Heh heh heh
HA HA HA HA!
......?!

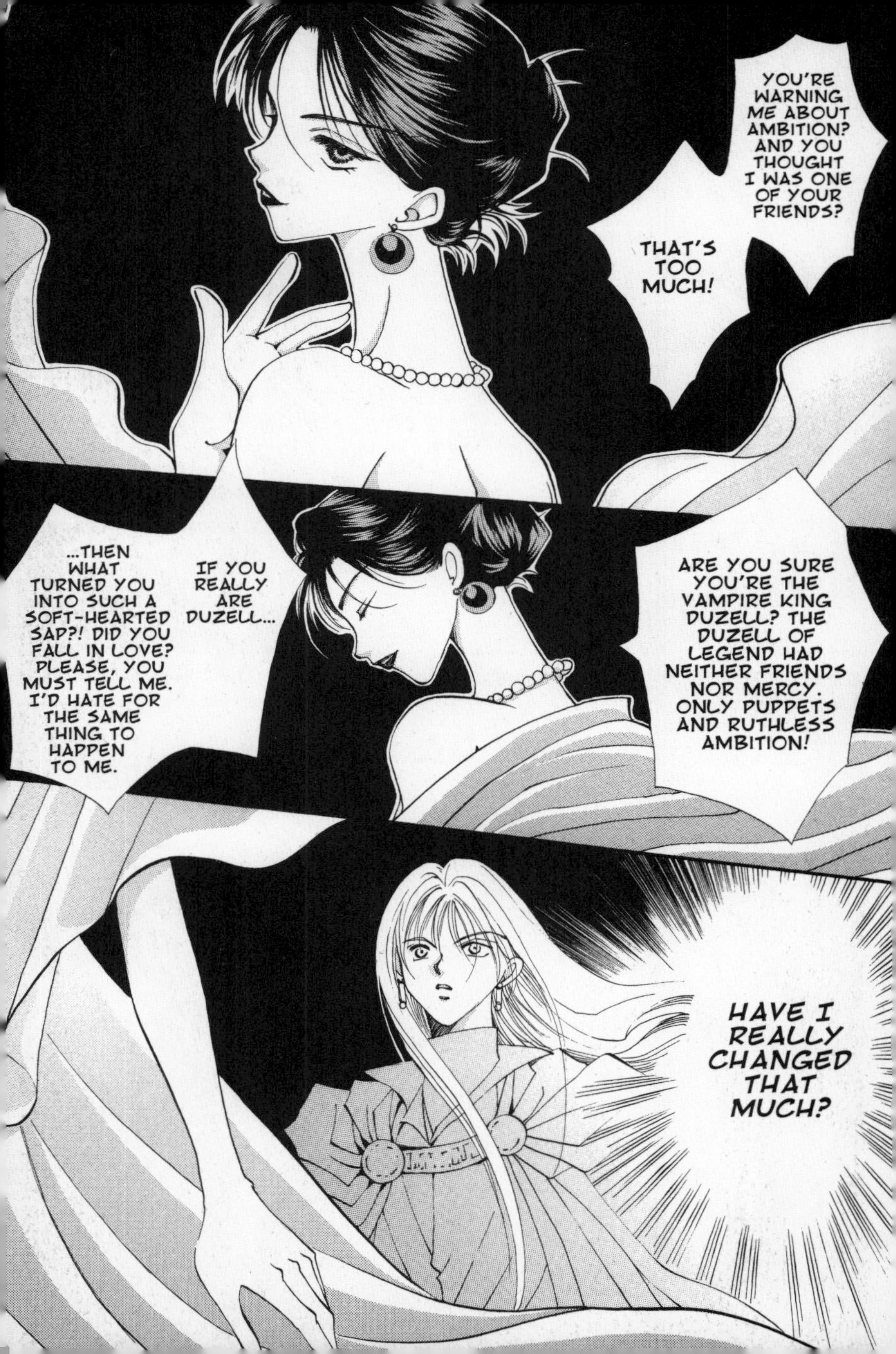
YOU'RE WARNING ME ABOUT AMBITION? AND YOU THOUGHT I WAS ONE OF YOUR FRIENDS?
THAT'S TOO MUCH!
ARE YOU SURE YOU'RE THE VAMPIRE KING DUZELL? THE DUZELL OF LEGEND HAD NEITHER FRIENDS NOR MERCY. ONLY PUPPETS AND RUTHLESS AMBITION!
IF YOU REALLY ARE DUZELL...
...THEN WHAT TURNED YOU INTO SUCH A SOFT-HEARTED SAP?! DID YOU FALL IN LOVE? PLEASE, YOU MUST TELL ME. I'D HATE FOR THE SAME THING TO HAPPEN TO ME.
HAVE I REALLY CHANGED THAT MUCH?

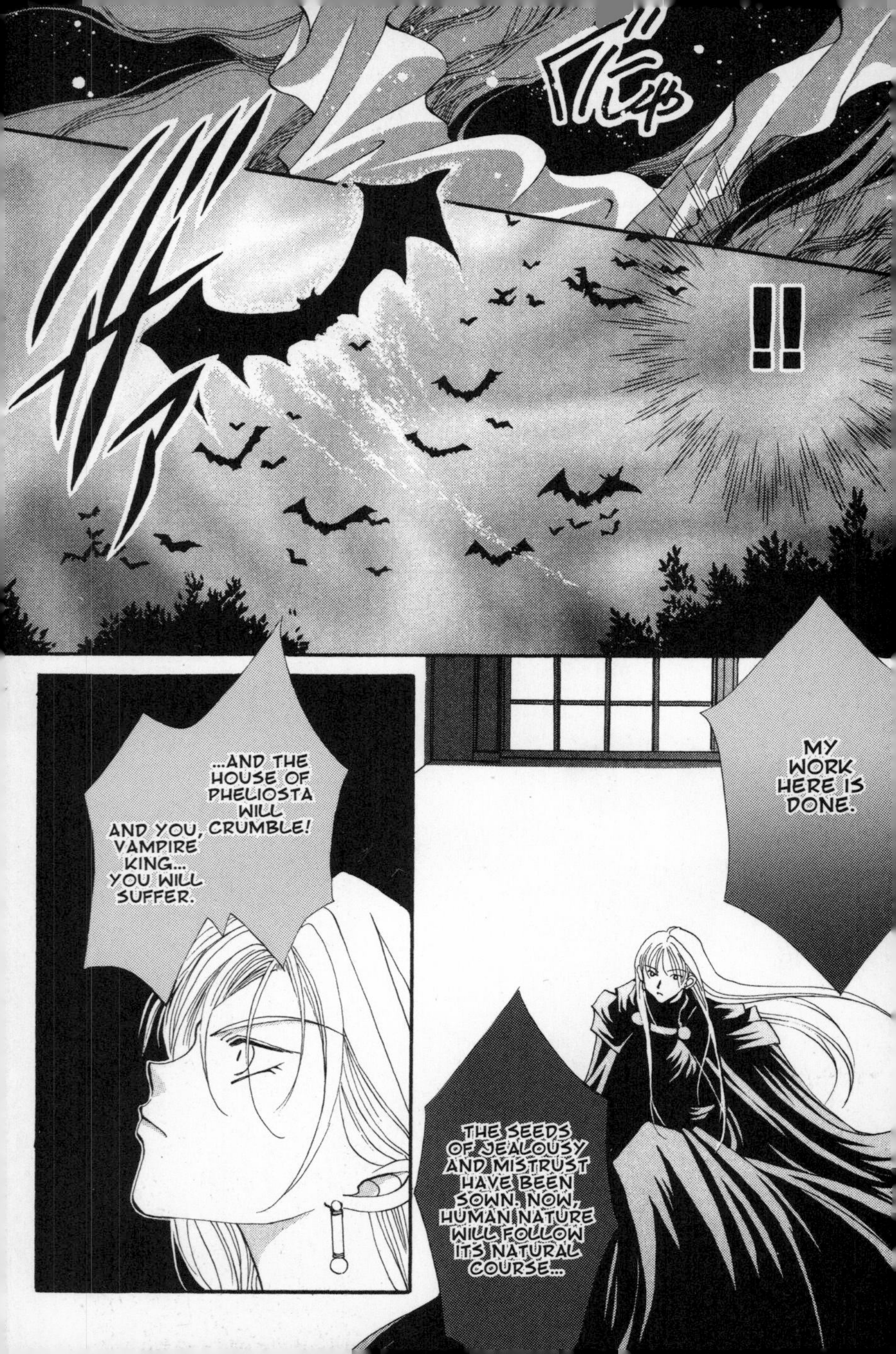
!!
MY WORK HERE IS DONE.
THE SEEDS OF JEALOUSY AND MISTRUST HAVE BEEN SOWN. NOW, HUMAN NATURE WILL FOLLOW ITS NATURAL COURSE...
...AND THE HOUSE OF PHELIOSTA WILL CRUMBLE!
AND YOU, VAMPIRE KING... YOU WILL SUFFER.

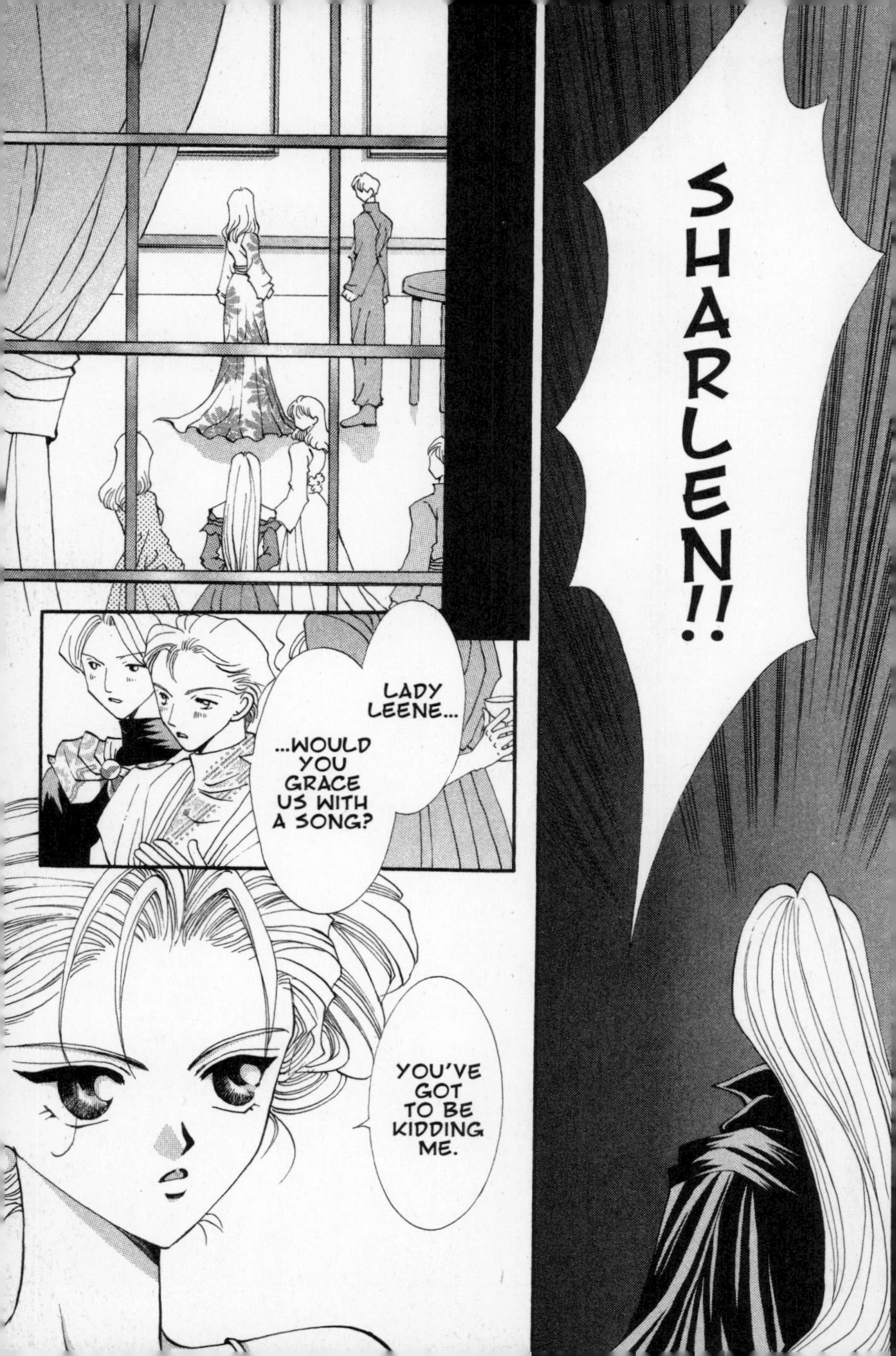
SHARLEN!!
LADY LEENE...
...WOULD YOU GRACE US WITH A SONG?
YOU'VE GOT TO BE KIDDING ME.

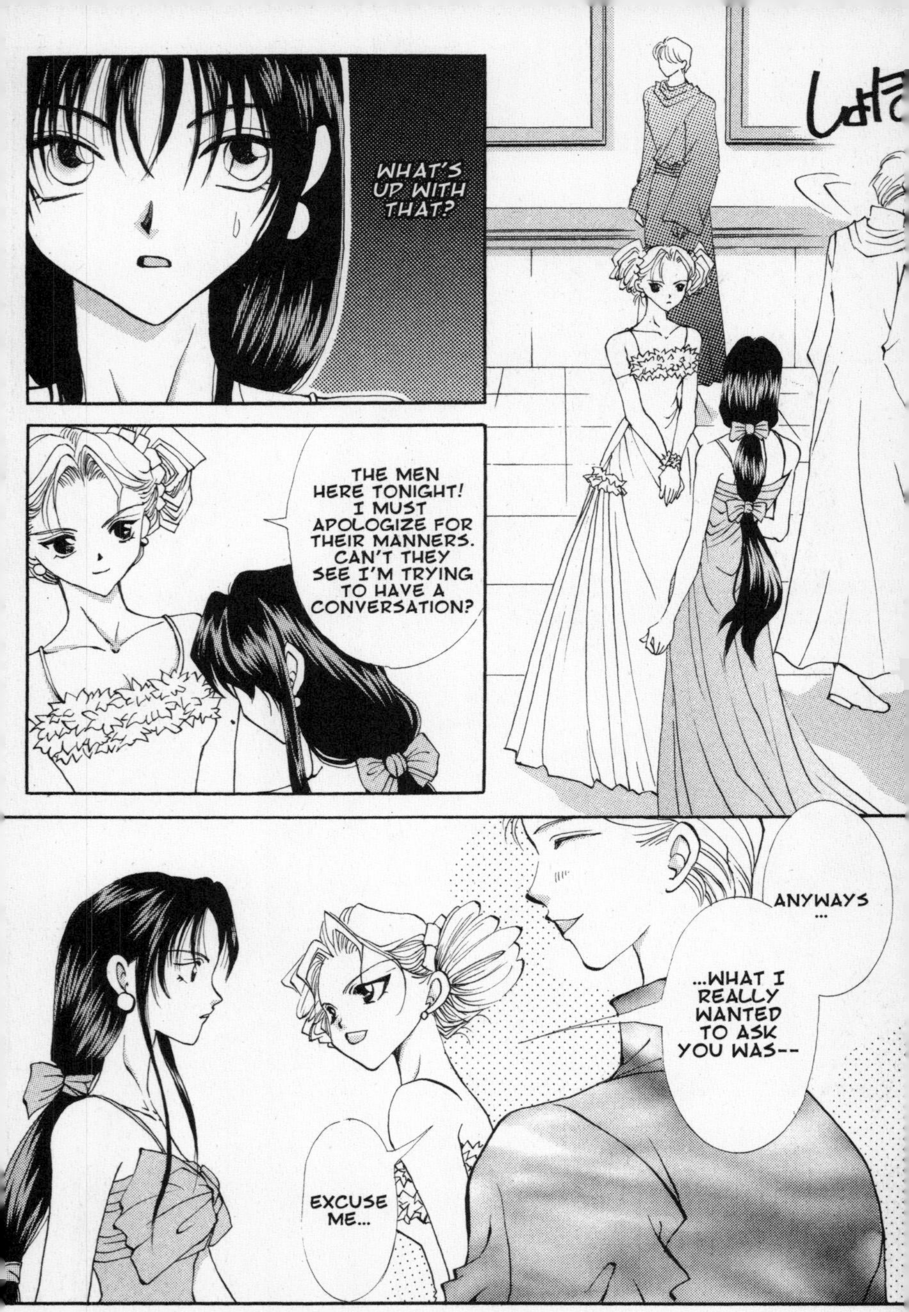
WHAT'S UP WITH THAT?
THE MEN HERE TONIGHT! I MUST APOLOGIZE FOR THEIR MANNERS. CAN'T THEY SEE I'M TRYING TO HAVE A CONVERSATION?
ANYWAYS ...
...WHAT I REALLY WANTED TO ASK YOU WAS--
EXCUSE ME...

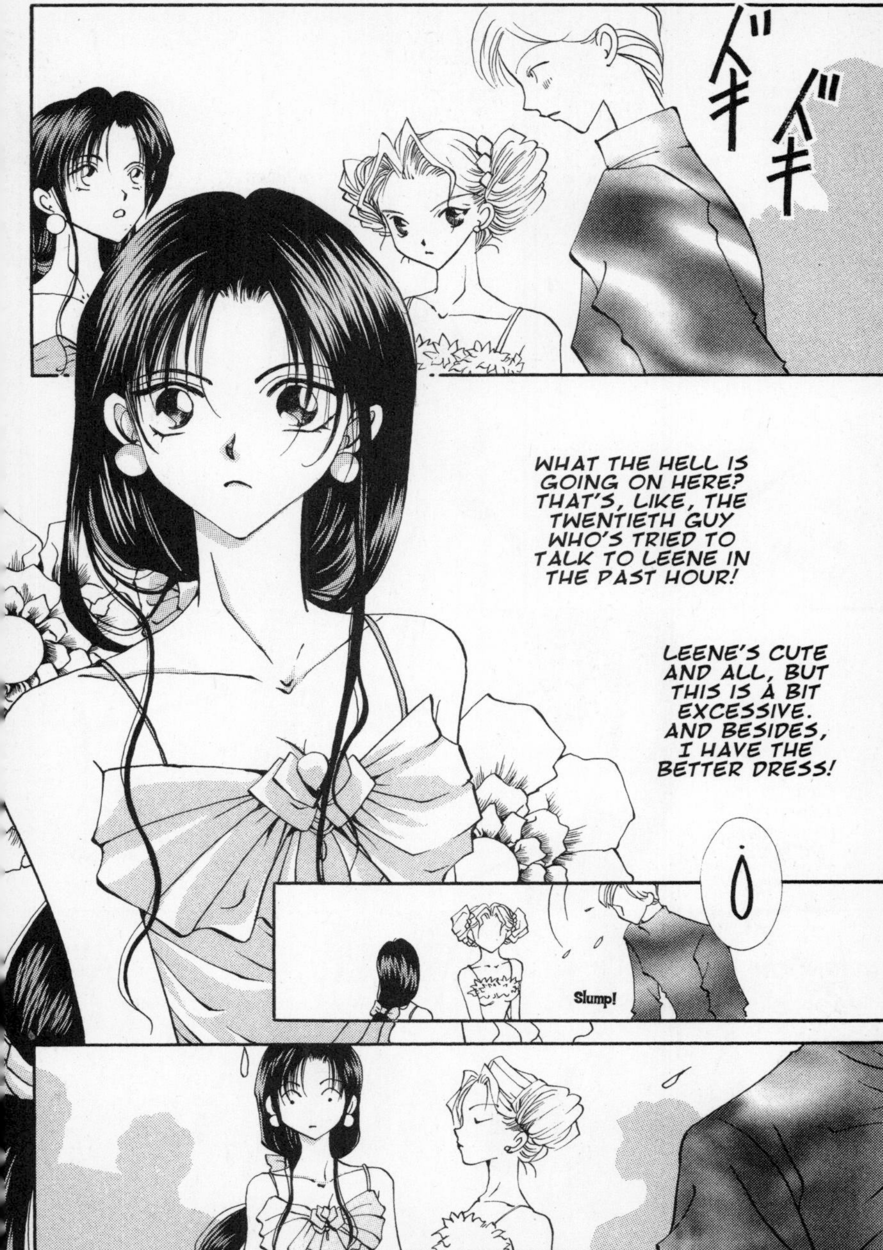
ギイ ギイ
WHAT THE HELL IS GOING ON HERE? THAT'S, LIKE, THE TWENTIETH GUY WHO'S TRIED TO TALK TO LEENE IN THE PAST HOUR!
LEENE'S CUTE AND ALL, BUT THIS IS A BIT EXCESSIVE. AND BESIDES, I HAVE THE BETTER DRESS!
Slump!

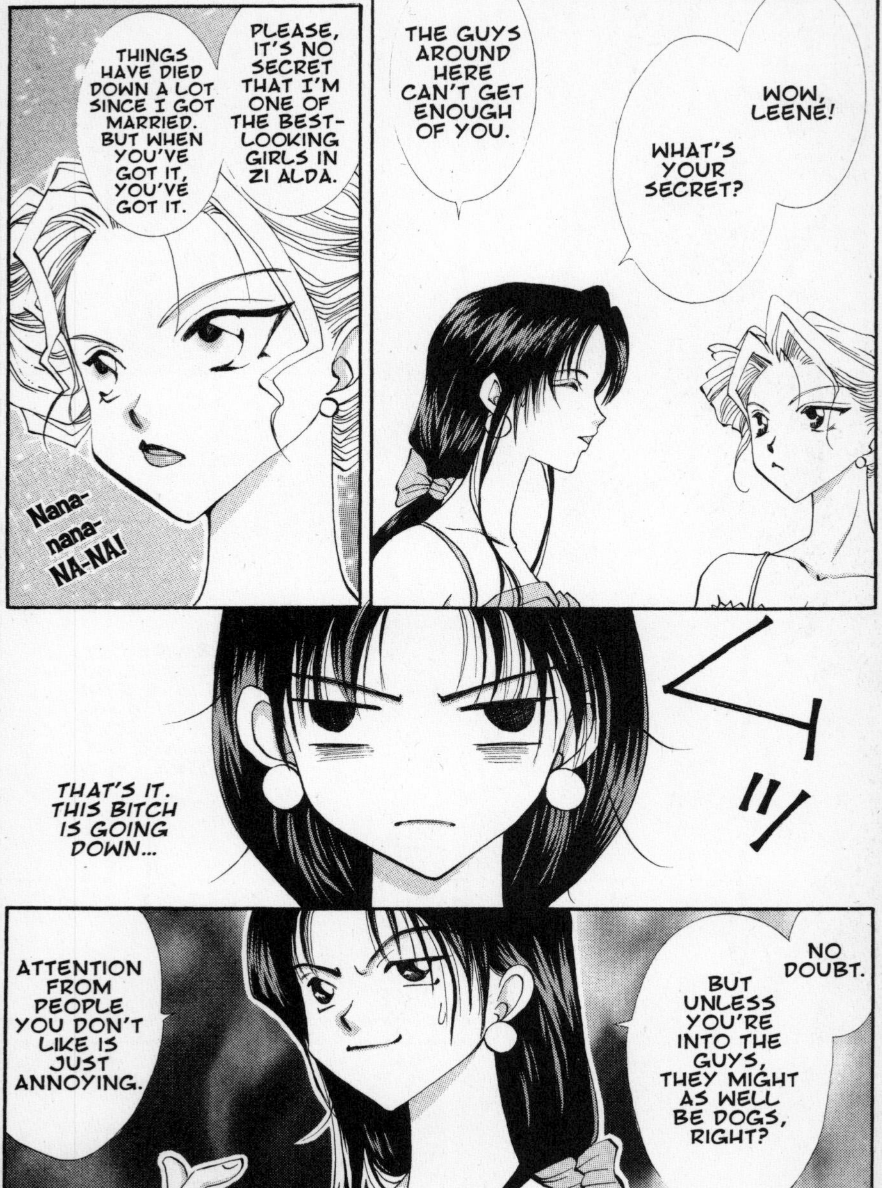
WOW, LEENÉ! WHAT'S YOUR SECRET?
THE GUYS AROUND HERE CAN'T GET ENOUGH OF YOU.
PLEASE, IT'S NO SECRET THAT I'M ONE OF THE BEST-LOOKING GIRLS IN ZI ALDA.
THINGS HAVE DIED DOWN A LOT SINCE I GOT MARRIED. BUT WHEN YOU'VE GOT IT, YOU'VE GOT IT.
Nana-nana-NA-NA!
THAT'S IT. THIS BITCH IS GOING DOWN...
NO DOUBT. BUT UNLESS YOU'RE INTO THE GUYS, THEY MIGHT AS WELL BE DOGS, RIGHT?
ATTENTION FROM PEOPLE YOU DON'T LIKE IS JUST ANNOYING.

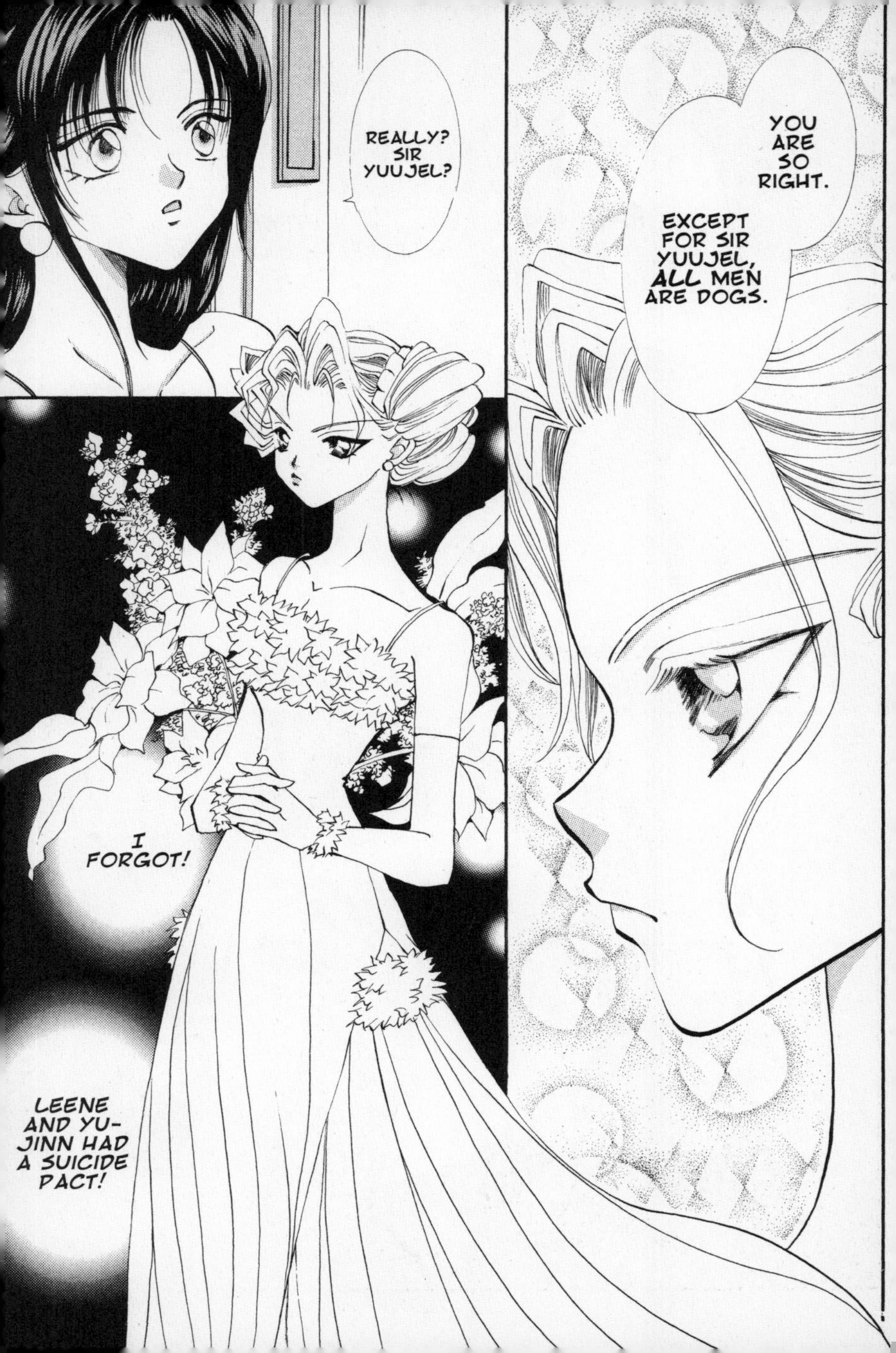
YOU ARE SO RIGHT.
EXCEPT FOR SIR YUUJEL, **ALL** MEN ARE DOGS.
REALLY? SIR YUUJEL?
I FORGOT!
LEENE AND YU-JINN HAD A SUICIDE PACT!

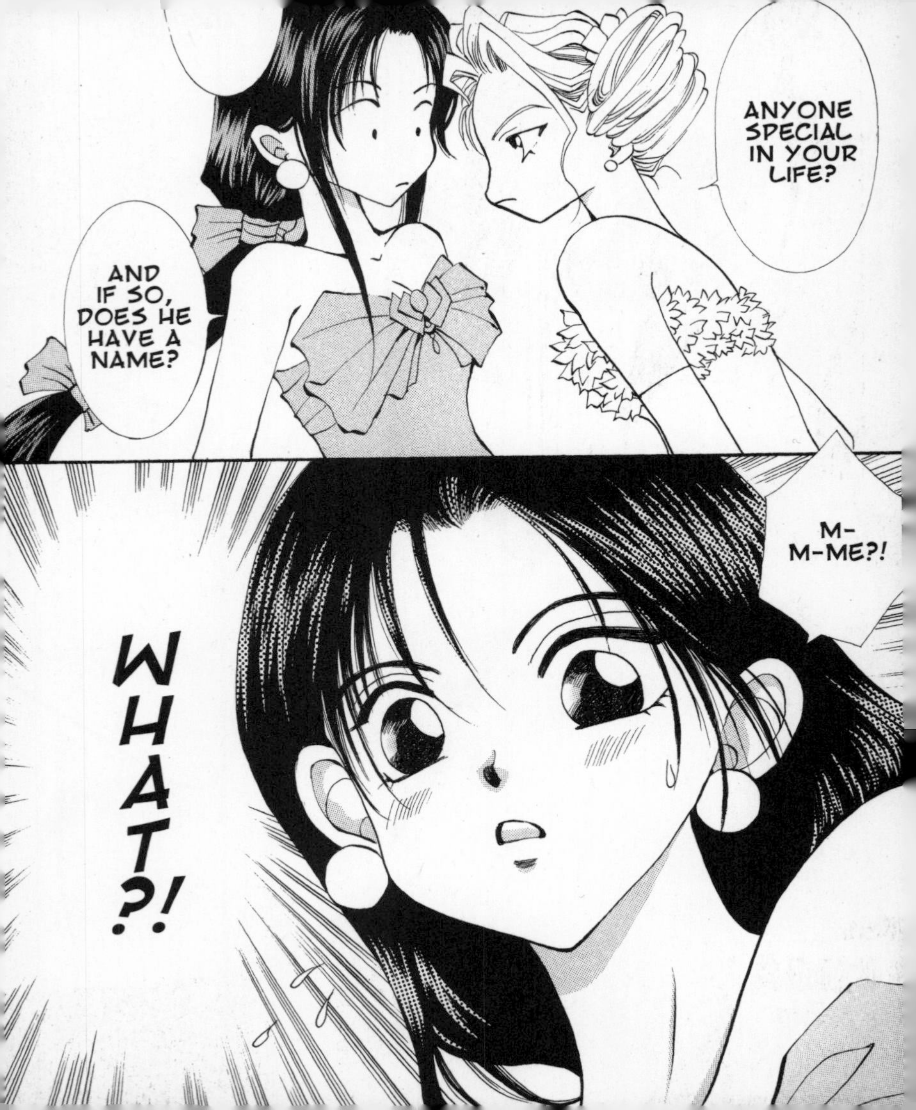
ANYONE SPECIAL IN YOUR LIFE?
AND IF SO, DOES HE HAVE A NAME?
M- M-ME?!
WHAT?!

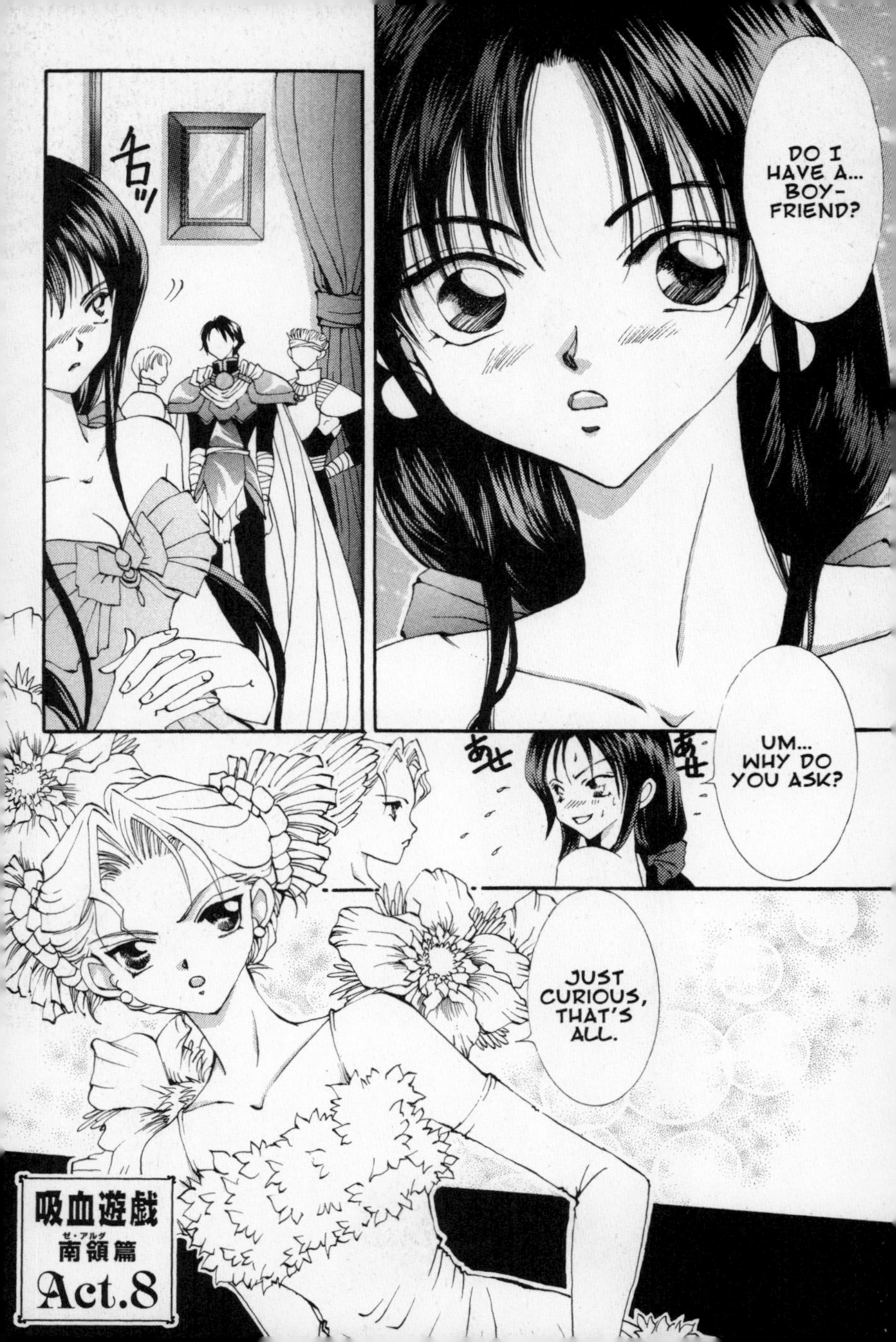
DO I HAVE A... BOY-FRIEND?
あせ
あせ
UM... WHY DO YOU ASK?
JUST CURIOUS, THAT'S ALL.
吸血遊戯
ゼ・アルダ
南領篇
Act.8

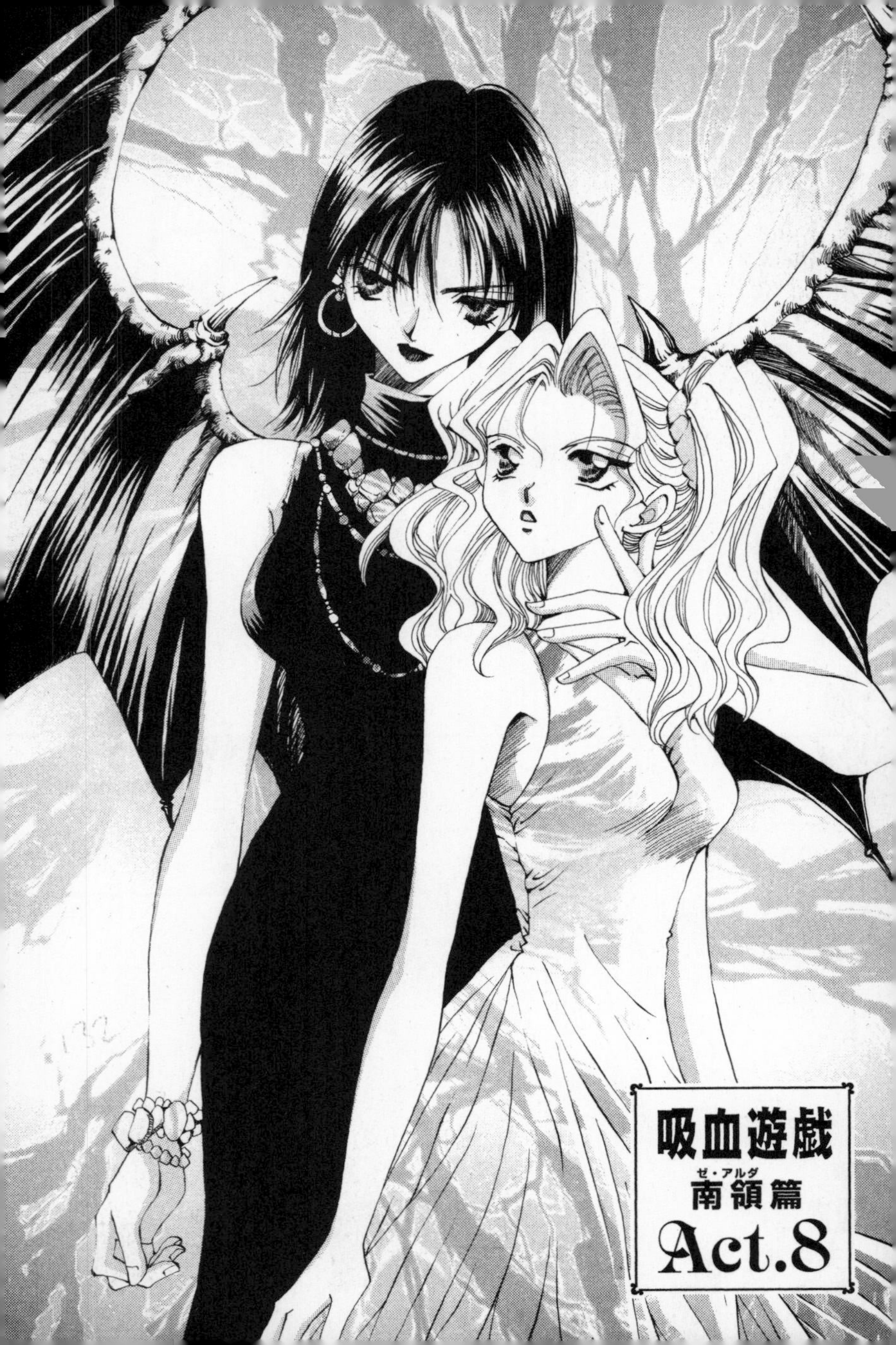
吸血遊戯
南領篇（ゼ・アルダ）
Act.8

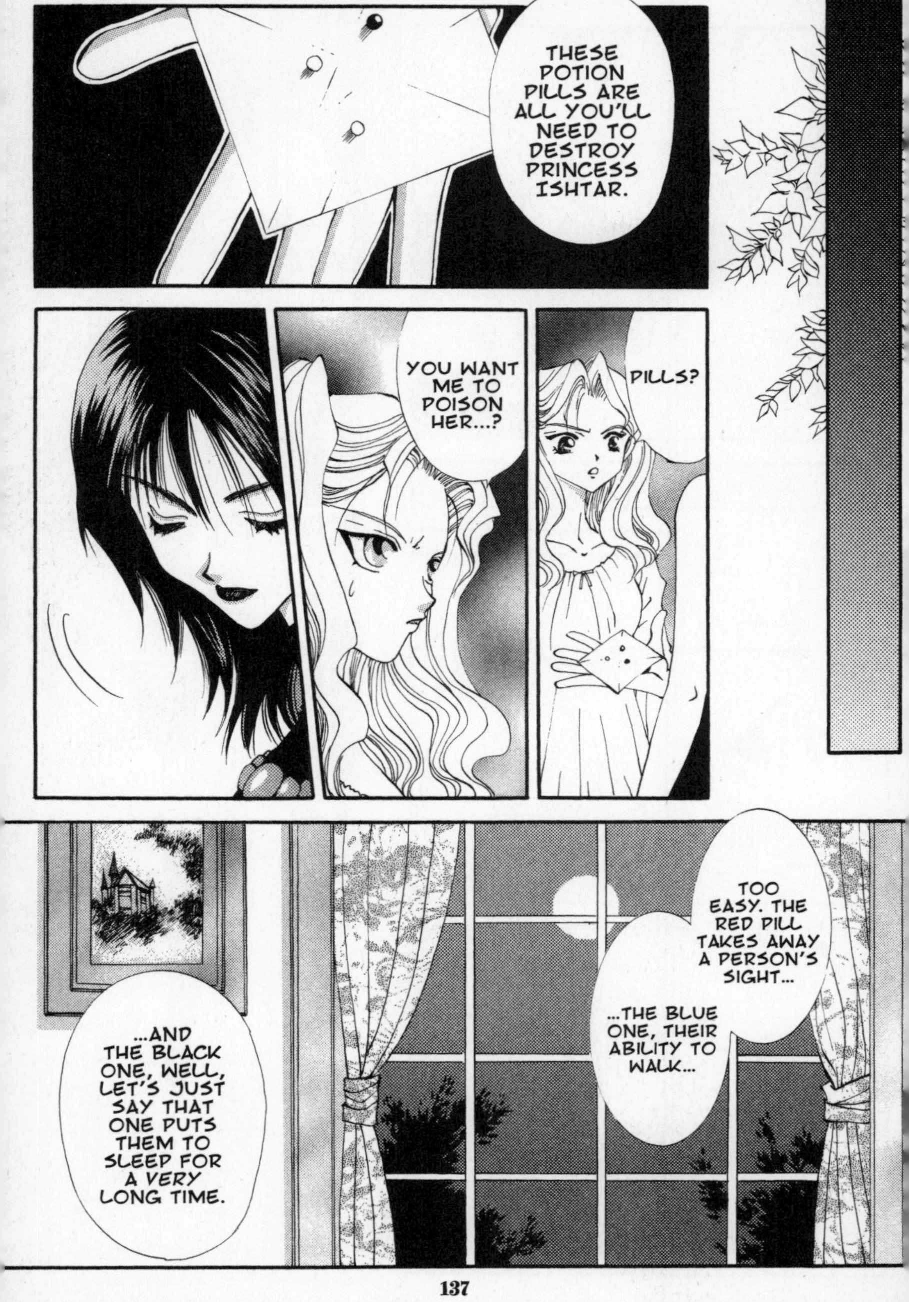
THESE POTION PILLS ARE ALL YOU'LL NEED TO DESTROY PRINCESS ISHTAR.
PILLS?
YOU WANT ME TO POISON HER...?
TOO EASY. THE RED PILL TAKES AWAY A PERSON'S SIGHT...
...THE BLUE ONE, THEIR ABILITY TO WALK...
...AND THE BLACK ONE, WELL, LET'S JUST SAY THAT ONE PUTS THEM TO SLEEP FOR A VERY LONG TIME.

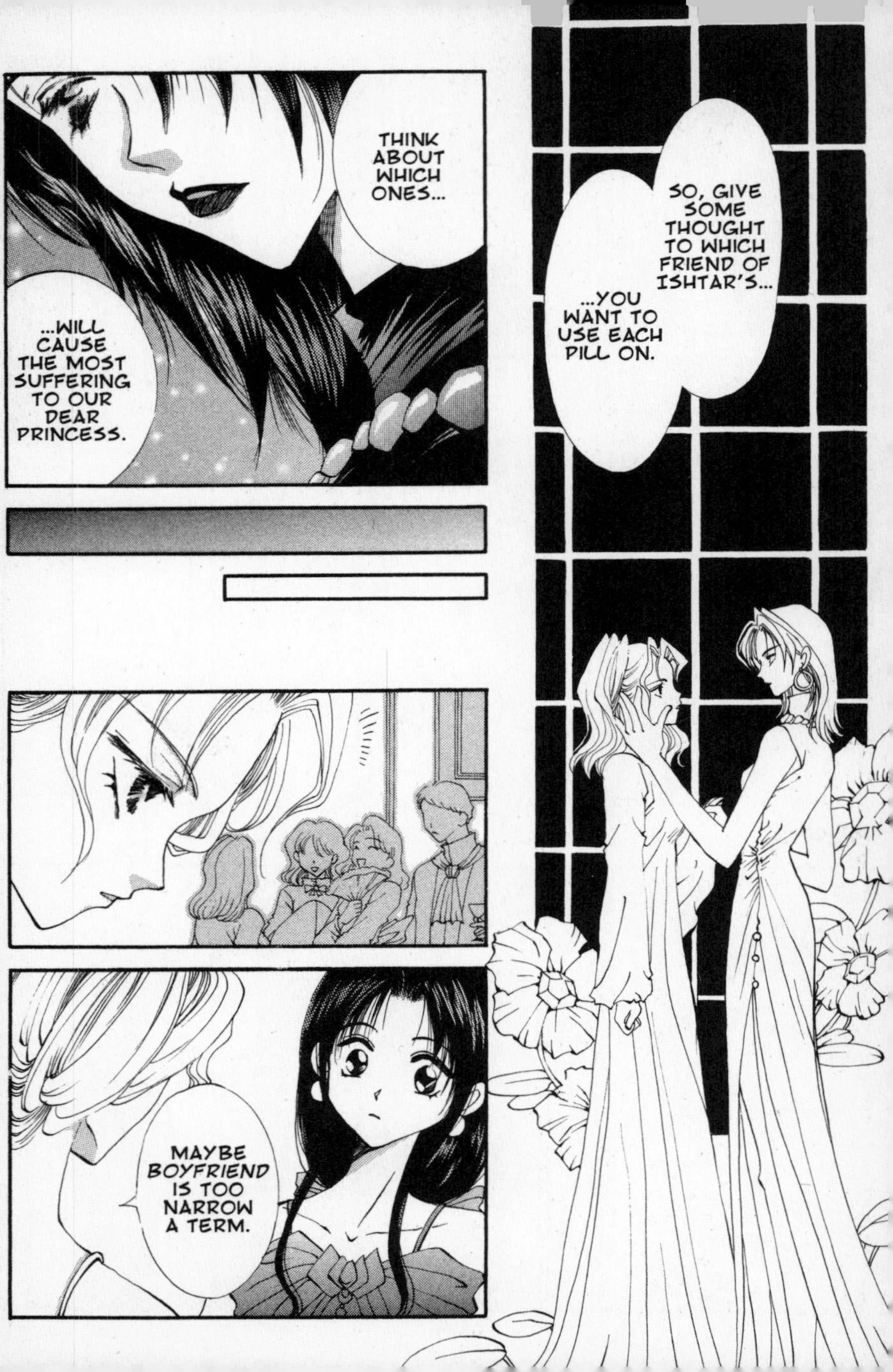
SO, GIVE SOME THOUGHT TO WHICH FRIEND OF ISHTAR'S...
...YOU WANT TO USE EACH PILL ON.
THINK ABOUT WHICH ONES...
...WILL CAUSE THE MOST SUFFERING TO OUR DEAR PRINCESS.
MAYBE BOYFRIEND IS TOO NARROW A TERM.

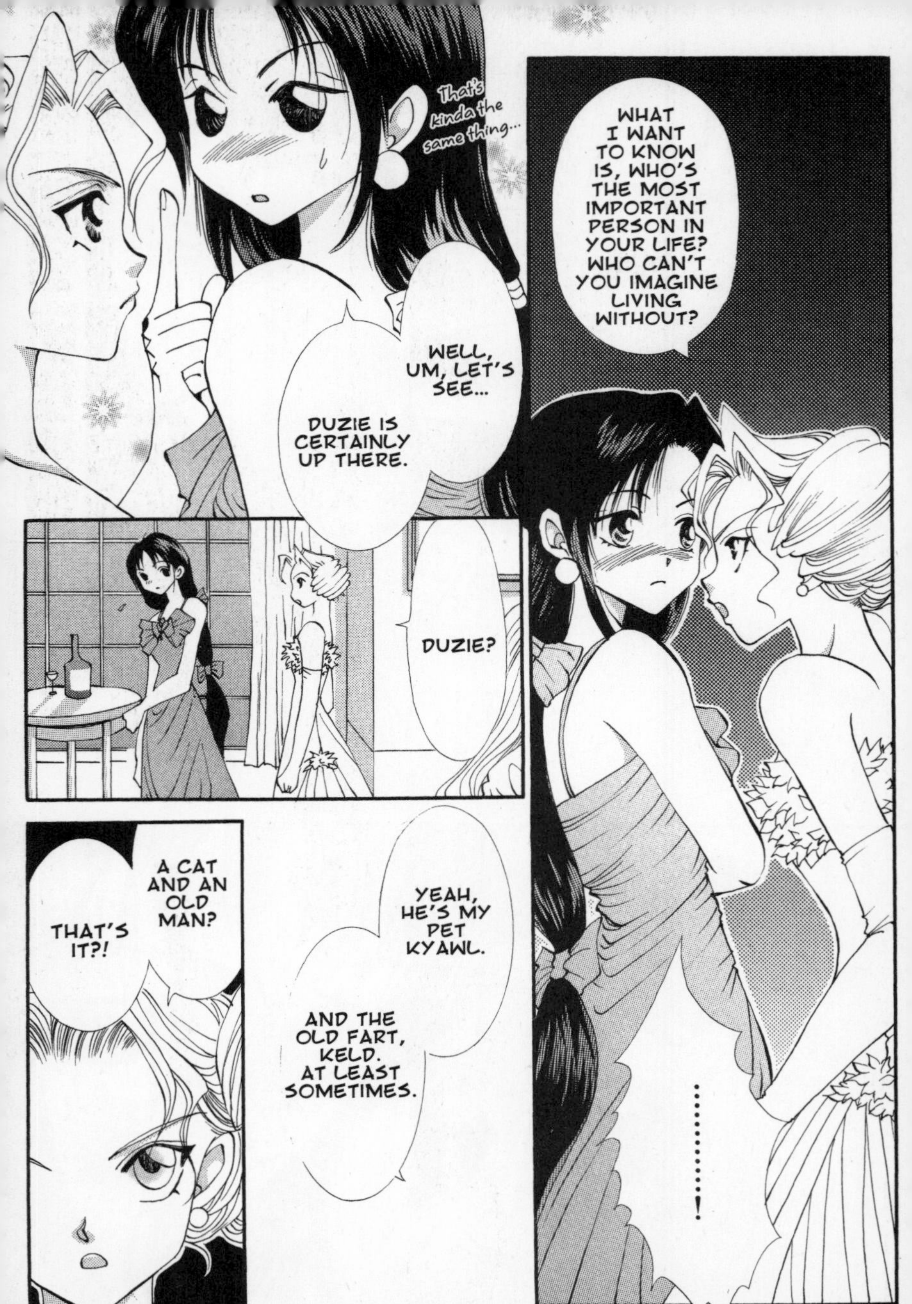
WHAT I WANT TO KNOW IS, WHO'S THE MOST IMPORTANT PERSON IN YOUR LIFE? WHO CAN'T YOU IMAGINE LIVING WITHOUT?
......!
That's kinda the same thing...
WELL, UM, LET'S SEE...
DUZIE IS CERTAINLY UP THERE.
DUZIE?
YEAH, HE'S MY PET KYAWL.
AND THE OLD FART, KELD. AT LEAST SOMETIMES.
A CAT AND AN OLD MAN?
THAT'S IT?!

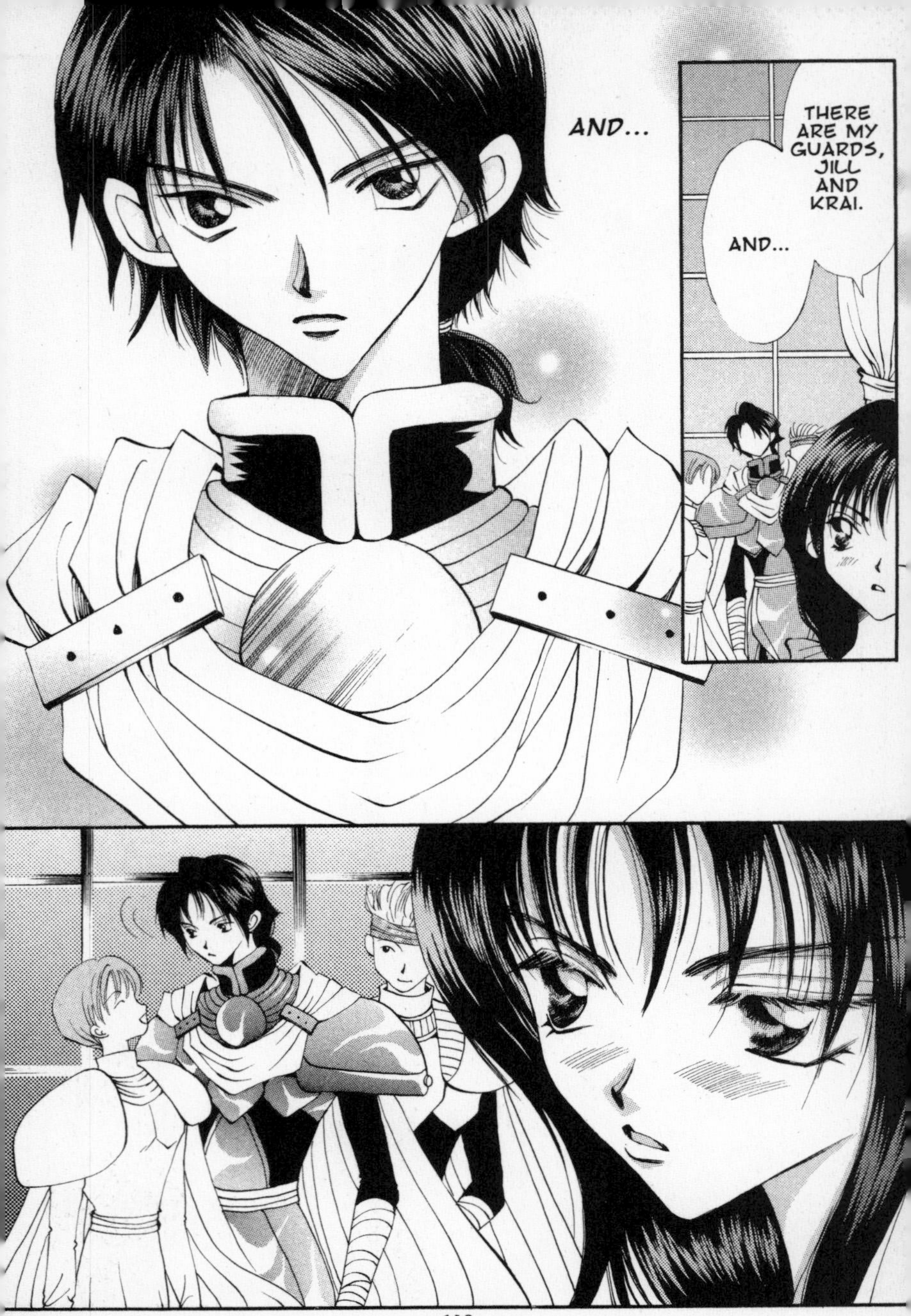
THERE ARE MY GUARDS, JILL AND KRAI.
AND...
AND...

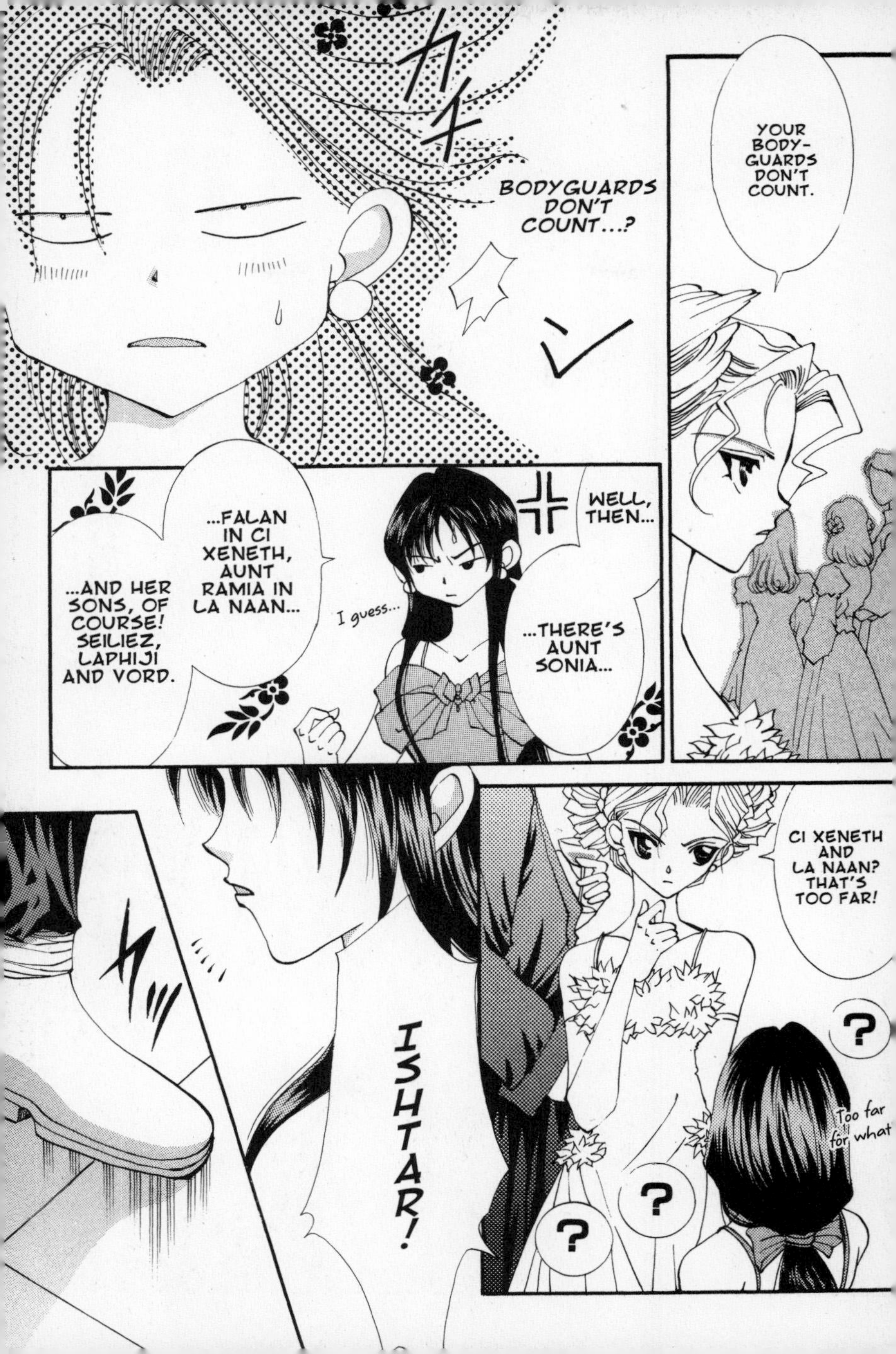
YOUR BODY-GUARDS DON'T COUNT.
BODYGUARDS DON'T COUNT...?
WELL, THEN...
...THERE'S AUNT SONIA...
I guess...
...FALAN IN CI XENETH, AUNT RAMIA IN LA NAAN...
...AND HER SONS, OF COURSE! SEILIEZ, LAPHIJI AND VORD.
CI XENETH AND LA NAAN? THAT'S TOO FAR!
Too far for what
?
?
?
ISHTAR!

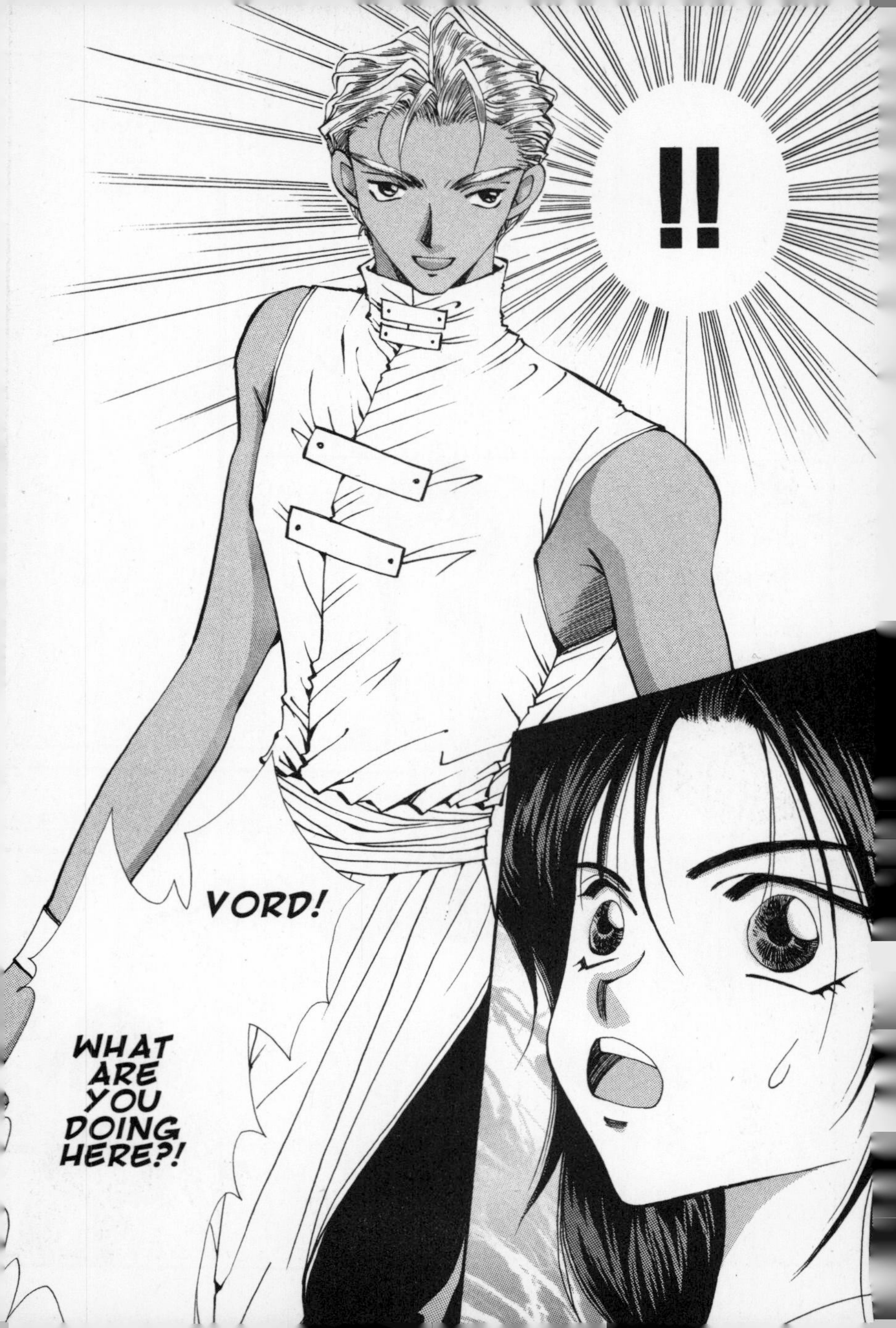
!!
VORD!
WHAT ARE YOU DOING HERE?!

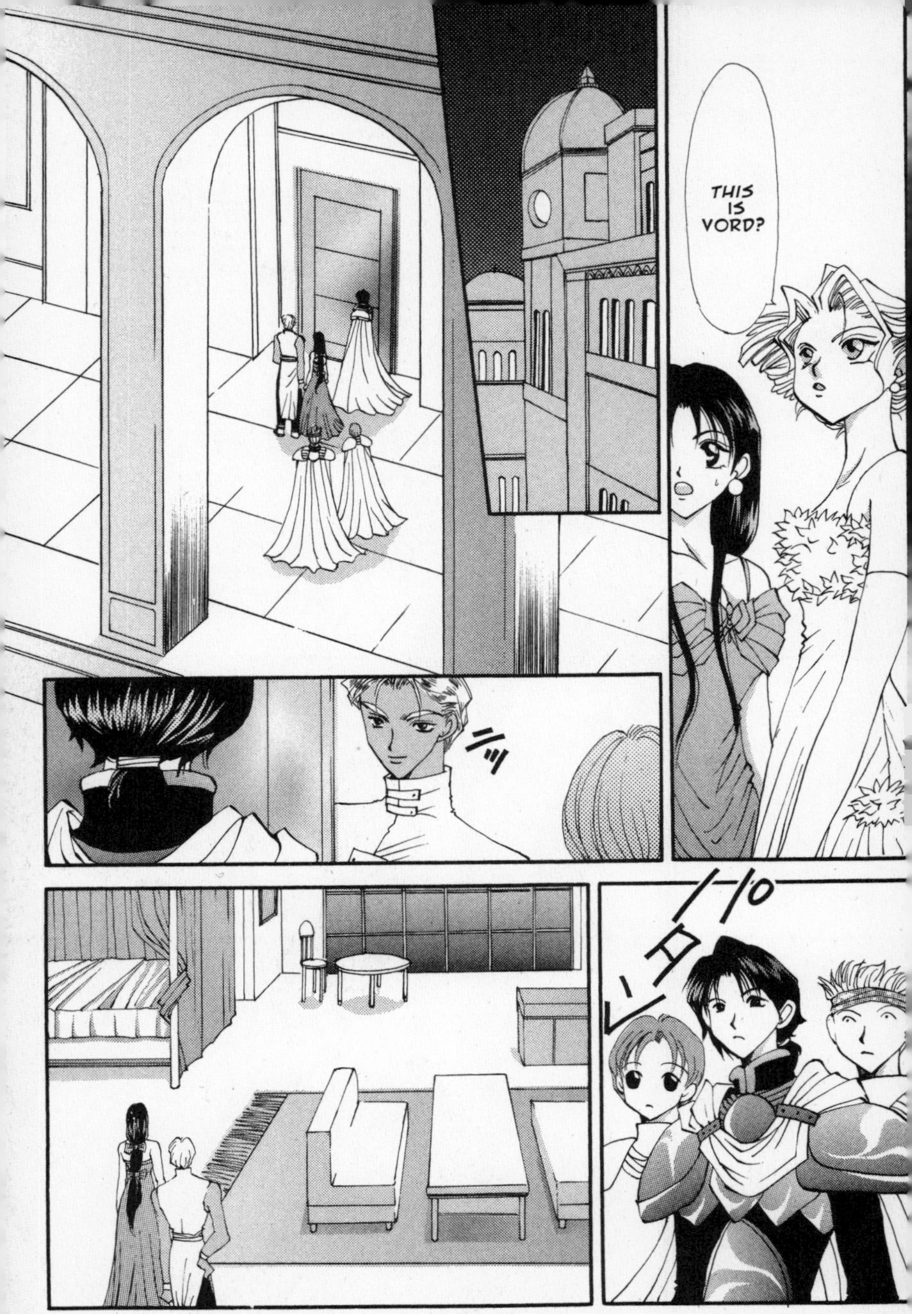
THIS IS VORD?
ニッ
パタン

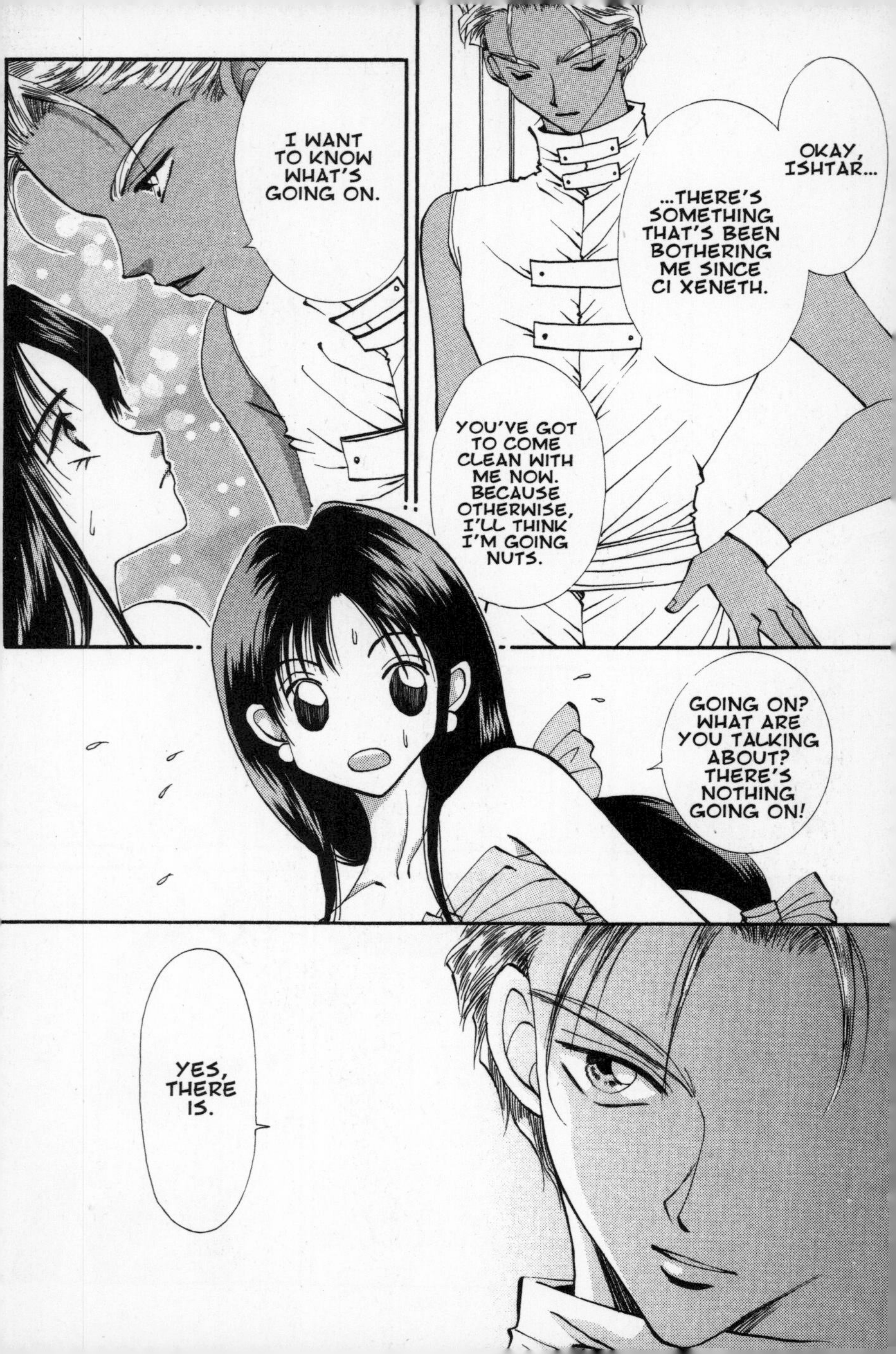
OKAY, ISHTAR...
...THERE'S SOMETHING THAT'S BEEN BOTHERING ME SINCE CI XENETH.
YOU'VE GOT TO COME CLEAN WITH ME NOW. BECAUSE OTHERWISE, I'LL THINK I'M GOING NUTS.
I WANT TO KNOW WHAT'S GOING ON.
GOING ON? WHAT ARE YOU TALKING ABOUT? THERE'S NOTHING GOING ON!
YES, THERE IS.

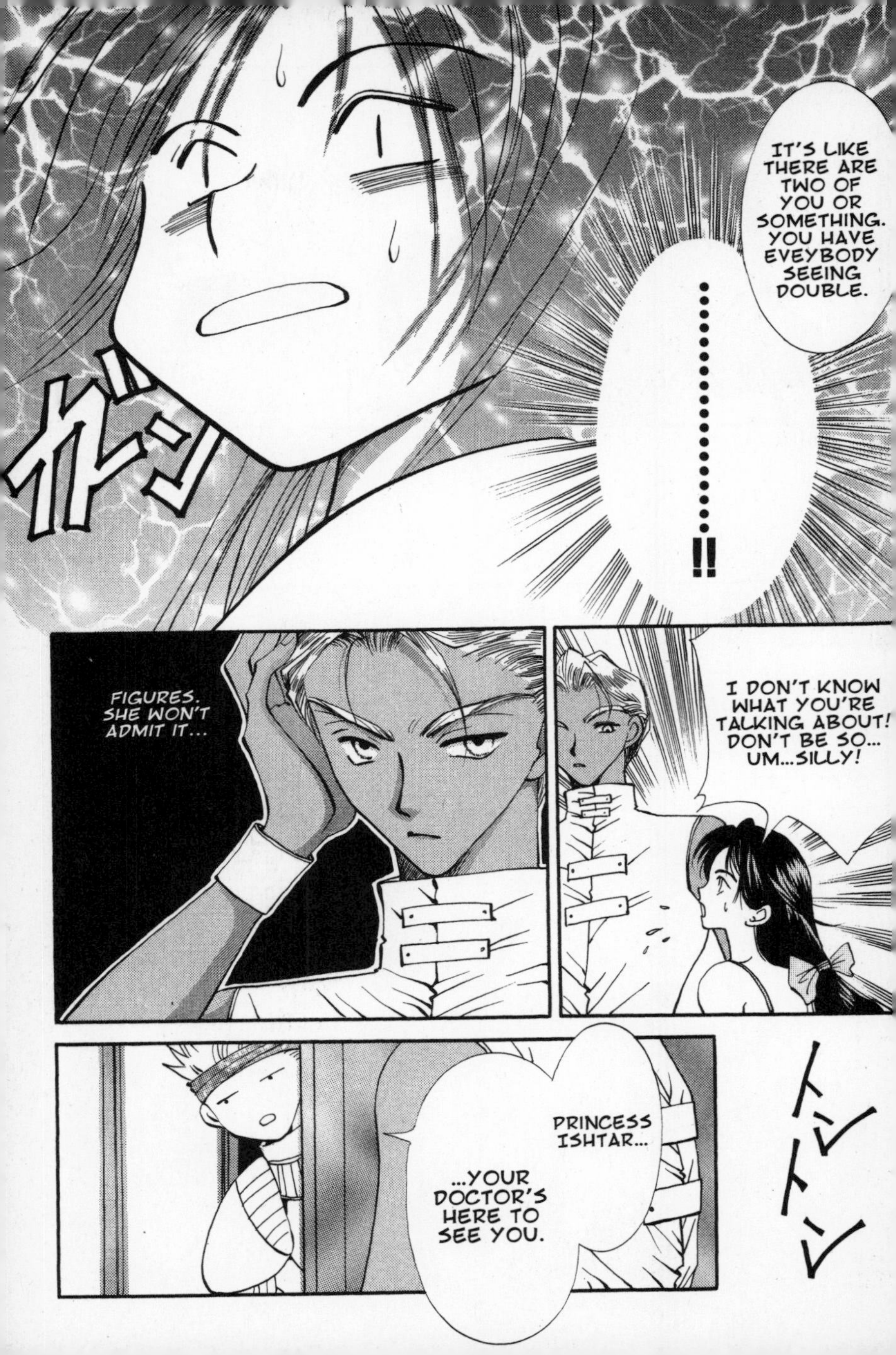
IT'S LIKE THERE ARE TWO OF YOU OR SOMETHING. YOU HAVE EVEYBODY SEEING DOUBLE.
.........!!
I DON'T KNOW WHAT YOU'RE TALKING ABOUT! DON'T BE SO... UM...SILLY!
FIGURES. SHE WON'T ADMIT IT...
トントン
PRINCESS ISHTAR...
...YOUR DOCTOR'S HERE TO SEE YOU.

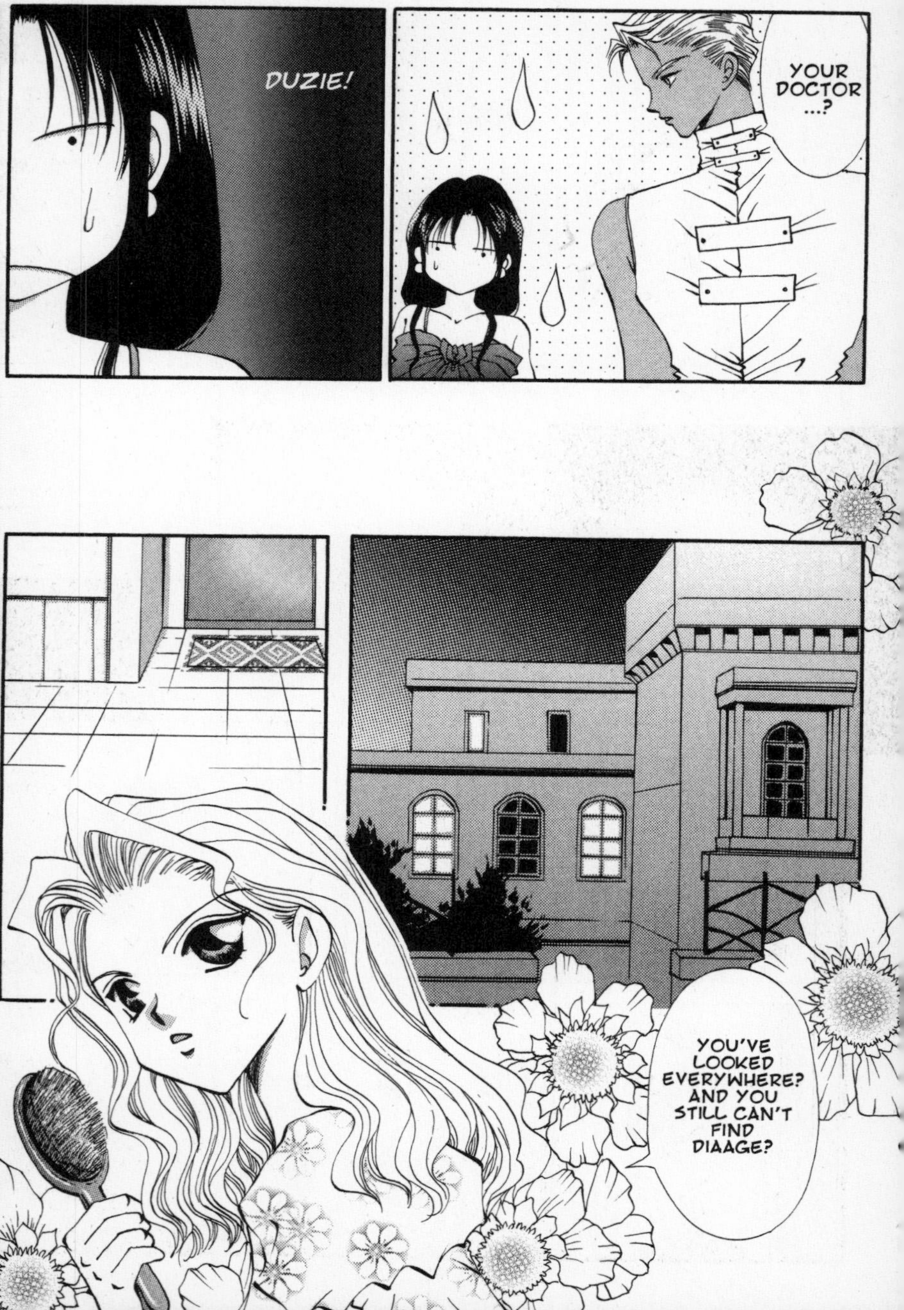
YOUR DOCTOR ...?
DUZIE!
YOU'VE LOOKED EVERYWHERE? AND YOU STILL CAN'T FIND DIAAGE?

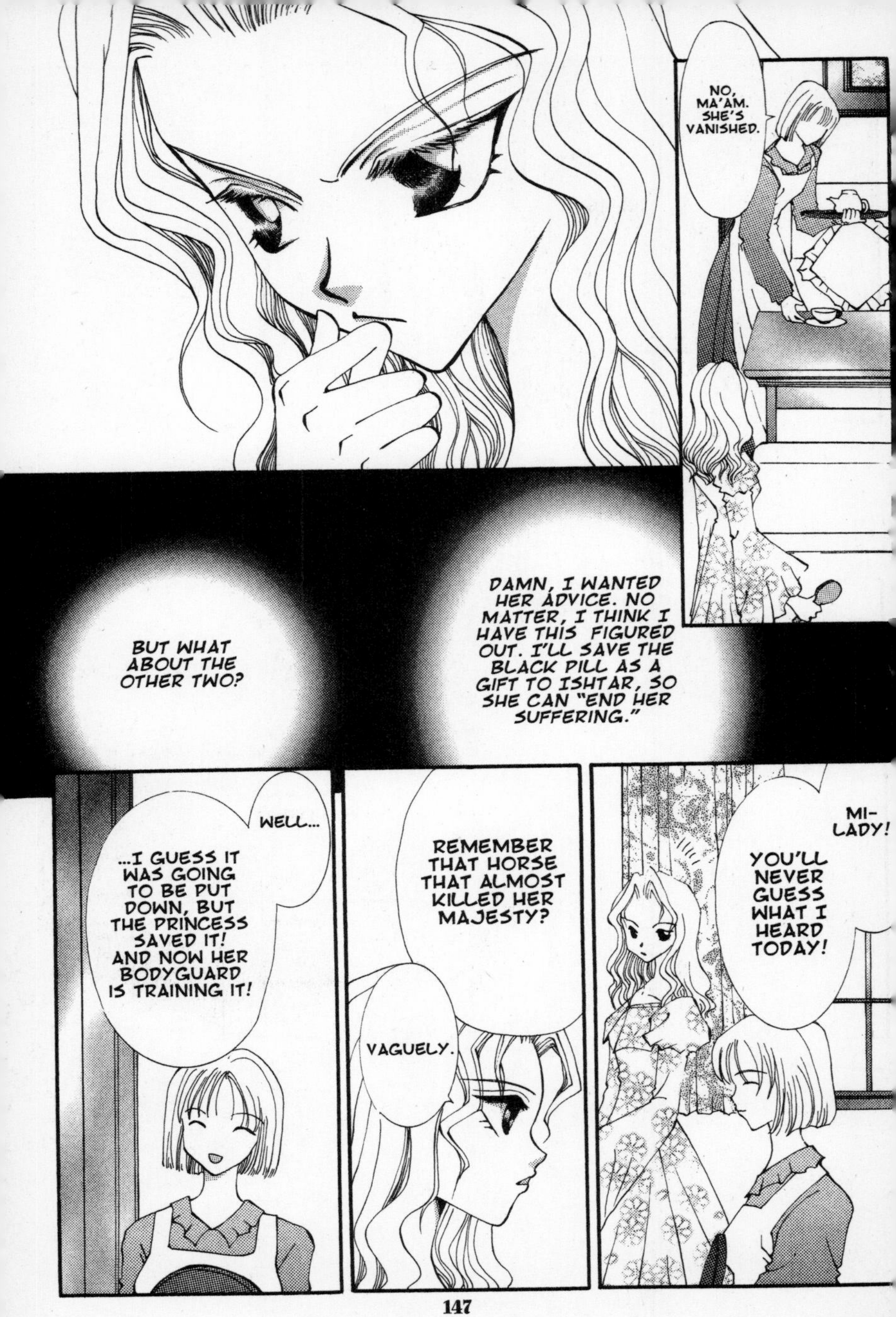
NO, MA'AM. SHE'S VANISHED.
DAMN, I WANTED HER ADVICE. NO MATTER, I THINK I HAVE THIS FIGURED OUT. I'LL SAVE THE BLACK PILL AS A GIFT TO ISHTAR, SO SHE CAN "END HER SUFFERING."
BUT WHAT ABOUT THE OTHER TWO?
MI-LADY!
YOU'LL NEVER GUESS WHAT I HEARD TODAY!
REMEMBER THAT HORSE THAT ALMOST KILLED HER MAJESTY?
VAGUELY.
WELL...
...I GUESS IT WAS GOING TO BE PUT DOWN, BUT THE PRINCESS SAVED IT! AND NOW HER BODYGUARD IS TRAINING IT!

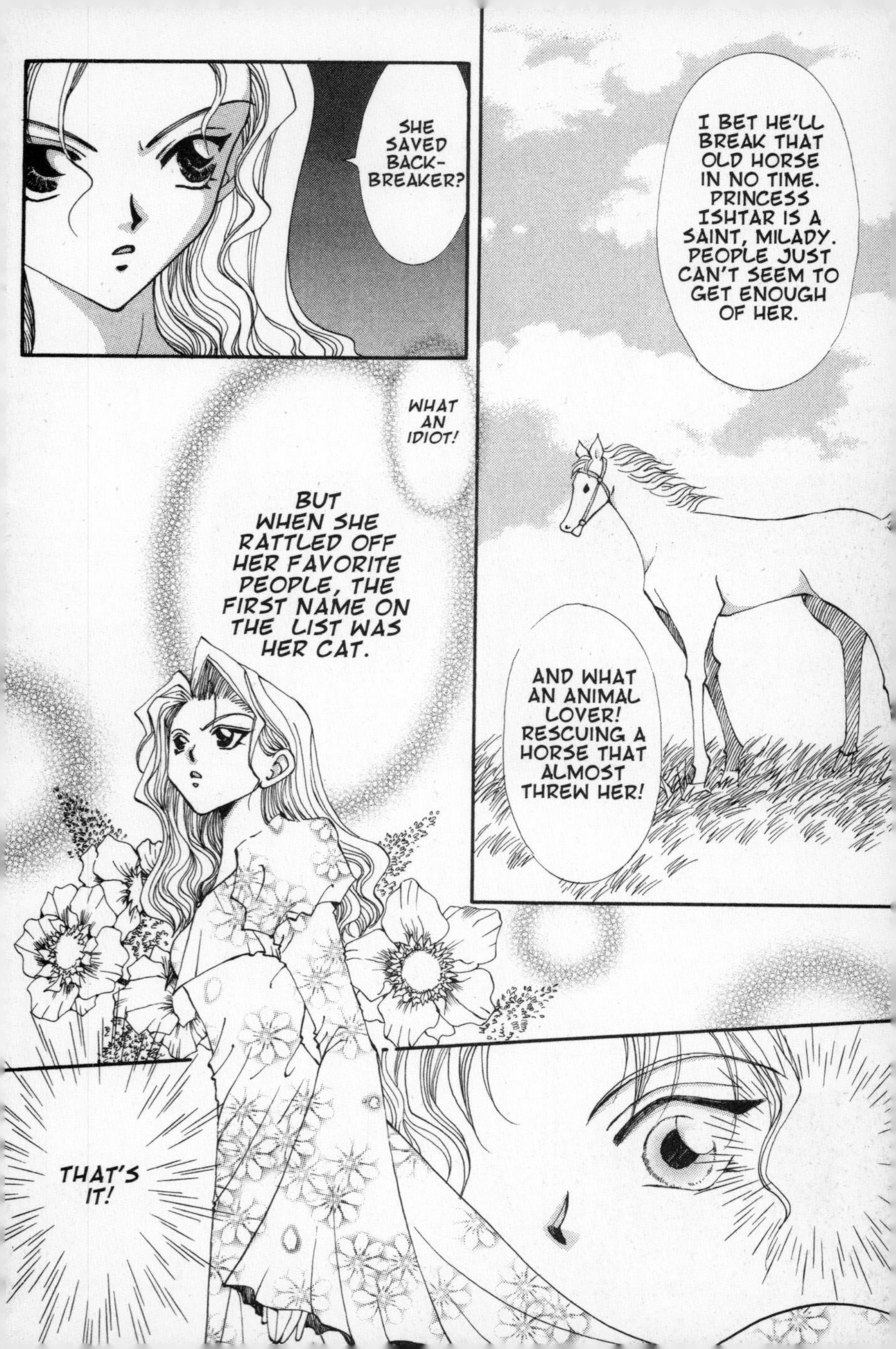
I BET HE'LL BREAK THAT OLD HORSE IN NO TIME. PRINCESS ISHTAR IS A SAINT, MILADY. PEOPLE JUST CAN'T SEEM TO GET ENOUGH OF HER.
AND WHAT AN ANIMAL LOVER! RESCUING A HORSE THAT ALMOST THREW HER!
SHE SAVED BACK-BREAKER?
WHAT AN IDIOT!
BUT WHEN SHE RATTLED OFF HER FAVORITE PEOPLE, THE FIRST NAME ON THE LIST WAS HER CAT.
THAT'S IT!

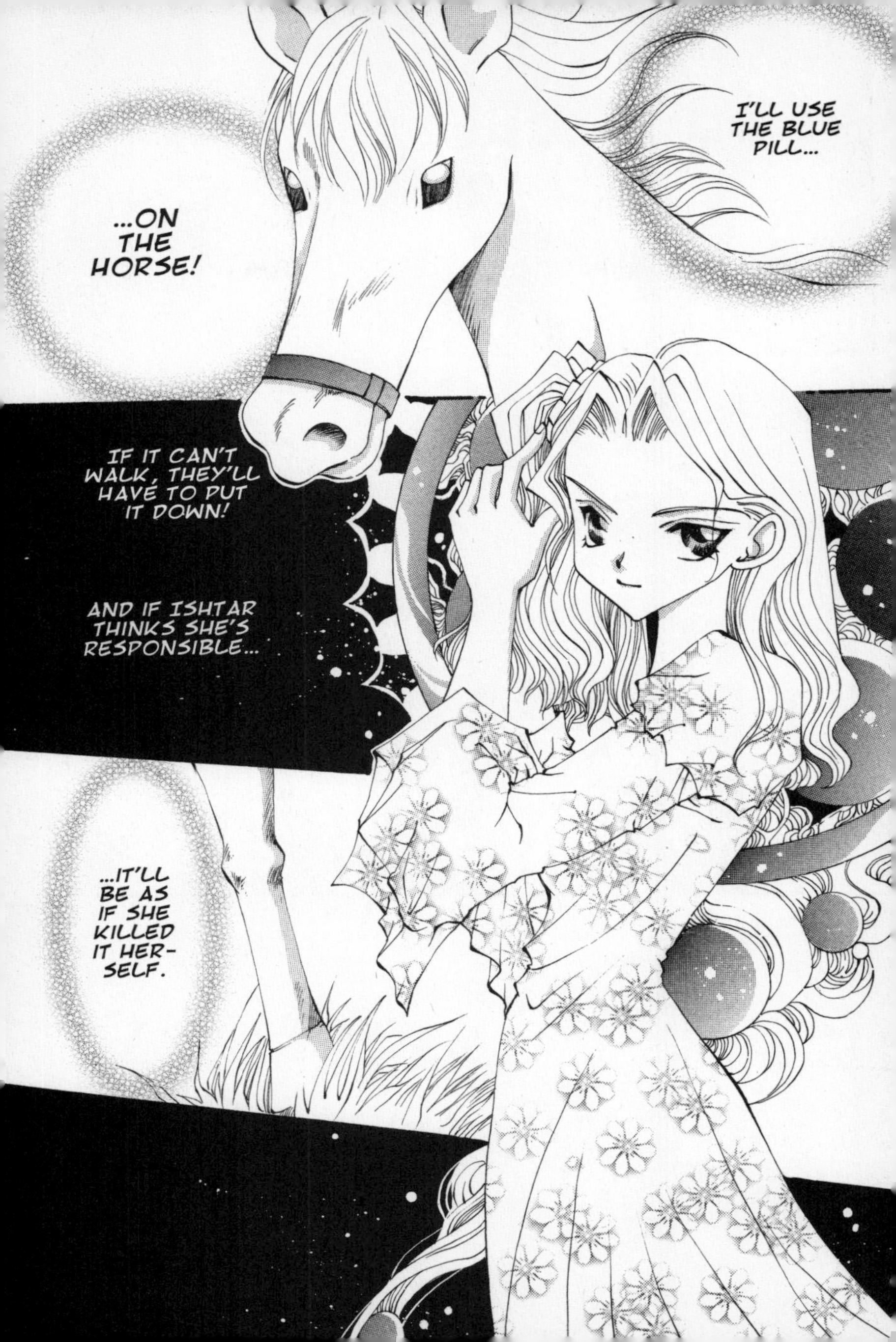
I'LL USE THE BLUE PILL...
...ON THE HORSE!
IF IT CAN'T WALK, THEY'LL HAVE TO PUT IT DOWN!
AND IF ISHTAR THINKS SHE'S RESPONSIBLE...
...IT'LL BE AS IF SHE KILLED IT HER-SELF.

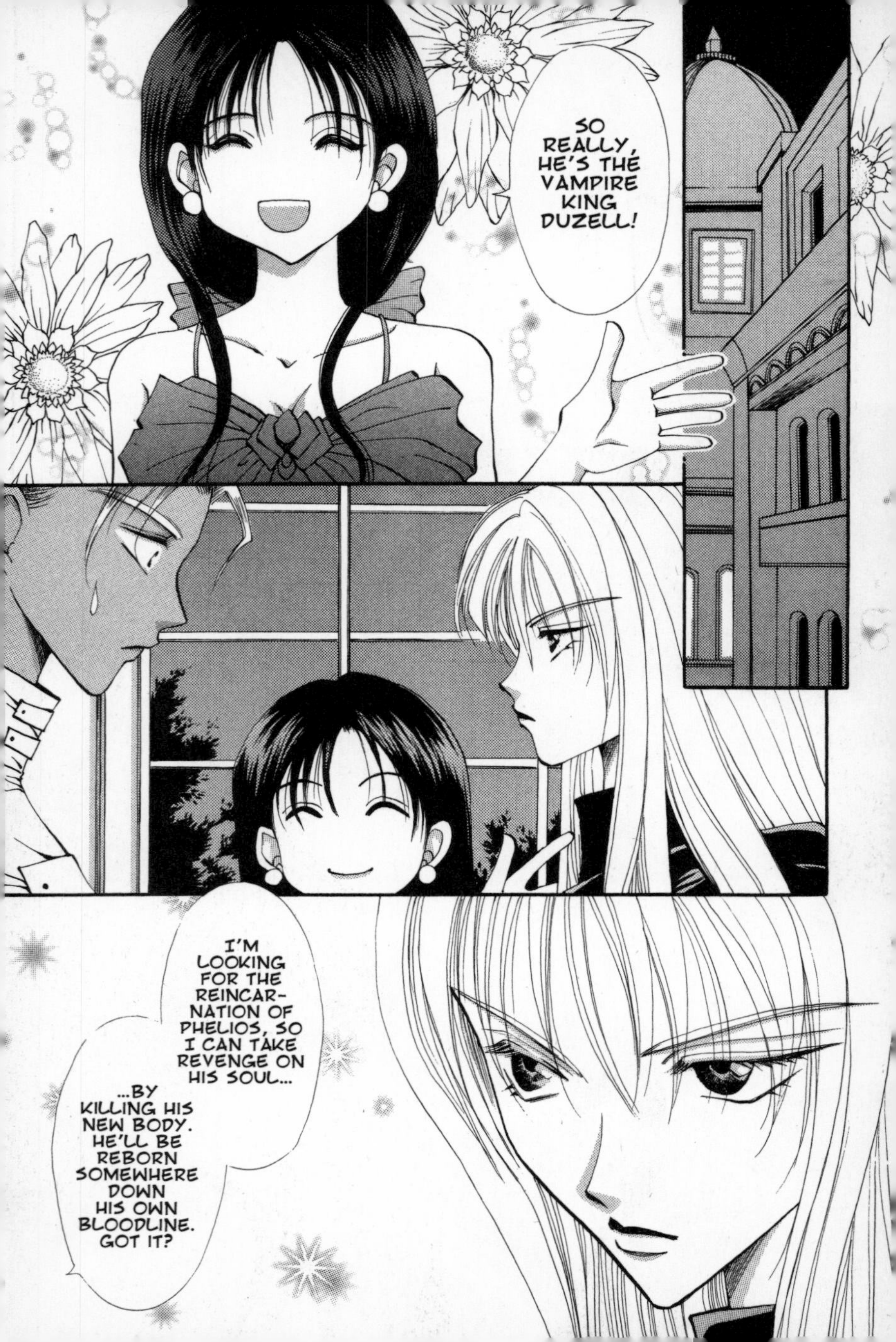
SO REALLY, HE'S THE VAMPIRE KING DUZELL!
I'M LOOKING FOR THE REINCAR-NATION OF PHELIOS, SO I CAN TAKE REVENGE ON HIS SOUL...
...BY KILLING HIS NEW BODY. HE'LL BE REBORN SOMEWHERE DOWN HIS OWN BLOODLINE. GOT IT?

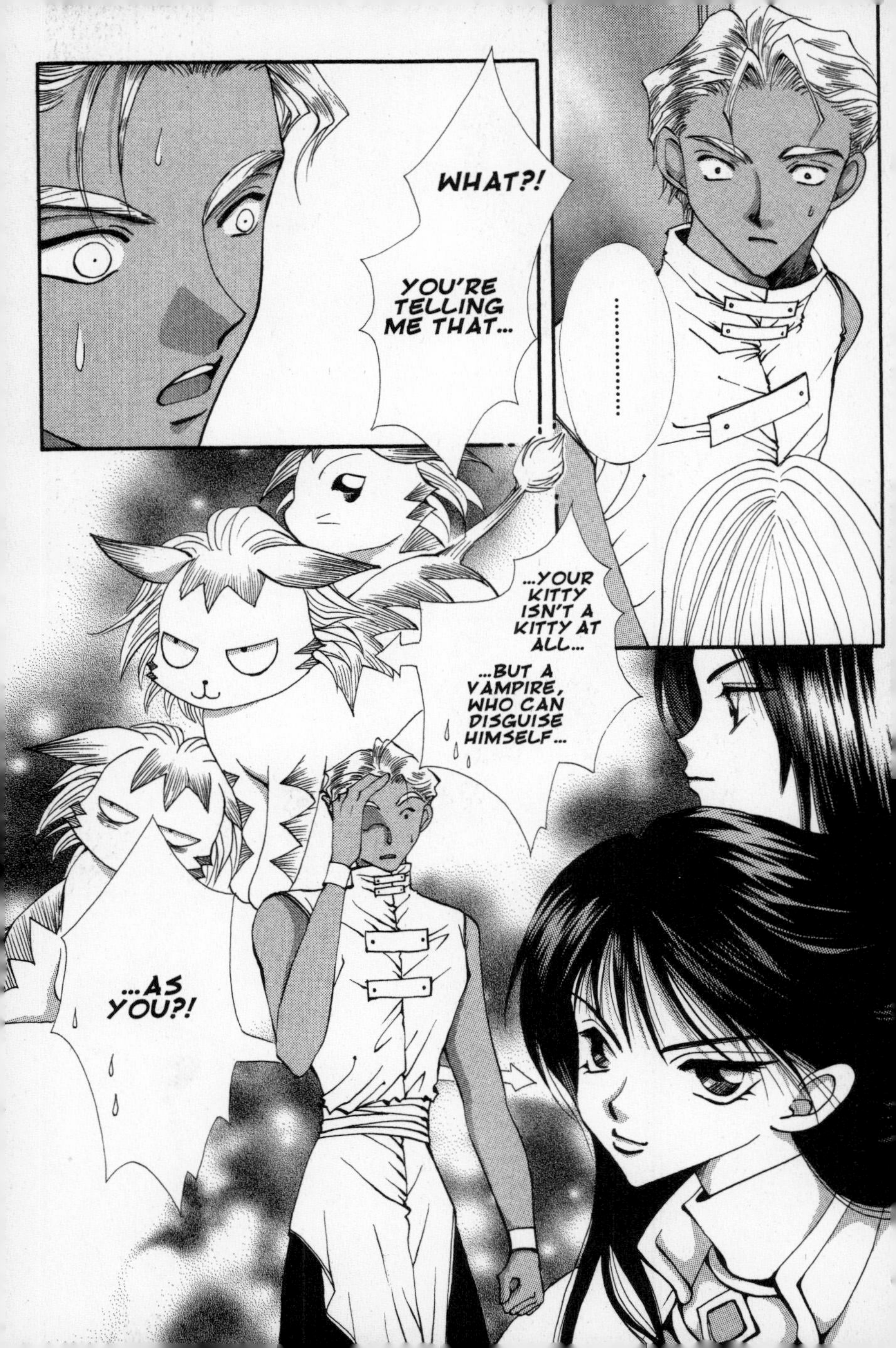
......
WHAT?!
YOU'RE TELLING ME THAT...
...YOUR KITTY ISN'T A KITTY AT ALL...
...BUT A VAMPIRE, WHO CAN DISGUISE HIMSELF...
...AS YOU?!

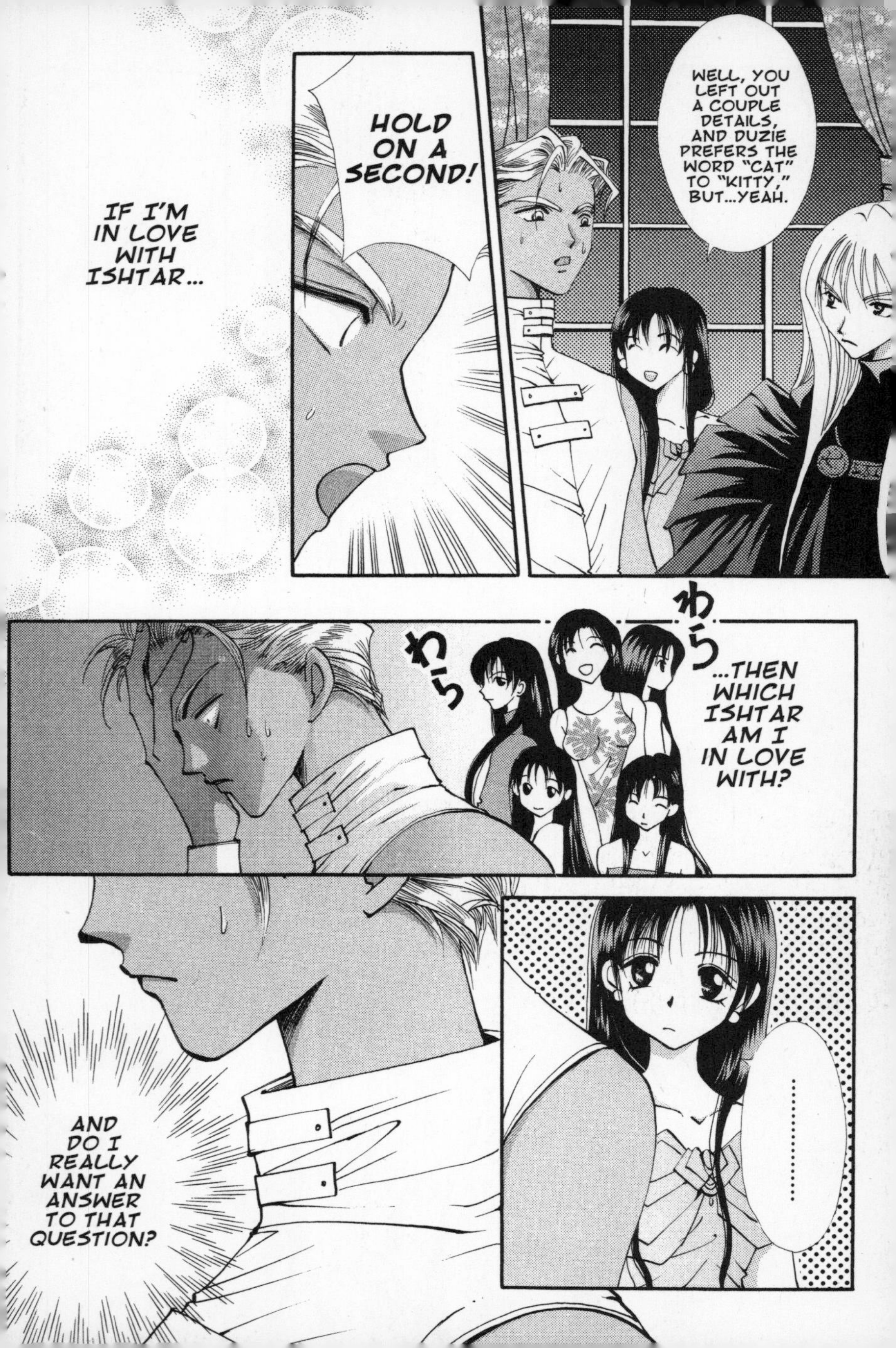

WELL, YOU LEFT OUT A COUPLE DETAILS, AND DUZIE PREFERS THE WORD "CAT" TO "KITTY," BUT...YEAH.
HOLD ON A SECOND!
IF I'M IN LOVE WITH ISHTAR...
わら
わら
...THEN WHICH ISHTAR AM I IN LOVE WITH?
......
AND DO I REALLY WANT AN ANSWER TO THAT QUESTION?

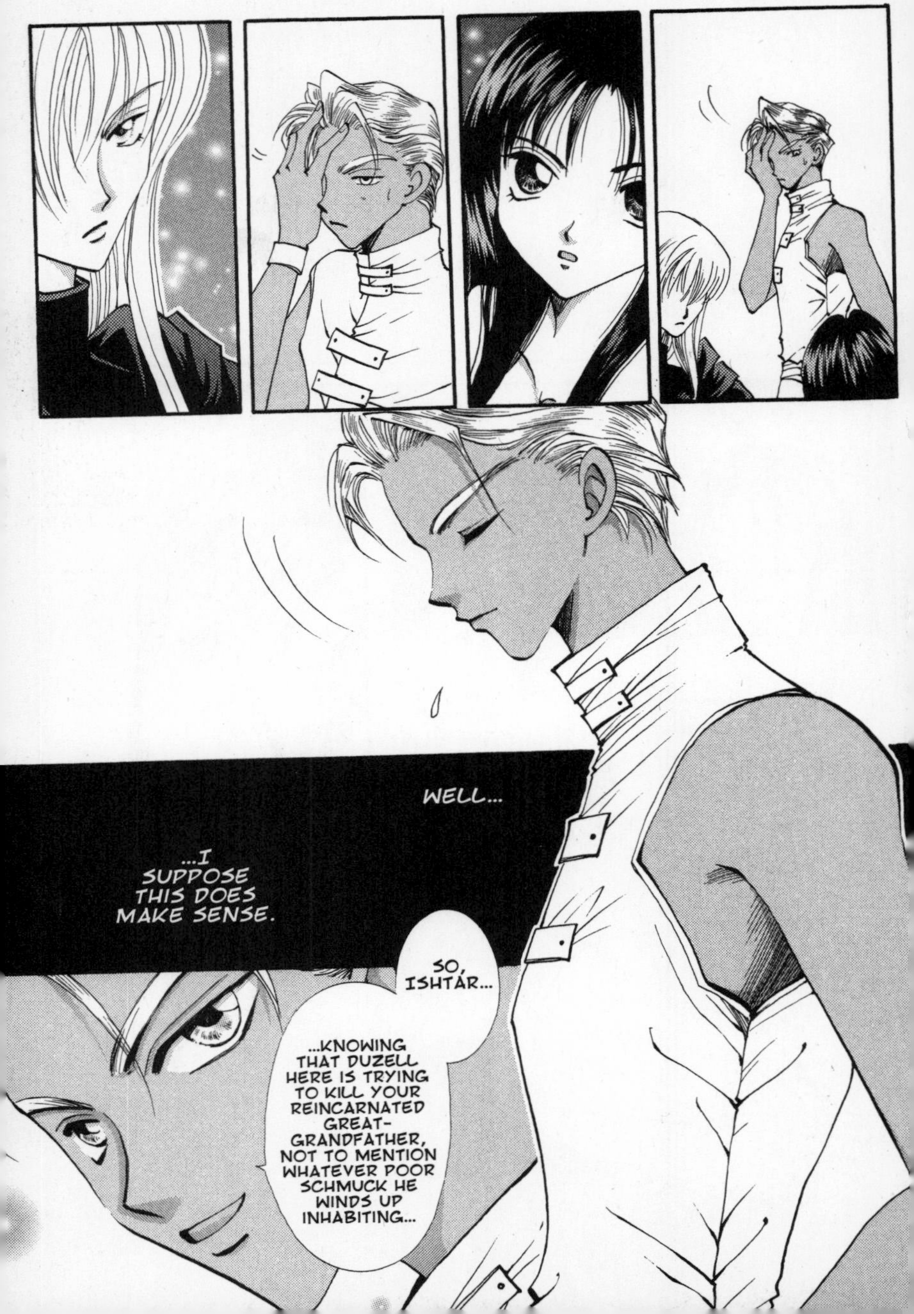
WELL...
...I SUPPOSE THIS DOES MAKE SENSE.
SO, ISHTAR...
...KNOWING THAT DUZELL HERE IS TRYING TO KILL YOUR REINCARNATED GREAT-GRANDFATHER, NOT TO MENTION WHATEVER POOR SCHMUCK HE WINDS UP INHABITING...

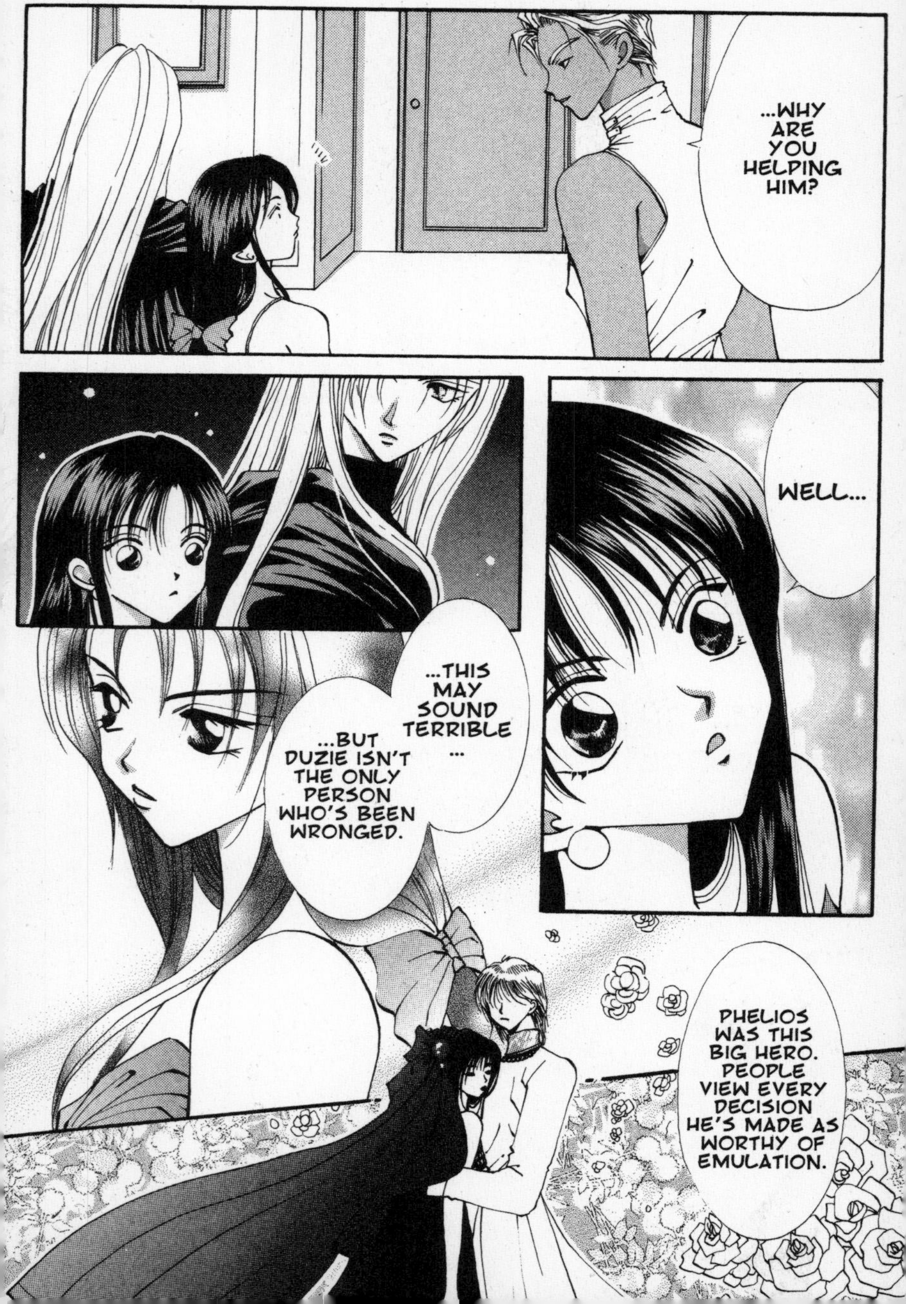
...WHY ARE YOU HELPING HIM?
WELL...
...THIS MAY SOUND TERRIBLE ...
...BUT DUZIE ISN'T THE ONLY PERSON WHO'S BEEN WRONGED.
PHELIOS WAS THIS BIG HERO. PEOPLE VIEW EVERY DECISION HE'S MADE AS WORTHY OF EMULATION.

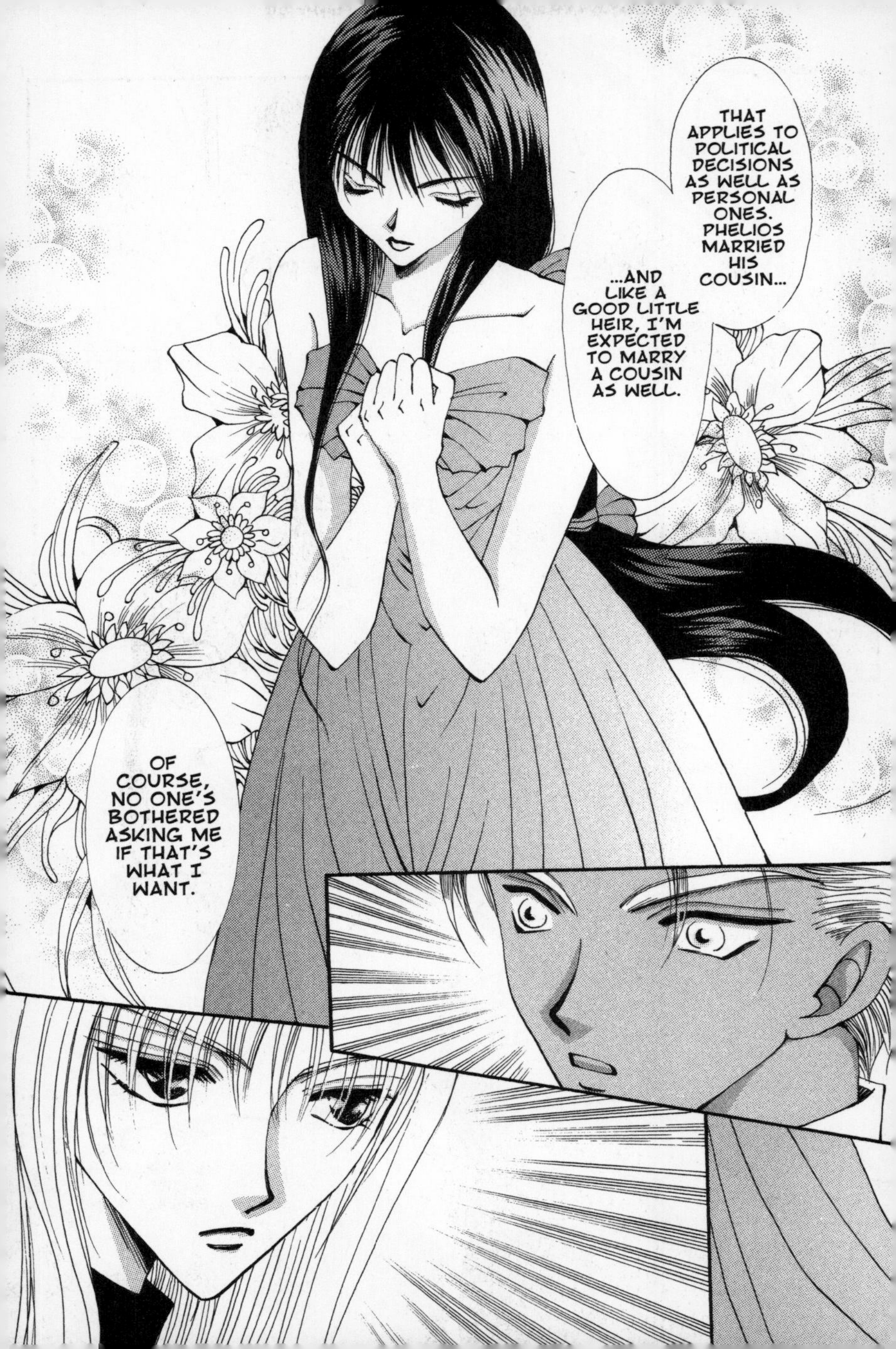
THAT APPLIES TO POLITICAL DECISIONS AS WELL AS PERSONAL ONES. PHELIOS MARRIED HIS COUSIN...
...AND LIKE A GOOD LITTLE HEIR, I'M EXPECTED TO MARRY A COUSIN AS WELL.
OF COURSE, NO ONE'S BOTHERED ASKING ME IF THAT'S WHAT I WANT.

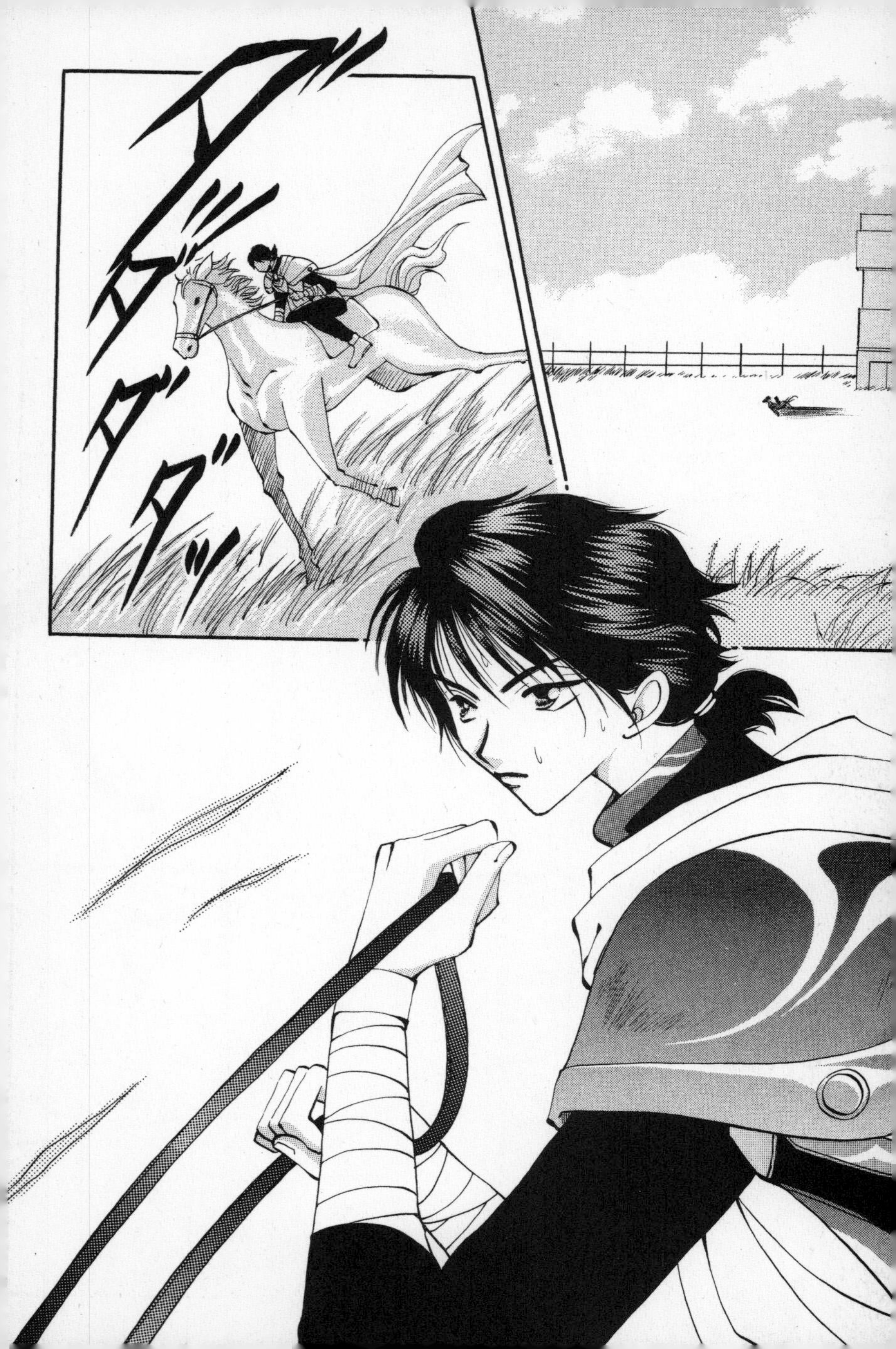
ズダダダッ

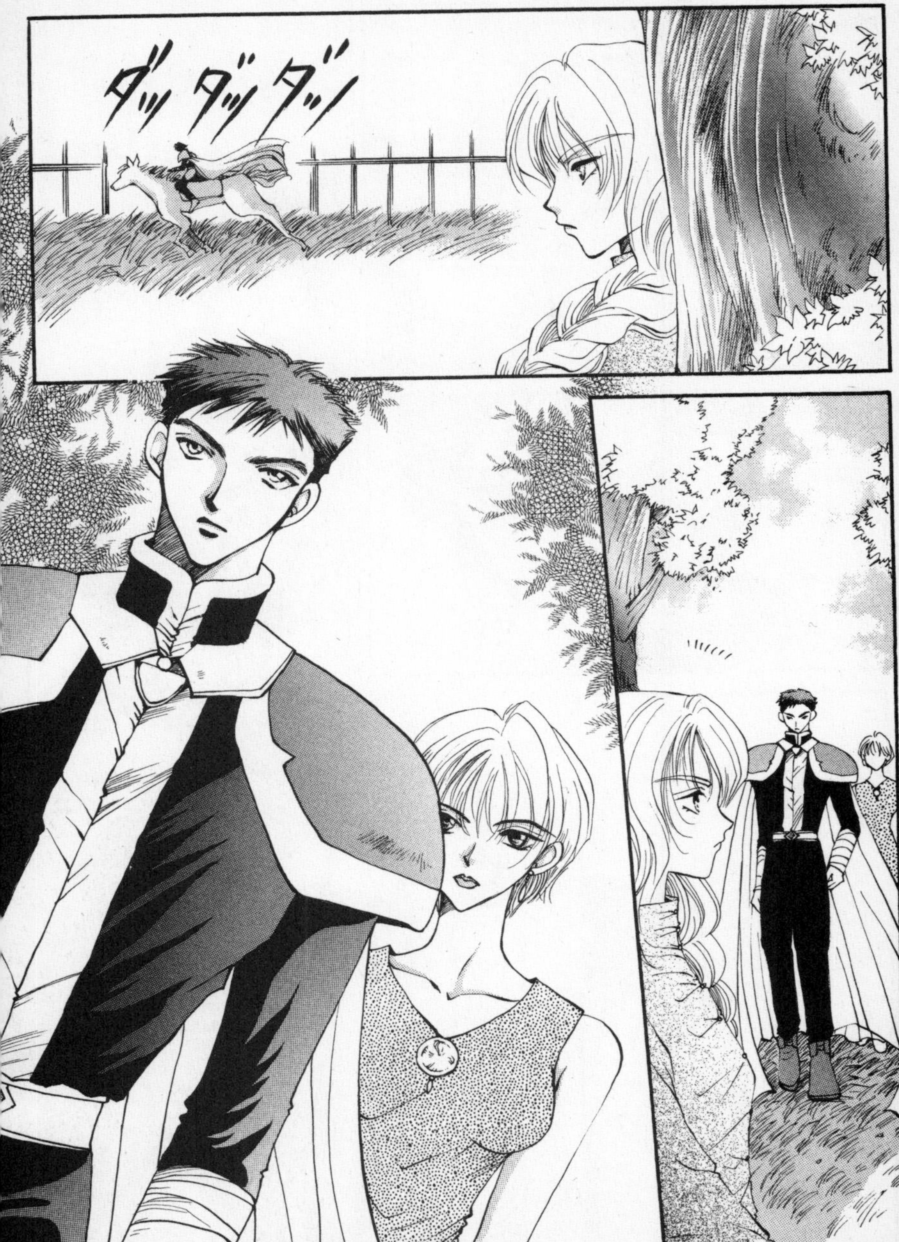
ダッ ダッ ダッ

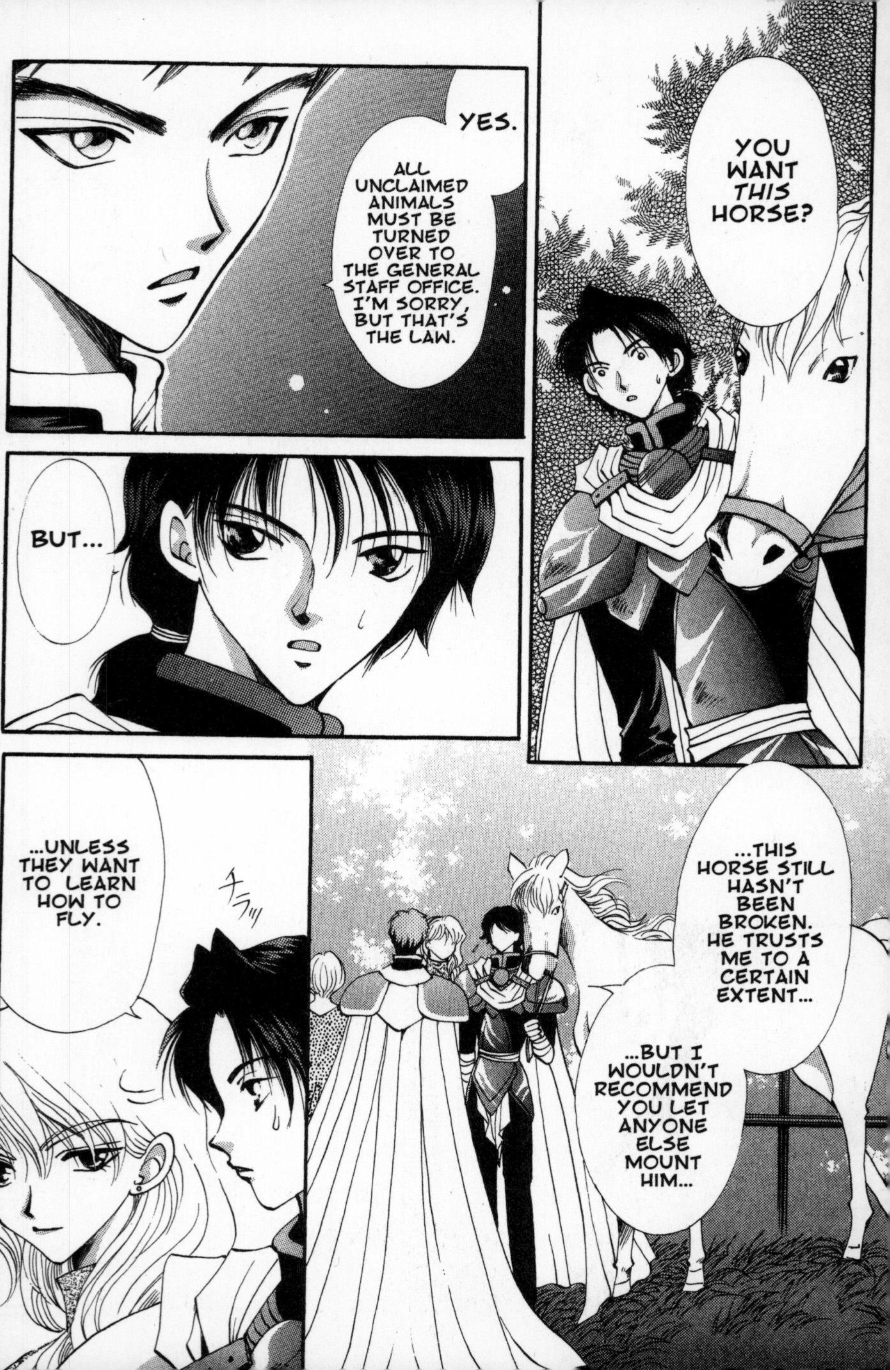
YOU WANT THIS HORSE?
YES.
ALL UNCLAIMED ANIMALS MUST BE TURNED OVER TO THE GENERAL STAFF OFFICE. I'M SORRY, BUT THAT'S THE LAW.
BUT...
...THIS HORSE STILL HASN'T BEEN BROKEN. HE TRUSTS ME TO A CERTAIN EXTENT...
...BUT I WOULDN'T RECOMMEND YOU LET ANYONE ELSE MOUNT HIM...
...UNLESS THEY WANT TO LEARN HOW TO FLY.
チラッ

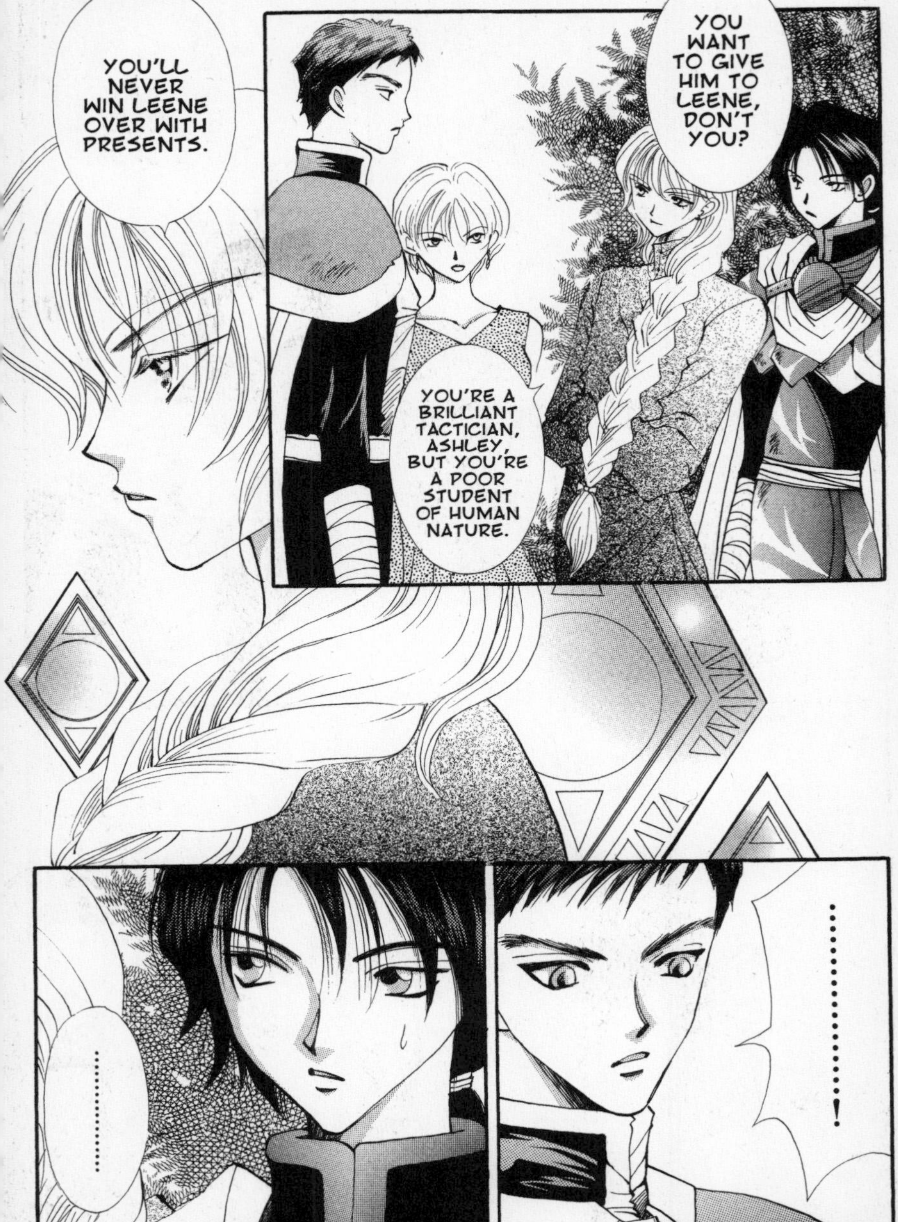
YOU WANT TO GIVE HIM TO LEENE, DON'T YOU?
YOU'RE A BRILLIANT TACTICIAN, ASHLEY, BUT YOU'RE A POOR STUDENT OF HUMAN NATURE.
YOU'LL NEVER WIN LEENE OVER WITH PRESENTS.
......!
......

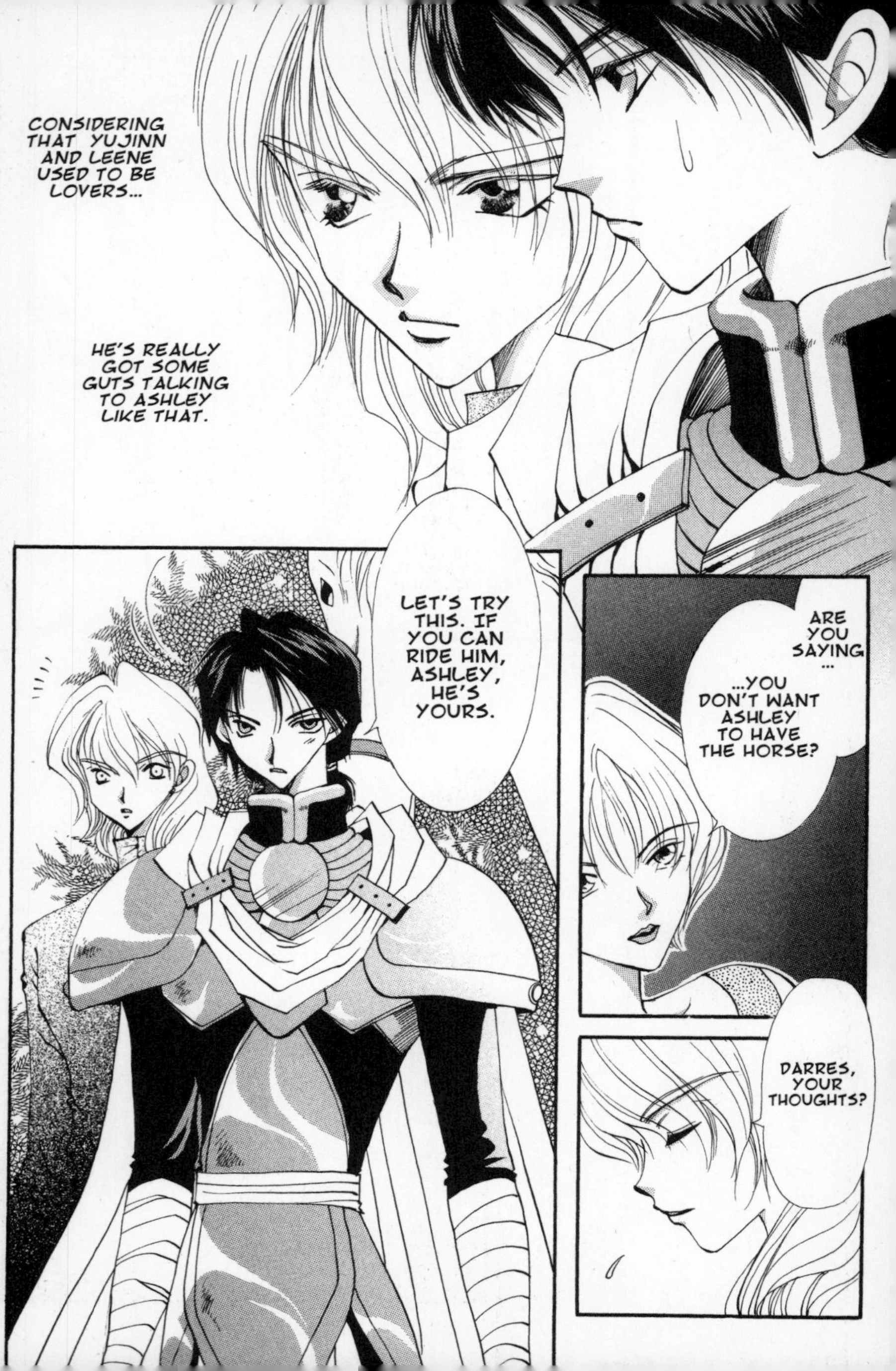
CONSIDERING THAT YUJINN AND LEENE USED TO BE LOVERS...
HE'S REALLY GOT SOME GUTS TALKING TO ASHLEY LIKE THAT.
ARE YOU SAYING...
...YOU DON'T WANT ASHLEY TO HAVE THE HORSE?
DARRES, YOUR THOUGHTS?
LET'S TRY THIS. IF YOU CAN RIDE HIM, ASHLEY, HE'S YOURS.

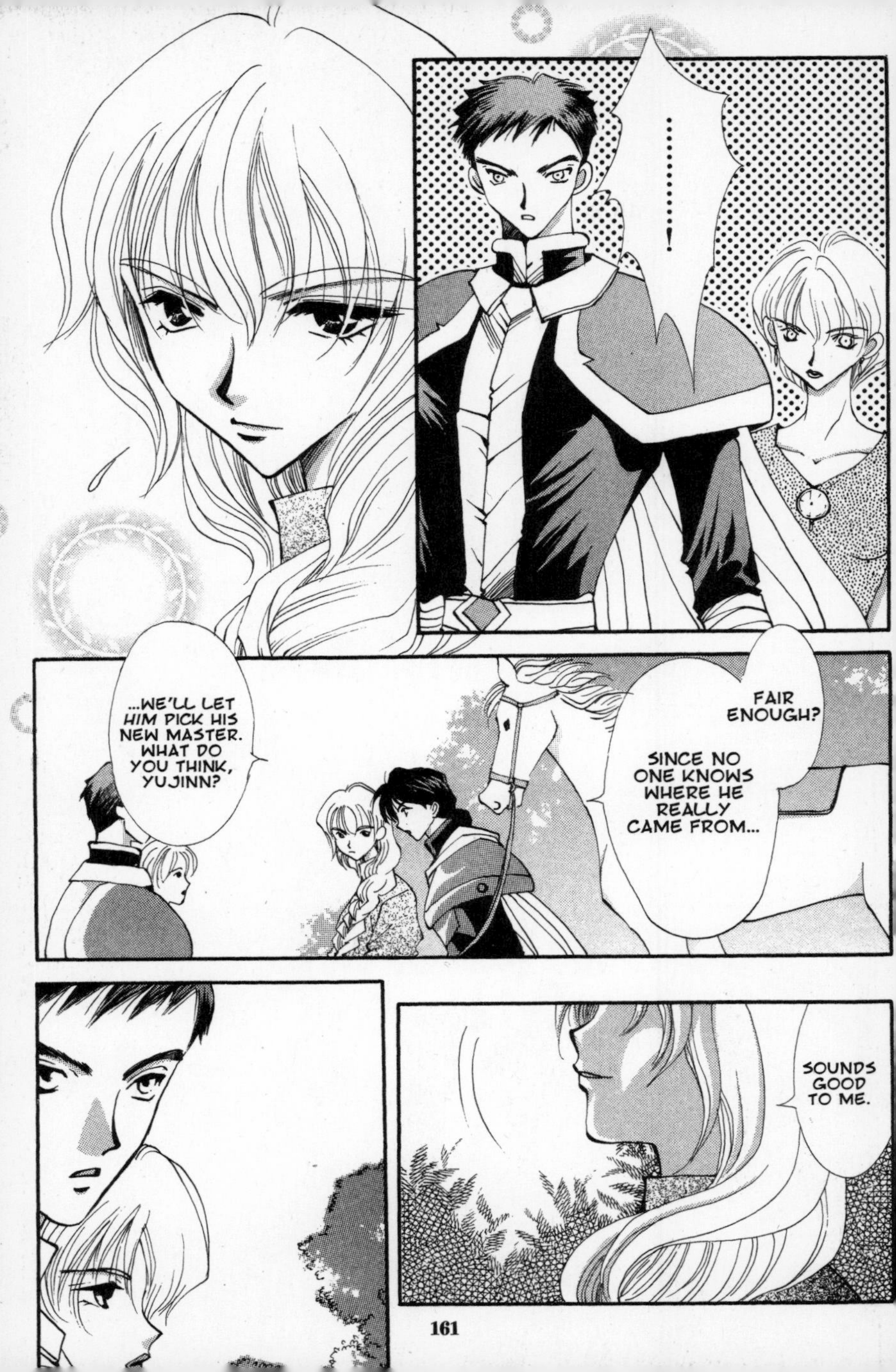
......!
FAIR ENOUGH?
SINCE NO ONE KNOWS WHERE HE REALLY CAME FROM...
...WE'LL LET HIM PICK HIS NEW MASTER. WHAT DO YOU THINK, YUJINN?
SOUNDS GOOD TO ME.

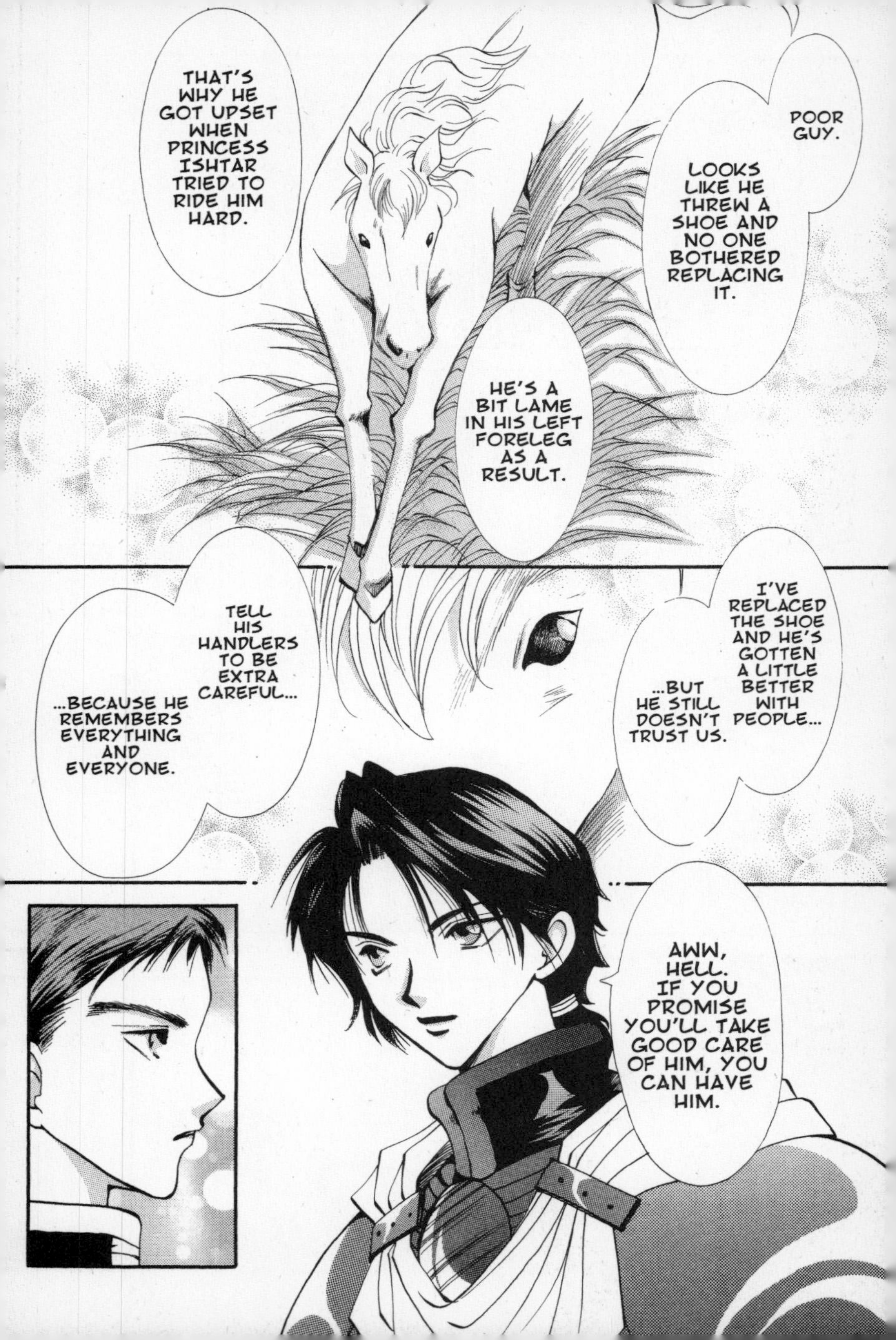
POOR GUY.
LOOKS LIKE HE THREW A SHOE AND NO ONE BOTHERED REPLACING IT.
HE'S A BIT LAME IN HIS LEFT FORELEG AS A RESULT.
THAT'S WHY HE GOT UPSET WHEN PRINCESS ISHTAR TRIED TO RIDE HIM HARD.
I'VE REPLACED THE SHOE AND HE'S GOTTEN A LITTLE BETTER WITH PEOPLE...
...BUT HE STILL DOESN'T TRUST US.
TELL HIS HANDLERS TO BE EXTRA CAREFUL...
...BECAUSE HE REMEMBERS EVERYTHING AND EVERYONE.
AWW, HELL. IF YOU PROMISE YOU'LL TAKE GOOD CARE OF HIM, YOU CAN HAVE HIM.

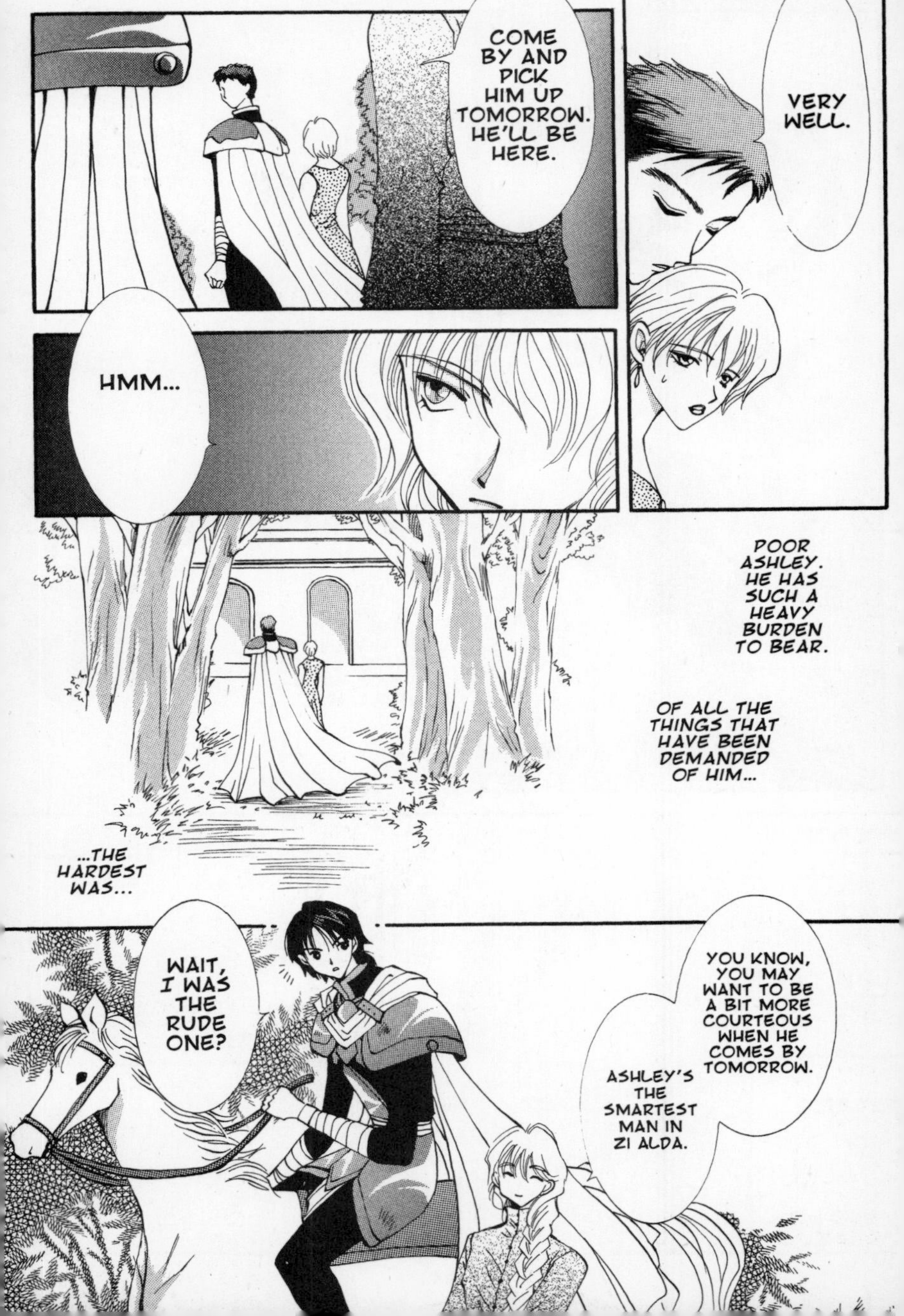
VERY WELL.
COME BY AND PICK HIM UP TOMORROW. HE'LL BE HERE.
HMM...
POOR ASHLEY. HE HAS SUCH A HEAVY BURDEN TO BEAR.
OF ALL THE THINGS THAT HAVE BEEN DEMANDED OF HIM...
...THE HARDEST WAS...
YOU KNOW, YOU MAY WANT TO BE A BIT MORE COURTEOUS WHEN HE COMES BY TOMORROW.
ASHLEY'S THE SMARTEST MAN IN ZI ALDA.
WAIT, I WAS THE RUDE ONE?

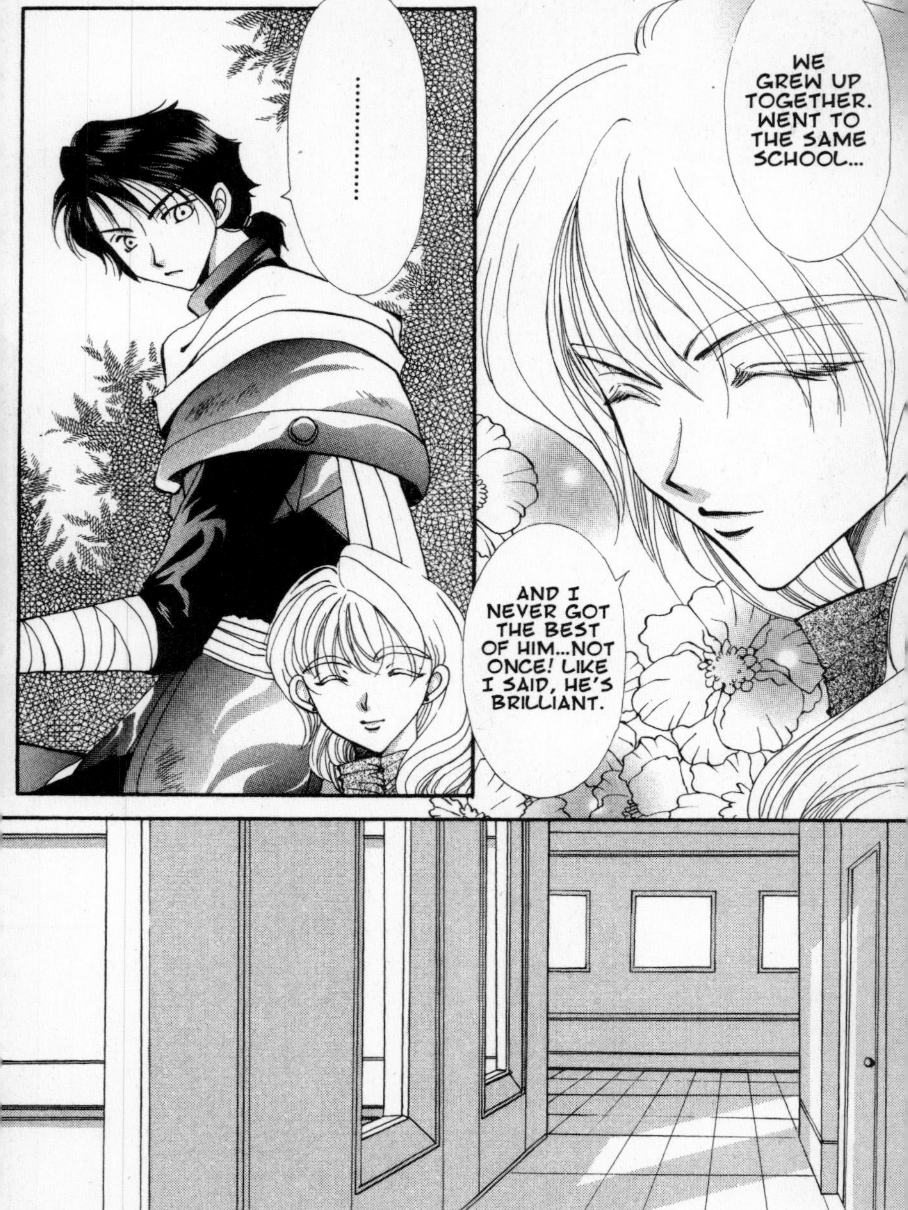
WE GREW UP TOGETHER. WENT TO THE SAME SCHOOL...
AND I NEVER GOT THE BEST OF HIM...NOT ONCE! LIKE I SAID, HE'S BRILLIANT.
....

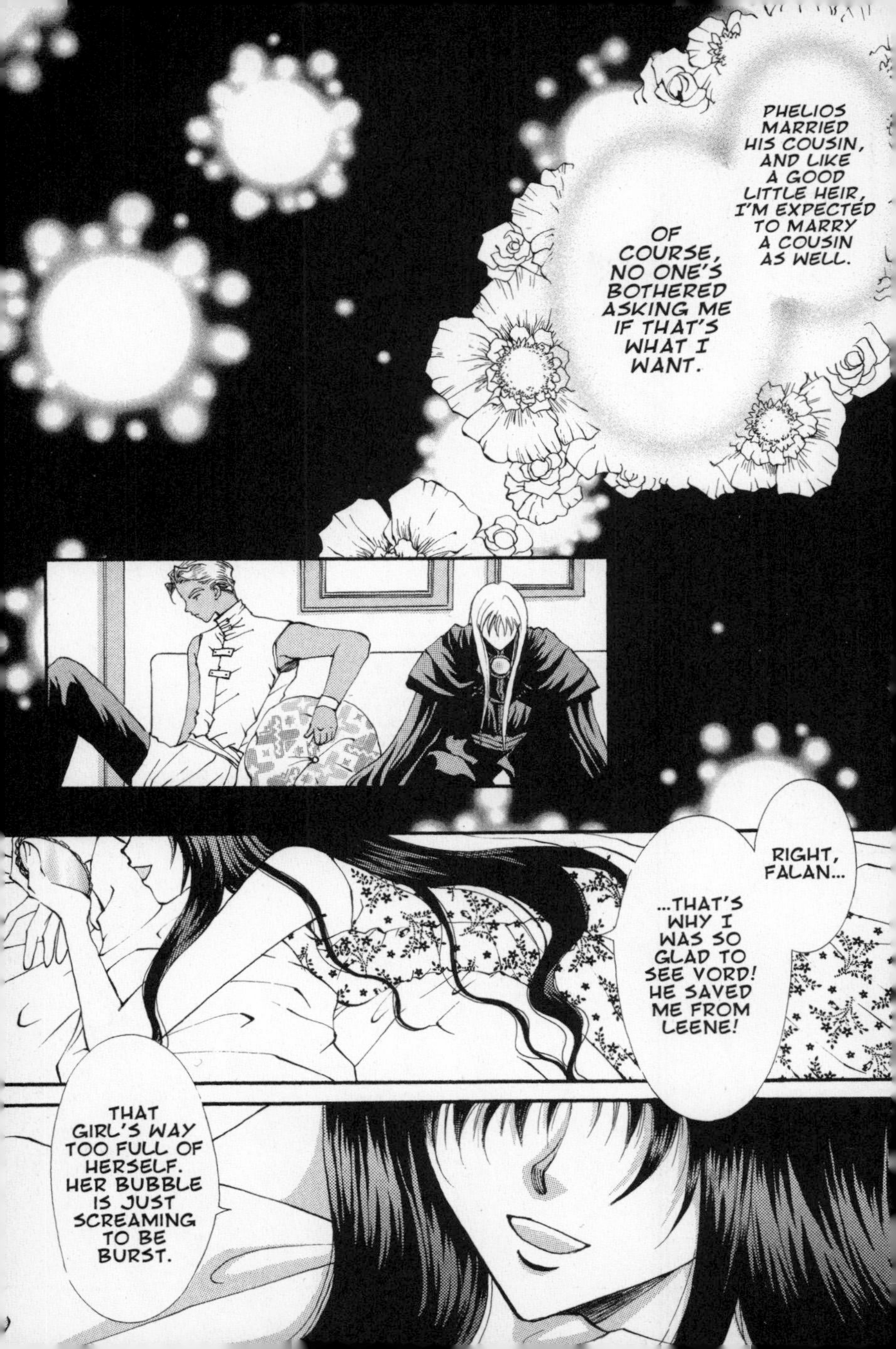
PHELIOS MARRIED HIS COUSIN, AND LIKE A GOOD LITTLE HEIR, I'M EXPECTED TO MARRY A COUSIN AS WELL.
OF COURSE, NO ONE'S BOTHERED ASKING ME IF THAT'S WHAT I WANT.
RIGHT, FALAN...
...THAT'S WHY I WAS SO GLAD TO SEE VORD! HE SAVED ME FROM LEENE!
THAT GIRL'S WAY TOO FULL OF HERSELF. HER BUBBLE IS JUST SCREAMING TO BE BURST.

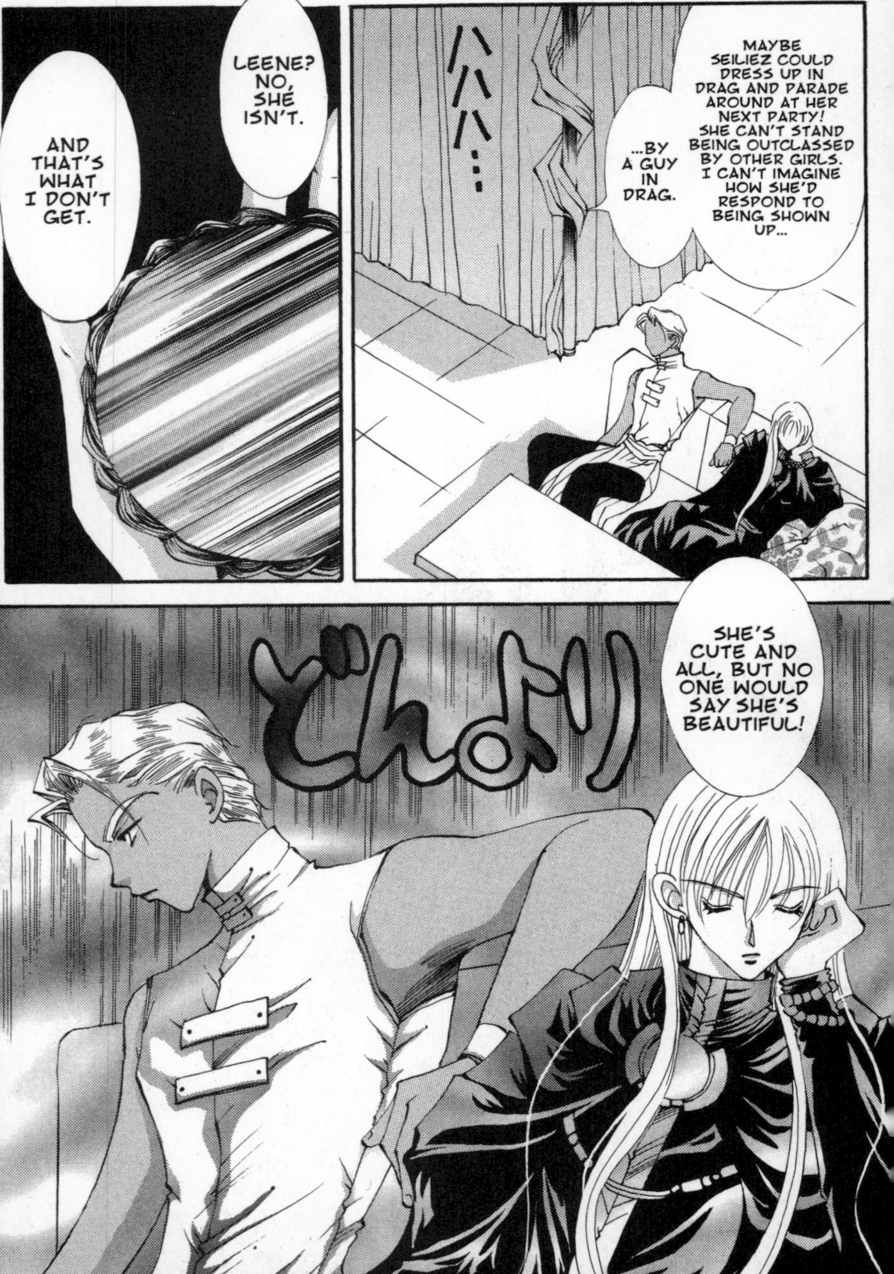
MAYBE SEILIEZ COULD DRESS UP IN DRAG AND PARADE AROUND AT HER NEXT PARTY! SHE CAN'T STAND BEING OUTCLASSED BY OTHER GIRLS. I CAN'T IMAGINE HOW SHE'D RESPOND TO BEING SHOWN UP...
...BY A GUY IN DRAG.
ハハハ…
LEENE? NO, SHE ISN'T.
AND THAT'S WHAT I DON'T GET.
SHE'S CUTE AND ALL, BUT NO ONE WOULD SAY SHE'S BEAUTIFUL!
どんより

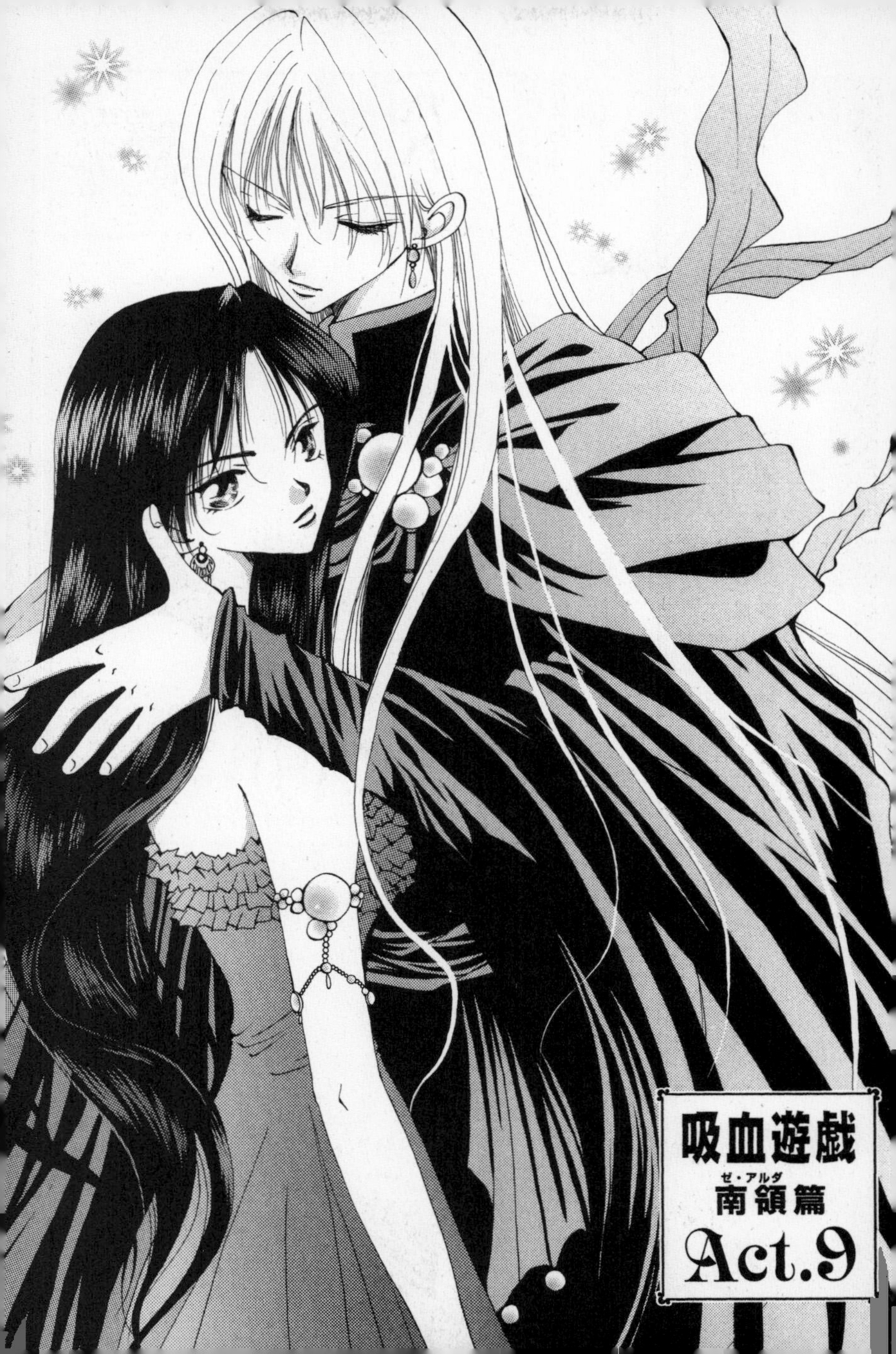
吸血遊戯
ゼ・アルダ
南領篇
Act.9

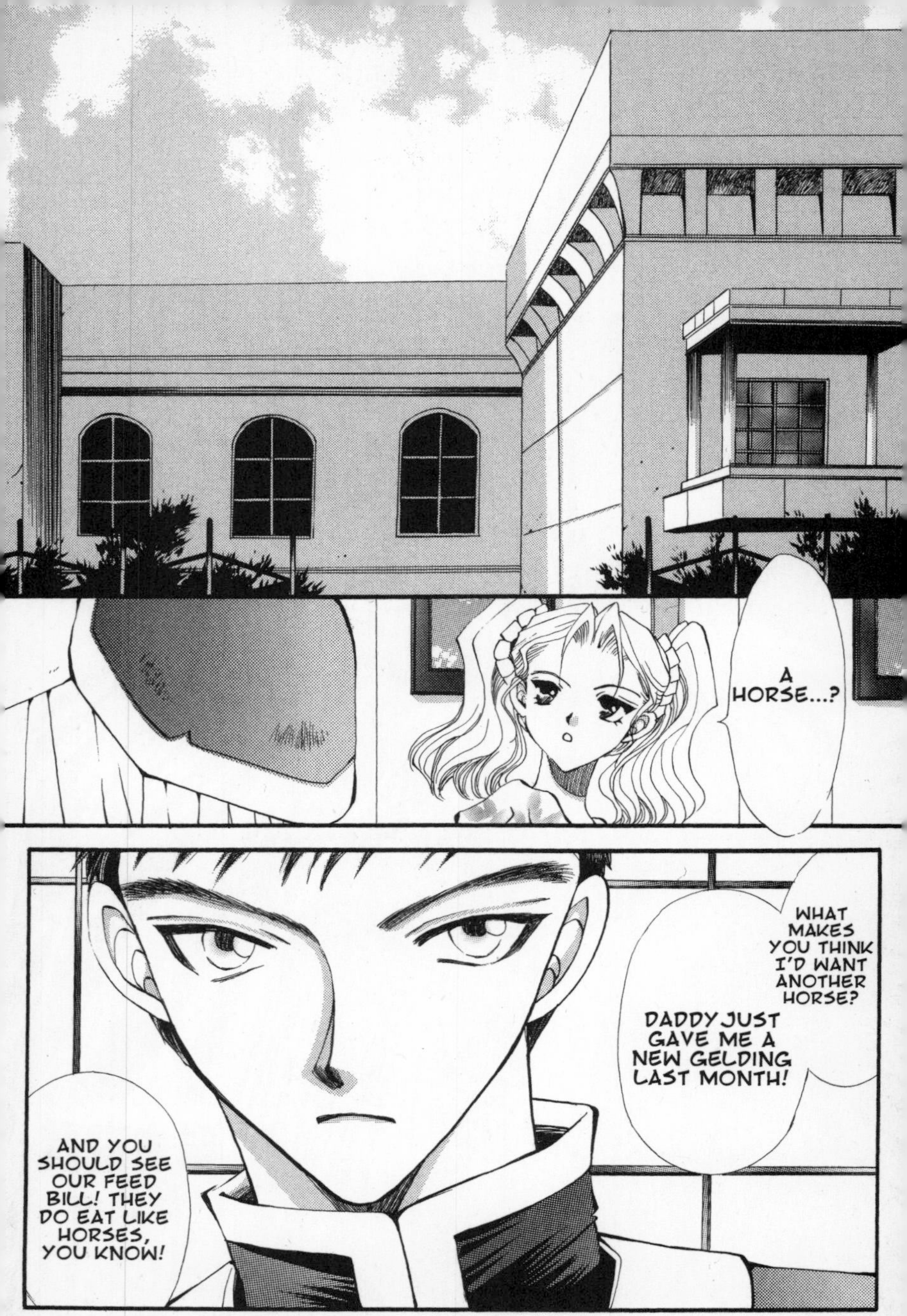
A HORSE...?
WHAT MAKES YOU THINK I'D WANT ANOTHER HORSE?
DADDY JUST GAVE ME A NEW GELDING LAST MONTH!
AND YOU SHOULD SEE OUR FEED BILL! THEY DO EAT LIKE HORSES, YOU KNOW!

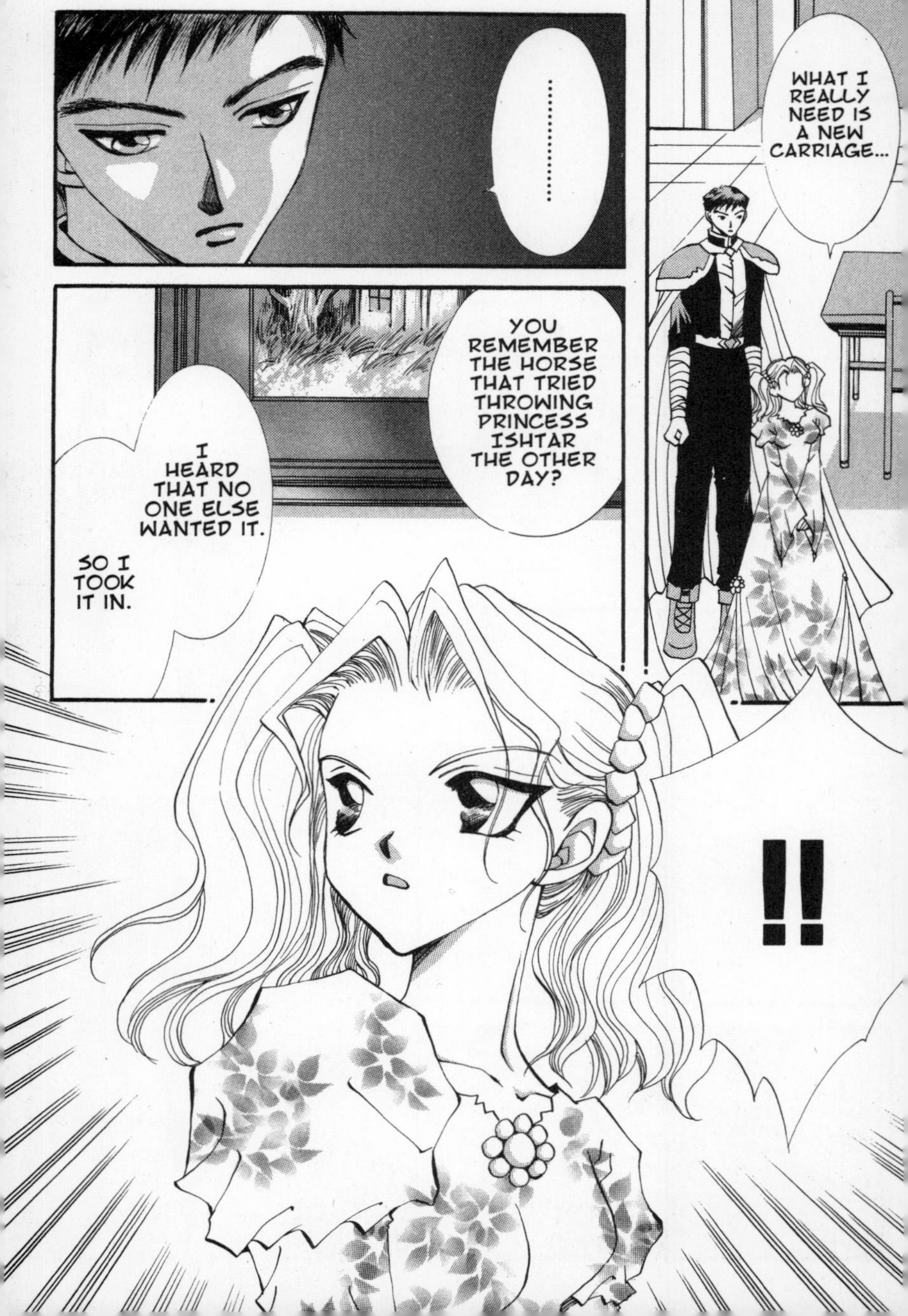
WHAT I REALLY NEED IS A NEW CARRIAGE...
......
YOU REMEMBER THE HORSE THAT TRIED THROWING PRINCESS ISHTAR THE OTHER DAY?
I HEARD THAT NO ONE ELSE WANTED IT.
SO I TOOK IT IN.
!!

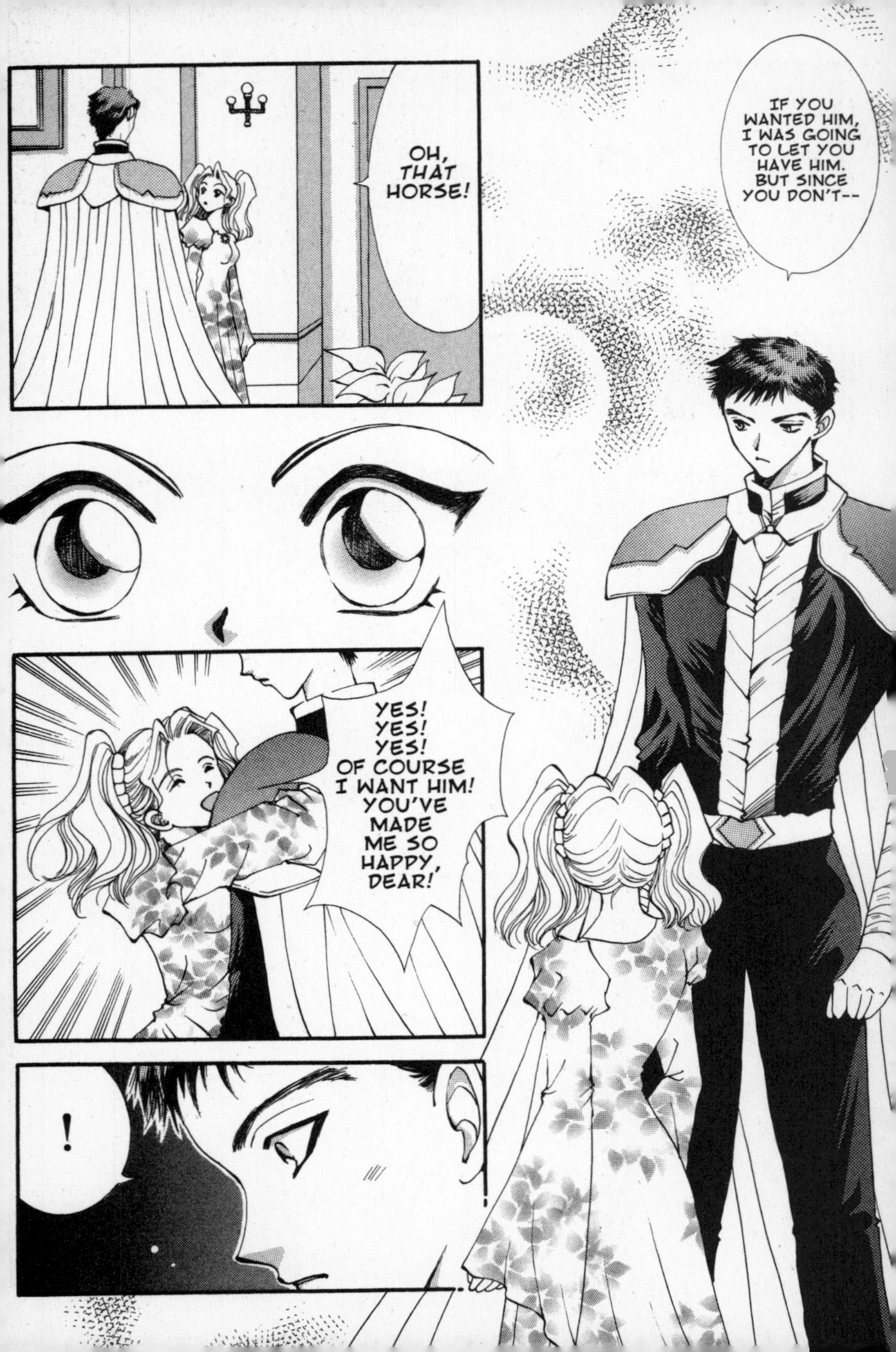
IF YOU WANTED HIM, I WAS GOING TO LET YOU HAVE HIM. BUT SINCE YOU DON'T--
OH, *THAT* HORSE!
YES! YES! YES! OF COURSE I WANT HIM! YOU'VE MADE ME SO HAPPY, DEAR!
!

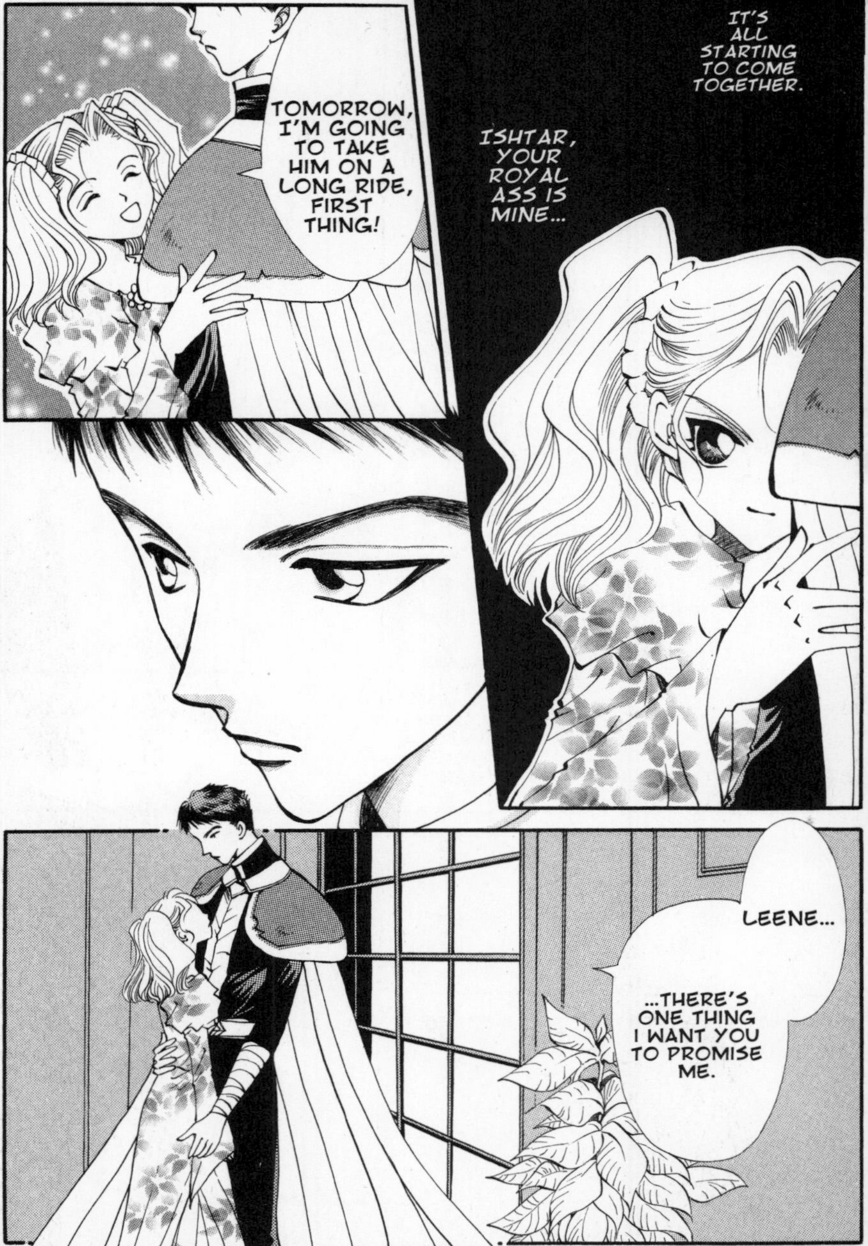
IT'S ALL STARTING TO COME TOGETHER.
ISHTAR, YOUR ROYAL ASS IS MINE...
TOMORROW, I'M GOING TO TAKE HIM ON A LONG RIDE, FIRST THING!
LEENE...
...THERE'S ONE THING I WANT YOU TO PROMISE ME.

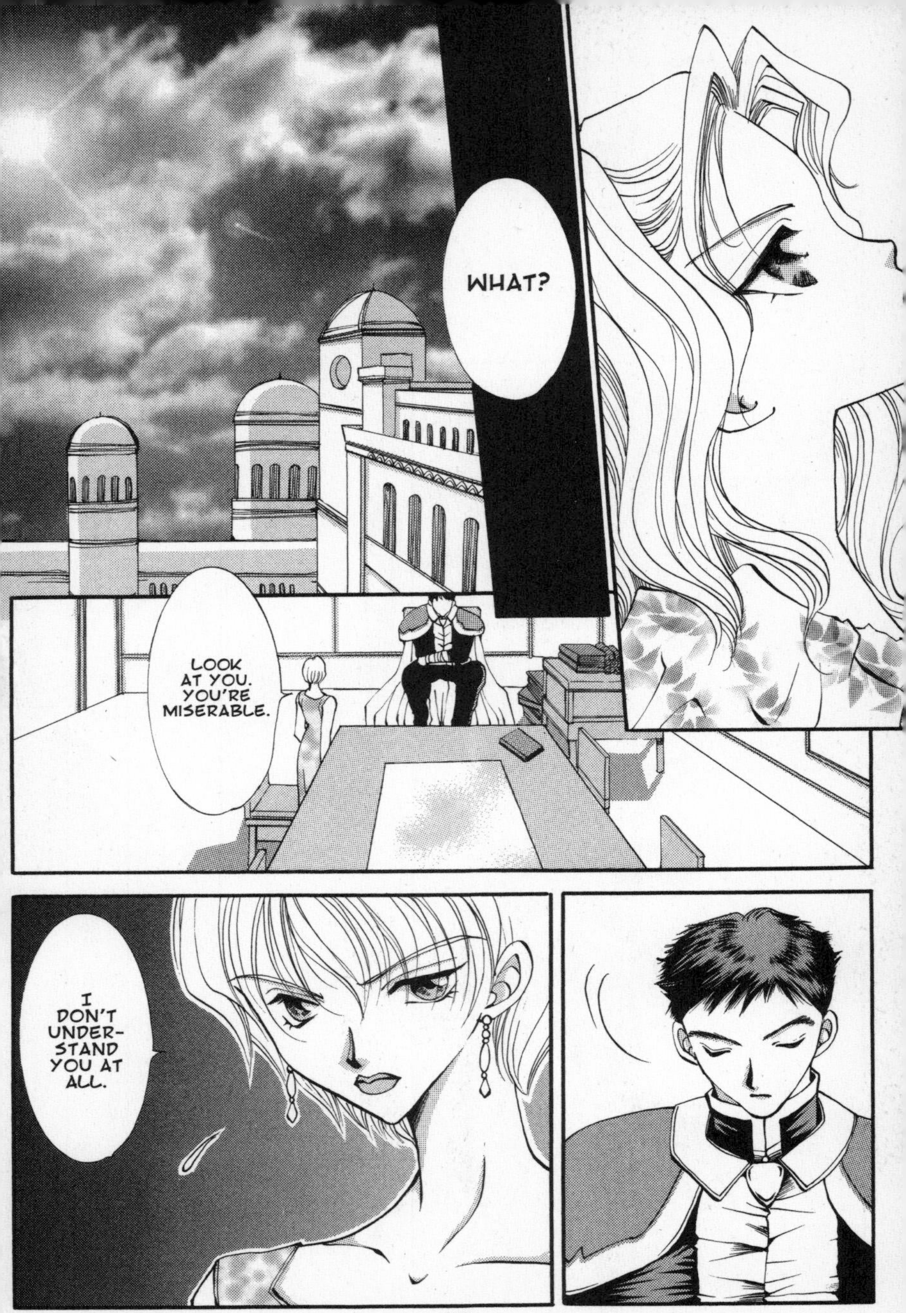
WHAT?
LOOK AT YOU. YOU'RE MISERABLE.
I DON'T UNDER-STAND YOU AT ALL.

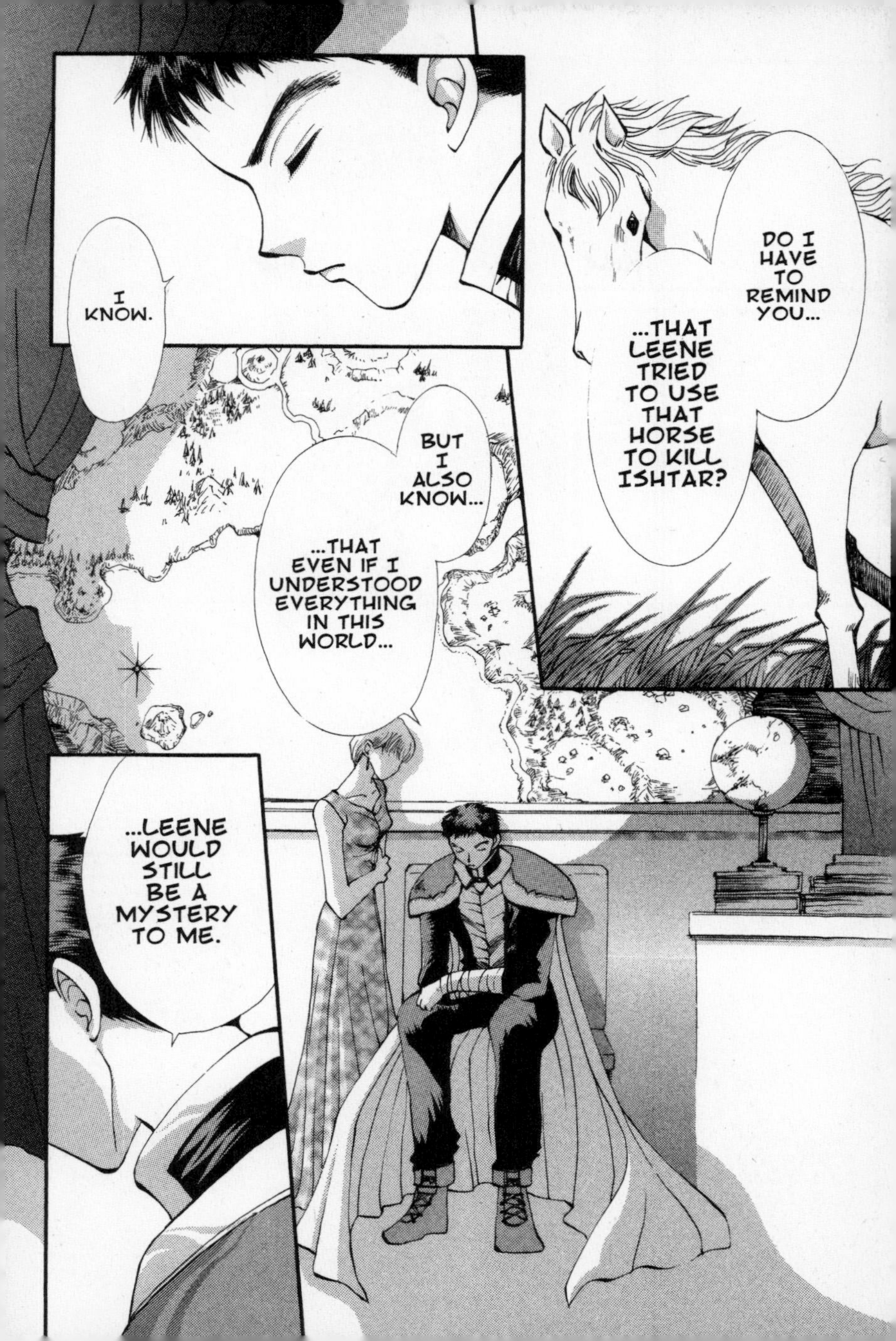
DO I HAVE TO REMIND YOU...
...THAT LEENE TRIED TO USE THAT HORSE TO KILL ISHTAR?
I KNOW.
BUT I ALSO KNOW...
...THAT EVEN IF I UNDERSTOOD EVERYTHING IN THIS WORLD...
...LEENE WOULD STILL BE A MYSTERY TO ME.

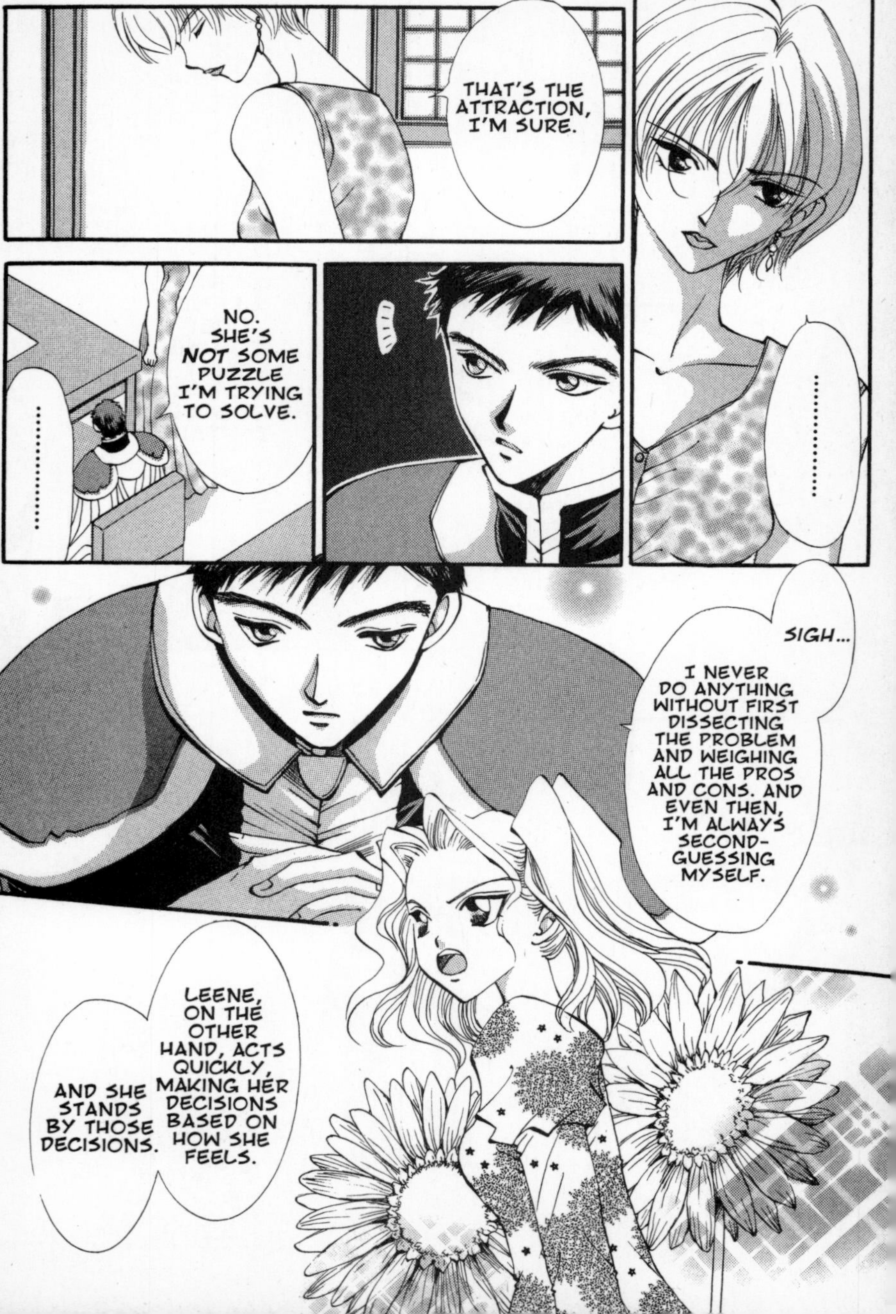
......
THAT'S THE ATTRACTION, I'M SURE.
NO. SHE'S NOT SOME PUZZLE I'M TRYING TO SOLVE.
......
SIGH...
I NEVER DO ANYTHING WITHOUT FIRST DISSECTING THE PROBLEM AND WEIGHING ALL THE PROS AND CONS. AND EVEN THEN, I'M ALWAYS SECOND-GUESSING MYSELF.
LEENE, ON THE OTHER HAND, ACTS QUICKLY, MAKING HER DECISIONS BASED ON HOW SHE FEELS.
AND SHE STANDS BY THOSE DECISIONS.

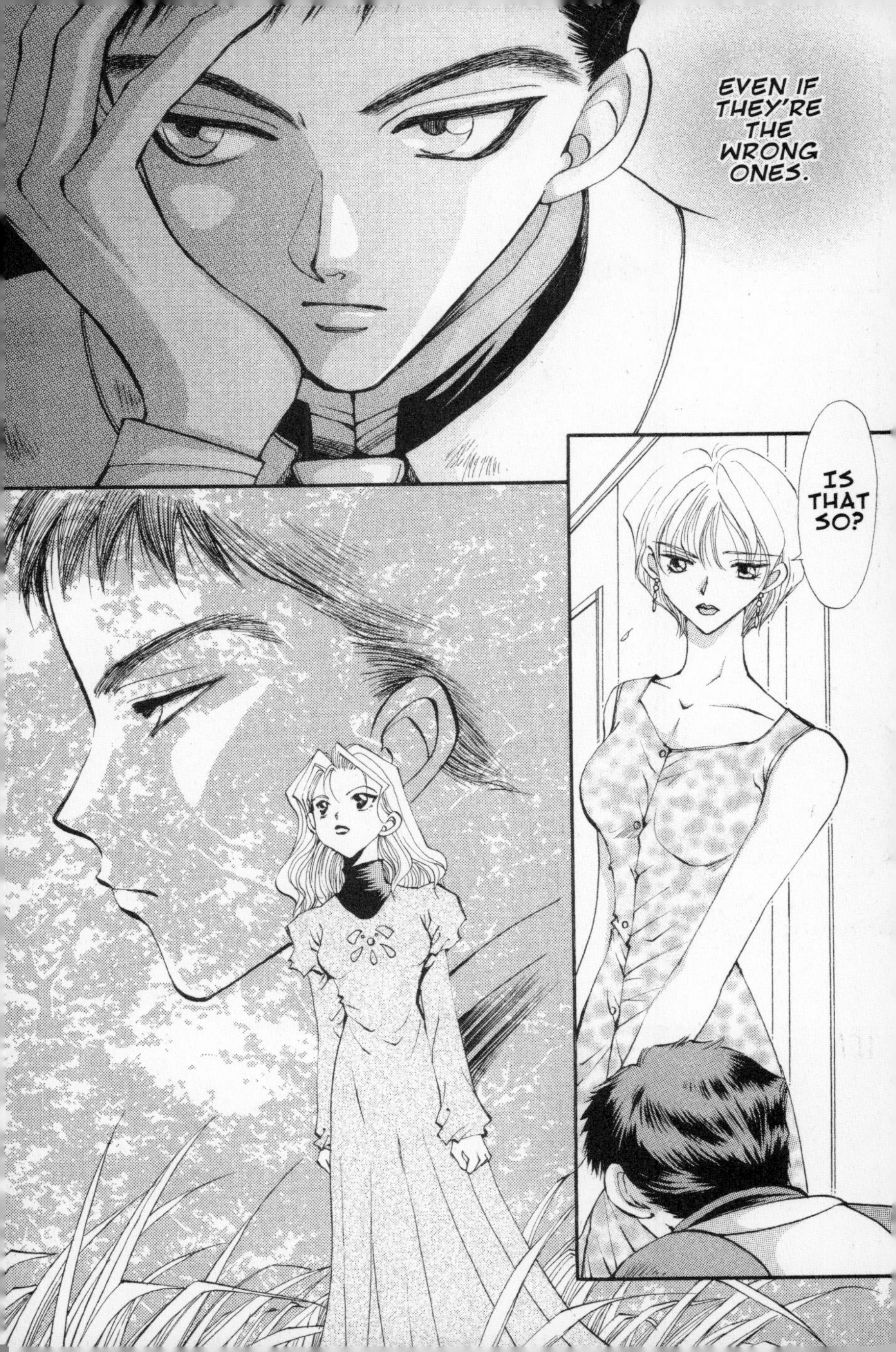
EVEN IF THEY'RE THE WRONG ONES.
IS THAT SO?

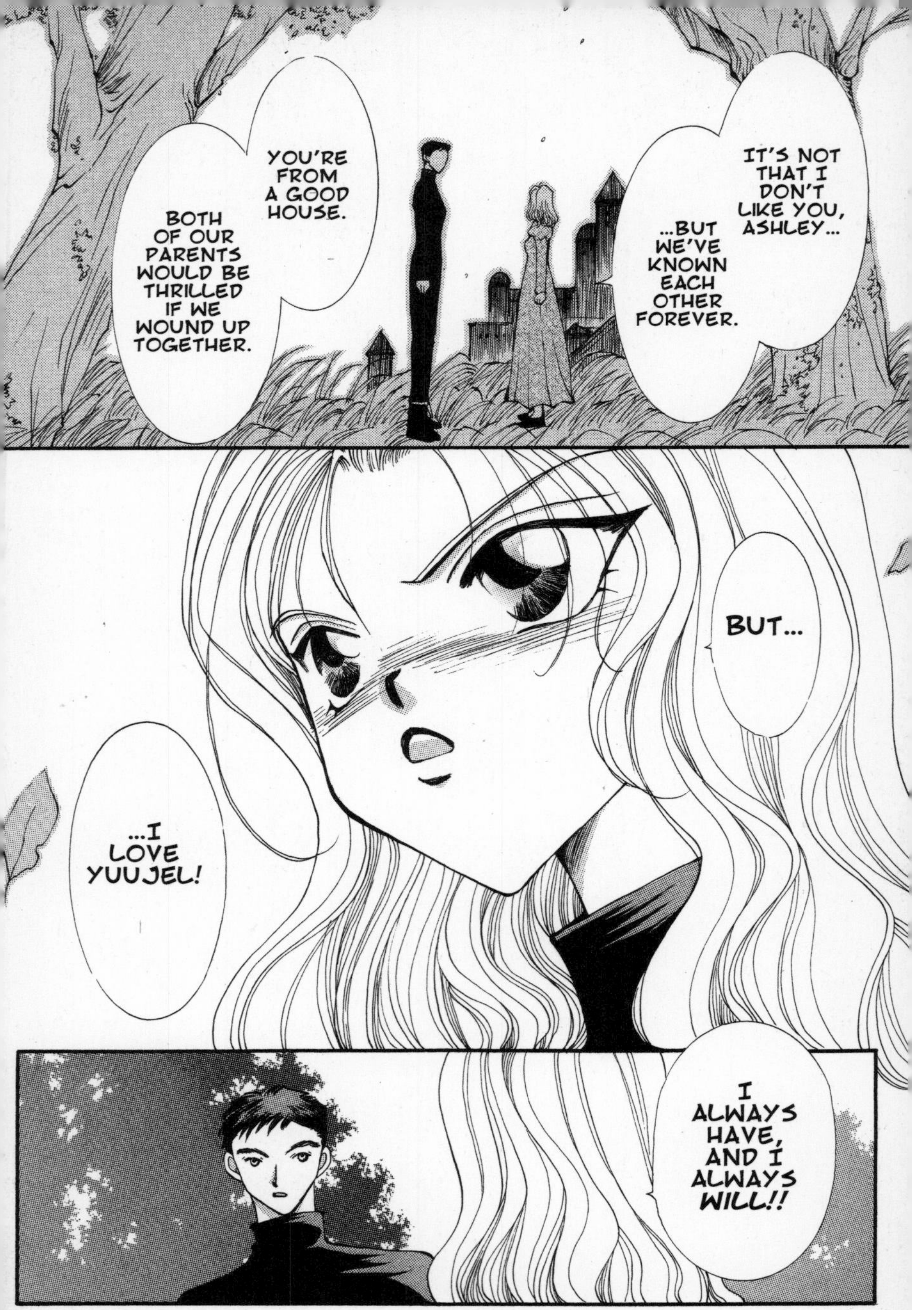
IT'S NOT THAT I DON'T LIKE YOU, ASHLEY...
...BUT WE'VE KNOWN EACH OTHER FOREVER.
YOU'RE FROM A GOOD HOUSE.
BOTH OF OUR PARENTS WOULD BE THRILLED IF WE WOUND UP TOGETHER.
BUT...
...I LOVE YUUJEL!
I ALWAYS HAVE, AND I ALWAYS WILL!!

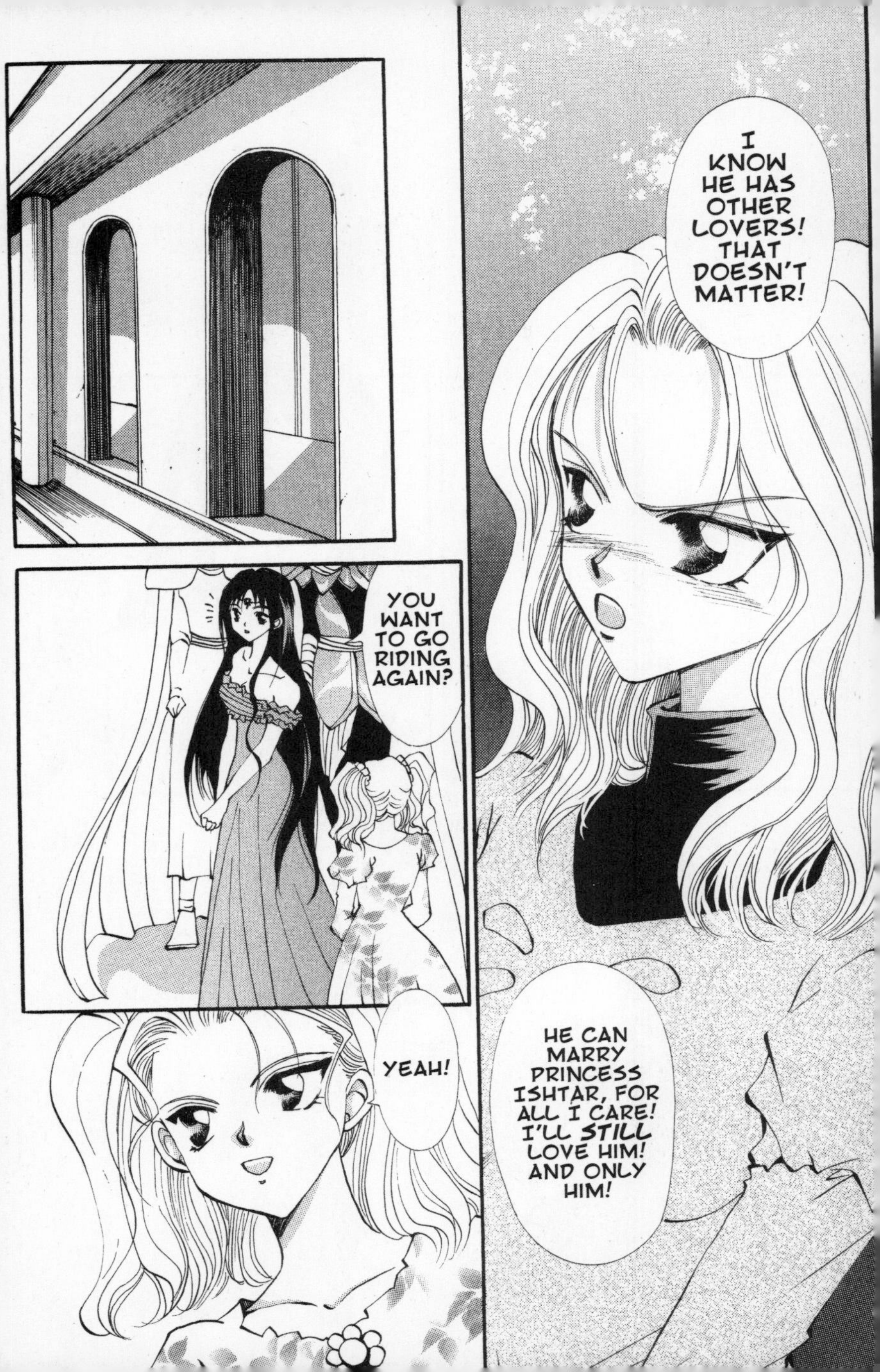
I KNOW HE HAS OTHER LOVERS! THAT DOESN'T MATTER!
HE CAN MARRY PRINCESS ISHTAR, FOR ALL I CARE! I'LL *STILL* LOVE HIM! AND ONLY HIM!
YOU WANT TO GO RIDING AGAIN?
YEAH!

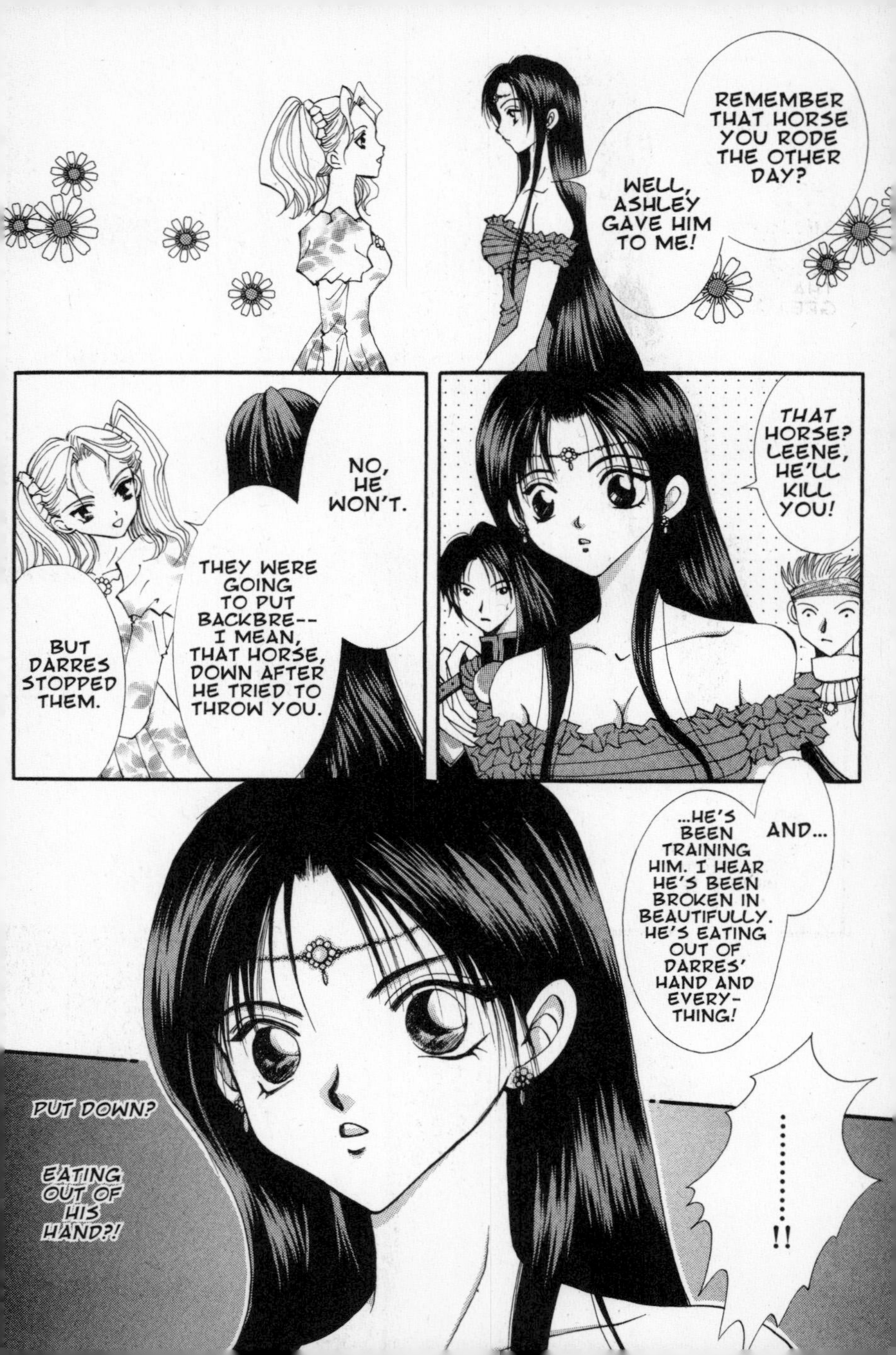

REMEMBER THAT HORSE YOU RODE THE OTHER DAY?
WELL, ASHLEY GAVE HIM TO ME!
THAT HORSE? LEENE, HE'LL KILL YOU!
NO, HE WON'T.
THEY WERE GOING TO PUT BACKBRE-- I MEAN, THAT HORSE, DOWN AFTER HE TRIED TO THROW YOU.
BUT DARRES STOPPED THEM.
AND...
...HE'S BEEN TRAINING HIM. I HEAR HE'S BEEN BROKEN IN BEAUTIFULLY. HE'S EATING OUT OF DARRES' HAND AND EVERYTHING!
......!!
PUT DOWN?
EATING OUT OF HIS HAND?!

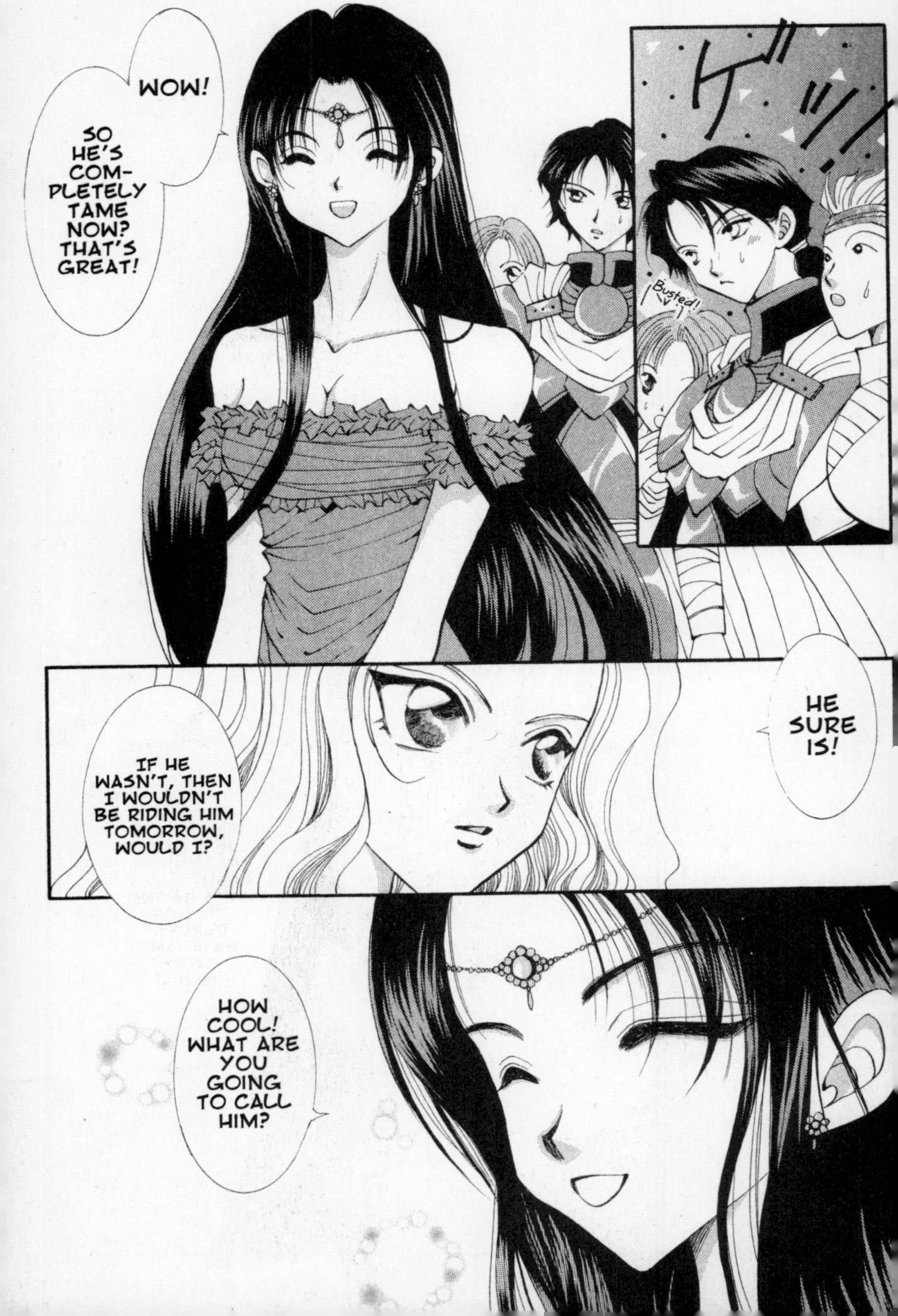
WOW!
SO HE'S COM-PLETELY TAME NOW? THAT'S GREAT!
Busted!
HE SURE IS!
IF HE WASN'T, THEN I WOULDN'T BE RIDING HIM TOMORROW, WOULD I?
HOW COOL! WHAT ARE YOU GOING TO CALL HIM?

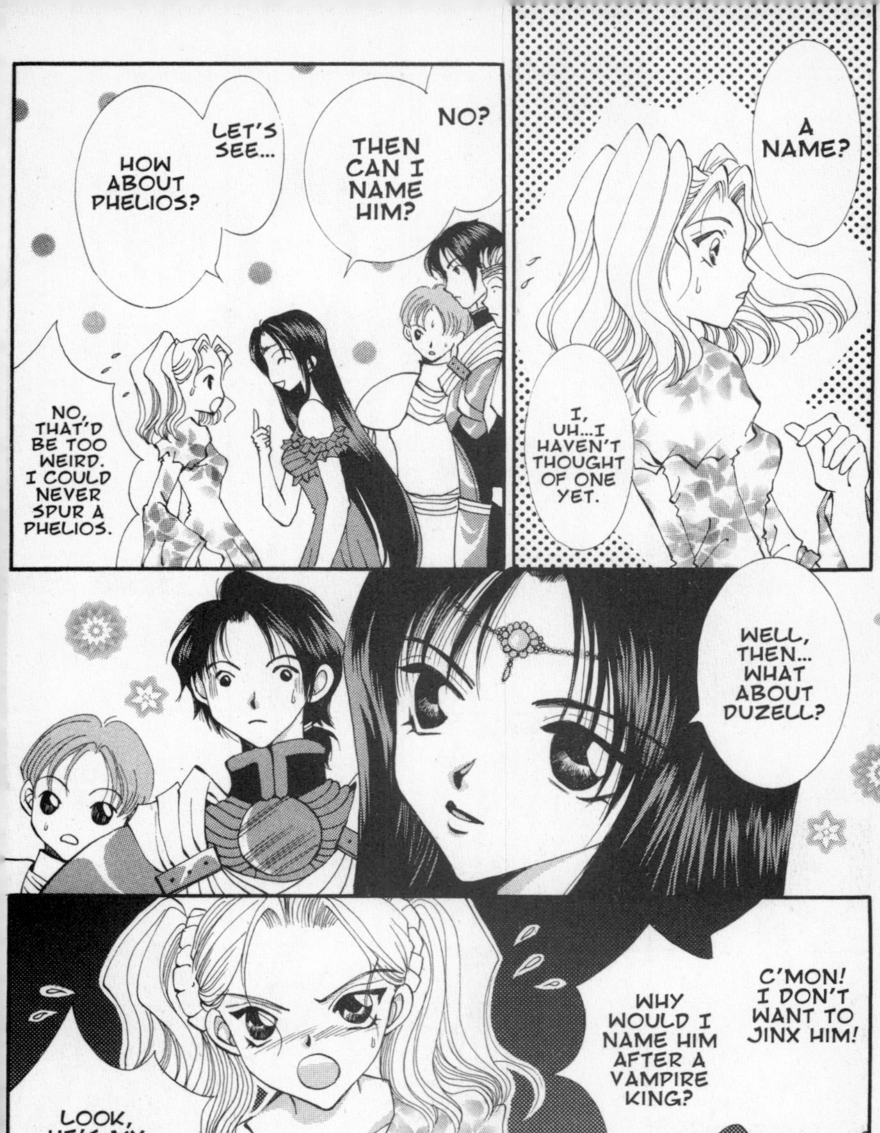
A NAME?
I, UH...I HAVEN'T THOUGHT OF ONE YET.
NO? THEN CAN I NAME HIM?
LET'S SEE... HOW ABOUT PHELIOS?
NO, THAT'D BE TOO WEIRD. I COULD NEVER SPUR A PHELIOS.
WELL, THEN... WHAT ABOUT DUZELL?
C'MON! I DON'T WANT TO JINX HIM!
WHY WOULD I NAME HIM AFTER A VAMPIRE KING?
LOOK, HE'S MY HORSE, OKAY? **I'M** GONNA NAME HIM!

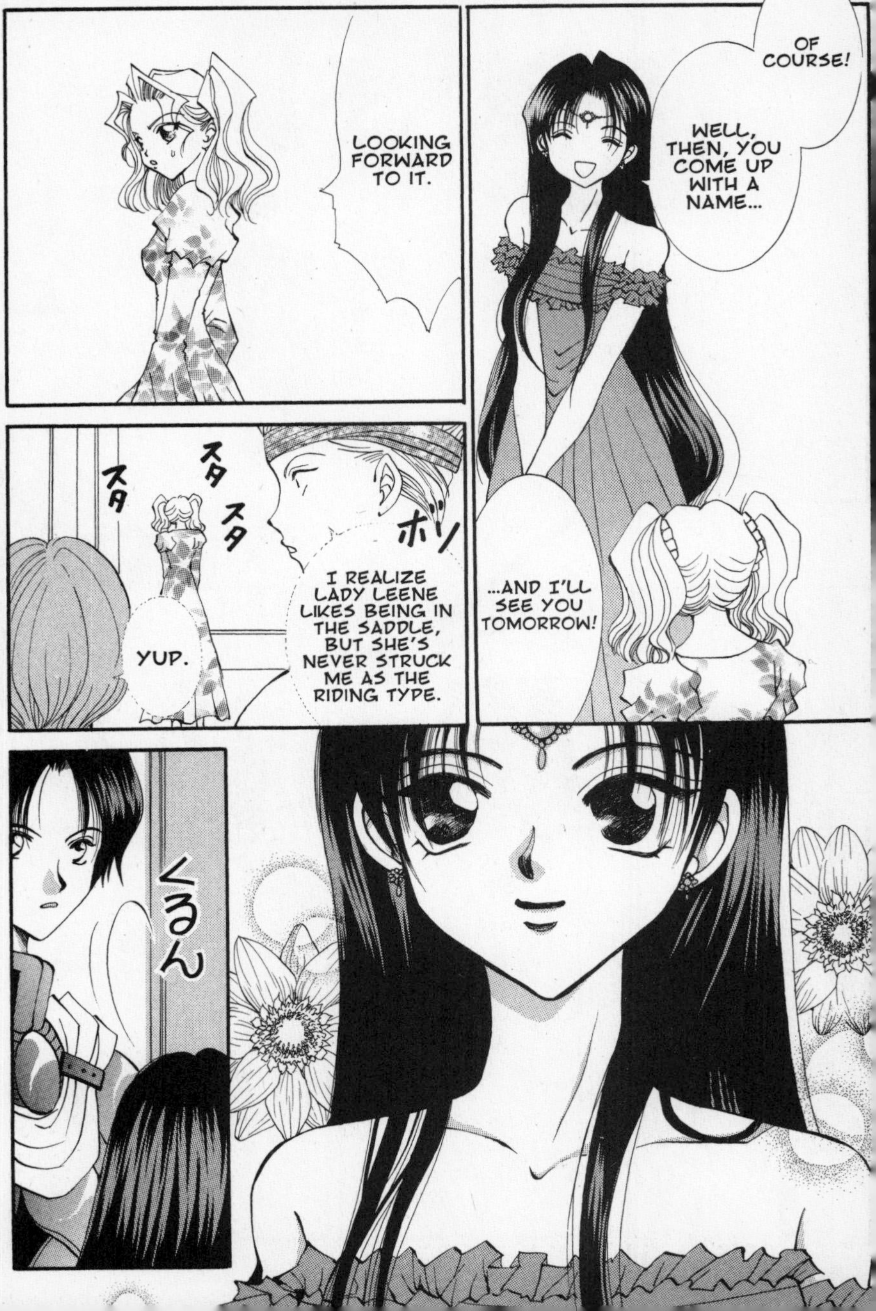
OF COURSE!
WELL, THEN, YOU COME UP WITH A NAME...
...AND I'LL SEE YOU TOMORROW!
LOOKING FORWARD TO IT.
ボソ
スタ
スタ
スタ
I REALIZE LADY LEENE LIKES BEING IN THE SADDLE, BUT SHE'S NEVER STRUCK ME AS THE RIDING TYPE.
YUP.
くるん

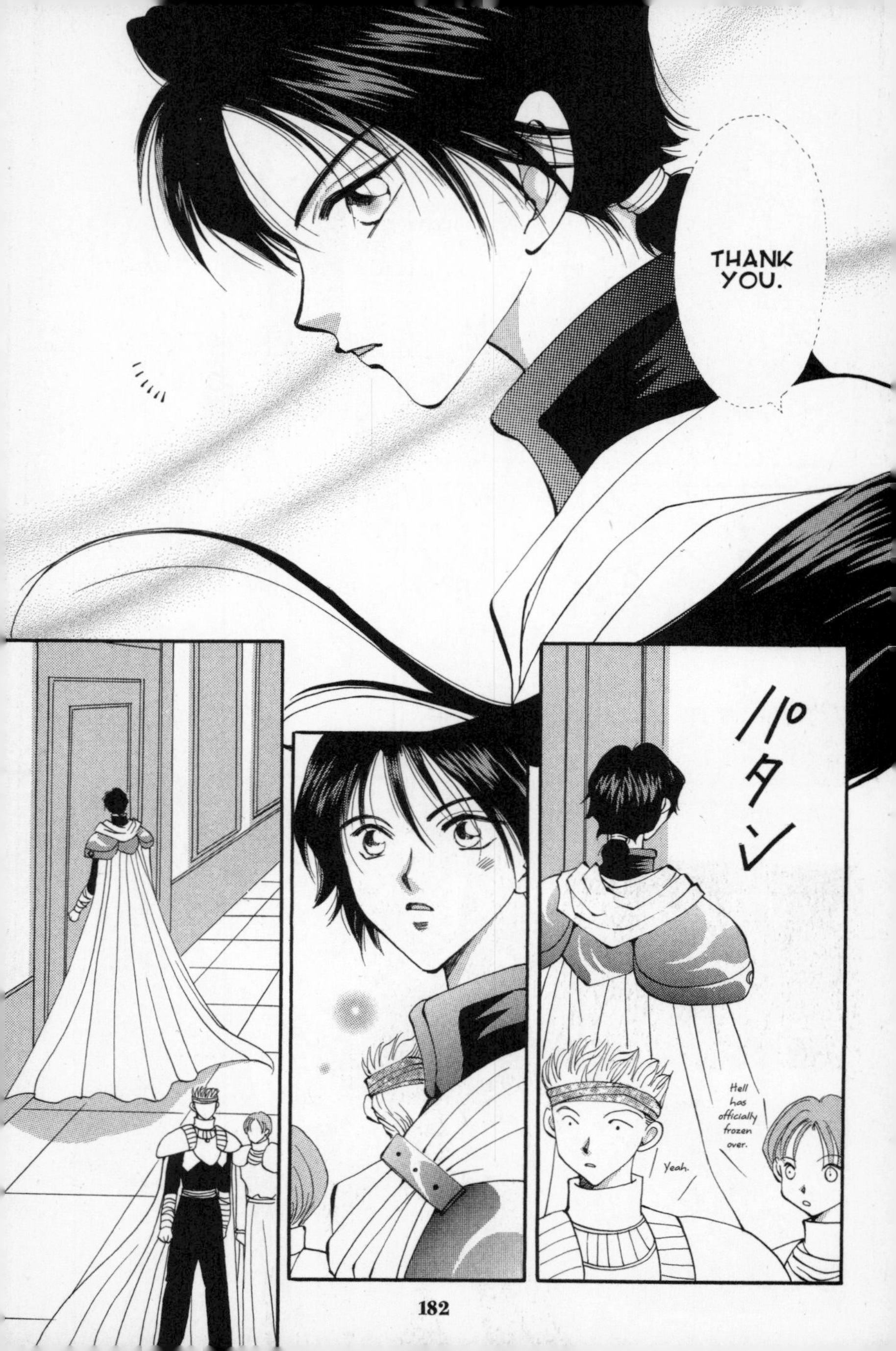
THANK YOU.
パタン
Hell has officially frozen over.
Yeah.

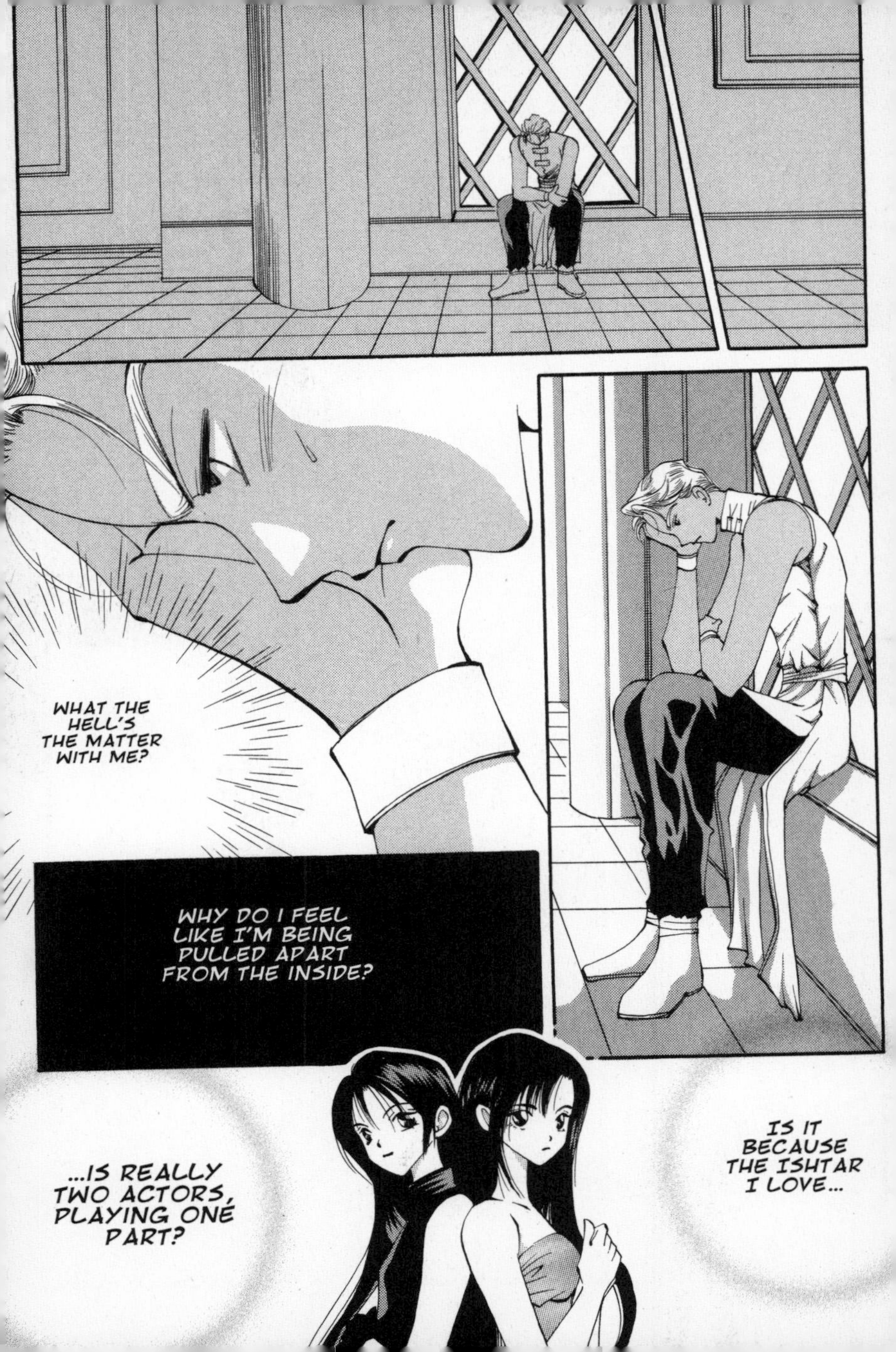
WHAT THE HELL'S THE MATTER WITH ME?
WHY DO I FEEL LIKE I'M BEING PULLED APART FROM THE INSIDE?
IS IT BECAUSE THE ISHTAR I LOVE...
...IS REALLY TWO ACTORS, PLAYING ONE PART?

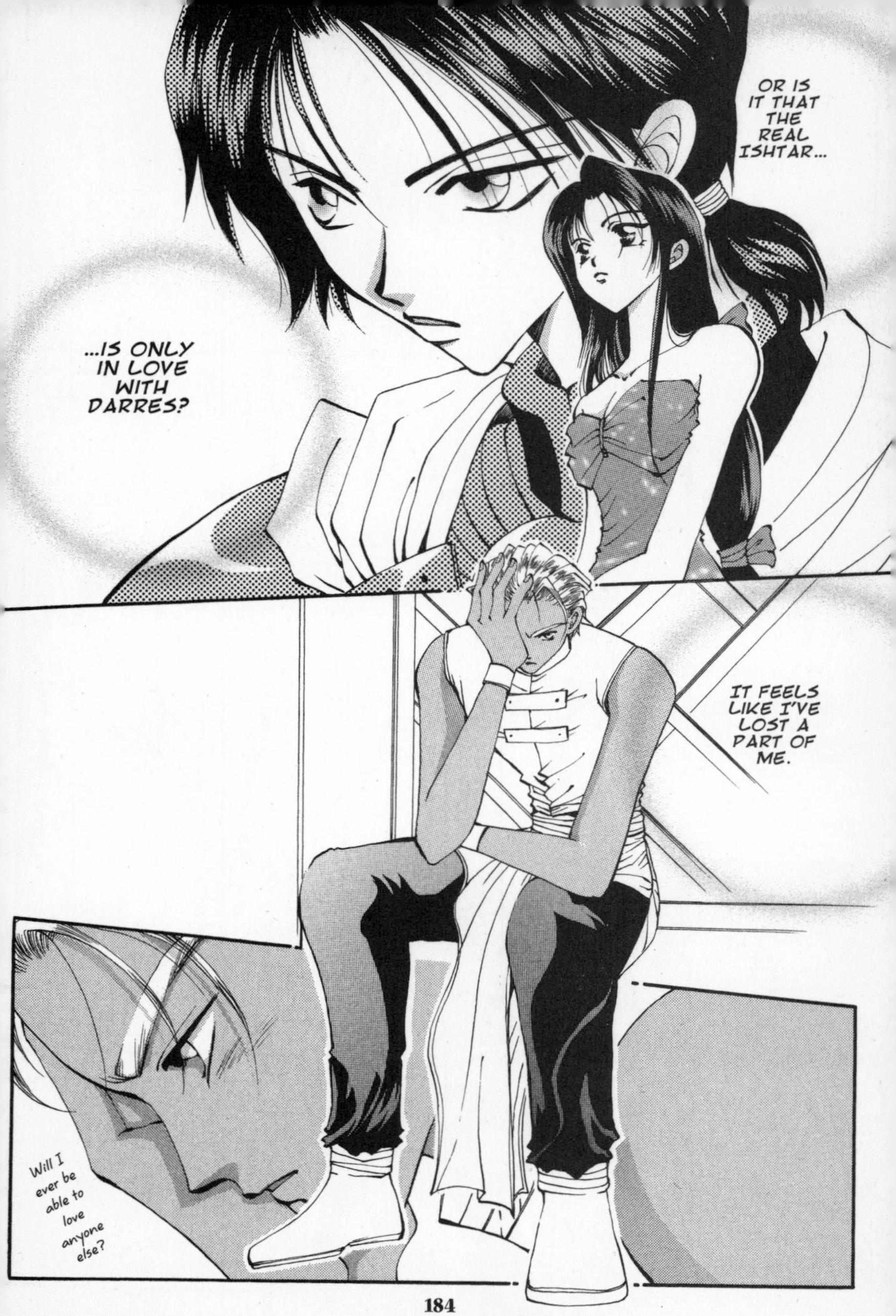
OR IS IT THAT THE REAL ISHTAR...
...IS ONLY IN LOVE WITH DARRES?
IT FEELS LIKE I'VE LOST A PART OF ME.
Will I ever be able to love anyone else?

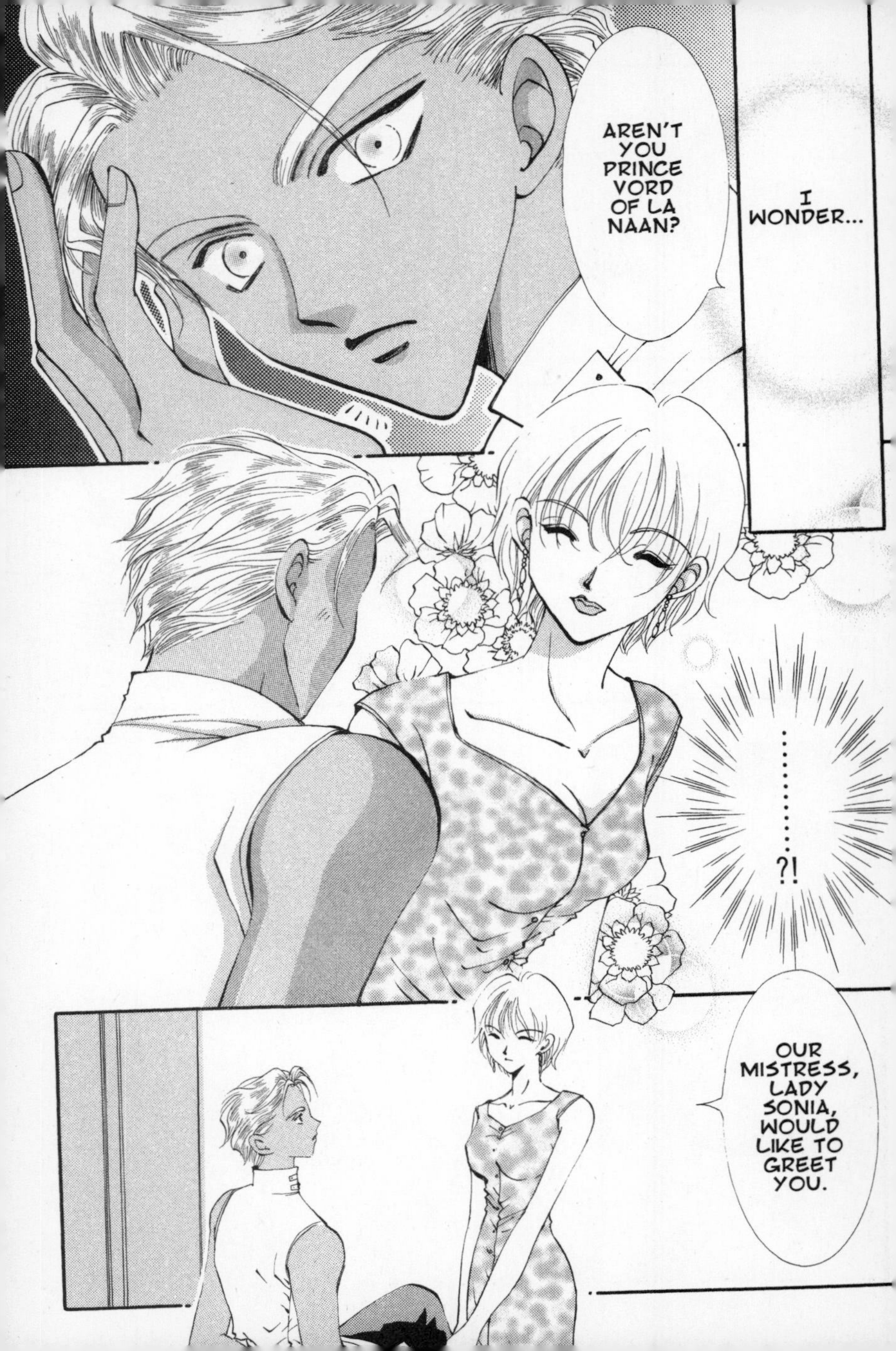
I WONDER...
AREN'T YOU PRINCE VORD OF LA NAAN?
......?!
OUR MISTRESS, LADY SONIA, WOULD LIKE TO GREET YOU.

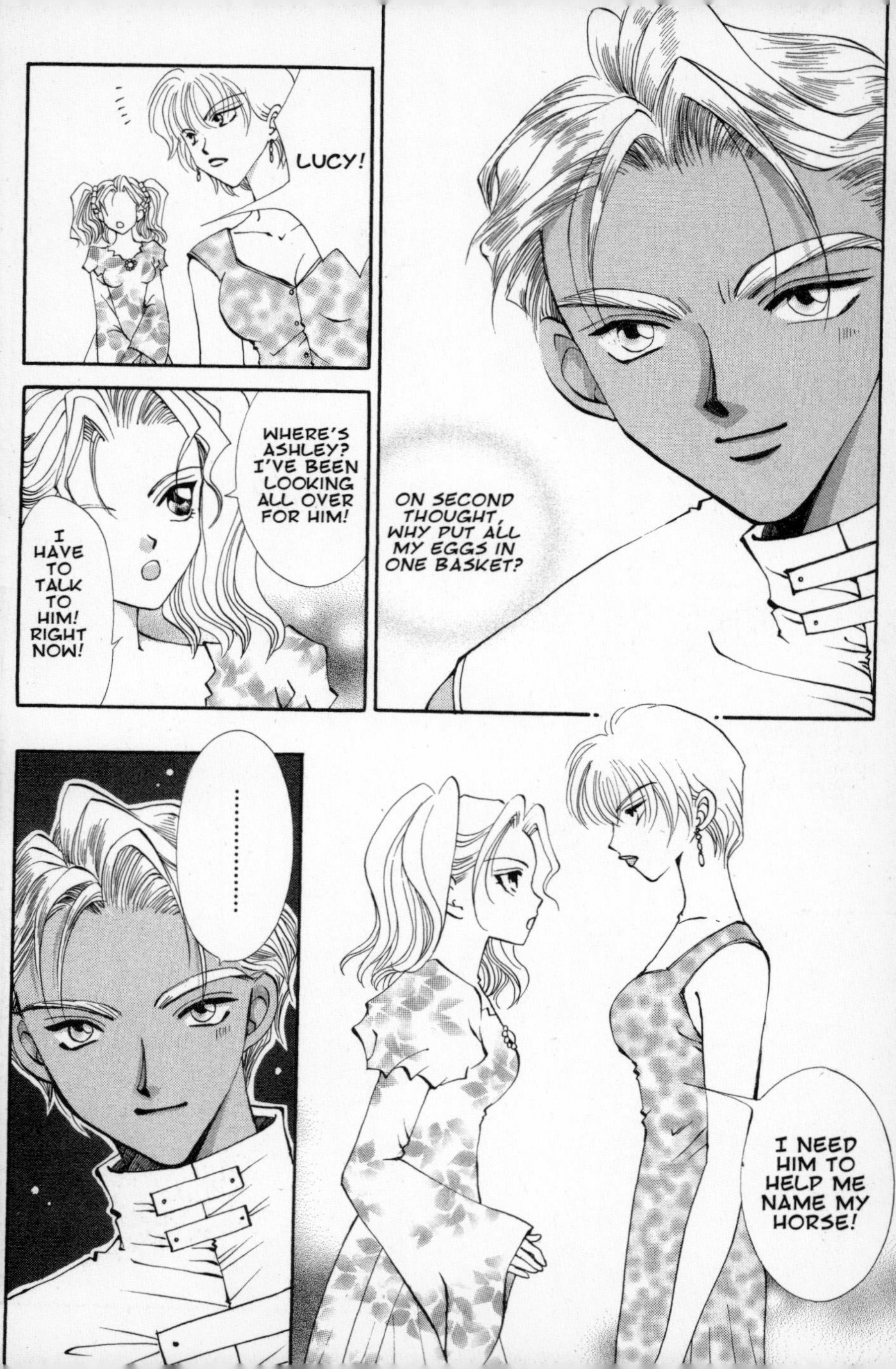
ON SECOND THOUGHT, WHY PUT ALL MY EGGS IN ONE BASKET?
LUCY!
WHERE'S ASHLEY? I'VE BEEN LOOKING ALL OVER FOR HIM!
I HAVE TO TALK TO HIM! RIGHT NOW!
I NEED HIM TO HELP ME NAME MY HORSE!
......

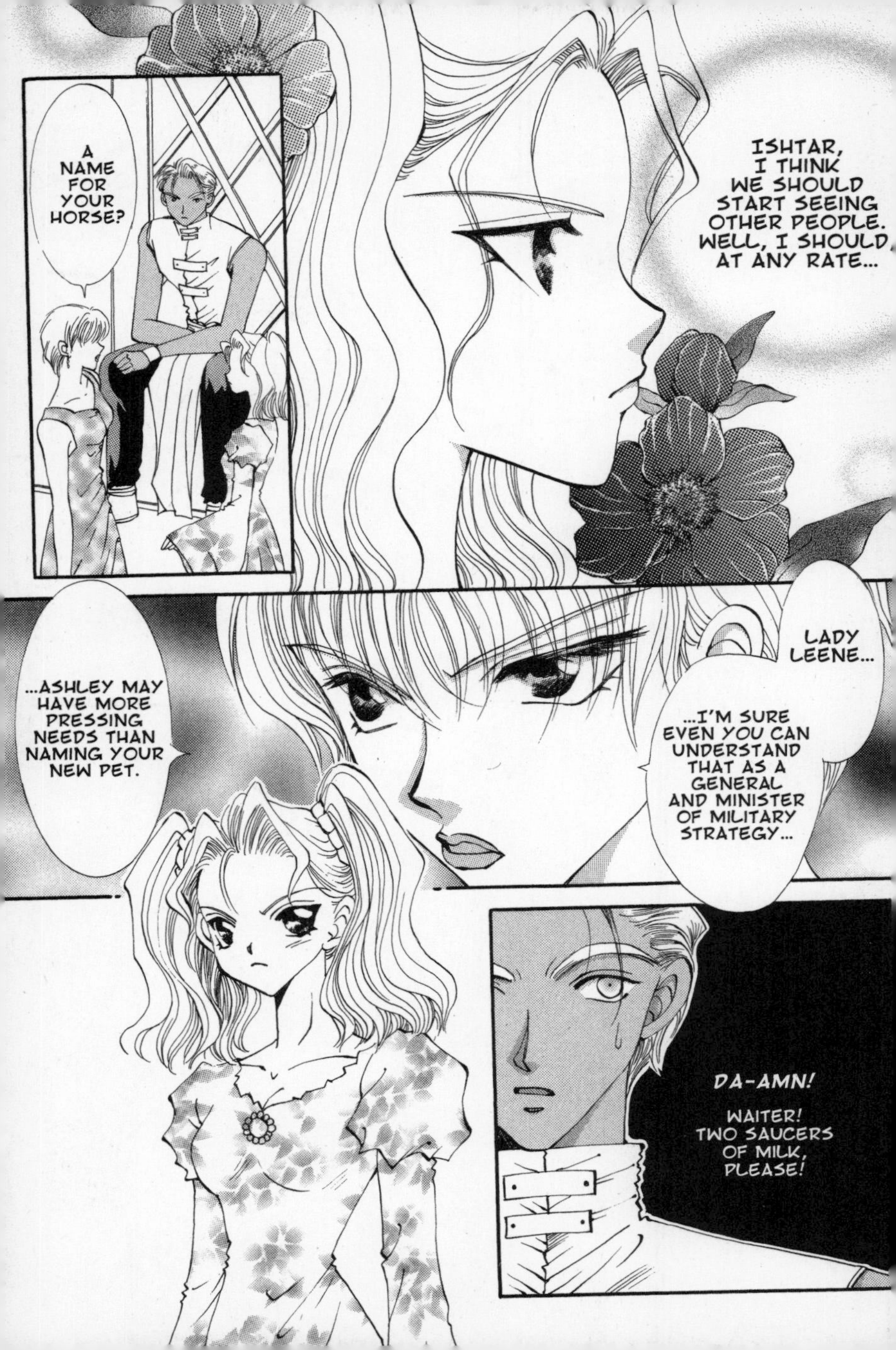
ISHTAR, I THINK WE SHOULD START SEEING OTHER PEOPLE. WELL, I SHOULD AT ANY RATE...
A NAME FOR YOUR HORSE?
LADY LEENE...
...I'M SURE EVEN YOU CAN UNDERSTAND THAT AS A GENERAL AND MINISTER OF MILITARY STRATEGY...
...ASHLEY MAY HAVE MORE PRESSING NEEDS THAN NAMING YOUR NEW PET.
DA-AMN!
WAITER! TWO SAUCERS OF MILK, PLEASE!

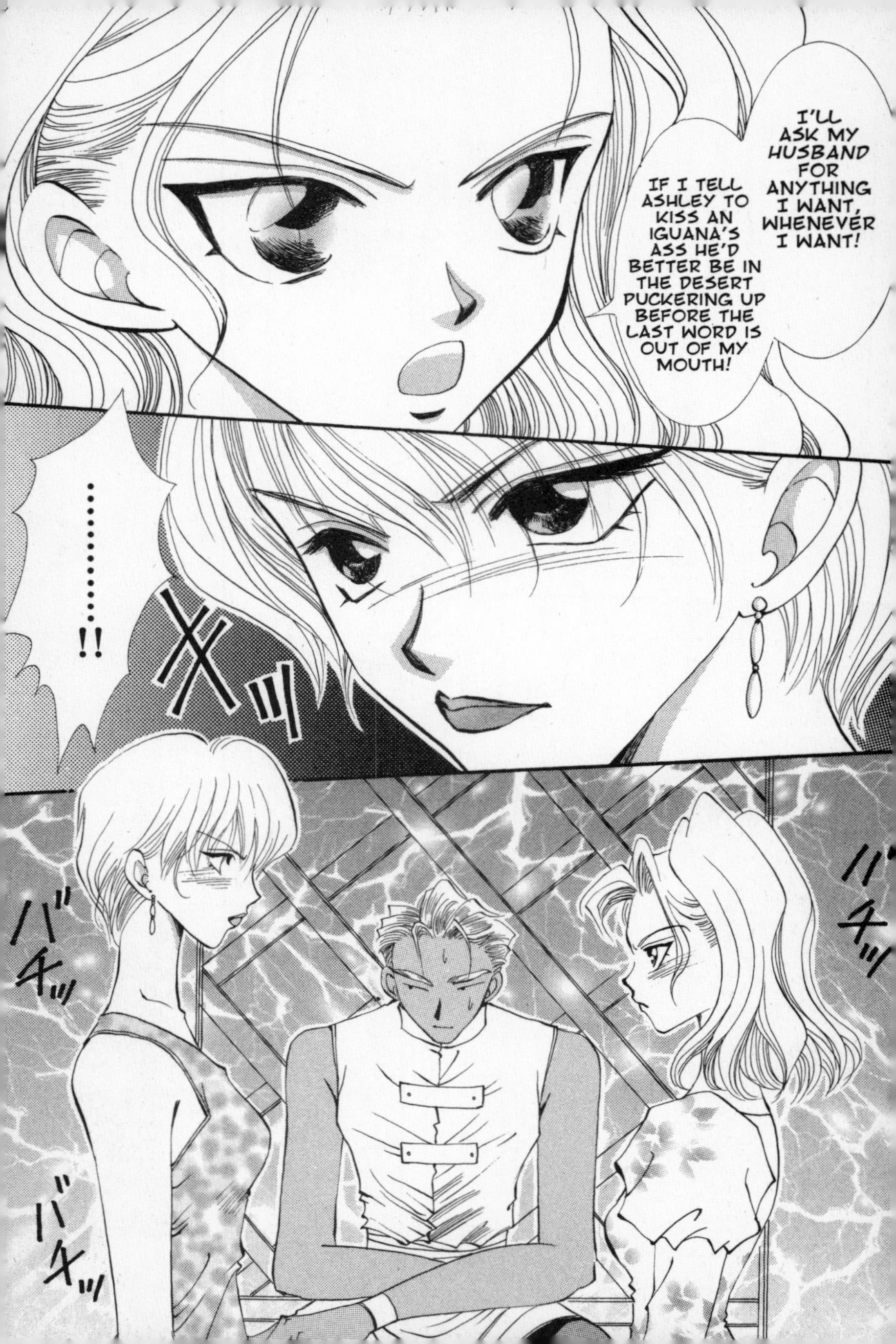
I'LL ASK MY HUSBAND FOR ANYTHING I WANT, WHENEVER I WANT!
IF I TELL ASHLEY TO KISS AN IGUANA'S ASS HE'D BETTER BE IN THE DESERT PUCKERING UP BEFORE THE LAST WORD IS OUT OF MY MOUTH!
......!!
バチッ
バチッ
バチッ

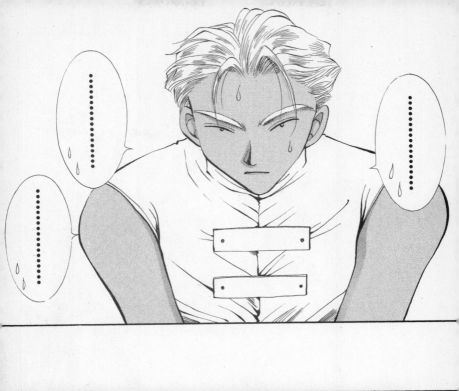

HAVE I
REALLY
CHANGED
THAT MUCH?

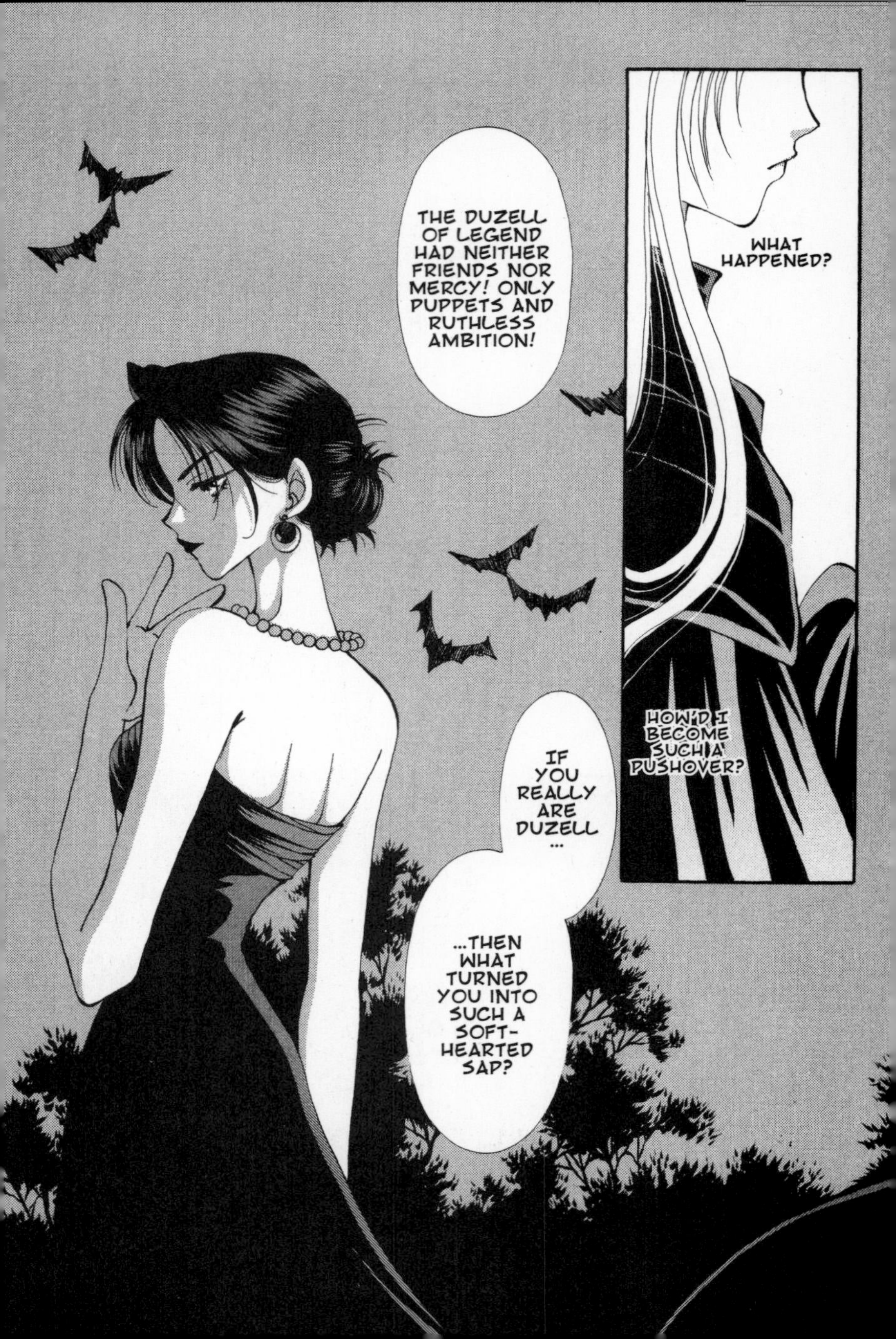
WHAT HAPPENED?
HOW'D I BECOME SUCH A PUSHOVER?
THE DUZELL OF LEGEND HAD NEITHER FRIENDS NOR MERCY! ONLY PUPPETS AND RUTHLESS AMBITION!
IF YOU REALLY ARE DUZELL ...
...THEN WHAT TURNED YOU INTO SUCH A SOFT-HEARTED SAP?

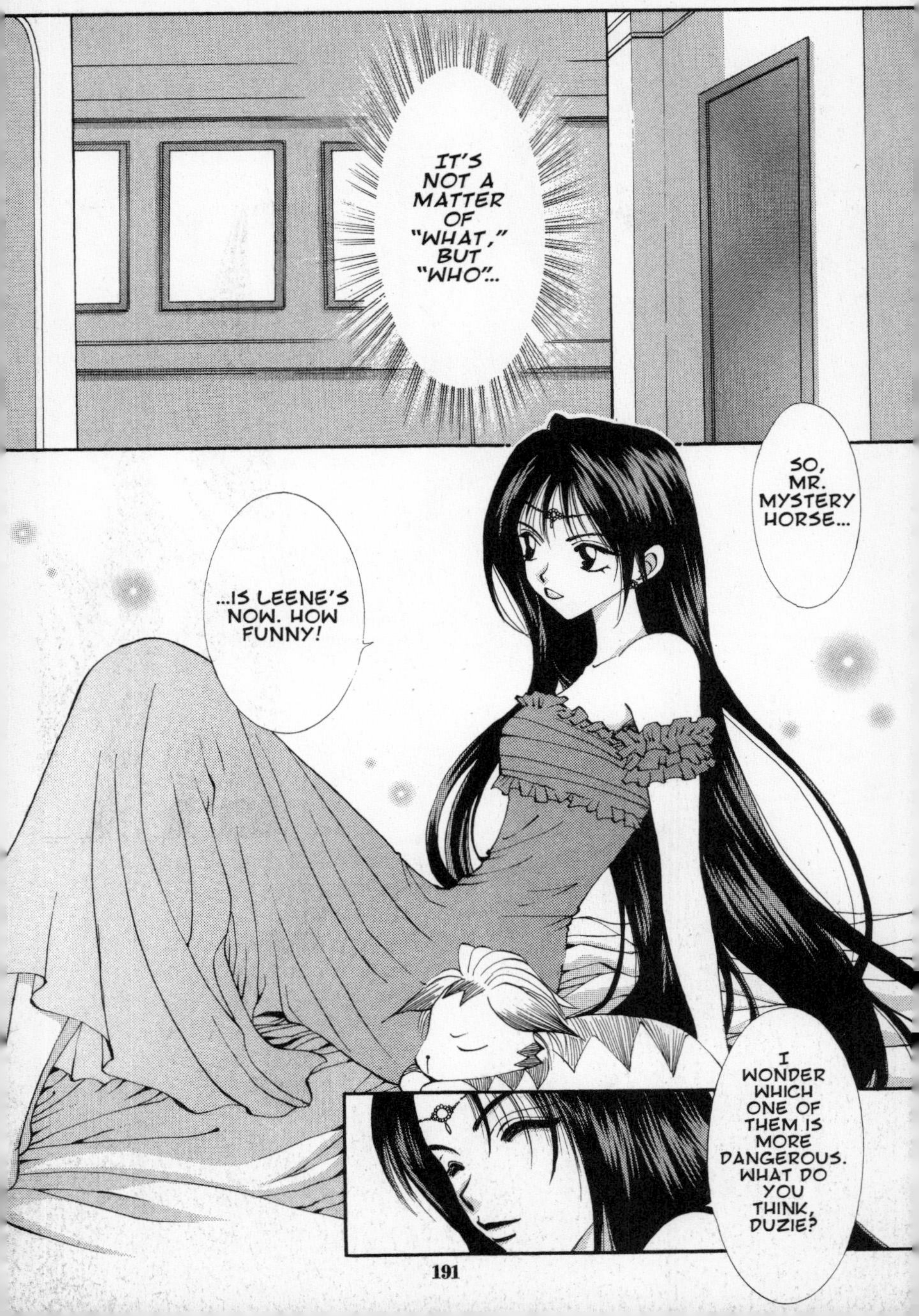
IT'S NOT A MATTER OF "WHAT," BUT "WHO"...
SO, MR. MYSTERY HORSE...
...IS LEENE'S NOW. HOW FUNNY!
I WONDER WHICH ONE OF THEM IS MORE DANGEROUS. WHAT DO YOU THINK, DUZIE?

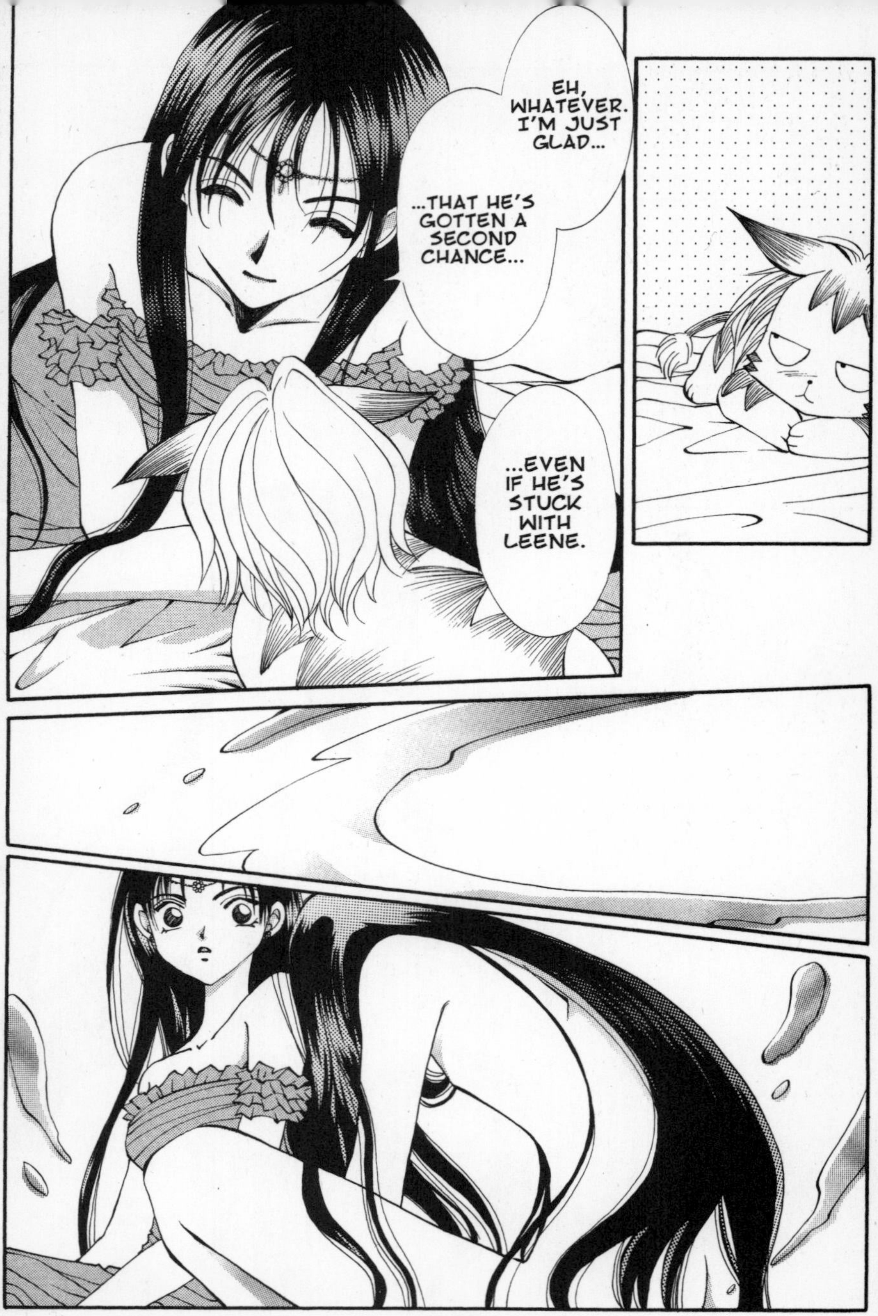
EH, WHATEVER. I'M JUST GLAD...
...THAT HE'S GOTTEN A SECOND CHANCE...
...EVEN IF HE'S STUCK WITH LEENE.

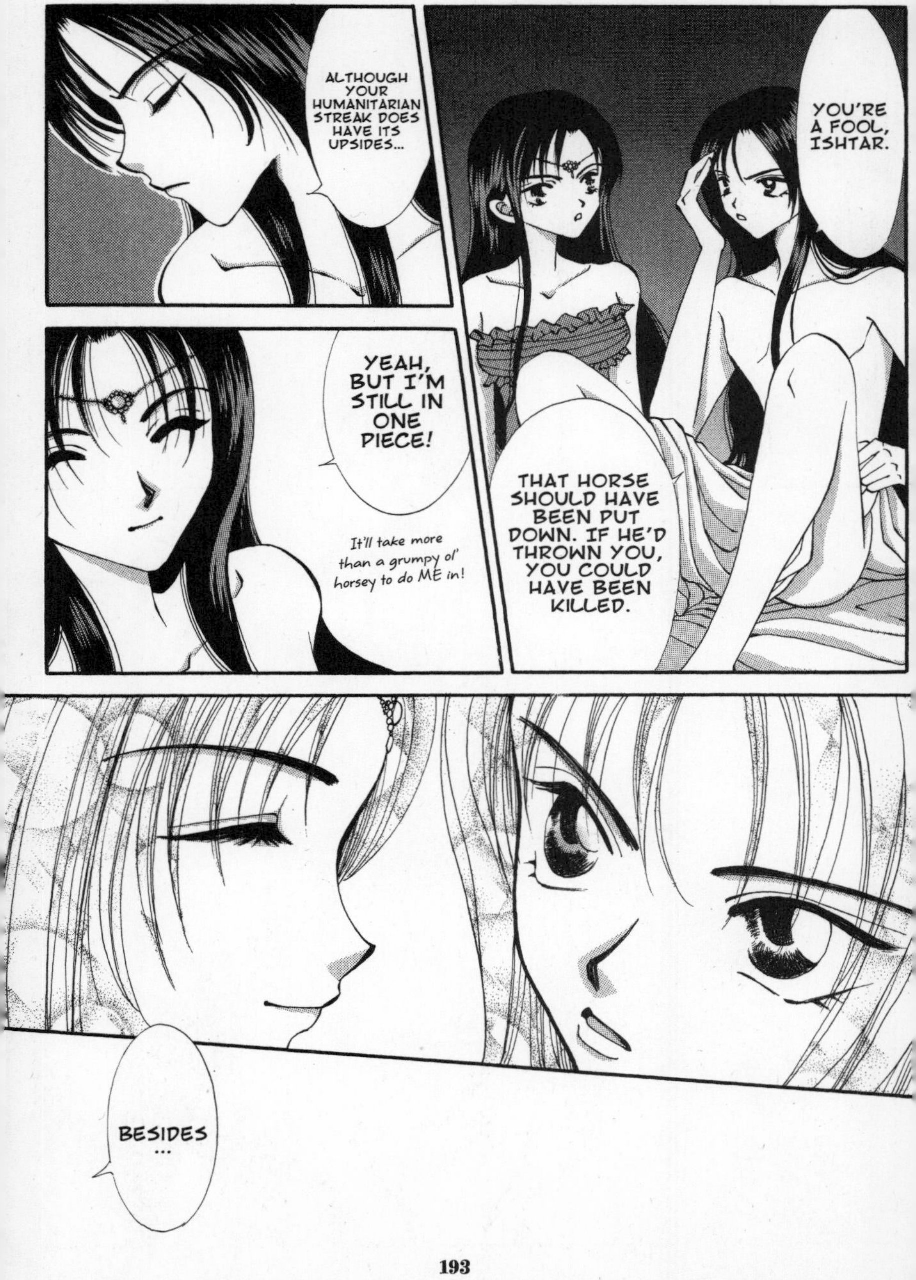
YOU'RE A FOOL, ISHTAR.
THAT HORSE SHOULD HAVE BEEN PUT DOWN. IF HE'D THROWN YOU, YOU COULD HAVE BEEN KILLED.
ALTHOUGH YOUR HUMANITARIAN STREAK DOES HAVE ITS UPSIDES...
YEAH, BUT I'M STILL IN ONE PIECE!
It'll take more than a grumpy ol' horsey to do ME in!
BESIDES ...

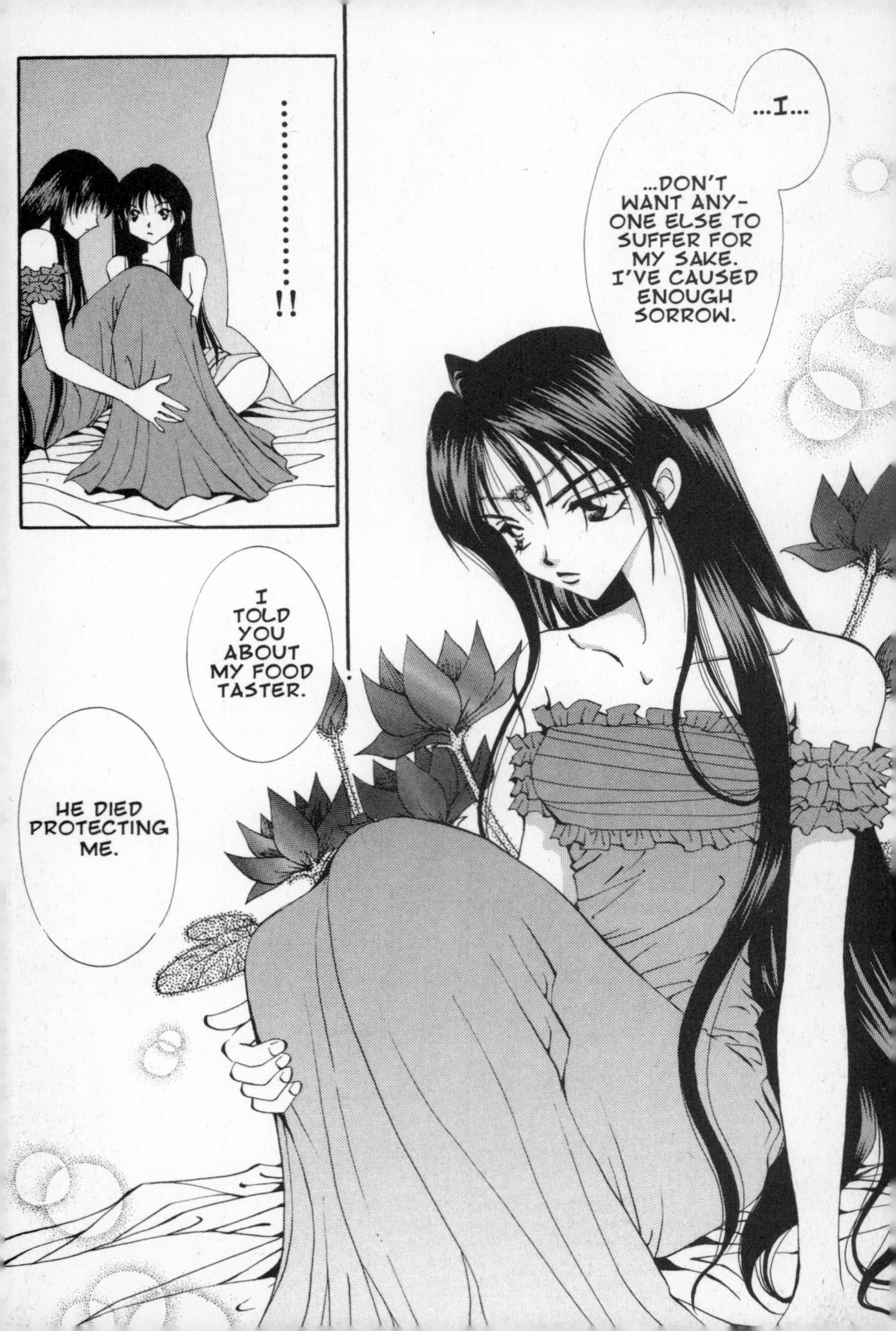
...I...
...DON'T WANT ANY-ONE ELSE TO SUFFER FOR MY SAKE. I'VE CAUSED ENOUGH SORROW.
......!!
I TOLD YOU ABOUT MY FOOD TASTER.
HE DIED PROTECTING ME.

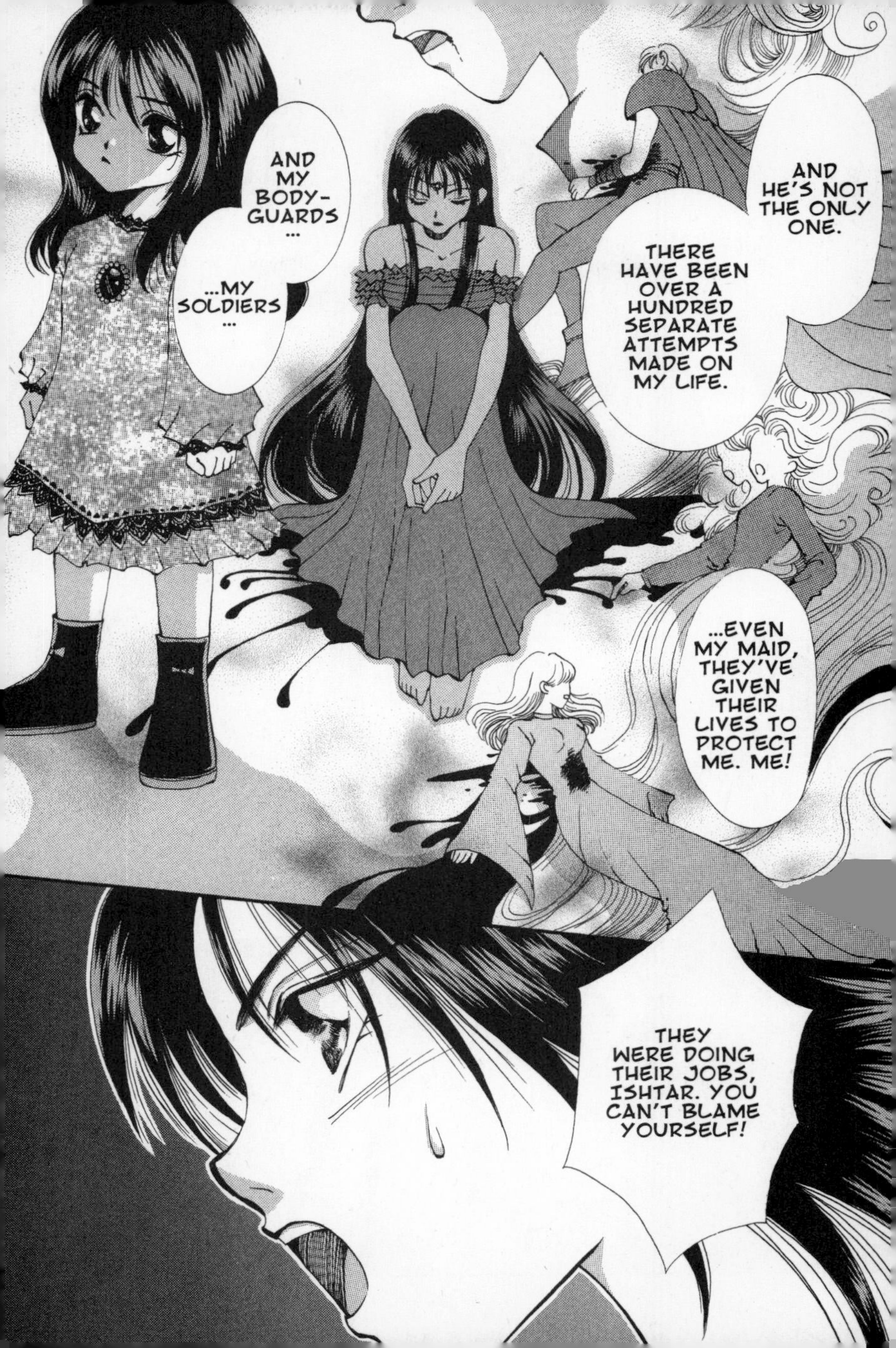
AND HE'S NOT THE ONLY ONE.
THERE HAVE BEEN OVER A HUNDRED SEPARATE ATTEMPTS MADE ON MY LIFE.
AND MY BODY-GUARDS ...
...MY SOLDIERS ...
...EVEN MY MAID, THEY'VE GIVEN THEIR LIVES TO PROTECT ME. ME!
THEY WERE DOING THEIR JOBS, ISHTAR. YOU CAN'T BLAME YOURSELF!

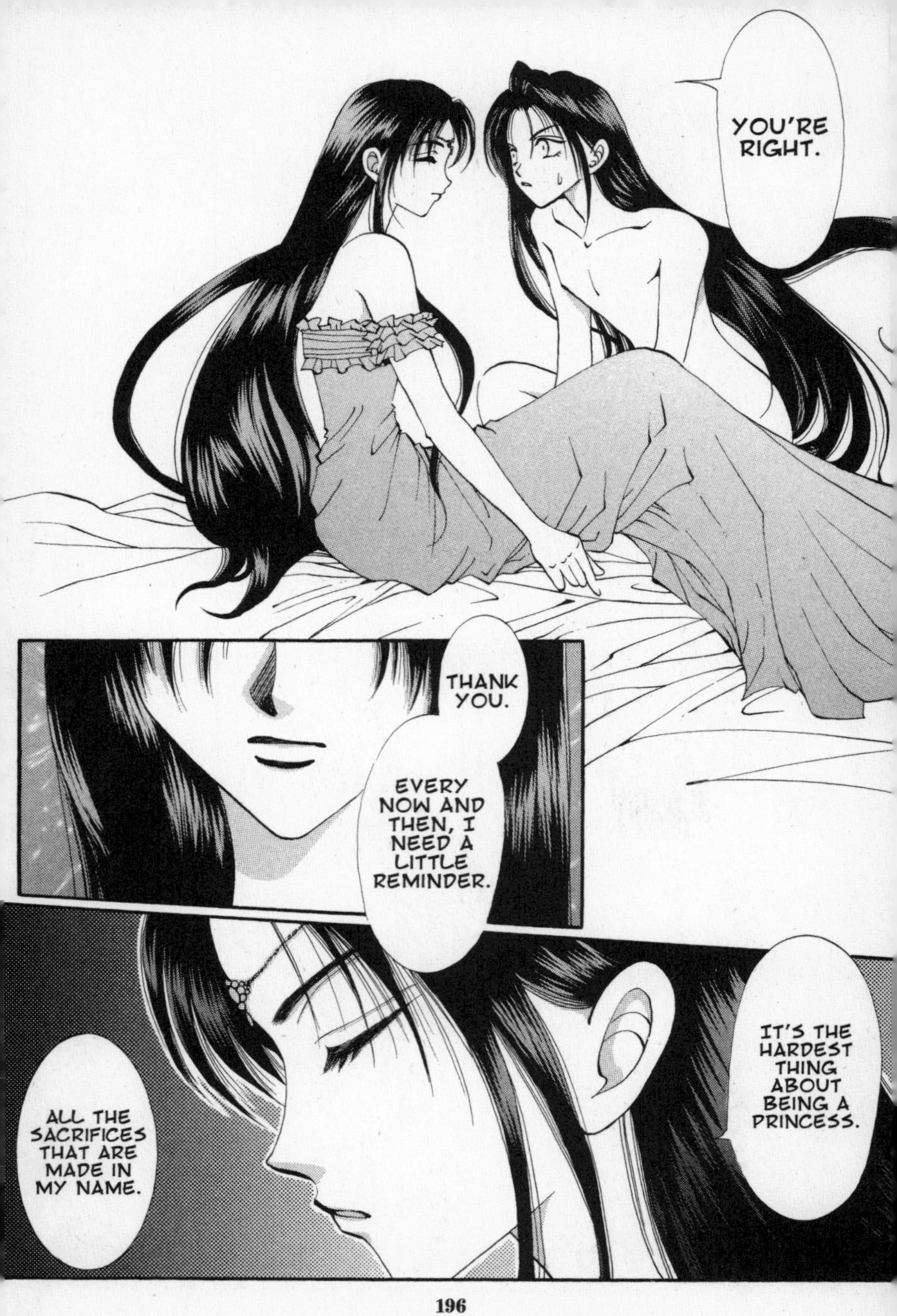
YOU'RE RIGHT.
THANK YOU.
EVERY NOW AND THEN, I NEED A LITTLE REMINDER.
IT'S THE HARDEST THING ABOUT BEING A PRINCESS.
ALL THE SACRIFICES THAT ARE MADE IN MY NAME.

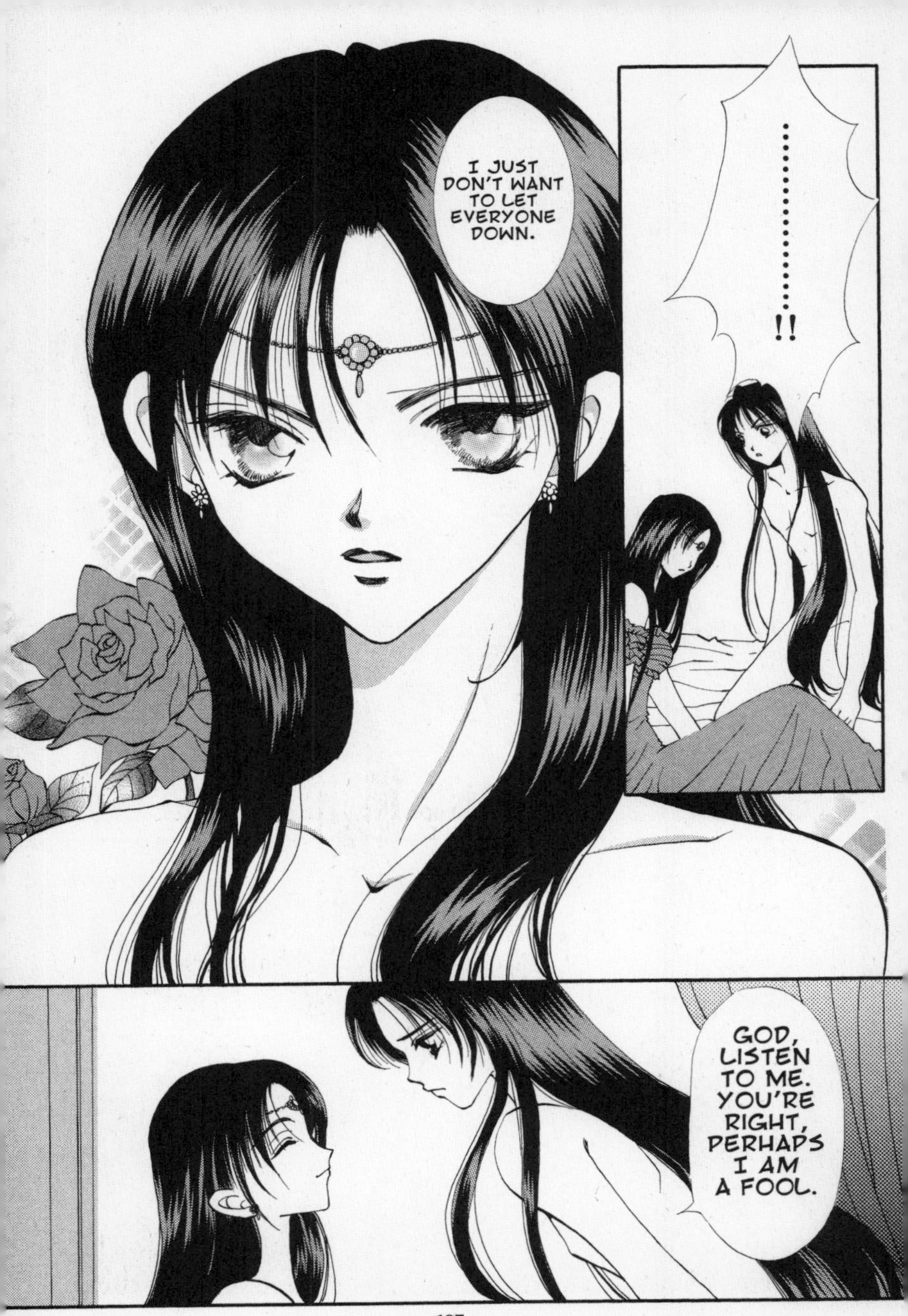
......!!
I JUST DON'T WANT TO LET EVERYONE DOWN.
GOD, LISTEN TO ME. YOU'RE RIGHT, PERHAPS I AM A FOOL.

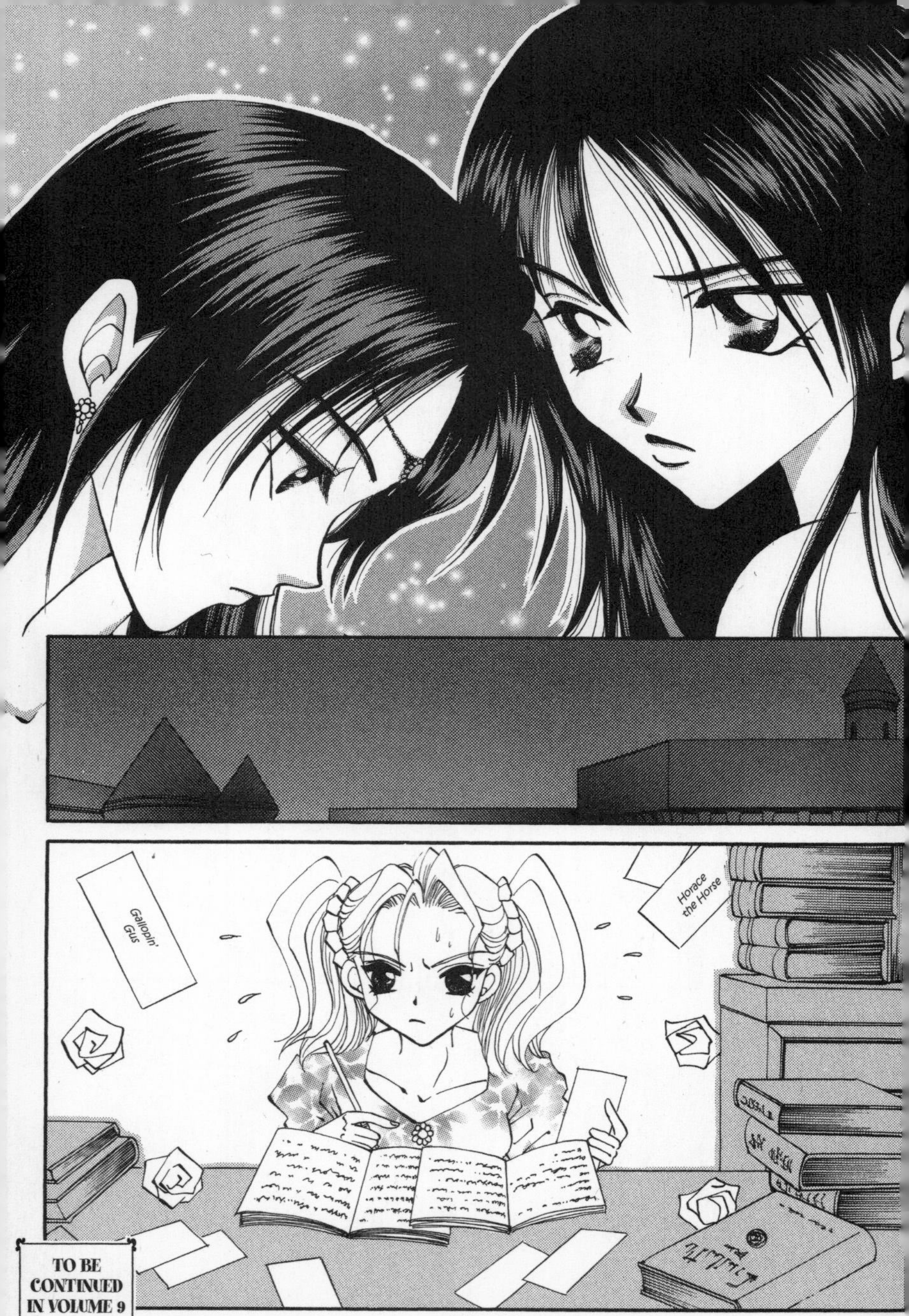
Horace the Horse
Gallopin' Gus
TO BE CONTINUED IN VOLUME 9

Not Your Average Afterword

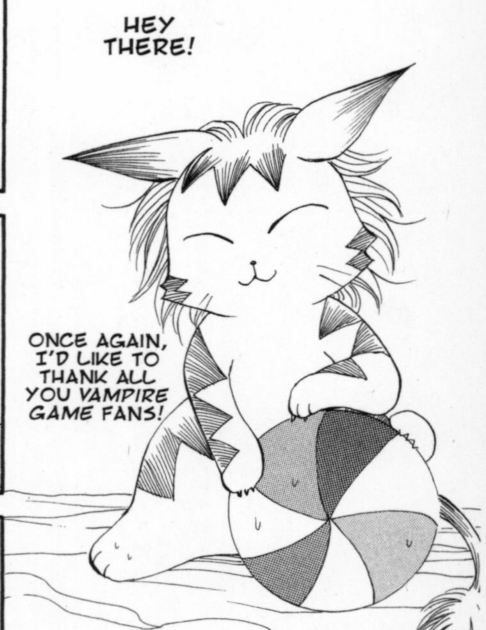
HEY THERE!
ONCE AGAIN, I'D LIKE TO THANK ALL YOU VAMPIRE GAME FANS!

Hey There!

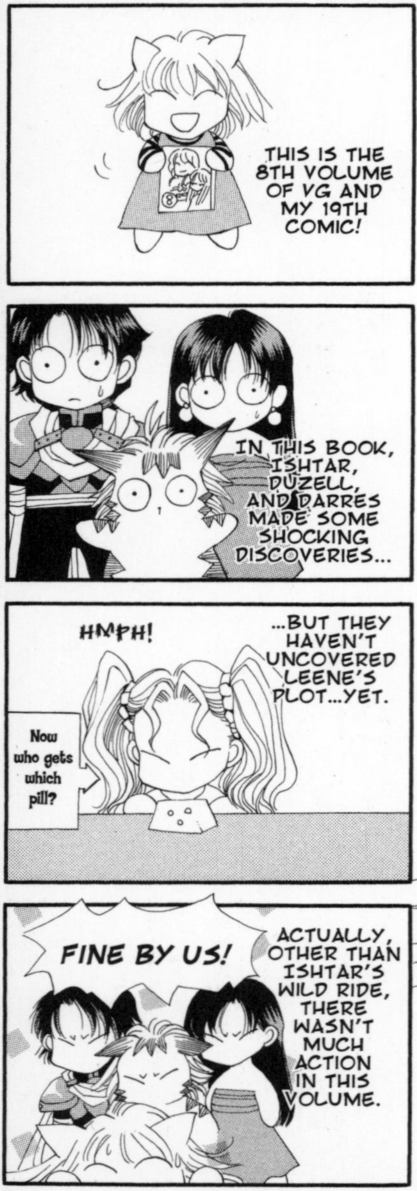
THIS IS THE 8TH VOLUME OF VG AND MY 19TH COMIC!
IN THIS BOOK, ISHTAR, DUZELL, AND DARRES MADE SOME SHOCKING DISCOVERIES...
...BUT THEY HAVEN'T UNCOVERED LEENE'S PLOT...YET.
HMPH!
Now who gets which pill?
ACTUALLY, OTHER THAN ISHTAR'S WILD RIDE, THERE WASN'T MUCH ACTION IN THIS VOLUME.
FINE BY US!

Yujinn / Yuujel

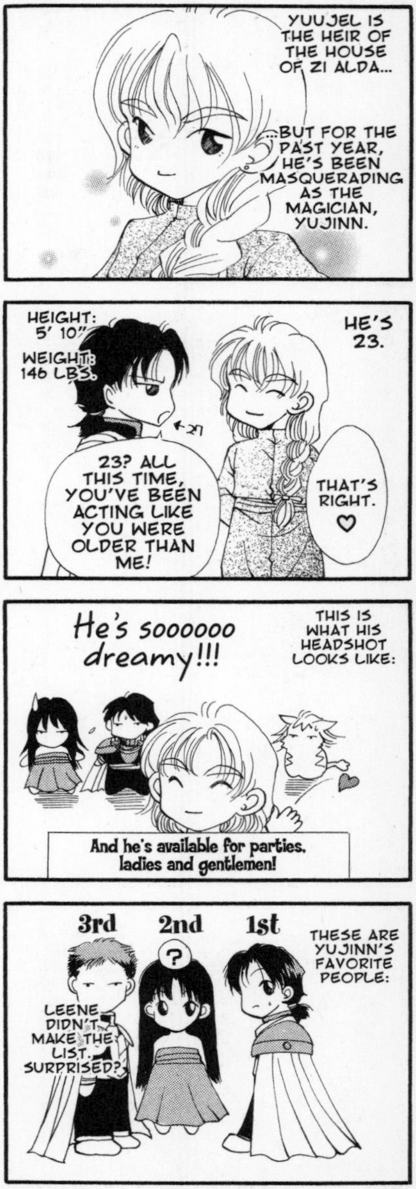
YUUJEL IS THE HEIR OF THE HOUSE OF ZI ALDA...
...BUT FOR THE PAST YEAR, HE'S BEEN MASQUERADING AS THE MAGICIAN, YUJINN.
HE'S 23.
HEIGHT: 5' 10"
WEIGHT: 146 LBS.
THAT'S RIGHT. ♥
←27
23? ALL THIS TIME, YOU'VE BEEN ACTING LIKE YOU WERE OLDER THAN ME!
THIS IS WHAT HIS HEADSHOT LOOKS LIKE:
He's soooooo dreamy!!!
And he's available for parties, ladies and gentlemen!
THESE ARE YUJINN'S FAVORITE PEOPLE:
1st
2nd
?
3rd
LEENE DIDN'T MAKE THE LIST. SURPRISED?

Lady Leene

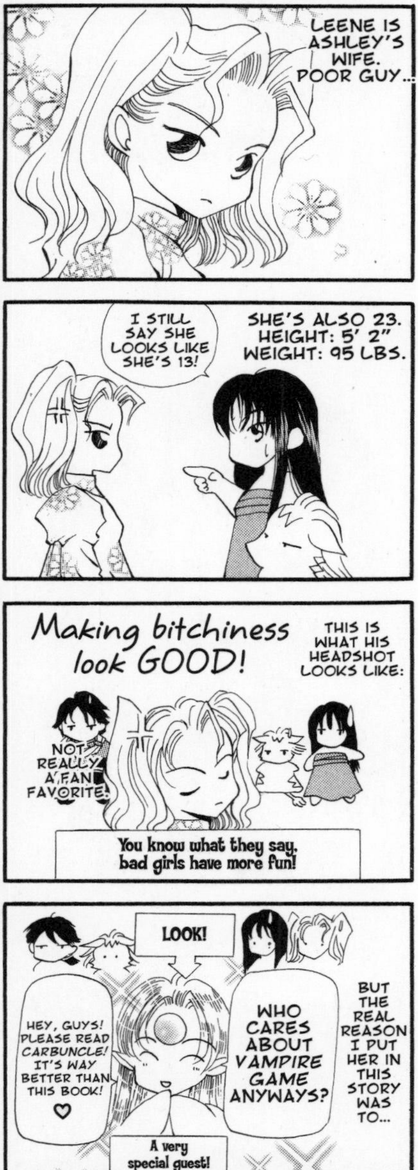
LEENE IS ASHLEY'S WIFE. POOR GUY...
SHE'S ALSO 23. HEIGHT: 5' 2" WEIGHT: 95 LBS.
I STILL SAY SHE LOOKS LIKE SHE'S 13!
THIS IS WHAT HIS HEADSHOT LOOKS LIKE:
Making bitchiness look GOOD!
NOT REALLY A FAN FAVORITE.
You know what they say, bad girls have more fun!
BUT THE REAL REASON I PUT HER IN THIS STORY WAS TO...
WHO CARES ABOUT VAMPIRE GAME ANYWAYS?
LOOK!
HEY, GUYS! PLEASE READ CARBUNCLE! IT'S WAY BETTER THAN THIS BOOK! ♥
A very special guest!

Editor's note: *Carbuncle* is another popular manga series by Judal.

Carbuncle

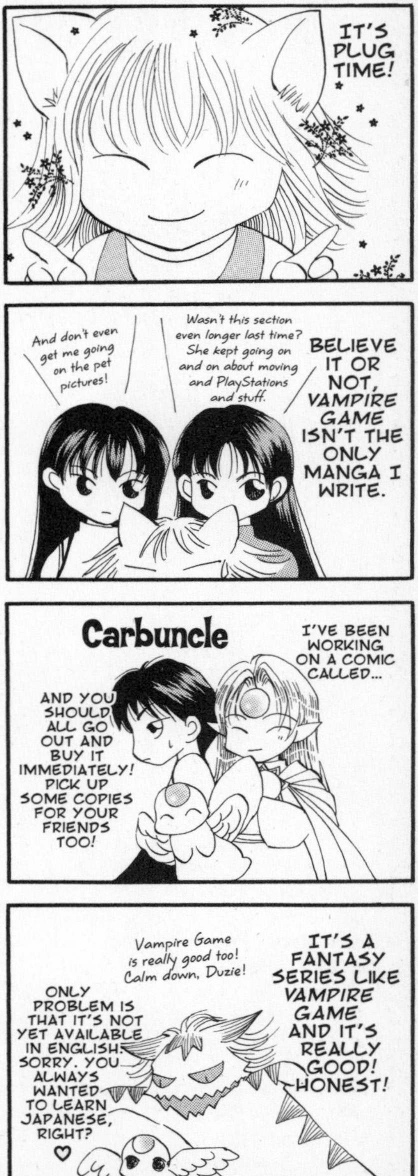
IT'S PLUG TIME!
BELIEVE IT OR NOT, VAMPIRE GAME ISN'T THE ONLY MANGA I WRITE.
Wasn't this section even longer last time? She kept going on and on about moving and PlayStations and stuff.
And don't even get me going on the pet pictures!
I'VE BEEN WORKING ON A COMIC CALLED...
Carbuncle
AND YOU SHOULD ALL GO OUT AND BUY IT IMMEDIATELY! PICK UP SOME COPIES FOR YOUR FRIENDS TOO!
IT'S A FANTASY SERIES LIKE VAMPIRE GAME AND IT'S REALLY GOOD! HONEST!
Vampire Game is really good too! Calm down, Duzie!
ONLY PROBLEM IS THAT IT'S NOT YET AVAILABLE IN ENGLISH. SORRY. YOU ALWAYS WANTED TO LEARN JAPANESE, RIGHT? ♡

Postscript

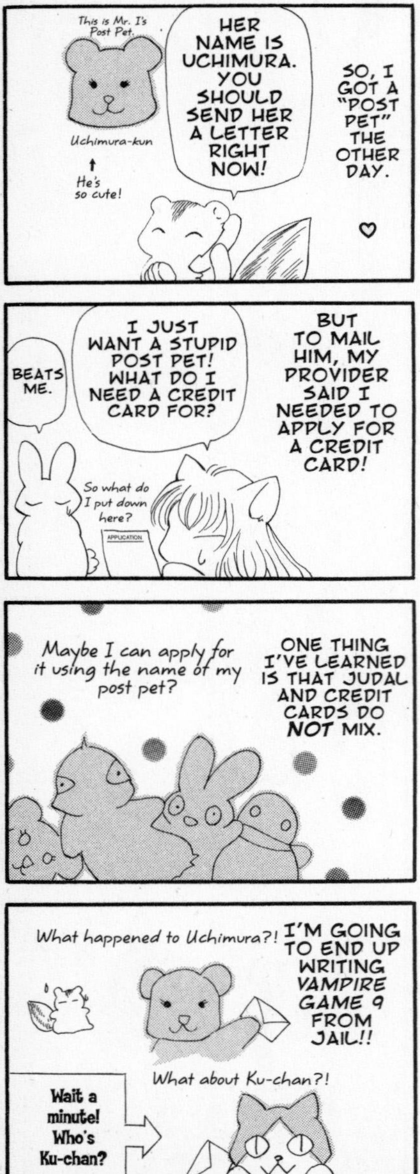
SO, I GOT A "POST PET" THE OTHER DAY. ♡
HER NAME IS UCHIMURA. YOU SHOULD SEND HER A LETTER RIGHT NOW!
This is Mr. I's Post Pet.
Uchimura-kun
He's so cute!
BUT TO MAIL HIM, MY PROVIDER SAID I NEEDED TO APPLY FOR A CREDIT CARD!
I JUST WANT A STUPID POST PET! WHAT DO I NEED A CREDIT CARD FOR?
BEATS ME.
So what do I put down here?
APPLICATION
ONE THING I'VE LEARNED IS THAT JUDAL AND CREDIT CARDS DO NOT MIX.
Maybe I can apply for it using the name of my post pet?
I'M GOING TO END UP WRITING VAMPIRE GAME 9 FROM JAIL!!
What happened to Uchimura?!
What about Ku-chan?!
Wait a minute! Who's Ku-chan?

VAMPIRE GAME

Next issue...

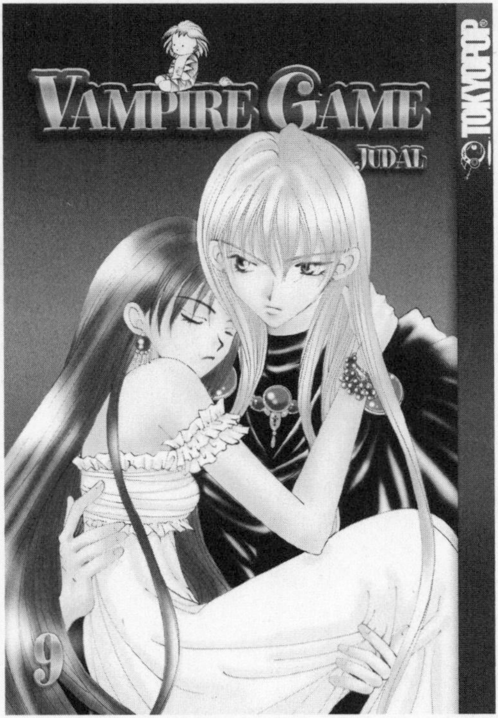
VAMPIRE GAME
JUDAL
TOKYOPOP
9

Leene literally picks her poison. With three different poisons to choose from, Leene is armed to avenge the woman she believes is responsible for steeling Yuujel's heart. The first of the three toxic pills causes blindness, the second makes the victim go lame, and the third brings about an untimely death. Yet despite all evidence to the contrary, Leene does have a conscience. Dealing in death is not her forte, and the fact that she's beginning to like Princess Ishtar certainly doesn't help.

Meanwhile, the rest of our crew must decide what to do if she does go through with her plan. And while the issue may be clear-cut to Darres, Yuujel and Lucy, it's not to Ashley. Leene is his wife, after all. Ashley has sworn an oath to defend Zi Alda and by extension, Pheliosta, but how can he possibly choose between the woman he loves and the country he's sworn to protect?

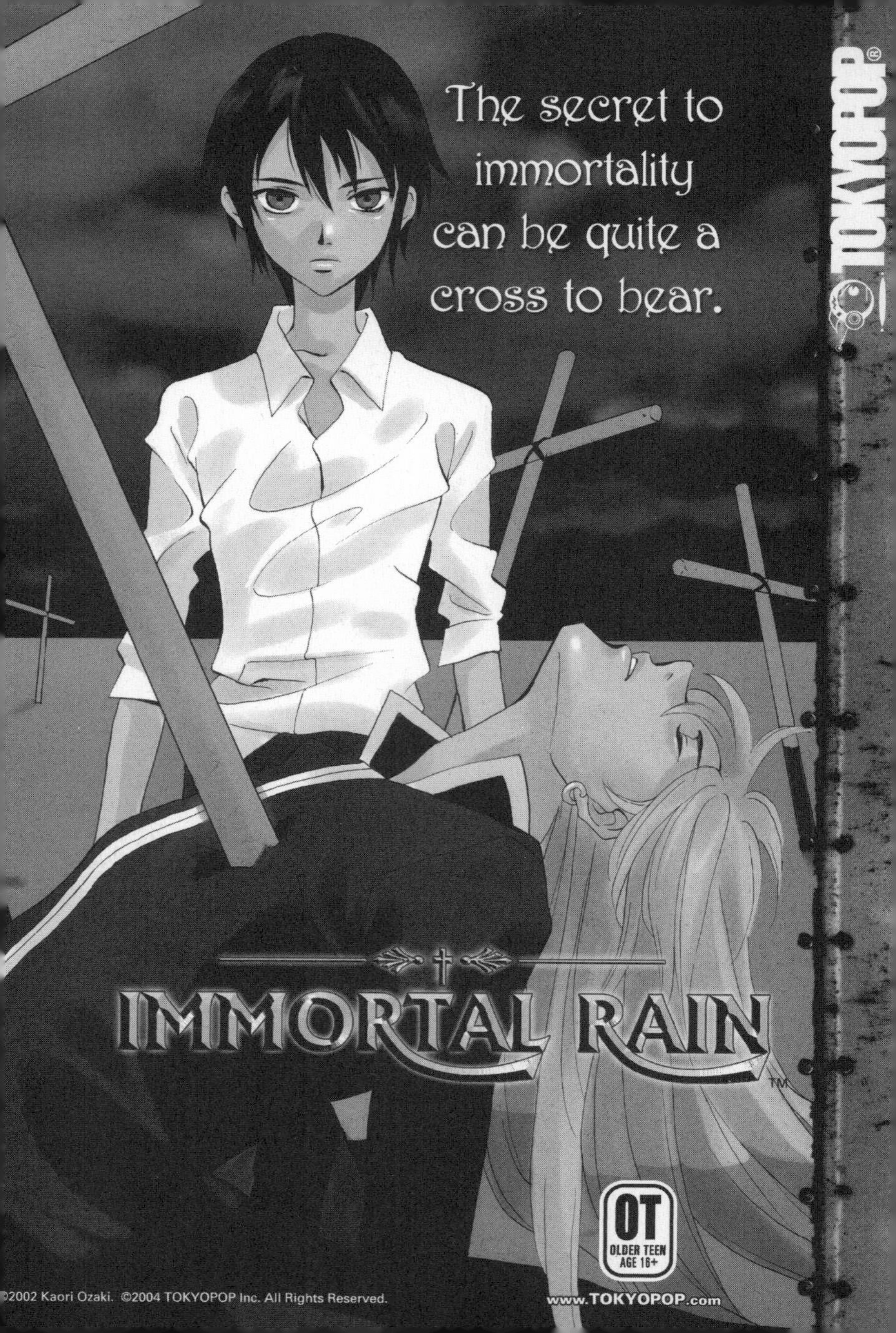

The secret to immortality can be quite a cross to bear.
TOKYOPOP®
IMMORTAL RAIN™
OT
OLDER TEEN
AGE 18+
©2002 Kaori Ozaki. ©2004 TOKYOPOP Inc. All Rights Reserved.
www.TOKYOPOP.com

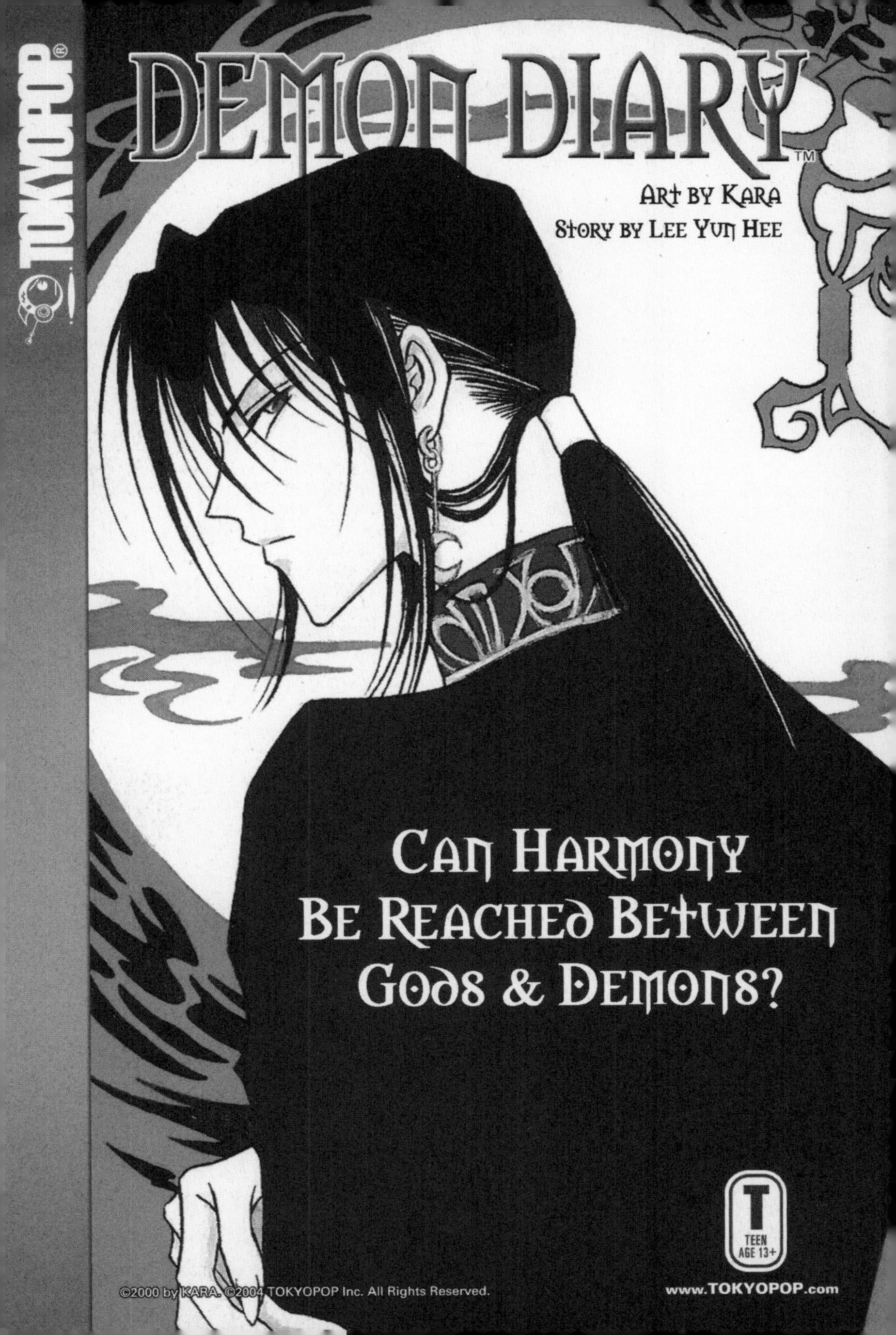
TOKYOPOP®
DEMON DIARY™
ART BY KARA
STORY BY LEE YUN HEE
CAN HARMONY
BE REACHED BETWEEN
GODS & DEMONS?
T
TEEN
AGE 13+
©2000 by KARA. ©2004 TOKYOPOP Inc. All Rights Reserved.
www.TOKYOPOP.com

ALSO AVAILABLE FROM TOKYOPOP®